She reached p[...] eyes fell on the fullness of her bosom, reminding him of his promise to get rid of the shirt at the earliest opportunity. His finger reached, popping the next two buttons free. When she looked at him, he watched her eyes and flicked open another button.

"I like this shirt," she said.

"I'll buy you another." His fingers closed on the shirt and they both watched the last buttons fly across the bathroom floor when he pulled.

"What the heck." Rissa beat his fingers to the hem of her skirt by less than a second and yanked it high above her hips before she pushed his robe open. Straddling him, she pushed close to find him ready and waiting for her. Anticipating the urge of his hands against the hot skin of her thighs, she caught her breath when his strong fingers traveled higher, breaking the fragile lace that might have kept them from joining.

"I'll buy more," Dench promised against her mouth. Like a woman closed too long from love, she pressed closer, straining to feel him grow, throbbing within her boundaries, and he knew she wasn't listening anymore.

DREAM KEEPER

GAIL McFARLAND

Genesis Press, Inc.

INDIGO LOVE STORIES

An imprint of Genesis Press, Inc.
Publishing Company

Genesis Press, Inc.
P.O. Box 101
Columbus, MS 39703

Copyright © 2009 Gail McFarland

ISBN: 13 DIGIT : 978-1-58571-366-0
ISBN: 10 DIGIT : 1-58571-366-x
Manufactured in the United States of America

First Edition

Visit us at www.genesis-press.com
or call at 1-888-Indigo-1-4-0

DEDICATION

In order for all good things to come to an end,
They must have a great beginning.
To that end,
I am eternally grateful for prayer, and endlessly thank those who love me.
I appreciate your helping me to find the good things in my life.

No man is truly married
until he understands
every word his wife is NOT saying.
- Anonymous -

Once in a while,
Right in the middle of an ordinary life,
Love gives us a fairy tale.
- Anonymous -

CHAPTER 1

"There she is!"

Walking fast, Marissa Yarborough Traylor swung into lobby of the Hanover Building. Her dark glasses and long, sleekly tailored black wool coat fooled none of the waiting reporters. They knew her the second she pushed through the cold glass doors. Balancing her briefcase and purse, she plucked black leather gloves from her hands. Her pace never faltered as she held her head high and her smile in place. She had no words for the gentlemen of the media.

"Is it true? Is it true? Is Kadeem Gregg staying in Atlanta? Did you really broker the deal for Gregg and Sawyer?" someone yelled as she passed.

"Word is, Traylor is moving back here as a defense coach. Is the ink dry on the contract?" Ben Thomas was sweating as he jockeyed for position, trying to keep pace with her. "You shopping runners for your old man these days? Is that why you latched onto those boys out of Tech?" Rissa spared him a sidelong glance and a half-smile as she stepped a little faster.

"Yeah, we know they both play strong 'd', and that's gonna be Traylor's place on the team, right? Right? Coachin' 'd', right?"

She brought a slim, honey-colored finger to her lips, raised her brows, and held her smile.

"Come on, Rissa, give us *something*! It's three days before Christmas and you're acting like Scrooge! We know you know sports and we know you know the players. Hell, you did a great job of agenting for AJ. But you know we know you're married to the new defense coach, too. Is this going to shape up as a conflict of interest for you? For him? You pullin' a team together for Atlanta to keep your husband on the job?"

"And don't forget, you got James Clarence, too," José Christopher called. "Middleweight contender going pro, gonna be champ. You're either living right, or you're a witch!" He grinned when Rissa tossed her head and her hand went to her hip. But not a word passed her lips.

"She's too damned good lookin' to be so smart," another man whispered.

"You didn't give us an answer, Rissa." Thomas got louder. "How you gonna leave us hangin'?"

She pivoted, looked him in the eye, and winked. "Wait and see, boys. You'll get a press release when the deals are done, and then you'll know what I know." Rissa laughed, cutting across the marble-floored lobby and heading for the security stairs. Just steps ahead of dark, panther-like Adrian Kessler and his network cameraman, she managed to slip her card key free and into the reader. The door clicked and she eased inside, pulling the door closed behind her. Kessler would have caught the door edge and pulled if the beefy security guard trailing Rissa had been looking the other way, but he wasn't.

"Don't tell me she's taking the stairs," Christopher groaned. "She's a woman in heels, for Pete's sake."

"A woman in heels, with legs like a racehorse," Ben Thomas commiserated, watching the security guard. "Elevator's over there."

"Might be better to wait for the statement. She's got my number." Kessler watched two other reporters leave.

"Mine, too," Thomas said, nodding to his cameraman. "Come on, I'll treat you to Starbucks." Assuming inclusion, Kessler followed.

"I got Christmas shopping to finish, anyway." Christopher jammed his hands into his coat pockets and slunk off with a final glance at the still-guarded stairwell door.

Listening for trailing footsteps, Rissa stopped climbing stairs on the fourth floor. Stepping out of the stairwell, she looked left and right, scanning the modern polished steel and glass-walled corridor. Seeing no one, she headed for the ladies' room. Once inside, her back to the door, she listened again—nothing. Good. She tucked her briefcase under her arm and dipped her other hand deep into her red leather tote bag. Her fingers searched the contents and stopped when they found the small white CVS bag. Content that she was alone, she pulled the bag free as she hurried past the mirrored walls and polished marble vanity.

A woman was entitled to privacy, but it was hard to come by these days. Darned reporters were already suspicious of a woman handling the lives and careers of big million-dollar men. That she had just scored fantastic deals for two young players who might have otherwise managed second-round NFL draft status was front-page news, as far as they were concerned, so they were following her. But right now, for Rissa, the placement, the money, those kids' careers, all took a backseat to the small package she'd picked up at the drugstore.

Taking a deep breath, she brushed back her long coat and walked the line of stalls. "Okay, now this is just damned creepy," she admitted, pushing doors to make sure they were empty—they were. Mentally apologizing, she hip-checked the door to the handicapped stall and pushed it closed behind her. She needed space for what she was about to do.

Her heartbeat was hard and fast when she jerked her purse, briefcase, and coat to the hook on the back of the door, and she was almost panting when she dumped the contents of the CVS bag into her hand. Opening the small box, Rissa read the instructions on the back. "Good, it's exactly like the other one," she muttered, taking a deep breath and hiking up her skirt.

The box was open and the little wand was in her hand when she realized something was missing—Dench. "He needs to be a part of this," she whispered, reaching for her purse and knowing that she was not about to call him on her cellphone. If what she suspected was true, he didn't need to hear it over the phone. And if it wasn't true, he didn't deserve the hurt and disappointment. But if she was right . . .

She dug for her wallet, realized that she was holding her breath, and inhaled, gulping lavender and Lysol-scented air when she found their picture. Just looking at him in the photo and remembering almost stopped her heart—it had been taken on their honeymoon. Standing in front of a low and impossibly full moon on the sugar-white sand of Seven Mile Beach in Negril, he'd kissed her and promised that there was nothing in this life that he wouldn't give her.

"And I believed you, baby, then and now." Rissa Yarborough Traylor couldn't have cared less who heard her as she stood with her skirt bunched up around her hips in a public bathroom holding her honeymoon photo and a home pregnancy kit, whispering to her husband's image. "Baby, you've been nothing but luck for me, and I want to give that back to you. Maybe this time," she sighed. "It's Christmastime, a season for miracles, for children, and maybe good luck for . . . us." She kissed the photo and set it on top of her purse where she could see it. Opening the box, she looked at her smiling husband again. "Bring me luck now, baby. Please."

After that, everything went quickly. When she opened her eyes, she saw the tiny plus sign and nearly fainted. Her breathing was shallow as she stood staring at the little wand. "Pregnant."

Four years of trying, and now this. "Pregnant."

And right here at Christmas. Now she had something to really celebrate. She'd only agreed to put up the big tree at the last minute, trying to get over the disappointment of having it just for herself and Dench—again. Even when her brother's children worried about the tree, she'd almost refused, but now there was something to celebrate, a reason to anticipate.

The single word felt good as it crossed her lips and she couldn't stop herself—she said it again and loved each syllable. "Pregnant."

Righting her clothes, collecting her things, flushing the toilet, washing her hands, leaving the restroom—all mechanical things she would never remember doing. There was no room in her head or her heart for more than the one thought she nursed all the way back to the elevator: *I'm pregnant!*

She pressed the button and when the elevator arrived, she stepped on board, the very image of a dignified business woman. The doors whispered shut and she couldn't help herself. "Baby," she shouted to the empty car. The word was out and she felt better for it, but she needed just a little bit more. Digging into her personal boogie groove, she broke down and did her funky little dance until she felt the car slow. When it stopped, so did she.

Stepping off the elevator in front of MYT, Unlimited, Marissa Yarborough Traylor took a deep breath and promised herself that she would not skip through the doors and do a repeat of her happy dance in the lobby— that just wouldn't be dignified. She and her partner had earned their elegant seventeenth floor offices in the prestigious Hanover Building in Buckhead's Tower Place complex. Being women, relatively young women at that, they'd worked hard to establish themselves as more than pretty faces with law degrees and knowledge of sports. Rissa had no intention of sullying that reputation.

It was hard, though, especially when she was carrying the kind of news that she had. Rissa had to stop herself from biting her lip as it occurred to her why her brother, her husband, her sister-in-law, and even her mother always said the same thing about her: "That girl's mouth won't hold water!" And it was pretty much true, she had to admit. Keeping secrets had never been her forté, but this one was for Dench.

"Of course, after I tell him . . ." The list of people she would tell was a long one. Rolling her shoulders back, she stood taller, lengthening her long frame as she made a mental list of the first people she would tell after Dench. Mom first, then there was Marlea, her sister-in-law, and Marlea would tell AJ if Dench didn't beat her to it.

And Yvette, her friend and partner, who would have a happy dance of her own. Yvette had been listening to Rissa's baby blues almost from the first time they'd met back in law school. Over the years, she'd listened to Rissa coo over babies every time they went out for lunch, shopping, a movie, or . . . pretty much always, and she wanted nothing more for Rissa than motherhood.

Rissa felt the nervous flutter in her belly. It mirrored the flutter of happiness in her heart and she pressed her lips together, reaching for composure. *I need to calm my happy self down. This little test could be wrong; it happens sometimes. I need a confirmation, so I can't say anything until I talk to my doctor.* A big breath and the narrow shot of logic did a little to calm her nerves. But the damned smile on her lips just wouldn't die.

Doing the best she could, determined to hold onto her secret, Rissa shifted her coat to the other arm and raked fingers through the short, razored thickness of her hair. She pushed through the door of her office suite, where the countdown to Christmas was in full swing.

"Looks like Santa Claus exploded up in this camp," Rissa said, looking around.

Eggnog seemed to be the drink of choice and was available from a crystal punchbowl perched on a corner of the receptionist's light- and tinsel-edged desk. Lifting her cup in salute, Karee, the receptionist, licked her lips and seemed to be enjoying it. Somewhere along the hall to the left, Rissa heard the Temptations singing about Rudolph, and one of the paralegals was handing out something wrapped in red and green paper. A ten-foot-tall, brightly sparkling pine tree held a place of honor near the door, and the mound of wrapped gifts for the Toys for Tots campaign had doubled in the time she'd been gone.

"Yvette, you and Helen have driven these people Christmas crazy in less than three hours. That's got to be some kind of record—even for you two."

Helen, passing by with a clutch of color-coded folders and wearing twinkling reindeer antlers, raised a hand and kept walking. Even in the spirit of the season, she had an office to manage.

Yvette Trask was another story. "Pump up the spirit, girl, 'tis the season. Cookie?" Wearing a fetching red and white Santa's cap, she strolled up and held out a festive, fully-laden tray. "Eat up, girl, eat up," Yvette urged, taking a cookie for herself. "I was up all night baking these, my grandmother's recipe. They're totally delicious and if I could, I would eat them by the dozen."

"You do anyway," Rissa grinned, taking a cookie. She pressed her cheek to her partner's, then bit into her cookie. "Oh, my God, this is delicious," she said, chewing behind her hand. "I can taste the butter and eggs. I feel my arteries clogging. I swear, if these things weren't so good, I would just slap them on my hips and lick my fingers, like you do."

"Don't hate, I didn't get all this just from cookies." Yvette accepted the air kiss, took another cookie and handed the tray off to one of the interns. Chewing, she said, "If you worked at it, you too could be the bearer of similarly luxurious amplitude. But no, you're just too lazy to eat wrong and ignore exercise."

"Right, *sensei*, 'cause I know you know what you're talking about."

At a shade over five feet in height, and looking up at her taller friend, Yvette slid a hand over her full hip and shook her head. "I would say something, but we have guests. Your four o'clock is here, and he brought his mama with him."

"Four? It's only a little after three." Rissa's eyes followed her partner's pointing finger to James and Brenda Clarence.

"Well, they're here now, and they're waiting for you, so don't shoot the messenger. Now, where did those cookies go?" Yvette turned, gave her red sweater a tug in the right place, and marched off, following her nose.

Seated in a soft, taupe-colored, corner-angled suede chair beneath a giant wreath, Rissa's newest client looked scared. At average height and weighing in at about one-fifty, James was all muscle and wound tight as a spring. Maybe it had something to do with the fact that she would be his first professional agent, or maybe because he was about to sign a major representation contract. But Rissa figured the truth was that his mother, Mrs. Brenda Clarence, was seated next to him, and Mrs. Brenda Clarence was a formidable woman—*I'd be scared of her, too.*

Pasting on a professional smile, Rissa started toward James Clarence and his mama. Mrs. Clarence sighed, lifting her full bosom and the plump hands she held folded across her stomach. On his own, James was a handsome, charismatic, talented boxer. In the company of his short, heavyset, low-voiced mother, he was little more than a kid. Brenda Clarence had raised her boy alone, and she had taken the job seriously. She had raised him to be strong and honest, and her own integrity radiated from his bright brown eyes—when he raised them from the floor to meet Rissa's.

"I, uh, we're early," he said softly when Rissa stopped in front of him. His mother nudged him and narrowed her eyes. He blinked rapidly, then tried again. "Miz Traylor. I know we're early, Miz Yarborough-Traylor. Sorry."

"Not a problem." Rissa shifted her coat, tote, and briefcase again as she reached for Mrs. Clarence's hand. Closing her fingers over the other woman's warm hand, she smiled. "If you can give me a moment to make a phone call, I'll be ready for you."

"Sure, sure." Mrs. Clarence gave Rissa's hand a final pat as she settled her hips further back in her chair. She watched Rissa turn and head for her office, admiring her trim figure and neat suit, then leaned close to her son. "Now that's a lady. You want to get married," she whispered, "you get yourself one like that."

"Yes, ma'am." James lifted the little cup of now-warm eggnog to his lips, swallowed hard, and hoped Rissa's call would be brief.

In her office, Rissa dropped her things in the chair nearest the door and headed for her desk. Lifting the phone, she stood for a moment fighting the urge to call Dench and scream into the phone. "Too early," she breathed, wishing that it wasn't. Instead, she pulled her directory closer and dialed her doctor.

Joyce Ashton was a Morehouse Medical School graduate and alone in her Collier Road office. It seemed that everyone else on her staff was still trying to finish Christmas shopping. Pushing back the heavy flow of her locked hair, she refused to be judgmental, though she thought procrastination deserved a place on the list of deadly sins. She would never understand why people put shopping off until the last minute, but it was nice to have this quiet time to herself. Sitting at her desk, reviewing files, she didn't hesitate to answer when the phone rang.

"Rissa, good to hear from you! How is everything?"

"Fine." Suddenly shaky, Rissa clutched the phone in both hands and sucked in a big breath. "Joyce, I know that so close to Christmas this is short notice, but I need a favor. I need an appointment."

"An appointment?" On her end, Ashton wrinkled her forehead. "Well, sure. May I ask why?"

"I know I just saw you three months ago, but . . ." Air sizzled past Rissa's teeth. "I think, uh, I could be . . . pregnant."

"Oh, Rissa! When?"

"Today. I was, you know, late. So I figured . . . I took a home test today. But I need to be sure before I tell, so I'm calling you."

"Confirmation, of course. I understand." Dr. Ashton smiled.

On her end of the line, Rissa blinked and leaned against the desk. "Joyce . . . Am I asking too much? Am I hoping too much? Am I just wanting too much?"

"Rissa, I'm only a doctor, but the way I see it, you and Dench have pretty much got everything going for you that any couple could ask for. You've got a hot career and he's coming into the new defensive coach slot for Atlanta. You've built and furnished that beautiful home off Cascade, and even better, you're both blessed with good health and you were born for each other."

"But a baby, Joyce. We both want a baby so much. And after all this time and all those fertility tests . . ." Rissa's chest rose and fell when she closed her eyes on the sigh. "If I am, I mean, if the test is right and I am pregnant . . ." Swallowing hope, she opened her eyes. "Well, I won't know if I don't check, right? When can I take a test?"

The doctor flipped her calendar. "I can see you first thing in the morning, say seven?"

"Fine, I'll be there at seven on the dot." Rissa could almost hear Joyce smile into the phone, and it warmed her. "I'm taking the test, but I'm telling you, I already know the result." Joyce's light laughter echoed Rissa's as the call disconnected. Dropping the phone into the cradle, unable to move for fear of singing like somebody in a crazy musical, Rissa tried not to think too far ahead and found herself doing it anyway.

"Baby, baby, baby," she sang softly, then caught herself imagining . . . a boy first and then a girl, just like for AJ and Marlea. Tall, of course. *How could our children be anything else?* Dench was a couple of inches over six feet, and though her own five-nine hadn't counted for much when she tried out for the WNBA, she was fairly tall for the average woman. So, yes, the children would be tall, and cinnamon-skinned like Dench, Rissa decided. And they would have Dench's eyes, deep and brown with wildly emotional flecks of gold and green.

She was still imagining when the phone buzzed beneath her fingertips, and Karee's voice came from the intercom. "Rissa? Its ten minutes 'til four and Mrs. Clarence wants to know if you're ready for them?"

"Yes, certainly. Send them right in." Lord, Rissa wondered, rising, is this what it's going to be like working with James Clarence? Pulling his file from a drawer, she placed it on the small table in the center of a three-chair conversational area facing away from her desk. She added three Mont Blanc pens—already guessing that Mrs. Clarence would need a souvenir of the signing. Smoothing her skirt, she crossed the room and opened her office door.

With all the grace of a small yacht, Mrs. Clarence flowed into the room, her sharp dark eyes calmly taking in Rissa's framed degrees, signed photos of her brother and other clients, and the subtly feminine lamps and artwork. Leaning, she inspected a photo of Rissa in action.

"That's you back in 2000, the finals." She nodded at the photo of the young woman who had rushed the camera and taken to the air with a hook shot. "I remember that. I saw that game on ESPN. I never played, but I know class when I see it, and you were really something." Clutching her purse, Mrs. Clarence's dark face dimpled when she followed Rissa's gesture and sat in one of the bright red chairs with a solid thump. "You should have gone to the WNBA, but I guess we can't all be Lisa Leslie, can we?"

"No, ma'am, we can't, and it's too bad because at six-five, *she* can dunk." Rissa smiled. "But that's okay because she's an awesome player and an awfully nice woman." She looked back at her client and indicated a chair. Looking like he'd rather be anywhere else, James sat facing his mother and his agent.

Mrs. Clarence looked at her son and realized his lips were still. Drawing herself up in her chair, she sniffed delicately as she pointed at the file on the table. "Are those the contracts?"

Rissa nodded and opened the file, setting three sets of contracts in front of her client. Brenda Clarence reached for one set and read it quickly. James turned the pages and let his eyes slide across the pages.

Brenda tapped the edges of the pages together when she finished reading and looked squarely at Rissa. "We're here because you strike me as smart, and because you believe in my boy. You took good care of your brother, and I believe you'll take care of my son."

Rissa nodded at the mother and smiled at the son. James looked up and smiled back. "My husband says that you're easily the most exciting fighter in the game today, James. I watched you fight and I agree. If I didn't, we wouldn't be here today. As a boxer, you have your flaws, but you seem consistently able to overcome them with sheer offensive might, and you sure as heck are getting hit a lot less often. You're a good, potentially great, fighter, and I am going to take very good care of your career."

"That's what I'm talking about." Brenda Clarence flapped her large leather bag at her son. "That's exactly what I'm talking about."

"Mrs. Clarence," Rissa as she turned slightly to face the older woman, "I appreciate what it must have taken for you to turn your son's career over to me, but I need you to realize that once he signs these contracts, the job is mine, all mine—and I will be working for him, not you. Are we all clear?"

Shifting in her seat, Brenda Clarence looked annoyed, concerned, then resigned. Her lips pushed together and she took a deep breath before nodding slowly. Across from her, her son almost sagged with relief. He reached for one of the Mont Blanc pens and began signing the contracts in front of him.

His mother watched in silence, finally turning her narrowed gaze to Rissa. Her eyes were hard and appraising when James passed the signed documents back. "You'll take responsibility for my boy?"

"Yes, I will." Rissa never blinked. "Full responsibility."

"Good. Well, now that that's done, I guess I'm satisfied." Brenda Clarence was satisfied enough that she stood and offered her hand to Rissa. Nodding, she gripped Rissa's tightly and smiled when Rissa neither flinched nor grimaced.

James stood beside his mother and offered his hand, as well. "Thank you, Miz Yarborough-Traylor. I never really saw this coming, this agent thing, but I'm glad it did and I'm glad to be working with you. Thanks. Can I keep this pen? For a souvenir?" His mother cleared her throat loudly. "And one for my mother, too?" On Rissa's nod, James smiled and tucked the pens into his jacket pocket.

"James, let me know if there's anything I can do for you, any questions I can answer for you, okay?" The boxer nodded and Rissa walked the Clarences to her office door. Walking behind his mother, James's feet suddenly slowed.

"Uh, did you mean it? I can ask you anything?" Whispering, the boxer's face was tense, almost like when he stood facing an opponent across the ring. His mother kept walking.

"Well, sure. I'm your agent." Rissa wasn't sure why she was whispering, but he'd started it.

"Can I come talk to you? In the morning? Early?" He cast a furtive glance over his shoulder; his mother was sampling cookies.

"Early, sure, but . . ."

"I just have something to . . . to talk to you about. It won't take long, but it's important. Really."

"No problem, I'll be here."

The boxer's fisted hands pumped air and he grinned. "Great. Thanks again."

Rissa watched his back when he hurried toward his mother. His shoulders and spine seemed straighter and stronger, as though a weight had been lifted. "Whatever it is, at least he has faith in me."

She would have watched longer, but the phone on her desk rang. Turning, she noticed that it was her direct line, the number that only her family used. Picking up the phone, she waited a beat before saying anything, then before she could, Dench's warm tenor filled her ear, "Hey, baby, how's it going?"

"Good, and guess what . . ." She caught herself just in time.

"What?"

Damn! Didn't mean to say that! Pushing her chair away from the desk, she dropped into it and turned to face the window. "I made a run to Macy's and picked up the tablecloths today. I'm so excited about doing Christmas Eve at our house, and . . .you will be here, won't you?"

"Dude, that is so not what I called to say," her husband laughed. "I was just sitting here closing out some paperwork and you were on my mind." He laughed again. "You must be real tired, 'cause you've been running through my mind all day."

"Oh, I am not nearly as tired as that joke."

"Come on, give a brother a break. I worked hard on that."

She shook her head. "And for that I got you the big bucks?"

17

"Naw, baby. You got me the big bucks 'cause I'm sexy."

"Yeah," Rissa sighed into the phone. "There is that."

His voice dropped, the growl making her cross her legs tightly. "And because you know I love you like . . ."

"Jesus loved the church," she finished with him. The biblical words from *Ephesians* had been a part of his marriage vow to her—he claimed that he remembered them from childhood Sunday school. Now, every time he said the words, she felt bound to him by a wash of love so deep that it defied passion and defined him as the only man she would ever love. "Nice to know you love me."

"I do, Rissa. I always have. I always will."

"I know," she whispered into the phone. Turning her chair to the Buckhead skyline, she bit her tongue and closed her eyes. *Don't tell him. Not yet.* "I know."

"I just wanted to let you know that I found something for your mother." Dench cleared his throat proudly. "I found the perfect thing."

"What? You found about a million flashbulbs for that old camera of hers?" Rissa laughed, thinking about her mother's old Kodak Brownie Hawkeye. "Goodness knows, she needs them, because she's never going to use the digital camera we gave her."

Dench laughed, too, and the sound made Rissa hold the phone closer to her ear. "Okay, so I didn't find a million, but do you think she'd go for a gross? That's a hundred and forty-four, babe. I got two gross, and a case of one-ten film to go with it."

"Oh, see? That's just one more reason I love you. And, AJ'd better watch out because you know that you're going to be Mom's favorite now."

"I know, I know," Dench crowed. "But I also know you're at the office, so I'm going to go now. I just couldn't wait to tell you." His voice slowed, longing evident. "Maybe you're rubbing off on me."

"I'll have to check on that when you get home." Rissa heard her own longing surface. "And just so you know, I'm planning a *very* close inspection."

"I'm looking forward to it. Love you, babe."

"Love you more," she whispered as the call disconnected. She sat for a long moment with her hand resting on the phone.

"He's going to call back tonight." He always did when he was away, and those late night calls were always interesting. *Nobody told me about those calls when I got married.* She smiled. *Nobody told me how interesting phone sex with my husband could be.* Imagining made her blush with anticipation. Then she sat up in her chair, remembering. "I just have to figure out a way to keep my mouth shut until he gets here."

CHAPTER 2

"James?" Stepping off the elevator, Rissa almost tripped over her own feet when the boxer grinned up at her from the floor. "What the hell are you doing down there?"

He gathered his compact body and got to his feet. "I don't like being late, so I left home early and then traffic was pretty light, so I got here even earlier than I planned. Nobody was in when I got here, so I waited." His grin slipped a little bit and he held a small Starbucks bag and two large cups of coffee forward. "I brought coffee, not too light and one sugar. Will it help?"

"Couldn't hurt." Rissa shrugged and reached for one of the cups. A quick glance at the container showed steam, and the smell was inviting, not that she needed the caffeine jolt to wake her up. Not after last night—after Dench's call and all the crazy things he promised, she couldn't eat, couldn't sleep, didn't dare call anyone, and after hours of tossing and turning in the empty bed, she was afraid of oversleeping. She knew from the clock at her bedside that she had gotten exactly three hours of sleep the night before.

And then there was the test. *I swear, I haven't been this nervous since I took the LSAT,* she'd told the doctor. Now, waiting for the results and facing a client who looked as antsy as she felt, Rissa was so wide awake that her nerves shimmered and jangled. "A woman working on three hours of sleep deserves coffee," she muttered, bringing the cup to her lips. It was perfect. "Where's Karee?"

James's shoulders rose and fell. "Not here yet."

Behind them, the elevator chimed and Karee rushed off, keys and knit hat in hand. "I took the train this morning, and you know how it can be some days, but I'm here now." Breathless, she eyed the cups Rissa and James held. "Smells good. Only two cups, huh?"

Rissa raised an eyebrow and sipped deliberately. "That we'll probably finish before you get some made."

"I'm on it, boss." Karee pressed her full lips into a thin line and unlocked the door. She waited for Rissa and James to enter, then followed. "Should I order up a box of pastries?"

James lifted his small bag. "I brought muffins: cranberry and blueberry."

Karee stopped, gave Rissa a quick glance, then peered into the bag. "I love cranberry," she said, taking a muffin and hurrying to her desk. "Thanks."

"Welcome," James mumbled, following Rissa back to her office. Crossing the threshold, he headed for the bright red chair he'd sat in on his last visit. He put the bag of muffins in the center of the small table and set his cup down beside it. Unzipping his jacket, he pulled it off and laid it across the back of the chair. Then he sat in silence, expectantly watching Rissa remove her coat and hang it up. When she brought her cup to the table and sat across from him, he leaned forward to rest his elbows on his knees and waited.

"James?" His eyes found hers and their brightness softened. Rissa tried again. "James, you said you had something important to talk about. You want to tell me what it is?"

"You don't have to keep calling me James," he said. His eyes went back to his coffee and he picked up the cup, turning it between his palms. "That sounds too formal. Could you call me Jimmy? I'd like it if you did."

"Okay, Jimmy it is."

He passed one hand over his close-cut hair and nodded. Rissa could see the creeping path of an almost too youthful blush climbing his bronzed throat and clean-shaven cheeks. Opening and closing his mouth, he made a couple of false starts. "Okay," he finally said. "You met my mother. She's all about support, doing things right, you know?"

Now, where, Rissa wondered, *is this going?*

"Well, she doesn't take, uh, disappointment too well. Right now, she's kinda disappointed in me. She doesn't think I'm ready to take on marriage." His shoulders pulled up around his ears and he sat a little lower in his chair. "That and Sierra."

"Sierra?" Rissa knew that the obvious question was all over her face.

The name infused Jimmy with new energy and he set the coffee on the table and shifted to pull his wallet from his pocket. "Here," he said, pulling a small photo free and offering it to Rissa. "This is Sierra. She's pretty, huh?"

"Very," Rissa agreed, looking down. A young and beautiful oval face remarkable for its knife-sharp cheekbones, almost feline long-lashed eyes, and red-touched ebony skin smiled up at her. "Your girlfriend?"

Smiling, the boxer nodded as he passed his hand over his head again. "Yeah, my girlfriend and my problem—part of it, anyway. The other part is my mother—she thinks Sierra is good enough for a girlfriend, but not a wife. Especially not for *my* wife."

Rissa passed the photo back. Now it was beginning to make sense. "You want to marry her, in spite of what your mother has to say." He nodded, just as she'd known he would, and she straightened in her seat. "Jimmy, look, I'm your agent and my job is to do what's good for your career—not your love life. You've got looks, talent, a very defensive and supportive mother, and a problem that I can't fix. Who you marry is entirely up to you."

"See, I know that, but there's more. Sierra's pregnant."

"Does your mother know?" Rissa folded her fingers in her lap and waited. When Jimmy's eyes darted away, she knew the answer. "You haven't told her yet. Why not?"

"Because . . . I don't know. Maybe I don't want to hurt her feelings." He shrugged and slid lower in his chair. "She already thinks I'm too young to be a husband. I don't know what she'll say about my being a father, but it won't be good. I'm all, maybe not all, she's got, but she's invested so much of herself in me. I don't want to hurt her. And Sierra, she says she won't marry me. We've been together since we were sixteen, just kids, and I thought she loved me enough." He finally let his eyes find Rissa's and shrugged. "I know I sure do love her enough to last me for a lifetime."

"You look miserable." Rissa scooted into the chair next to him and softened her voice. "Why did she say she wouldn't marry you?"

"Because she's pregnant. Does that make sense? She said I waited too long. What does that mean?"

"It means that she doesn't want you to marry her *because* she's pregnant." Tickled, Rissa tapped Jimmy's knee and smiled. "Jimmy, honey, are you really that young? Don't you see, she wants you to want *her*. She wants you to marry her because you love *her*, because you want to build a life with *her*, because *she's* the only woman in the world you can see as being the mother of your child. You should definitely love the baby, too, but she doesn't want her only identity to be as the mother of your child." *Something that would never happen with Dench*, she didn't say.

Confusion was deep and swirling in the boxer's brown eyes. "But ma'am, I do love her. I bought her this to show her how much." He pulled a jeweler's box from his pocket and flipped it open. Glittering against dark velvet, the diamond shone like a small star and Rissa sighed.

Rising, she walked around her chair to stand behind her new client. "Jimmy, you're going to have to do more than just show her the pretty ring. You're going to have to do music and candlelight, and get down on one knee. If she's old-fashioned, you're going to have to go see her father and ask for her hand in marriage. You're going to have to share finances and life insurance, and make a home for her if you want a wife. You're going to have to promise this girl a lifetime of love, for better or for worse, even if it ticks your mama off—and then you're going to have to be a man of your word. You're going to have to commit all that you are to her and make her see it."

"Aww, that's lame."

Rissa's nut brown eyes narrowed and the corner of her mouth ticked. "You've been your mother's boy all your life. You want to be this woman's man, you're going to have to man up."

"So lame."

He jumped when Rissa swatted the back of his head. "That's why she won't marry you, boy."

"Ow." Jimmy slid a slow hand over the smarting spot her palm left behind. He looked at her, started to speak, then thought better of it.

Seating herself, Rissa looked into his face. "Now Jimmy, I've gotten you the contract you wanted because that's my job. I've gotten you the endorsements you wanted—hell, baby, you're going to be an action figure. And now you want a wife. I've told you what to do, it'll work, and you'd better treat her right because I am not going to do a press cleanup for you. Clear?"

"Yes, ma'am."

"And your mama? Buy her something nice for Christmas. You can afford it. Then introduce her new daughter-in-law as the woman you love and intend to spend your life with."

The boxer looked queasy. "She's not going to like it . . ." Rissa's lips pushed together, a charming pout, but James read seriousness in the look she gave him. "Maybe I could just . . ."

"Boy, don't make me slap you again." Rissa leaned forward with narrowed eyes and Jimmy reflexively sat a little farther back in his chair. "Man up. Don't debate it, just do it. Tell your mother where your life is headed, because once you get to the part about the pretty grand-babies, I can assure you, she'll get over it."

"Pretty babies," he muttered, then brightened. "They will be pretty, won't they? Like Sierra and maybe a little like Mom. She'd like that."

Rissa turned palms to the sky and looked wise.

"Merry Christmas, Miz Traylor. And thanks." Standing, he dug deep into the pocket of his jacket and slid a small red ribboned box across the small table. "This is for you. Thanks for, you know, everything." He turned and hurried from her office.

Shaking her head, she watched him leave with the ring in his other pocket. "He's going to be fine," she promised herself.

Lost in thought, Rissa almost missed the ring of her cellphone. Shifting professional gears, she put James Clarence out of her thoughts. Flipping the phone open, she barely got her name out.

"Merry Christmas, the test is back," Joyce Ashton fairly sang. "Back and positive."

"Positive? Really?"

"Did I stutter?"

Clapping a hand over her phone, Rissa squeezed her eyes shut and blew out hard. Reaching for composure, she took a deep breath and opened her eyes. "I'm really pregnant."

"Yep. I want to talk to you about it, but it's a definite positive."

"Holy . . ." Without thinking, Rissa clicked the call off. "Finally," she breathed. Folding the phone between her palms, she squinted, thinking. "Now, who can I tell?"

Forgetting her earlier list, her thoughts raced, checking and discarding. *Call my mother, and I might as well call the* Journal-Constitution. *Could tell Yvette, but she's not in yet and knowing her, she wouldn't be able to keep it to herself either; she'd be on the phone to Dench in a New York minute.*

Connie and Jeannette? Anxious fingers tapped the phone. *They're nurses and they have had my back right from the very first fertility test. I know they'll be excited for Dench and me. They've always been great, even from the first time they reached out to Marlea in Grady Hospital's Emergency Room after her accident. They're a part of our lives now, but as much as I love them, they're friends, not family. I want to share this with my family. I could tell AJ, though . . . but he would knock Marlea over, running to Dench, and I want to tell Dench myself—in person, not over the phone.*

"But Marlea . . ." *Now, there's a thought. Goodness knows, she can keep a secret. Humph, I would run out of fingers and toes if I tried to count the things she's kept her mouth shut about just since I've known her. Besides, she loves me. I'm the sister she never had.*

Rissa flipped the phone open and hit speed-dial.

"Hello?"

Rissa congratulated herself; this had to be fate. Marlea had picked up the phone and answered on the first ring. "What are you doing?"

"What do you mean, what am I doing?" Marlea screwed the lid onto the small pink sippy cup and passed it to Mrs. Baldwin, who in turn passed it into Nia's eager little hands. "I'm trying to get breakfast into my children, and then . . . hold on."

"Apple, please." Jabari swung his feet and watched Marlea juggle the phone, his apple, and a paring knife. When Mrs. Baldwin moved to collect the apple and the knife from his mother, the little boy grinned. "I like apple in my oatmeal," he informed the housekeeper as his mother made good her escape.

Easing her hip onto a high stool at the granite counter, Marlea moved the phone to her other ear. "Now, I can talk. What's going on?"

"I need to talk, but not on the phone. Can you get away? I don't have any other appointments this morning, and I'll meet you wherever you say. Just make it somewhere nice, okay?"

"Rissa, it's not even ten in the morning on Christmas Eve, and my two little hooligans are up and in full effect." Marlea paused when her children began to shout greetings at the sound of their adored aunt's name. "They're saying good morning, Merry Christmas, and . . . something special in Nia-speak. Oh, it's 'love you,' I think. Anyway, what's up?"

"I already told you that I couldn't tell you over the phone, and it's important. Really important. Mrs.

Baldwin is there, she'll watch the kids. How soon can we meet and where?"

Aware of the housekeeper listening, Marlea tucked stray hairs back into her ponytail and lowered her voice. "I need to change, but give me an hour. I'll meet you at Starbucks around the corner from your office."

Rissa sucked her teeth. "You most certainly will not! I said somewhere nice."

"Beggars can't be choosers, but since it's you, how about Arcadia? I think that it qualifies as a nice, by your terms, beautiful, restaurant, with good food and great service. They open early."

"Arcadia's good. Eleven-thirty?"

Marlea agreed, dropping the phone when she bent to pick up her free-roaming toddler.

The phone clicked in her ear, and if anyone had asked, Rissa would have sworn that she felt some of the pressure of secrecy rise from her shoulders. Pocketing her phone, she walked around her desk to gaze out of her broad window. She was only vaguely aware of the hand she slipped across the flatness of her belly. "Well, baby," she whispered, "it won't be long now."

The woman in the slate gray suit and kente shawl looked irritable and the tight line of her mouth made Rissa lay the spoon carefully on the china saucer and fold her hands into her lap. She offered a small smile of apology. *Wonder if it would make a difference if I told her*

that I was tapping the spoon because I was nervous. If I told her it was because I'm pregnant? The woman gave Rissa a final evil glance before turning back to her companion.

"Well, maybe not but dang, I didn't even realize I was doing it until she looked at me like that," Rissa muttered into her delicately curved teacup.

"Talking to yourself, just like your brother," Marlea said, making Rissa jump. "I'm going to have to watch Nia and Jabari." She shook her head and sat across from her sister-in-law.

"You weren't here. You don't know . . ."

"Whatever." Marlea waved a dismissive hand as she jammed her gloves into her coat pocket and pulled the scarf from her neck. Unbuttoning her coat, she flipped it over the back of her seat and looked at Rissa. "So, what's going on?"

"Have some coffee first, catch your breath and relax."

"Relax? Now, that's a word I don't think I've ever heard from you." Marlea accepted the menu from the waitress and squinted across the table. "Who are you, and what did you do with Rissa?"

"I don't know what you mean." Rissa sipped tea before smiling up at the waitress. "She'd like coffee, I'd like another pot of tea, and we'll both have the Cobb salad, please. We'll decide on dessert later." She turned her attention to the woman across from her. "You look good, for a woman in a hurry."

"Which is a minor miracle, considering I had to sneak past a toddler to get here. Thank goodness our tree was trimmed weeks ago, because the kids are so excited, I don't know how we could ever manage to do it now." Marlea fingered the soft collar of her blue sweater, a gift from Rissa. The woman might be crazy, but she did have good taste. "What's up with the madonna act? Why are you so serene, all of a sudden?" The waitress left the table and Marlea narrowed her eyes. "The pod people got to you, didn't they?"

"Don't talk crazy." Rissa sipped again.

"What's *really* in that tea?" Marlea leaned across the table to inspect the small teapot. Lifting the lid, she sniffed, then turned the tags on the teabags. "And since when do you drink herbal tea?"

"Since I found out I was pregnant."

"Since you . . . what?" Suddenly frozen, Marlea's eyes rose and locked on Rissa's.

"Just this morning," Rissa said. "Nine weeks."

Marlea fumbled the glass of water the waitress set in front of her. Eyes still on Rissa, she finally found her mouth and drank deeply. When the glass was empty, she set it on the table and stared. "After all this time?"

And all those tests and false alarms.

"Can you believe that finally your kids are going to have a cousin? Maybe even the first of many?"

"Have you told Dench yet?"

"No, I have not yet told my husband," Rissa said carefully, even as his name made her grin like a fool. Dench: Big hands, big feet, long limbs, sheets of muscle, warm lips, and a heartbeat like music. "Not yet. I'm thinking that this will make the best possible Christmas present for him." She hugged herself, almost feeling the heat and warmth of him course through her.

"And you."

"And me," she agreed. "Dench has always wanted a family, growing up the way he did, just him and his Aunt Linda." She stopped and looked at Marlea. "I didn't mean . . ."

"I know," Marlea said. Losing parents and being raised by their aunts was something Marlea and Dench shared. Marlea had lost both parents almost before birth. Dench had been left behind first by his father and then his mother, and his aunt had never been able to tell him any more about them before her death; but she'd always loved him and he'd always known that. "I know exactly what you mean, no harm, no foul."

"I want him to have a family, Marlea. I want it for him as much as he wants it for himself. Maybe more."

"Definitely more."

Rissa's fingers framed her plate and she sat looking down at it for a moment. "Nobody ever told me that it would be this hard, getting pregnant, you know? I thought I would be like you, find Mr. Right, have a beautiful wedding, a sexy honeymoon, and a gorgeous baby nine months later. Besides, I'm black. Black women are fertile, everybody knows that. They don't have trouble getting pregnant, right? Unless they're me."

"Aw, Rissa . . ."

Rissa shrugged, a wry smile on her lips. "I have a new client and he came to me with a problem today. His girlfriend is pregnant. Just like that, and it was a problem because neither of them was sure of what to do next. And would you believe that even though I know that in the same circumstances, Dench and I would never have that problem, I was jealous—just a little? And I was jealous because there was a baby in the equation." She shook her head.

"Aw, Rissa . . ." Marlea reached for her hand and settled for linking her fingers with Rissa's.

"No, I'm over it now. Really, I'm okay, it's just that I always dreamed of having children of my own, of having my babies growing up with a lot of love, the way AJ and I did. After you married AJ and got pregnant, I was thrilled. I married Dench and couldn't stop dreaming of all the vacations and stuff my kids would share with yours and then when I couldn't . . . didn't . . ." She almost choked when the hurt ambushed her. "But it's okay, because now . . ."

"Now we've got to plan a baby shower, and you haven't even told him yet. Maybe we should cancel the tree trimming tonight." Marlea lifted her fork and pushed at her salad. Looking up, she tried a smile.

"And have us face Christmas morning alone with a big old naked tree? No, thank you. We'll see you at seven tonight. Bring the babies."

"I can't get over your not telling him yet. I mean, I understand your wanting to tell him face-to-face, but you know that you of all people can't keep a secret, Rissa, especially not a secret like this. When are you going to tell Dench?"

"I was thinking that I could tell him Christmas morning—kind of a gift, you know?"

"Uh-huh, yes. I can see that happening." Marlea's eyes shifted to the ceiling and she snorted laughter. "You keeping a secret, especially one this big? And overnight, too? Bet you can't do it."

"Oh, yeah?" Rissa leaned toward her sister-in-law. "How much you want to lose?"

"Invest, you mean? Let me see." Fork on her plate, Marlea snorted again and reached for her purse. "I've got a fifty, and here's another. That's a hundred dollars I'm betting that Dench won't make it through your front door tonight before you tell him, and definitely that you can't hold out until Christmas morning. And I'll even trust you to tell me the truth, 'cause you know I'm right."

"Honey please, you're an evil woman and I don't know why I chose you to be the first one I told."

"I can tell you why you chose me," Marlea drawled. "You chose me because you couldn't keep it to yourself, and you love me, and you know I won't tell AJ until you say I can. Now, what about that bet? A hundred dollars?" She stuck out her hand. "Shake on it."

Rissa made a face as she reached to shake hands, but her eyes were bright when her fingers closed on Marlea's. "I've waited all my life to share this with the right man. Besides, I only have to keep it from him until Christmas morning, right?"

"Christmas morning, and then all bets are off."

CHAPTER 3

The heavy thump beyond her kitchen made her heart lurch. "Garage door," Rissa whispered, her eyes going to the clock on the kitchen wall. *He's home and I only have to make it to midnight. Marlea thought she was funny making me promise to hold out 'til Christmas morning, thought I couldn't make it. Well, the joke is on her. I get through the next six hours and it's midnight. One minute past and it's Christmas morning, and I can tell Dench over and over again.*

His car door slammed, and she looked around her kitchen. "Marlea didn't say I couldn't give him any hints." She took a quick look at the steamer. Tender baby asparagus and new potatoes were ready, with baby carrots on the side. In the oven, baby back ribs were done to perfection, and baby Bibb lettuce leaves topped the salad cooling in the refrigerator.

"Whatever is clever, and clever would be me," Rissa congratulated herself. "If he guesses, it's not my fault." Placing the arrangement of red rose buds, fern, and pine in the center of the table, she knew she'd certainly set the scene for revelation.

Beyond her table, a wall of windows set along a stone terrace looked out onto a hilly expanse of pine and fern, the trees visible even in the dark because of the miles of tiny white lights strung through their branches. Centered on a slight rise, a pool, beautiful in wintry stillness, reflected a small waterfall and the starry winter sky, cold and breathtaking.

Indoors, Rissa had lined the dozen windows with red and silver ribboned poinsettia plants. Across the room, the fire she'd lit burned brightly and filled the room with warmth. Pine boughs, punctuated by tall red candles in pewter holders, draped the mantle, adding softness to the light and scenting the air around her, making the rooms homey and romantic at the same time. Around her home, comfortable furniture in shades of blue, green, and chocolate brown, rested in pooling shadows created by the moving light. *And it all feels so wrong. Looks pretty, but this is not where I want to tell him. It has to be perfect, a memory for our children*, she shivered, *for our grandchildren.*

But if I feed him, maybe he'll figure it out on his own and that will be a memory worth keeping. Rissa loved the sight of the small candlelit wrought iron table by the windows. *Small and intimate, just the two of us for dinner and a memory,* she approved.

His key turned in the lock. *I get to greet my husband and welcome him home. AJ, Marlea and the kids will come by to trim the tree, stay for a couple of hours, and then I'm home free.* The door handle turned and she blew out hard. *I'm as ready as I'm going to get, and maybe,* she smiled, *since we started this in bed, that might be the perfect place to tell him—after midnight.*

A second later, he stood framed in the doorway. "Hey, baby." When he walked toward her, his stride careless and long, she memorized every move. Three steps into the room, her resolve broke and the squeal that escaped her as she launched herself into his arms made him laugh. The arms that caught her made her want to cry—she'd missed him that much.

"Welcome back." She pushed her weight against him, throwing him back against the wall and pressing her lips to his, drawing away only a hair's breadth when his hands pulled her closer, and she found herself against the wall, clutching his jacket, holding him in return. His mouth on hers and his hands moving beneath her shirt claimed her.

His breath was hot and moist against the column of her throat. His voice, striped with low, growling hunger, tightened her core. "Girl, you don't know how much I missed you, 'cause you know I love you like . . ."

"Jesus loved the church," she whispered, crushing her mouth to his, her long leg wrapping his and binding him close. The taste and feel of him was everything she remembered, wanted, and craved. "Dench," she whispered, needing to say his name.

"Tell me you missed me."

"I did, I do. Always and endlessly." Clarity reared its silly head when his hand slipped past her waistband. "We're in the kitchen, Dench."

"It's paid for." He grinned and hummed when his tongue licked at her ear. "And we're grown."

"And we've got company coming. Later." Her teeth closed lightly on his lower lip.

He hummed again and felt his hunger surge when her hand found skin beneath his shirt. "Bedroom might be better."

Rissa didn't know whether to scream or swoon when he swept her up and over his shoulder. She settled for looping an arm around him as he carried her through the house, and she tangled herself with him when her feet hit the floor at the side of their bed. Pulling him with her, she enjoyed the tumble as they fell together. "This is the bedroom." Her voice was low and husky. "Show me how it's better."

Desire fanned her words and heat licked at his soul. She could feel it steaming from him in waves, from his hands as they touched her, from his skin against hers. She felt it burn and strain when he kissed her, and her urgency aroused him, made him more than he'd ever meant to be for anyone. A wisecrack died on his tongue. In her arms, captured by desire, he found himself linked to her by more than passion-flavored sex when her long legs climbed his back.

He felt himself fall away when the taste of her filled him and the lean curving length of her entranced him. Going deeper, he plundered all that she held for him. A tender cry passed her lips, creasing the night around them, and buried in her, he knew he was home. His lips, hands, and body stoked her yearnings and their cries became a shared moan as he met her call to parts of him that no other woman would ever touch in the same way.

"Rissa."

She heard her name, distant as the stars, and as close as his heartbeat.

"Rissa."

Her fingers gliding along the planes of his back tattooed him. Her eyes soft, her smile languid, her fingers held his face. Tracing his eyes, the bridge of his nose, his lips, she sighed softly. *The hell with Marlea.* Looking up into his face, feeling the rise and fall of his chest against her breast, Rissa took a deep breath, her lips parted—and her words were stopped by the distant sound of door chimes.

"Dude, is that the door?" Dench moved, switching on a bedside lamp.

"Crap!" Rissa sat straight up and glared at the bedside clock—seven on the dot. "AJ and Marlea," she growled. "Damn her prompt little heart. They're here to trim the tree. You let them in while I grab a shower."

"What?" Propped on an elbow, his chest bare, Dench raised an eyebrow at his wife. "And I should just walk around smelling like sex all night?"

"Now, Dennis Charles Traylor, is that really what you think I would have you do?" The eyebrow dropped and he looked sheepish. "I'm going to grab a quick shower and then you can have one. I'd offer to share, but I know how you are and we can't just ignore them—as much as I might want to." She scooted from the bed and headed for the bathroom. At the door she turned slightly, suggestion in her eyes. "We'll finish this a little later, okay?"

"I'll meet you right here." Admiring his wife's rear view, Dench nodded and swung his legs off the bed. He pulled on jeans and a shirt and headed for the front door. Still buttoning his shirt, he looked out to find Marlea and AJ. Standing slightly behind them, Mrs. Baldwin stood patiently holding Nia and Jabari's hands. Opening the door, he saw Connie in the driveway, climbing out of her car. Jeannette emerged from the other door with a shopping bag.

Wouldn't be a party without them. "Looks like a full house." He grinned. "Come on in!"

"House this big will never be full." Connie squeezed Marlea and AJ into a hug.

"Y'all hungry? I know Rissa's got some . . ."

"I'm saving my appetite for those cookies I know Mrs. Baldwin's baking!"

"Thought you were on a diet." Connie looked critical.

"That's why I saved my appetite," Jeannette explained patiently.

"Mebby Kismas!" Nia and Jabari waved frantically up at their godmothers. Connie and Jeannette returned the enthusiastic greetings and bent to kiss cold cheeks before the children were hustled through the door, barely managing to keep up with Mrs. Baldwin's longer stride. The housekeeper smiled, nodded, muttered something about cookies, and aimed the children toward the kitchen. Seconds later, the house sound system came up and the air was filled with Christmas carols.

"Come on in, it's cold out there." Dench ignored the look on AJ's face and waved them all in. Marlea took two steps past him and looked back at AJ, who grinned.

"I take it you just got home?" Marlea didn't try to hide her smirk. "Catching up on things with Rissa? All the news?"

"He just got here," Rissa insisted, appearing at the end of the hall. "We didn't have time for dinner, let alone current events."

"Or shoes," Marlea teased. Dench shoved one bare foot behind the other and looked more than a little guilty when she passed her family's coats to him. She watched him walk away, then turned to Rissa. "What did you do, jump on the man the second he got through the door?"

"He was gone for two weeks."

"So you tried to cripple him when he got back?"

Before Rissa could answer, Nia threw herself against her mother's legs, nearly buckling her knees, and clung there with tears glazing her cheeks. About the time Marlea hoisted the little girl to her hip, Jabari burst from the kitchen. Seeing his mother's occupation, he headed for his father and promptly climbed into his arms.

"What in the world?"

"See what you have to look forward to?" Marlea whispered, producing a tissue and soft words for her daughter. Her palm pressed against her daughter's back and smoothed away the hiccups and sniffing. "Nia? Jabari?"

Needing little urging, Jabari blurted, "I'm good, Mommy. Nia, too. Real good." His balled fist scrubbed at his runny nose before he burrowed his face into AJ's shoulder, and Rissa's heart nearly broke—he just looked too damned much like AJ.

Rissa's hand flattened over her stomach. *My baby's going to look just like Dench.*

Connie came quickly around the corner from the kitchen, waving her finger. "It's Jeannette's fault. She was in there talking bad about Santa Claus."

"All we did was walk through the door." Hands raised in defense, Jeannette followed. "Then all I said was that Santa only visits good girls and boys. I never said a word about . . ." She hunched her shoulders and looked innocent.

"Fine co-godmother you are, scaring the babies like that," Connie sniffed.

"I'm a good godmother and they love me." Jeannette tossed her head as she reached to lay a hand on Nia's head. At her touch, the little girl sighed and Jeannette smirked. "See?"

Connie's hands went to her hips. "She's young yet."

"I swear." Mrs. Baldwin brought up the rear, shaking her head and dusting her hands on her apron. "They have three godmothers and these are the two who always show up." She held out her arms to Nia, who pushed her face against her mother's before going into the other woman's arms.

"You are two quick little monkeys, but you're my little monkeys," Mrs. Baldwin said softly, holding out a hand to Jabari, who looked at his father and then slid to the floor and walked over to take the housekeeper's hand. "Now, let's go finish those cookies before Santa Claus gets here, because he is coming and he'll be hungry. And you two," her nod was for Connie and Jeannette, "stay out here and share your Christmas spirit."

She huffed, and, for a heartbeat, no one said anything.

Jeannette watched her leave the room with the children. "Guess I know where we're not wanted."

Connie looked around, the expression on her face clear: *Is it just me?*

Rissa caught her head shaking when she looked at Marlea and AJ. They stood with eyes on each other and lips pressed together, trying not to laugh, but when Dench walked into the room fresh from his shower, they couldn't help themselves.

"What's up?" Freshly showered, his eyes were heavy lidded and his smile was slow when he looked at them, but it grew wider and more inviting when his eyes fell on his wife. Shifting his hips and broad shoulders, he shoved a hand into his pocket and waited.

Marlea pressed two fingers to her lip and AJ's smile grew casual and sexy. "Kids."

"You didn't hear them?" Jeannette grunted when Connie's elbow nudged her.

"It's Christmas, you're supposed to hear kids," Dench said, his eyes collecting a suddenly blushing Rissa. "I guess they're excited."

"And they're not the only ones," Marlea muttered. Connie and Jeannette watched Dench watch his wife and hid smiles behind their hands. "Yeah," Marlea finished. "Kids."

Dench nodded as if the one word answered all his questions. "You want to help me grab the tree, AJ?" Opening the French doors leading to the terrace, Dench led the way into the cold night and, between them, Dench and AJ hauled the twelve-foot spruce into the house while Rissa signaled the other three women to follow her down the hall.

"Guess you're glad to have Dench home, huh?"

"Always. This big house is lonely when he's away." Rissa's hand seemed to tremble slightly when she reached for the wall panel.

"How about that big bed?" Jeannette danced away from Connie's swatting hand.

"You need to stay out of grown folks' business." A quick and delicate flush blossomed along the column of Rissa's throat and climbed to her cheeks.

"Guess she told you." Connie folded her arms and looked totally self-righteous.

Turning, Rissa opened a closet door and hauled out a series of marked boxes. "Okay, now these are the special decorations, the ones my mother gave me from when AJ and I were growing up, so we have to be careful."

"Yeah, 'cause they're old," Marlea whispered a little too loudly. The nurses snickered.

Rissa didn't miss a beat. "No, those were the ones she gave to you and AJ—from *his* childhood. These are newer—from *my* childhood." She cheerfully placed a box in Marlea's hands and ignored her when she stuck out her tongue. Connie and Jeannette looked at each other, snickered again and stepped back as Rissa led the way back down the hall.

Humming "Jingle Bells," Jeannette set her box down and looked toward the kitchen, sniffing. "Those cookies sure smell good."

"Forget about 'em, you've tortured those children enough for one night." Connie opened a box labeled *LIGHTS*. "What you need to do is sit your Santa-slandering, cookie-lovin' self down and help me untangle these lights."

Chastened, Jeannette dropped her chubby body to the floor beside her friend.

"So that leaves you to help me grab the other stuff from the library." Rissa gave Marlea a nudge with her hip when the door to the garage opened and closed again. Dench and AJ emerged with ladders over their shoulders.

Turning quickly, Marlea managed to hook her arm through Rissa's, towing her down the hall. "So, what did he say when you told him?"

"I haven't told him yet, so you haven't won."

"Uh-huh, I saw how he looked at you, how he keeps looking at you. What happened? He got through the door, you got him in bed, and then you told him, didn't you? I mean, you have every right . . . but we had a bet."

"I didn't tell him, okay?" Refusing to face her, Rissa grabbed bags and loaded Marlea's arms. "Take them and go," she ordered, relieved when Marlea went. Following, trying to hum along with the music filling her house, Rissa prayed for an interruption, something to get Marlea off her trail.

"Raydeer claw!" Nia charged into the living room with Mrs. Baldwin in pursuit. "Raydeer claw!"

High on ladders, Dench and AJ looked down. "What is she saying?"

"Dude, that's your daughter."

AJ sent a dark look at Dench, then watched his happy daughter wade through a swath of tinsel toward her mother. "Raydeer claw, Mama!" Holding a frosted cookie in each hand, she graciously offered one to her mother.

Marlea looked from her daughter to Mrs. Baldwin. "Raydeer claw?"

Taking a second to straighten her snowflake etched sweater, Mrs. Baldwin laced her fingers in front of her and nodded. "Reindeer claws," she enunciated clearly. "The cookies are called reindeer claws. See the shape right there? Jabari fell asleep and I made those for her." Near her knees, Nia jogged in place and held onto her cookies.

"Did you say thank you to Mrs. Baldwin?" Nia nodded happily. Marlea bent to inspect the cookie Nia was trying to fit into her mouth. Smiling, she broke the treat in two, gave the child the smaller portion and folded the rest into a napkin. Aware of the reduction in size, Nia stopped jogging, but was more than ready to follow Mrs. Baldwin back to the kitchen. Connie and Jeannette tagged along, promising to bring a plate back.

"Bet they won't. They'll get in my kitchen, start sampling those cookies, and it'll be all over for the rest of us."

"Speaking of bets . . ." Marlea stuffed the napkin into her pocket and faced Rissa over an open bag. "The night is young, and I'm going to keep my eye on you."

"Over a silly bet? Girl, it is not that serious."

"Silly or not, you made the bet and I intend to collect on it."

"I know you're a teacher and they don't make a mint, but I thought my brother made a little bit of money. Why are you trying to hold me up for a hundred bucks?"

"You told." Marlea looked wise. "I knew you would."

"Did not," Rissa hissed back.

"Told what?" Climbing down from their ladders, AJ and Dench looked curious.

"Nothing," Marlea and Rissa said together.

"And you've just got to know that that means something," Dench said softly.

"I actually forgot to tell," Rissa said quickly. Marlea's neck gave a satisfying snap when she twisted to face her. Calmly, Rissa dug deep into one of the bags and pulled out a red beaded garland. "Mom called as I was coming in this afternoon."

"What's wrong?"

"Nothing, AJ. She's fine, loving Greece, but she's not going to make it tonight or tomorrow. Something about missing a plane and being stranded on Mykonos and not getting home for another week."

"Sounds like 'something' means 'someone.' " AJ grabbed a bundle of lights and handed one to Dench. "Does 'something' have a name?"

Dench slung his lights over his shoulder and swung a long leg onto the ladder. Climbing, he looked over at AJ. "Dude, you're wrong for that."

"Maybe." AJ stepped up on his own ladder and began to anchor the lights on the tree. "But I'm not the one sitting on an island in the Aegean sipping drinks with 'something.' "

"Hey, your mother is an attractive woman." Dench reached around the tree, exchanged light bundles with AJ, and moved down a step on the ladder. "She's done all she needs to do with you and Rissa, she's a widow, and in good health. She deserves some fun."

"Even if it is with 'something.' " Boxes of glass bulbs came out of Rissa's bags. She stole a glance at her watch. *Dang. Only eight-fifteen and I can feel Marlea watching me like a hawk, just lying in wait, trying to make me confess.*

Marlea looped small wire hangers into a dozen glass ornaments. "I'll know if you cheat."

"I'm married to the sexy man on the ladder over there, I don't have to cheat," Rissa hissed, trying to keep her voice low. "What do you think of these?"

"Love them." Marlea reached to hold a pair of the beautifully crafted African kings in her hand. Turning one, admiring the real silk of his purple and gold robes and turban, she sighed. "Maybe next year, when Nia is a little older, something like this will stand a chance at our house."

"A little problem I can't wait to have."

Marlea looked up. "You really didn't tell him?"

"Cross my heart."

"Hmm. AJ said . . ."

"*You* told," Rissa gasped. Her eyes widened and her mouth dropped. "All that about *me* telling, and *you* told!"

Marlea dropped the tiny king and clapped her hands over her mouth. Horrified, her eyes went to AJ and Dench—both apparently oblivious. "He guessed, sort of, but I never confirmed it! Rissa, I didn't think . . ."

"Damned straight, you didn't think." She eyed her brother closely, then snapped her attention back to Marlea. "No wonder he's been watching me since he came through the door."

"He was watching to see if you two could survive what you'd obviously started—him being half naked, and you looking like you needed a cigarette."

"Don't try to change the subject." Rissa struggled to keep her low voice from growing shrill. "What if he said something to Dench while we were out of the room?"

"He didn't. I just know he wouldn't. Besides, you're the one who can't keep a secret. That's why we made the bet, remember?"

"Don't you talk to me about bets and secrets, you old blabbermouth!"

Marlea's skin sizzled beneath the scathing look Rissa sent her way.

"I'm sorry, I don't know what I was thinking. When he said, wouldn't it be nice," Marlea shrugged helplessly, "I think I said something like this Christmas would be the nicest, and he said if you were pregnant, that's all. I wasn't thinking, and I said . . ."

"I guess we should have bet on whether or not you could keep *your* mouth shut."

Looking meek, Marlea tried again. "He's happy for you and Dench."

"What's not to be happy about?" Rissa folded her arms. The bright strains of "Joy To The World" rang through the air around them and it was hard to hold onto her anger. "He's my brother. He loves me."

"What he's really happy about is that you'll both have what you want so much, and even if he was sure of it, he would never tell, Rissa. Not until you told him that it was okay."

"I know."

"Forgive me?"

"Not yet." Rissa sucked in her cheeks and looked away. "I want to savor this moment of sanctimony first."

"And then you'll tell."

"Will not." Rissa's lips twitched and her resolve cracked. She tried to glare, but it washed away when she smiled. "You sure know how to suck the fun out of savoring."

Folding the ladders, AJ looked at his wife and sister, then across at Dench. "What do you think they're over there talking about?"

Dench shouldered his ladder and headed for the garage. "Dude, you know those two as well as I do, and I don't have a clue."

Following, AJ moved the ladder on his strong shoulder. "Then I guess time will tell."

An hour later, the tree was decorated, gifts were opened, cookies had been eaten, and carols sung. Two sleepy children were dreaming of Santa, their laughing parents were ready to assemble and play with the toys, and two grateful ER nurses were glad to have the weekend off. Mrs. Baldwin had plans of her own and nothing more was said about that as the front door closed behind everyone.

"Hungry?" Rissa watched Dench turn off lights. "I could warm up dinner, if you like."

"I'm not starving." Dropping onto the sofa beside her, his arm stretched long, and he gathered her close, his fingers stroking her shoulder. "What did we have?"

"Baby back ribs, baby carrots, baby asparagus, and baby . . ." He looked at her and she could see the question before he asked. Her stomach lifted and fluttered, but she couldn't look away. *Forget you, Marlea!*

"Are we eating on a theme?"

Pulling her knees up, tucking her legs beneath her, Rissa settled deeper into his embrace. "You could say that."

Pulling her close, Dench leaned back against the cushions and listened for her heartbeat against his own. "Baby back ribs, baby carrots," he repeated, "baby asparagus, and baby . . . baby . . . Baby?" He sat up carefully, large hands cradling Rissa's shoulders, and blinked at her. "Baby?" She nodded and his brown eyes misted, the gold and green flecks swimming in a sudden wash of emotion.

"Dench?"

He sniffed and turned his gaze to the ceiling, the fire, over her left shoulder, anywhere but her face as he struggled for control. *Tough guy*, Rissa thought. *My big old soft tough guy.* She let herself be folded into his embrace and waited.

"When did you find out?"

"Just this morning." She could feel his smile, his acceptance and grace as his chest rose and fell against her.

He pulled back and looked at her. "And you kept it to yourself? All day?"

"Yes, I did. Mostly."

He blinked and the green and gold flecks settled in his eyes. "Mostly?"

"Mostly . . ." Rissa scooted her hips into his lap and accepted the tiny kisses he placed along her cheek. "I can tell you that our little bundle of joy will be making an appearance in mid-July, Big Poppa."

"Big Poppa." He grinned. "Is that what you plan to call me?"

"Oh, yeah." Her hand slipped between them and squeezed.

"Dude!" He jumped and shifted, almost spilling her from his lap, but she held on. "You can't be doing that, not knowing that it will be a whole nine months before we can . . ."

"Now who told you that?" She squeezed again and laughed when he moaned. "We can have pre-baby sex." Rissa tightened her arms around his neck and brought her lips to his ear. "We can have really *great* pre-baby sex," she whispered. His mouth opened in wonder and closed in anticipation when she let her teeth close along his jaw line. "*Really* great," she whispered again, nudging his knees apart so that she fit between them.

"But what about . . ."

"The baby and my body?" She gripped his hands and led them beneath her shirt—no bra. "Yeah, well, these will change some."

"I can live with that," he said, easing his mouth along her neck, finding the spot she swore had a direct connection to her very core as his fingers danced over the fullness of her breasts.

"You should stop that . . .in a few minutes."

"Because I'm so good at it, right?"

She wanted to answer him, but his voice was part of the sensual haze drifting over her. Pressed against his chest, offering her mouth to him, her brain began to fog. The taste of him, already coded into her very DNA, came alive and she wanted more. Her heart hammered and she knew it had nothing to do with pregnancy. When she rose, holding his hand, he followed.

In their bedroom, cast in ambient light, she was warm and naked, and he didn't remember or care how she'd gotten that way. On their bed, she moved into his arms, as close as a dream, all scent and touch and shadow. His muscles tensed under her impatient hands, fueling them both, making them greedy for each other. Flesh pressed and she took him inside her, holding tight as the thrill rushed after him.

He moved and even from the beginning, she was hot, wet and trembling. With the first lift of her hips, his body quivered against her, fighting for control, until it shattered under need and pleasure. Blood pounded in his ears as he gathered for her, again and again. In his world, there was spinning and there was Rissa, color and scent gone mad, until the storm inside him was spent.

On his back, feeling his body cool, his desperate heartbeat slow, he smiled. Turning his head, he looked at his wife. On her back, the molten gold of her skin still warm and flushed, she used the back of her hand to brush hair back from her eyes. She smiled and Dench swore he would walk through fire for her.

"Does AJ know?"

"Not unless he guessed." Hoping her sister-in-law was right, Rissa's smile broadened, showing the bright white of perfect teeth. She linked her fingers with her husband's.

Dench looked at their fingers, then back up into her eyes. "Bet it killed you to hold out on him."

"Yeah, it did but, you know me . . ." She kicked at the top sheet until it was close enough to reach, then pulled it high enough to cover them.

"Yeah, baby—you're a rock. You told Marlea, didn't you?"

"Yes . . ."

"So I got it secondhand?" He pulled her close and the pat he gave her was anything but brotherly. It made her shiver. "It's okay, baby. I know that it must have killed you to hold it in for as long as you did, and you had to tell somebody."

"But Marlea . . ."

"Is pretty tight-lipped, so you trusted her."

"Yeah, because . . . well, can you think of anyone better? I wouldn't have stood a chance of telling you if Connie and Jeannette had known. And I didn't want to tell Mrs. Baldwin, or Jabari and Nia. But just think, Big Poppa, we're having a baby."

"Funny. I never thought about a baby for Christmas. I was going to ask if you wanted a kitten, just so there would be something small and cuddly in the house."

"I have you for cuddly, I don't need a kitten." She pushed her hips against him. "Just think, this will be the last time we have that great big beautiful tree just for us."

"And I guess I'd better buy a Santa Claus suit. You know, so that Big Poppa can make the kids smile—the kids and the grandkids. Grandkids, baby." He sighed. "From now on, everything . . . it's for our family." Rolling toward her, his face close, his fingers drifted over her skin. "Sure you don't want a kitten?"

"No way. I want a baby. Our baby."

"Good, and when it gets here, that's what we'll call it—Ours."

She punched his arm and made a face. "That's a horrible name for a little girl."

His lips were soft when he kissed her. "Or boy."

"Or boy," she agreed. Settled in his arms, her breath grew even and Rissa fell asleep dreaming of decorating their family Christmas tree, putting toys together for their children, baking cookies for Girl and Boy Scout meetings. She curled closer to Dench and inhaled deeply.

Her breath was a sigh. He watched her lashes drop, fall softly against the roundness of her cheek, and wondered what she'd begun to dream about when her lips curved into a graceful smile. *The baby, it has to be the baby,* he thought. *My son—or daughter—perfect and healthy. Is it too early to wonder about the baby's sex? What he, maybe she, will look like? Big Poppa, she called me. Yeah, that's me, Big Poppa.*

It's been a long time coming. Watching her sleep, Dench thought about all the stuff he'd heard about pregnant women. *They get fat and cranky and have strange cravings. That's what they say. They say that they have this glow, that they're beautiful.* Rissa had always been beautiful to him. *And we've waited four years for this baby—all that testing. Dude, when I think of all the tests we endured, how sick some of them made her—such a strong woman. Pregnant now, though. Finally.*

She moved in his arms and Dench was struck again by the miracle of this woman he loved more than he'd ever thought he could love any one human on the planet, and he was grateful. *With her I get everything a man is entitled to ask of this life—love, hope, and family. Sure wish Aunt Linda was here for this baby.*

Something thrummed in his chest and for a minute he missed his Aunt Linda so deeply that it hurt. Linda Traylor had been his mother, his conscience, and his pep squad, all rolled into one. She'd been there for him from childhood, right up until eight years ago when she'd passed in her sleep. Depression might have claimed him, if not for his friendship with AJ and his love for Rissa.

I know you're up there on a cloud, just watching. You always liked Rissa, he thought. *Now look what she's done for us.* The ache eased, went away, and he smiled. *Yeah.*

His hand slipped from Rissa's breast to her belly and he held his breath, wondering at the miracle of life. AJ said there was nothing like being a father—and, dude, AJ never lied when it came to Marlea and his babies. Rissa stirred gently, shifting in his arms. *She deserves children and she's gonna be the Mother of Life.*

Drifting, he closed his eyes. The phone rang, sounding far away. Recognizing the sound on the second ring, he struggled to pull himself up from sleep when Rissa made a purring sound. Fingers closing over the receiver, he had to smile. She might hate to miss out on a good secret, but his woman was a seriously sound sleeper. Almost as though she heard his thoughts, Rissa smiled, purred again and snuggled closer to his body.

"Hello?"

The man's voice on the other end was agitated when he asked to speak to Rissa, "Please."

"Who are you, and why are you calling my house at," Dench glared at the clock, "at eleven at night, and asking for my wife?"

"Maybe what I really need," the man said, "is to talk to you."

"To talk to me? What do you need to talk to me about?" Dench whispered into the phone, cupping a hand around the mouthpiece when Rissa moved against him. "Who is this?"

"It's . . . I'm . . . My name is James Clarence, sir. I'm one of your wife's clients and . . ."

"Clarence? The boxer?"

"Yes, sir, and see . . . I've got sort of a situation."

Dench passed a hand over the warm silky leg Rissa suddenly swept over him. "Do you need me to get her for you?"

"No! No, sir. Please don't. You answered, that's a good thing. I need to talk to you."

"About what?" Dench let toughness creep into his voice. "Dude, I'm football and you're boxing. What do we have to talk about?"

"Come on, man." James was pleading. "I need a man's opinion."

Not ready to give in, Dench could almost hear the younger man shrug and blink innocent eyes. "Dude," he finally said, "I am not your father and I'm not a priest."

"But you are a man, and what I need to hear right now is what a man has to say. I need your help. It's about a woman. My woman."

"So you thought you would just call here in the middle of the night and wake mine up?"

"Naw, man, it ain't like that. See, she gave me some advice and I'm going to take it. At least I think I'm going to take it." His voice dropped to a whisper. "I guess I just wanted to hear somebody say everything was going to be all right."

So this is going to take a minute, right? Moving carefully, Dench separated himself from the warmth of his wife and eased from the bed, taking the phone with him. Grabbing his robe, he pulled it over his arms and headed for the kitchen. Flicking on a light, he made a stop at the refrigerator for juice and poured a tall glass. "Tell me about it."

"Where do you want me to start?" James Clarence sounded about as miserable as one man could be.

Dench sipped juice. "Start at the beginning."

James did, spinning his tale of woe, confusion, and fractured love. When he got to the part where he would have reiterated his blues chorus, Dench stopped him.

"Look, dude. You love her, she loves you. You trusted each other enough to share your bodies and you trust her enough to want to entwine your life with hers. You're about to have a baby. If you don't man up now, when do you think would be a better time? I've seen you take some bad dudes out in the ring and you looked fearless. Why would you wimp out now, with so much at stake?"

"See . . ."

"Naw, dude. I don't see nothing but you blowin' smoke about how you don't want to hurt your mother's feelings. You need to talk to your woman and be done with it."

James blew out hard, and it carried across the line. "Man, all that talking stuff, it ain't for me. I'm a boxer, and I'm used to lettin' my hands do the talking for me."

"And now you want to be a husband."

"Uh. Yeah."

"Suck it up, dude—husbands talk. The truth of the matter is that if you love Sierra, your mother will love her better, especially when that baby gets here. Damn, when that baby gets here, your mother is going to forget all about you, and marrying Sierra will suddenly be her idea. Wait and see."

James laughed. "You're right. I guess it's just jitters. Nerves, you know, and it's not like I've got a dad or big brother around. But . . . thanks for steppin' in."

Dench rose, set his empty glass in the sink and looked out into the cold darkness beyond his cozy kitchen. "A man's got to know where his heart is," he said as much to himself as to the young man on the other end of the line. "A man, a husband, and a father have to know where that is, and then you've got to do everything you can to protect that. Good luck on the proposal, and let us know where to send the wedding and baby gifts."

"Will do. And just so you know I was listening, James Clarence does not need luck. I'm going to be marrying the right woman."

"Way to go, dude." Dench grinned and disconnected the call. He couldn't help feeling a little heroic when he turned off the light and went back to his bedroom. At his bedside, he paused to watch his wife. Rissa was still sound asleep, trusting him to be with her no matter what. Sliding into bed beside her, he touched her cheek and smiled, knowing one thing for certain: *I'm going to be here, no matter what.*

CHAPTER 4

Dench pulled the door closed and jerked at the seatbelt. On the other side of the truck, AJ clicked his seatbelt into place and settled back for the ride home. Flowery Branch was less than an hour's ride away, but he knew Dench was glad for the company. The Falcons' training camp was not exactly the kind of place a man wanted to take his wife while he was handling business, but as a former player, AJ enjoyed watching him on the job. He'd also enjoyed getting a look at the team that would hit the field for the last five games of their NFL season.

Dench pulled out of the parking lot and turned left toward Atlanta Highway. Eyes on the road, a corner of his mouth hitched into a grin. "So, what did you think?"

"I think that you've come a long way in six weeks. Has to be hard, trying to pull strong play at the end of January, from a team that you're just getting to know, but you're workin' it out, dude, you're workin' it out." AJ fiddled with the CD player, found something by Pieces of a Dream, punched buttons and nodded to the beat when sound filled the truck cab. "Rissa did good by you, the boys, and the team."

"I knew you were going to say that." Dench's grin widened. "Did you check out Sawyer and Gregg?" he laughed. "Kadeem Gregg, especially. Dude, I'm amazed he could run that fast and watch you at the same time."

"Hey, he's a good kid. He's got speed and good hands, and with some seasoning, he's gonna make a really fine player. They both will."

Dench merged into traffic, still laughing. "You'd say that even if they sucked. Those boys were treating you like the walking god of all football—and you were lovin' it. Go on and admit it, you loved it."

"Aww . . ." AJ pulled his cap lower and tried not to laugh out loud.

"And you didn't seem to mind when my whole back line came running off the field, begging for autographs like a bunch of star-struck kids. No shame, dude, you have no shame. I guess that's what Hall of Fame status will do for a brother."

"Hey, man, you knew what I was when you brought me out here. No shame in my game." Smoothing a hand over his cap, AJ sat straighter. "Besides, now I'm just a humble physical therapist."

"By day."

"Yeah, well, you'd have to ask Marlea about my nights. I'm too humble to speak on it myself," he sniffed.

Dench blew out and rolled his eyes. On the road in front of him, traffic slowed as it merged onto I-985. "And yet you were out there signing autographs like a pro—an old, retired pro."

"I am what I am. But, brother, you were out there taking charge like a real coach—gettin' results and everything. You looked good. I'm thinking Sunday will be a win for you."

"You think?" Dench hit the brakes when kids in a convertible cut him off. "For real?" When AJ nodded, Dench's grin lit his face. "That's high praise, dude. High praise, indeed."

"You deserve it. I saw you, I saw your team, and considering the time you've had with them, you did good." His eyes cut across the cab. "Have you thought about playoffs? Playoffs and Rissa?"

"Playoffs, Rissa, *and* a baby? Yeah, dude. I've thought of almost nothing else." Concentrating on the road ahead, Dench thought again. "She's a complicated woman and she's smart, but I know she's watching the calendar, counting down the days for this baby. Dude, she made me promise to pick up paint samples for the nursery." His eyes met AJ's. "Was Marlea like that?"

AJ shrugged, eyes on the road. "I think they all do that. It's natural."

"Yeah, maybe." Gripping the steering wheel, Dench made his way onto I-285. "Makes it hard to keep my head in the game sometimes."

"Gotta watch that."

"Dude, you think I don't know that?"

"I'm just sayin'."

"I know." Dench's mouth was suddenly dry, even after he found his bottle of water and brought it to his lips. He tried to think of how to say what was on his mind. AJ fiddled with another CD, and Dench tried to frame his thought. "Has she said anything to you—about the baby?"

"You know Rissa," AJ snorted. "Every chance she gets, she's talking about the baby. I thank God that she lives in your house instead of mine—even if it is only down the street."

"Yeah, I do know Rissa. Maybe that's why I think that there's something that . . . she's not telling me."

"Like what?"

"I don't know. Aw, come on AJ, don't look at me like that. I'm not trying to be all, you know, in touch with my feelings. I just know Rissa, and something's off."

"Marlea hasn't said anything—she would have told me if Rissa said anything to her."

"Huh. You sure?"

"Positive."

"Huh." Dench slowed and drove thoughtfully down the exit ramp. "She tell you what happened with her client?"

"Which client?" AJ drawled. "What happened?"

"James Clarence, she calls him Jimmy. He called after you all left on Christmas Eve, right? He had talked to her earlier, then he talked to me. Well, something one of us said must have been right because we woke up a couple days later with a chauffeur at the front door."

"You're joking."

"No, dude, for real. It was about eleven o'clock in the morning, and Rissa was buried under the covers when the doorbell rang, so I grabbed my robe and went to the door."

AJ snickered. "Probably shuffling like an old man in those leather house shoes the kids gave you for Christmas."

"Whatever, dude. I like the shoes. Anyway, by the time I got to the door, Rissa woke up and came running right behind me. You know how your sister is. I barely got the door open before she started asking questions." His voice rose to imitate hers. "Who is it? Is that a limo out there? Why is a limo out there? Is that man dressed as a chauffeur? Why is a chauffeur at our front door?"

"And she never took a breath in between, right?"

"Don't laugh, dude, you know she didn't. But when I opened the door there he stood, a chauffeur, uniform and all. He was even wearing these high, polished black boots like you see in the movies, and I promise, he bowed and all but clicked his heels when the door opened. I asked who he was and he handed over these two long white boxes. 'Courtesy of Mr. James Clarence,' he said."

Turning in his seat, AJ didn't know whether to laugh or not. "So what was in the boxes?"

"You're as bad as Rissa. He was a chauffeur, dude, pulled up in front of my house—that was enough for me."

AJ gave up and laughed.

"Dude just smiled, touched the brim of his cap and got back in the limo. By the time he drove off, Rissa had her box open. Red roses, a split of champagne, and imported chocolates—mine was the same. Don't ask, I guess he was so happy that it was all he could think of. Anyway, both cards had the same note. Seems the boxer is getting married, after all. Private ceremony, and oh, we've been invited to be godparents."

"Godparents, huh?" AJ's laughter simmered to quiet. "That's why you're wondering about Rissa? If this is too much for her, with her own pregnancy and all?"

"Yeah, and she's all over the godparent thing. Thinks it's sweet, thinks she can maintain professional distance as his agent and still be there for him and his wife." Making the turn off Cascade, Dench let his truck slow as he neared the gate to his own street. Pulling close to the electronic sentry he stopped the truck and sighed. Punching in the code, he watched the heavy gate slide open and drove through.

"You think it's too much," AJ finally said.

"And you know I'm right." Dench nosed the truck up the winding stone driveway and stopped at the side door of AJ's home.

"You say anything?" Sitting in the truck in the midst of the winter-bare stone courtyard, AJ saw the things that made his home his own: the rose garden he'd planted with his wife, the small blue boy's bike tilted on its training wheels, a Big Wheel with plastic rainbow streamers parked next to a pink-hooded doll stroller, and a pair of adult bikes neatly racked beside the narrow porch. At the door, several pairs of adult running shoes waited on a shelf next to plastic children's boots.

He couldn't help the sigh that escaped when Dench's glance answered his question. This man was as close as a brother, closer. *And he married my sister. Wish I could help, but . . .* "What did she say?"

"She's your sister, man. You already know what she said."

"And she's your wife. What did she say?"

"That she wanted to do it. That after everything we'd been through, it was a sign that things were going right for us." Dench slid low in the seat and finished off the water left in his bottle. "I opened the champagne and finished it off, then I said I thought it was a bad idea."

"Working up your nerve, huh?" AJ saw the fire build behind his friend's eyes. "What did she say?"

"*Fine.*"

"Damn! That's all she said?"

Dench crushed the empty water bottle and nodded. "Dude, you know that's the one word women use to end an argument when they've decided to be right . . ."

"And you need to shut the hell up." AJ looked across the courtyard and whistled softly.

"I told her that I was going to call Clarence and tell him to count us out, that we had too much on our plate already."

And now I know what a dead man looks like. AJ looked at Dench and shook his head. "What did she say to that?"

"*Go ahead.*"

"You know that was a dare and not permission, right?"

"Yeah, I know. But at least I got her to agree to think about it."

"Or at least that's what she's going to let you believe, for now." AJ shook his head. Across the courtyard on the porch, pretty white eyelet curtains moved in the window next to the door. He saw his sister's curious face appear, eyes bright, lips curling in a smile when she recognized the truck. "Speak of the devil . . ."

". . . and the imps appear," Dench finished, reaching for his door. "My Aunt Linda used to say that."

"Hope she was wrong this time," AJ muttered, climbing out on the passenger side.

The door opened and Rissa slipped out. She pulled the door closed behind her and stood waiting, her jeans and sweater shrouded in the blue afghan she'd pulled around her shoulders. Dench smiled and she smiled back. It amazed him how still she could be sometimes, and how perfect she could be in her stillness—like now. Poised with the dark slash of her hair and the warmth of her eyes contrasting against the rosy gold of her skin, she waited for him as if he were the only man in the world. When her full lips parted, flashing the brightness of her teeth, he felt his heart clench.

"Hey." Behind him, he heard AJ's voice. "It's my house, how come you get the hero's welcome?"

"Dude, 'cause I got it like that." Long steps took Dench to Rissa's open arms and he forgot all about AJ.

Knowing when his presence was not required, AJ stepped past them and pushed the door open. He grinned when his wife and children looked up at him from the middle of a room filled with women and children. *Play date*, he remembered.

Nia promptly stood from her seat on the bright-colored plastic see-saw, tipping another child over in her rush for her father. Jabari was close behind, and a laughing Marlea just shrugged as she came toward him. *It's good to be the king*, AJ thought, scooping up his daughter and son.

A king in his own right, Dench strolled in with his arm around Rissa's shoulders and surveyed the room. "What's with all the little people?"

"Play date," Rissa answered. "I'm not sure why Marlea thought the King holiday would be a good time to bring children together, but since Yvette and I closed the office today, I thought I would help." Her lips brushed his ear to whisper, "Besides, it's good practice."

"Speaking of practice," AJ leaned in and whispered into Dench's other ear, "let me show you what to do in a roomful of kids." He planted a loud wet kiss on Nia's cheek and one on Jabari's before letting them slide to the floor. They looked up at him with adoring eyes, then melted into giggles when he winked at them. Lifting his hands to the room at large, he looked at Marlea. She made a "mommy face" and the children took the hint.

"I'd better go help," Rissa chuckled, peeling away from Dench's side.

"And that's all there is to it," AJ grinned. "Let's get something to eat."

"Where's Mrs. Baldwin? You know she's got a thing about her kitchen."

"She's probably hiding in her apartment, or maybe on the phone in the den. You know she's got a boyfriend now."

"No kidding?" Dench followed AJ into the kitchen and pulled open the refrigerator door. "Same guy she was with Christmas Eve?"

"Far as I know." AJ set plates and glasses on the high granite counter. Turning to the range, he lifted lids from the pots and made a face. "Looks like the kids had spaghetti."

"I like spaghetti."

AJ shook his head at the pot. "Man, this is little kid spaghetti, all sweet and bland. No garlic, no oregano, no real seasoning. Trust me, this is not the spaghetti you want."

"How about this, then?" Dench popped a Tupperware container open. "Baked chicken?"

"From last night. Cool." Looking over his friend's shoulder, AJ pointed. "Grab that one, that one, and that one." Taking the containers from Dench, AJ opened them and approved the contents. "A couple of beers, and we're in business."

Heaping plates took minutes to heat in the microwave while the two men sat with their longnecks. In the rooms beyond the kitchen, they could see Connie lightly tossing a ball to Jeannette as a trio of three-year-olds chased them. Rissa sat in the middle of the floor with a thumb-sucking child in her lap, reading aloud, while Marlea sang about the wheels on the bus.

AJ shoveled in a mouthful of garlic-laced mashed potatoes, then pointed his fork at the scene before him. "Not sure why Marlea thought the Martin Luther King, Jr. holiday would be a good time to bring children together, but when you marry a teacher, even one who holds world records as a runner, you have to expect childhood enrichment." He dug his fork deeper into his potatoes. "Just think, in a few months, you'll be sitting here with one of your very own."

Dench swallowed hard and had to reach for his beer.

AJ jabbed his fork into the chicken. "Of course, they don't start out like that, running around, talking, eating spaghetti. Yours will be little, an infant."

"Right, all round and smooth and . . ."

"And then you'll have to feed it and burp it and change it, and man, when they need changing . . . whew!"

"Dude, you sure know how to take the joy right out of it, don't you?" Dench sucked at his beer again.

"Hey, I've done it twice. Just consider me the voice of authority."

"But you didn't do it alone."

Halfway to his mouth, AJ's fork stopped. "No, I didn't, and truth be told, I wouldn't have it any other way. Marlea made it so . . . right. That made it cool, a lot easier, and when your own baby looks up at you with eyes that trust you for everything . . . there's nothing like it, nothing like it in the world."

Imagining, Dench watched the other man's face. "Dude, you're just soft. You sound like a man in love."

"Hey, I am what I am." AJ laid his fork across his plate, his eyes fixed on his family. "Give it a minute. The woman, the children, they get to you like that."

"And what doesn't kill us makes us stronger."

"I like how strong she makes me, man. I like it a lot."

"Whipped," Dench whispered.

"Like puddin'," AJ agreed, taking up his fork again. "I wouldn't trade my life for anything. I can't imagine anything better."

"I wanna be just like you when I grow up." Eyes on Rissa, Dench tilted his bottle to his lips and drained it.

"Keep on living," AJ promised, finishing the last roll on the plate between them.

"It's a good thing you two didn't mess my kitchen up any more than those children did, or you'd be lucky to keep on living," Mrs. Baldwin muttered from the doorway. "I leave here for five minutes and you two come in here like twin tornados—and look at the food. Ought to change your last names to 'Hoover.' You suck up food like vacuums."

Dench made a face. "Where'd she come from?"

"Sneaky," AJ whispered.

"With really good ears," Mrs. Baldwin huffed. Whisking the men's empty plates from counter to sink to dishwasher took seconds. Mrs. Baldwin reached into the refrigerator and withdrew cold beer and set the tall bottles in front of the men. "Remember that the next time you want to discuss me."

"Okay."

Dench flinched, his shoulders rising. "Oh, you're just gonna take my life in your hands. You *know* that's a dangerous statement, coming from a woman."

Mrs. Baldwin pressed her lips together and looked over the top of her glasses.

"Not saying that I know all about every woman in the world," Dench amended, trying to mitigate the damage. AJ wrapped long legs around his high stool and looked from his friend to the housekeeper. "See, what I really meant was," Dench tried again and stopped when words failed.

AJ brought his fist to his mouth and succeeded in not laughing. "All I know is, I love my wife."

"So now you're going to throw me under the bus?" Dench's eyes filled with brief reproach that gave way to something more vital. "I love my wife, too. Even if she can be crazy sometimes."

"Marlea gets crazy, too. And stubborn, especially when it comes to doing what she thinks is right."

The lift of Mrs. Baldwin's eyes was an unspoken prayer for patience.

"Okay," AJ admitted, "we love them, we married them, and we will definitely keep them, no matter what. Maybe it takes some imperfection to make a woman perfect."

"Here comes the bus again. . . ."

"You've got more nerve than a brass-assed monkey." Hands on her broad hips, Mrs. Baldwin let her eyes lift again. "You both do. Neither one of you has got the sense to realize that those two women would probably be sane if they didn't have two slightly screwed up men to contend with. After all, I've had the chance to see you at your best and your worst." She looked directly at AJ and pushed her lips together. "Like that screaming fit you all went through when Marlea ran the race in New York that time. And I can always tell when you two have had a falling out because she wants to eat pancakes—like it's my fault."

"Dude, she called that, got you cold!" Dench hooted.

Mrs. Baldwin turned on him. "You're not much better: Rissa gets on your nerves and you practically move in here because you can't bear to be unhappy in her presence. Got that woman so spoiled she thinks the sun rises and sets on you, dares anybody to tell her different, and won't admit it to your face. Crazy, that's what it is."

"She told you, didn't she?" Dench watched the house-keeper's face soften.

"I might have heard something about you two adding a baby to the mix. Good luck with that."

Dench looked into the next room, to find Rissa looking back at him. "Yeah," he said, watching her blush and drop her eyes. "We're hoping for good luck with everything."

Connie caught the swift exchange, saw the look on Dench's face and the responsive flush of Rissa's skin. Her lips lifted. "Something's up."

Jeannette rolled the red, yellow, and blue ball across the floor and into the little hands of a delighted toddler. "What? What's up?" Capturing the returned ball, she looked from Connie to Marlea and Rissa.

"I don't know, but something's been in the air for the past few weeks. At first, I just thought it was you and Dench just doing what you do—rolling all over each other like puppies. But it's more." Connie's gaze narrowed, appraising Rissa. "What don't we know?"

Surprise washed across Marlea's face and she stopped singing, though the children continued, mangling the words as they went along.

Saint Rissa just smiled.

Knowledge dawned. Connie and Jeannette gasped. "You're pregnant! How did you keep that a secret?"

"I was going to tell you."

"When? You forget, we've known you ever since Marlea's accident."

Rissa tossed her head and wrinkled her nose. "You two are never going to forgive me for telling her who ran into her car, are you?"

"Of course we forgive you. Marlea did, why wouldn't we?"

Jeannette hummed assent and crossed her arms. "But AJ is right, you are kind of like the Mouth of the South. Remember when AJ stepped in and invited Marlea to live here after her accident, you had plenty to say—bringing her up to date. That's how long ago, Connie? Five? Six years?"

"Let's see . . . Jabari is nearly five, so that would be right at six years." Crossing her arms, Connie slipped a hand to her cheek. "And in all that time, you have never *ever* kept a secret—not your own or anybody else's. So, how far along are you?"

"Oh, and we have to plan a shower, too. Do we get to be godparents again?"

Connie huffed. "How far along are you?"

"And what about Libby? Is she going to be a godparent, too?"

"Don't look at me," Marlea said, dimpling when Rissa looked at her. "I already spent the hundred I won from you."

"Still can't believe you held me up for it when you were pretty much the one who told my business."

"But you were the one who had all the fun part of telling."

Rissa's grin was sly. "I did, didn't I?"

Marlea's hand fanned the air between them. "You might as well go on and tell the rest of it."

"Yes, hurry up and tell." A sleepy toddler crawled into Jeannette's lap and settled happily when Jeannette's arms closed around her. "Too bad Libby is working out of state, training a new runner. She's a good coach, but she's going to hate missing this."

"Don't worry, Dench and I will tell her."

"Lord, I can just imagine how she'll take the news, as excited as we all know she can get. I still remember her practically running the last hundred meters of your race with you in Barcelona," Jeannette laughed.

"She did, didn't she?" Marlea laughed. "I guess when you've trained someone for as long as she trained me, you start to take a lot of responsibility for them."

"We've all taken a lot of responsibility for each other, haven't we?" Connie turned and looked at Rissa, her eyes growing misty as she took her in fully. "We got AJ and Marlea married, saw you and Dench come together, and now . . ."

"Uh-uh, honey. There is no way you're taking credit for this baby." Rissa slipped a hand over her belly and looked elegantly radiant. "Dench and I did this all on our own."

Nia materialized at Marlea's side. Working the ends of a braid between her fingers, she curled an arm around her mother's neck and laid her head on her shoulder. Taking the cue, Marlea scooped her daughter up and began organizing the other women. "Mothers will be here in the next half hour, but pull out the mats and blankets. The children can nap until . . ."

"Just like a mother." Rissa grinned. Pulling a pile of colorful children's blankets from the table, she spread them over the children, who politely fell on the mats. "Me, I'm going to be so different, I'll break the mold. I'm going to be the sexy, sassy, have it all, do it all, 'Hot Mom.' You know, the one who's always in the know and has all the flavor, the 'Super Mom.' "

"Lord," Jeannette breathed, "don't let her start singing about bringing home the bacon and frying it up in the pan, I'll have to kill her if she does. Please, Lord, don't let her do it."

Connie wiggled her fingers for attention. "Anyway, 'Hot Mom' and Keeper of Secrets, when are you going to tell Libby?"

"Soon," Rissa simpered.

"Not over the phone, I hope."

"Please, not after the way she fussed when I told her that I was charting my temperature and trying to figure out our peak fertility periods. She pretty much dropped the phone and showed up at my door with baskets of eggplant, telling me that it would help me conceive." Rissa gagged daintily behind her hand. "Dench and I still can't stand to look at the things."

"We'll catch her up when she gets back." Marlea checked to see if one of the toddlers was wet or not, and was glad to find him dry. "She'll need some good news after national time trials. Sprinters are always so temperamental."

"Says the woman who ran us all ragged competing for a 400-meter gold medal." Jeannette turned on Rissa. "I'm still waiting for details, give us the details. . . ."

"Found out on Christmas Eve." Rissa giggled when Connie and Jeannette turned to each other and goggled. "I'm twelve weeks, due in mid-July. You can call Dench Big Poppa if you want to—I do, and he loves it."

"*You* kept a secret this big? And Dench is *letting* you call him Big Poppa?" Connie turned to Marlea. "I know you love her, but how are you putting up with all this?"

Marlea's shoulders rose and fell.

"Yeah, 'cause we've only known about the baby for five minutes, and we're ready to kill her," Jeannette said. "In fact, now that I think of it, I'm impressed with the fact that everybody around here seems to have patience with Rissa's highly active pregnant ass."

"Well," Rissa plopped into a chair and looked important, "my highly active pregnant ass could use some tea right about now."

"I'll get it." Marlea stood and nearly bumped into Mrs. Baldwin.

"I thought this might be timely." The housekeeper set the tray on a small table near Rissa's chair. Pouring quickly, she handed cups and sandwiches to the women. Turning to leave, she looked at Rissa, and all of the women could have sworn that she twinkled. "Let me know if you need more," she said, walking back to the kitchen.

Jeannette's head swiveled, tracking Mrs. Baldwin's progress. Turning back, mouth open, brow arched, she looked at Rissa. "That woman is totally charmed by you. I think she might have even *approved* of you."

"She's always liked me."

Jeannette snorted derision.

"It's the baby," Marlea guessed. "She knows, I don't know how, but she knows."

"Maybe she overheard you and AJ talking, or maybe it's because I told her." Rissa stirred honey into her tea. "I've gotten good at keeping my news to myself, but I occasionally choose to share it selectively."

"That charm doesn't just work on Mrs. Baldwin, either." Connie harrumphed, making the sound from deep in her throat.

"Dench is proof of that."

"Maybe it's something in the water," Connie ventured, raising her cup. "Then, we'd all be blessed, wouldn't we?"

Rissa fluttered her lashes, sipped her tea, and looked entitled.

"It must be something in those Yarborough genes. And it especially seems to always work on the opposite sex." Connie looked over her shoulder, back into the kitchen. The men had disappeared—maybe in search of something on ESPN. "Maybe that Yarborough DNA gives off some kind of pheromones, you know, so that they only attract people like themselves."

"Sexy people." Jeannette's eyes were sly. "How about it, Marlea? The Yarboroughs you and Dench got tangled up with are all tall and good looking, even their mother. Really attractive people, right? Did they charm you? Just draw you in?"

Marlea opened her mouth, but Connie reached out and slapped a quick high five on Jeannette's palm. "Oh yeah, you've got a point, girl. Don't you remember all those men following Mama Yarborough around at AJ and Marlea's wedding?"

"Uh-huh, and at Rissa and Dench's, the same thing happened. Mama was in there bringing sexy back in a big way. And don't forget that last minute Christmas Eve delay. By the way, did Mama Yarborough ever get back from Mykonos?"

"Next week," Rissa and Marlea said together.

"Lord, makes you wonder why the family business is not bottling sexy," Connie laughed. "They'd make a mint if they did."

"But that's beside the point." Jeannette leaned forward, suddenly intense. "We were talking about you being pregnant. How does it feel, Rissa?"

Rissa sighed and used the toes of one foot to push the shoe off the other, then repeated the process. "I feel fine."

"But you felt fine when you thought you were pregnant before, right?"

"I always feel fine." Rissa inspected the depths of her cup.

"And you're not spotting or anything? Has your doctor . . . said . . . anything?"

Marlea held her breath and silently cursed Connie for asking the question that had teetered on the tip of her own tongue for most of a month. Rissa looked fine, but when it came to pregnancy, looking good didn't mean a thing. The doorbell sounded and Marlea fairly leapt from her chair. "That's got to be somebody's mommy."

A child whimpered and both nurses turned to find several pairs of wide, watchful eyes measuring them. Naptime, however brief, was over. The mothers came in bunches after that. Ten spa-refreshed women, rejuvenated by afternoon retail therapy, were ready to resume active nurturing. Promising to return the favor in the near future, they spirited their children away. Left alone, Nia and Jabari looked lost until Mrs. Baldwin came along with the offer of a snack.

"Well, that was quite an afternoon, wasn't it?" Connie stretched her arms wide, yawning with satisfaction. "I think I need a nap, now."

"But wait a minute." Jeannette waggled a finger at Rissa. "You never said. Did your doctor say anything?"

Rissa swirled the contents of her teacup and looked bored. "Could you just go rain on somebody else's parade? My husband and I are making plans for our baby, and he's walking around with his chest poked out. We haven't decided on a color for the nursery, or a college yet, but I'll be sure to let you know when we do. Okay?"

Connie bit her lip and sucked air. Jeannette looked uncomfortable when she stood. "It's been a long afternoon, and I guess we should get going. We'll see you guys later."

Marlea stood and both nurses shook their heads. "That's okay, we know where the coats are. We'll just . . . See you."

Blinking, Marlea watched them go. She waited until she could see Connie's small car rolling down the driveway before turning to Rissa. "What was that about?"

"What?" Rissa struggled to keep her litigator's tone intact.

"Damn it, Rissa, don't make me call you names, 'cause I'm not scared of you. And, don't make me chase you for an answer, 'cause I'm faster than you've ever been. Besides, I married your brother. You have to talk to me."

Rissa set the cup on the table and sighed heavily. "About what, Marlea?"

Hands on her hips, Marlea bit at the inside of her cheek and stared. *Is she really going to make me say it out loud?* Sitting determined and silent, Rissa waited. "I want to know what they wanted to know, Rissa. Has your doctor said anything special about your pregnancy? About your ability to carry a baby to term?"

"Nothing, Marlea. Nothing at all."

For the briefest of moments, pain, fear, and anger chased through the depth of Rissa's gaze and she refused to let memory stake a claim on her thoughts. Months of costly fertility treatments, nausea, and cramping had seemed a small enough price to pay for a few weeks of breathtaking possibility in her quest for motherhood. And just when it seemed that her mission would bear fruit, there was nothing.

And if I could have kept my silly mouth shut about the possibility, they wouldn't all be looking at me like I was going to grow a third eye in the back of my head.

"Is this how everybody is going to treat me for the next six months? I'm not going to get to enjoy being pregnant, especially after waiting so long for it?" Rissa closed her eyes and blew out hard. She took a deep breath before she opened her eyes. "I've talked to my doctor, and I'm not worried. Why should you be? I can't wait to be this big." She stretched her arms wide. "Pregnancy is a condition, Marlea, not a disease, and I'm not worried." *Even if I don't tell you everything my doctor said.*

"Are you sure you're not doing selective listening? Only hearing what you want to hear?" Marlea narrowed her eyes. "I know you, Rissa. You've got a mouth like a sieve and a head like a rock."

"I hear everything my doctor says." *Even if I don't want to.* On her last checkup, Joyce Ashton had said something about her cervix. When Joyce said the words, they came out in slow, measured tones and Rissa barely recognized them even as she heard herself ask what they meant to her and her baby. Your cervix is short, the doctor said, almost as though it had been partitioned. *And what in the world did that mean?* When Joyce said something about high risk, Rissa had stopped listening.

Now, facing Marlea, Rissa knew she'd blocked most of the words—couldn't remember them if she had to. The only thing she remembered, she was afraid to admit, and could never say to Dench. Joyce had warned her that the heavier the fetus, the greater the possibility of losing it. *But just because there's a warning doesn't always mean that there's always danger ahead. I'm healthy.*

Sometimes warnings only exist to instill caution. And I've done my research. I'm cautious. I'm watching my weight, I'm not engaging in any dangerous activity, I don't smoke or drink . . .

Lifting her head higher, Rissa looked at Marlea and squared her shoulders. "I'm not worried about a thing."

CHAPTER 5

"You could call in, play hooky."

"No, I'll go in, make sure all the contracts are signed and be back in a few hours. I'm just jealous that you can spend the day working from home."

The arms that enclosed her came as no surprise. Distinctly male flesh, planes and strength, pressed at her back, supporting her softness. Bringing her hands up to trace the muscles of his arms, her fingers linked with his, and she found herself admiring the red-tinged bronze of his skin against the warm gold of her own. Looking up, she found his eyes in the mirror and smiled.

"Damn, our baby is going to be pretty." His breath was warm against her throat and she felt the words soak into her skin. "I'm going to have to start early, teaching him to use his powers for good."

"And if it's a girl?"

"I'm gonna buy a bat."

"Way to go, Big Poppa." Her fingers tightened on his, and though she didn't try very hard, she couldn't tear her eyes from the mirror. When his mouth closed on her throat, her knees softened and nearly gave way. "Keep doing that and I'm going to miss my meeting." Holding her closer he did it again, finding her rhythm this time.

His eyes laughed when her head fell back and she moaned, "You are a wicked, wicked man."

His fingers broke from hers and slipped low with wanton determination. She called his name when questing fingers found the lacy edges of a final barrier.

"Should I stop?"

"Wicked man," she whispered, gasping when his fingers answered.

Going with him, no fear of falling, Rissa dropped all pretense of thought. She forgot about work, the time it would take to redress, apologies she might have to make, and what anyone else might think. She gave herself fully to the joys of the only man who had ever stolen her breath.

Whimpers, sighs, moans, and the ocean of heat she brought with her burned his blood and cindered his thought. Ebbing and flowing with her hunger, knowing the keys to her satisfaction, Dench found himself before his wife with no words and he wanted to pull her deep into his heart, right through the very skin that separated them.

When she collapsed against his chest, wet and sated, he knew only two things: *I'm happy. She makes me happy.* His arms felt a little worn from the work of her, but she was always worth it. Looking at her, he was glad he'd made the effort.

"Wow," she breathed, pulling far enough away to look at him. Her eyes were soft and her lips swollen, and she looked ready to fall with him again. She sighed and laughed softly, then dropped her head to his chest. "I have to get to the office, but I don't want to move—not now, not ever."

His finger found a tear-shaped drop of sweat between her breasts. "That makes two of us, but we've got to do what we've got to do." His palm curved over the swell of her belly. "Don't want this baby to be homeless, right?"

"Wicked and practical, too. Such a complicated man." Her tiny kiss at the corner of his mouth grabbed his heart and held it tight when his hand travelled low again. She caught his hand and held it as she escaped his embrace.

Slipping across the radiant flooring and into the shower, Rissa turned on the water, admiring the flash of her wedding ring. It was always hard, coming back from a long weekend, particularly one as special as their Valentine's weekend at Biltmore Estate. Rissa closed her eyes and enjoyed the memory again. Long hours of touching and just breathing the same air had been better than anything she might have thought of on her own. Dench had thought of it and planned the weekend get-away to Ashville.

The car trip had been pleasant and the North Carolina countryside reminded her of a postcard. Ashville on its own was beautiful, but their sumptuous suite at the Biltmore was romantic enough to make her feel like a new bride again. *But this time, I'm the mommy, and goodness knows, the daddy sure did make me feel good about it.* Through the clear glass walling the shower, she saw Dench move in the room beyond where she stood and stroked the ring with her thumb, moving it against her skin.

Stepping under the spray, she stood tall and slender, with warm water pouring over her swollen breasts and exquisitely sensitized skin. *Almost five months,* she marveled. *Who knew the time could go this fast?* Filling her palm with the jasmine and honey shower gel Dench loved to smell on her skin, Rissa pushed her stomach out and laughed at her baby bump.

Sliding her hand over the swell of her baby as she saw her husband moving nearby made her smile—then she remembered. *Joyce wants me to see a specialist.* Rissa reached for a loofah and the smile slipped from her lips. Putting the appointment off couldn't make that big a difference. *I just wanted to enjoy the weekend first.* She scrubbed the loofah across her shoulders and ignored the little hair of concern that crawled across her psyche. *I told her I would, and I will.* Stepping closer to the falling water, feeling herself in his eyes, Rissa turned her head. Dench stood in the doorway watching her. She lifted her fingers to him and was pleased when he waved back.

I'll make the appointment today, she promised.

"So? How was Valentine's Day? Ashville is always so dreamy, and to have all weekend like that . . ." Yvette scrunched her cute face into a leer, then sighed. "Might as well have your fun now, because when the baby gets here . . ."

Rissa brushed past her and picked up a handful of mail as she passed Karee's desk.

". . . none of that slinky underwear is ever going to look the same. Oh, baby, and that's not all."

Reaching her office door, Rissa pushed it open and stepped through. Uninvited, Yvette followed. Crossing to the red visitors' chairs, she plopped into one and crossed her legs. "You know, I do believe your butt is getting big. Carrying the baby low, hmm, that means it's a boy."

"Look, Mother Wit, I can do without the comments, and don't look at me like that." Rissa dumped her coat, the mail and her briefcase on the desk and ignored Yvette when she pushed her lower lip out. Walking over to the chair facing Yvette, she sat and crossed her legs. "Ask me about our trip."

Determined to sulk, Yvette concentrated on her nails.

"Come on, ask me. You know you want to."

"All right, I will, but just to make you happy." Yvette feigned indifference, and then leaned in, succumbing to her natural impulse. "Tell me, did you have an amazing time? What did you do? Was Dench, like, world class romantic?"

"Yes, everything, and omigod!" Rissa's hands flew to her face.

"Girl, you're blushing like a virgin! Tell me everything!"

"You don't need to know *everything*." Hands still at her warm cheeks, Rissa giggled.

Yvette sat back and folded her hands in her lap. "Then give me the PG-rated version."

"Okay, here's what I can tell you." Rissa leaned forward, eager to share, but was interrupted by Karee pushing the office door open.

"Sorry." Karee's head bobbed from side to side when the women looked over at her. "I didn't mean to interrupt, but they're here, the Clarences."

"Oh, I'd better get out of your way, then." Yvette stood and looked back just long enough to make her point. "I expect you to finish telling me about your trip."

"I know you do," Rissa told her partner's back.

Sierra Clarence came through the door first, and she took Rissa's breath away. "My goodness, Sierra, you look like the maternity poster girl."

"Thank you, and you! You're still so slim, how many months are you?"

"We're almost to five," Rissa moved her hands over her stomach and hips proudly. "I just can't get over how good you look. You are going to look really good on camera, the perfect spokeswoman for child support products."

At Sierra's side, James beamed and nodded. Her doe-soft eyes were bright and she held her husband's hand. "We've got two months to go, and then you'll get to meet James Jr."

Lips parted, Rissa froze in her tracks. "I thought you didn't want to know the baby's sex!"

"It wasn't me." Lowering herself carefully into one of the red chairs, Sierra looked at James. "He couldn't take it, and you know you're never in this all by yourself, so I gave in."

"In my defense, she wanted to know, too," Jimmy laughed. "Especially after you came up with this deal for us to do the commercial series for BeaconGreen. She likes the idea of being able to stand up in front of the camera and talk about how we are going to bring our baby into a green world."

"And I'm not by myself."

"No, she's right. We got to talking about it after you got us the offer," the boxer drawled. "We liked the idea, and now she can be more specific. She can talk about our son."

"Knowing that we'll have a son makes everything more real." Under his eyes, Sierra smiled and pushed her coat from her shoulders. "I want to thank you for letting us do this."

"Yeah, thank you. I'm still surprised you used us for this group of commercials. The first time I heard about it, I expected you to use your brother and his wife."

"They're a little tied up right now." Rissa crossed her arms, holding the folder over her stomach. "They have two small children, AJ has his physical therapy practice and Marlea is still teaching at Runyon. On top of that, they're looking at expanding Project ABLE."

James perched on the arm of his wife's chair and gave a long low whistle. "I heard that Project ABLE is going international."

"In a couple of years, and when they do, they'll be active on three continents. So, I want to get this BeaconGreen project off the ground with you two as the initial spokespeople."

Bringing the contracts to the small table, she sat in one of the red chairs, produced a pair of the Mont Blanc pens she favored, and made quick work of explaining the contracts. Sierra lifted her pen to sign, but gasped sharply.

"Are you all right?" Out of her seat, Rissa was halfway to the door.

"Fine." Sierra blew out hard. Planting one hand on her belly, she gestured to Rissa with the other. "Come feel this."

Trying not to look as silly as she felt, Rissa walked back across the room. When James and Sierra reached for her, she let them place her hands on Sierra's stomach, and when they were quiet she was, too. Then she felt it; he kicked.

"Two times," James grinned. "Too bad Coach Traylor won't be around when my boy is ready for major league football. That was a field goal right there."

"He might be." Sierra's hand rubbed circles on her belly, and the baby kicked again. "You and Dench still haven't given us an answer."

Pressing her palms together and blowing softly between them gave Rissa a moment to think. Then she again pressed a hand to Sierra's stomach. She felt the ripple when the baby shifted and wanted to say yes, but Dench wanted . . . so, she bit her tongue and said, "Can I get back to you on that?"

"Just don't wait too long." The baby rolled and kicked again. Sierra's face lit with pleasure in her son's accomplishment. "Maybe you'll have a boy and our sons can play on the same team some day."

Someday, Rissa thought when she saw them to the door a few minutes later. A little jealous of Sierra's thickly ripe waddle, she made herself busy with the contracts and exchanging final information with her BeaconGreen counterpart. *I felt their baby move. I can't wait until my baby does that!*

She was still thinking about *someday* as she pulled into her garage. Stepping out of her car, she reached back to collect her purse, briefcase, and the books she'd made a special trip to MEDU for. The lady at the bookstore had been really nice, taking almost an hour to help her choose the right books, offering honey-laced tea, talking about her own pregnancy more than ten years earlier. And she'd walked out of the bookstore exhausted and carrying a couple of hundred dollars' worth of books.

Dench looked up when she pushed the door open, and his words felt like poetry to her. "Hey, baby, what have you got there?"

Standing in the center of the door that opened into her kitchen, Rissa couldn't help the smile Dench brought to her lips. He stood more than six feet tall and two hundred fifteen pounds, with broad shoulders, long arms, and a tightly muscled chest. Her husband wore jeans, a blue flannel shirt, Timberland boots, and a frilly yellow apron. He held a long-handled wooden spoon and the lid to a small saucepan. *Sexy.*

"I stopped at MEDU," she finally said and grunted a little when she held her full bag aloft. "What are you up to?" She walked closer, dumping the bag on a chair. "Smells good, what is it?"

"Dinner. Thought that since you had to work today and I was home, you might appreciate having dinner ready." He dipped the wooden spoon into a silky looking white sauce and offered it. Watching his eyes, she tasted. Smooth and buttery, the sauce slipped across her tongue, delighting her palate along the way. When she hummed satisfaction he smiled. "Alfredo. Good, huh?"

"Very." She licked her lips and looked at him. "A good looking man who can cook. I bless your Aunt Linda every day for raising you right."

"She did her best." Dench rattled pots and pans, then stirred the sauce again when Rissa reached for her bag of books. "You had a call today."

"Oh. Who was it?"

"Joyce Ashton."

Something in his voice made her stop. An odd thread of doubt unraveled along her spine. Forcing calm she could not claim, Rissa looked at him. "Did she say what she wanted, or leave a message?"

Dench jammed an oven mitt over one of his big hands and pulled a pan of rolls from the oven. Settling the rolls, he pulled the mitt off and dropped it on the counter. "She said that things are going well, so far."

Rissa felt her heart stutter.

"She wanted to know if you had contacted the other doctor yet." His eyes darkened and all of the laughter that came so easily to him seemed to drain away. "What other doctor, Rissa? Why do you need to consult with another doctor?"

"It's just a precaution, Dench. Nothing to worry about."

"Then why didn't you say something?"

"And scare you to death? You were scared enough when we heard the baby's heartbeat for the first time, remember?" Rissa let the bag fall to her feet and walked toward him. As she'd known he would, he opened his arms, accepted her. "Dench, we have gone through so much and come so far to have this baby, I didn't want to alarm you. I made the appointment today—I'll see the doctor on Monday."

His arms tightened and he laid his cheek against her hair. "And you'll tell me what the doctor says?"

"Every word," she promised, leaning into him. Her stomach rumbled between them and they shared soft laughter. "We'd better eat now, your baby is hungry."

"So is my baby's mama."

"Then I think you'd better feed me." Suddenly tired, she kicked off her shoes and rested in his arms a little longer. Her yawn caught her off guard and she felt the worry shadowing his eyes. "Wow, hungry and tired."

"Then how about you take your time, get settled, and I'll put dinner on trays."

She looked hopeful, glad that forgiveness came easily to him. When he picked up her shoes, she took them from him and yawned again. "Bring that tray to bed, and I'll show you what I bought for you."

"You bought something for me? What is it?"

"Bring me food and I'll show you." Picking up the bag of books, the shoes dangling from her fingers, she walked to their bedroom. The bag of books grew heavier with every step she took.

"Long day," she decided, sliding out of her pants suit in the dressing room. Unbuttoning the white ruffled shirt was more than she felt like doing, so she pulled it over her head and left it piled with the suit in the middle of the floor. Reaching into a bureau, she found a simple white eyelet nightgown and remembered what Yvette had said about sexy underwear after babies. Shaking the sheer cotton gown open, Rissa pulled it over her head. Big, soft and roomy, there was nothing sexy about the gown and she tried to remember where it had come from because it was like nothing she'd ever purchased for herself. It was definitely designed for comfort.

Yvette has a point. The baby's not even here, and I'm already going for the comfort—Dench will just have to forgive me this time. Climbing into bed, she heard him coming with the tray. Even as her stomach grumbled, she yawned and knew that sleep was going to win.

From the bed, the bag of books was just in reach and she pulled it closer. Getting a good grip, she levered it up on the blue and brown comforter and spilled the books across her lap just as Dench rounded the corner.

Holding the bed tray, Dench looked from her face to her lap and back again. "Is that my surprise?"

She held *Daddy for Dummies* aloft. "Is that my dinner? If it is, Big Poppa, then this book is for you."

One-handed, Dench planted the loaded tray in the center of the bed and sat next to Rissa. Taking the book from her hands, he flipped pages, studied a picture and flipped more pages. "So do you think this book is good?"

"I bought it, didn't I? I wouldn't buy you a book that wasn't good." Snagging a roll, she bit into it, chewed, and slid a little lower in the bed.

He swung his legs up on the bed and rolled to his side, reading. "Did you know that right now, the baby weighs about three ounces? Damn, baby, that's about the size of a hotdog."

Stuffing the last of the roll into her mouth, Rissa chewed. Dench turned another page, read and then looked at his hand.

"What?"

"Six and three-tenths inches," he said reverently, his eyes alive with swirling flecks of green and gold. "That's how big the baby is right now." He turned more pages, reading along the way. "And teeth, it says that all the teeth have formed." Rissa nodded sleepily and curled on her side as he continued reading. "This book is cool. Now I don't have to listen to AJ's nonstop commentary on the mysteries of childbirth. I've got my own reference tool."

When Rissa didn't answer, he looked over at her. Sprawled at an impossible angle, her head was thrown back and one foot dangled from beneath the covers. Her chest rose and fell with her breathing and an insolently sudden snore. Moving carefully, trying not to wake her, Dench eased from the bed. Sliding the tray away from her body, he stood and watched her sleep. When she started to drool, he set the tray on the floor and reached for a tissue—for better or for worse went a long way.

It's a good thing I love you, girl. He dabbed at the corners of her mouth and she smacked her lips in return. *And I love you like a shoe loves a sock.*

Her hearty snore was answer enough for him.

Rissa spent most of the night snoring and slept so deeply that she didn't hear Dench rise before daylight. His stealthy movements were so quiet that she never heard him dress or leave the house for Flowery Branch. Surfacing from sleep, she caught a trace of sweetness on the air, and it made her think of him. Refusing to open her eyes, sensing the stillness of her home, she knew that she was alone. *I didn't hear the alarm clock go off. Where's Dench?*

Oh, yeah, she recalled, liking the teasing floral whisper. *He said something about team assessment and medical reviews.* Yawning, still tangled in sleep, she managed to open her eyes. A glance at the clock told her that she could afford to sleep longer, but the delicate fragrance persisted. Turning her head, she found the source of the scent, soft, pink and velvety, in the center of his pillow. *A rose, he left a rose for me. And when did he get it?* She reached out, touching the bloom with a single finger and smiled. *Wonder what I did right to deserve a man like him?*

She stroked the rose tenderly. *Cathi,* she remembered sleepily. *I haven't thought of Cathi Jennings in forever. Wonder what she's doing now?* Rissa sighed and drew the rose across the pillow, closer to her face. *That girl was crazy about AJ. She was the reason I noticed Dench in the first place. We were twelve years old and she said he was fine, but AJ was finer. Said he was 'foine' . . . Then, she dared me to kiss him, and I did . . . almost twenty years ago . . .*

Her breathing deepened and Rissa closed her eyes and drifted. *He was more than 'foine.' He fell out of that tree trying to get my cat that time—I guess that's the first time I knew he was special, right for me. He's funny and sweet, and he loves me. Promises that he loves me like Jesus loved the church and I guess I've always known it.* Fingering the rose, she floated off to sleep.

And would have slept far later, if not for the annoyingly insistent alarm of the clock at her bedside. Rissa stirred, wanting to get rid of the heinous sound, but . . . maybe it wasn't a sound so much as a feeling, and the feeling was wrong. She knew it the second she moved her head.

Her body was hot and felt like it was . . . Her mind floundered, searching for the right word. B*uzzing,* she thought. *Why would I be . . . buzzing?* The pain that knifed through her back made a sudden detour down one leg and she gasped, her hands flying to her belly. *My baby?*

Her usually agile mind stumbled into stupid and her mouth filled with salty water. *This is not right. Something is wrong . . .* Sitting up, she pushed back the bed sheets and stared in horror. *This is wrong, horribly, horribly wrong . . .*

Wadded around her legs, the bed sheets lay where she'd pushed them, sodden, soaked with her blood. Rissa closed her eyes and tried to keep breathing. "Dench?" His name was a deadened croak when it crossed her lips, and she knew he wasn't there.

Terrified and fearing the damage, her eyes refused to leave what she didn't want to believe. Reaching without looking, she found the phone and pressed buttons. She babbled something to the 911 operator and pressed more buttons. Sitting in the bed with the awful sheets growing cold and stiff around her, she held the phone and prayed, afraid to move. Feeling her body begin to shake, Rissa ignored the lightning galloping through her body and made herself still. Maybe being still would save the baby. *Maybe . . .*

"Hi, Rissa," Marlea finally answered the phone. "What're you still doing at home? Don't you have any . . ." The line was too silent, for too long. Marlea's eyes went to Mrs. Baldwin, who stopped in her tracks. "Rissa?"

"What?" Mrs. Baldwin looked concerned when Marlea shrugged.

"Rissa, are you alright?" When she heard nothing, Marlea pitched the phone to Mrs. Baldwin and ran.

"Mommy runs fast!" Jabari told the housekeeper.

The 400-meter run had always been Marlea Kellogg's best event; she'd even won gold medals and set a world record. Running to Rissa's house, she proved that she was as fast as she'd ever been. Running the distance, her feet only slowed when she jammed the keys in the door and pushed it open. Running through the house screaming Rissa's name, she was too afraid to wonder what she might be running toward.

"Rissa!" Marlea nearly fell over her own feet when she reached the master suite. The set of rooms, shaped so like those in her own home, were different this morning—

quiet, except for muffled sounds from the bedroom. Slowing, her heart pounding, Marlea trailed her fingers along the wall, not knowing what to expect. "Rissa?"

"Here."

Sirens wailed in the distance, and Marlea's stomach wrenched when she stepped fully into the warm and stylish bedroom. Eyes adjusting to the sun-filled room, she looked toward the bed and her mouth dropped. "Rissa . . ."

Sitting in the middle of the bed, still holding the telephone, fat tears spilled down Rissa's face and she swallowed hard. "I don't know what happened, Marlea. My baby . . ." Her eyes dropped and the tears came faster. "My baby . . ."

"Help is coming," Marlea promised and hoped she was right. In the distance, she heard people talking, paramedics, she hoped. Somebody told them to go to the bedroom. *Maybe Mrs. Baldwin followed me*, she guessed, not concerned with whether she was right or not. Help had arrived. Concentrating on Rissa, she moved to the bed. Sitting carefully, she opened her arms and braced herself when Rissa collapsed against her.

"My baby," Rissa whimpered.

"Is going to be fine."

"You don't know that."

"I know that I'm not going to let you out of my sight until we both know." She rubbed circles on her sister-in-law's back and laid her cheek against her short, silky hair.

The paramedics, two strong-looking women, strode into the room and bent immediately to their work. Rissa was quiet as they fastened a blood pressure cuff to her arm and threw back her bed linens, preparing to shift her to the cold, white-sheeted stretcher they moved to her bedside. Her breathing was shaky and her fingers cold as she held Marlea's hand tightly.

"Stay with me," Rissa whispered and Marlea nodded, not knowing whether the words were for her or the baby.

CHAPTER 6

Lips pressed tight, the tall paramedic checked the blanket pulled over Rissa and looked to her partner. The chubby blonde nodded and grabbed the strap near Rissa's feet. Towing the stretcher, she started off at a determined jog, her partner working with her. Marlea grabbed Rissa's purse and ran with them, matching their every step.

"You have a hospital preference?" the tall one asked, never looking back.

Outside, the paramedics stopped and the back door of the ambulance slammed open. The wheels of the gurney clicked as the two women adjusted and lifted it. Rissa moaned softly as it clicked into place. "Monitoring is on you," the chubby blonde said and headed for the driver's seat.

"I'm on it." The tall one slammed a door shut and started to climb in. "Hospital?"

"Southwest is closest, right?" Rissa's golden skin had a distinctly ashen cast and her lips trembled when Marlea spoke for her. "Southwest."

"Right." The woman reached for the door, but Marlea was faster. She pulled and stepped up at the same time, landing on her knees at the foot of Rissa's stretcher. The paramedic's eyes widened, and her mouth opened.

"I'm going with her, and you can't stop me," Marlea said. The woman's gloved hand moved toward her radio and Rissa moaned again. Marlea's dark eyes narrowed when she squeezed onto the aluminum jump seat at Rissa's side. "You won't stop me." Holding Rissa's hand, she looked at the paramedic. "She's my sister, and I'm going."

The tall woman nodded and pulled the door closed. She pressed a button on the wall, murmured the name of the hospital, and the sirens started. The ambulance rolled and she took the jump seat on Rissa's other side. Her eyes moved when she checked the blood pressure gauge still attached to Rissa's arm. When she looked up, she was smiling. "You're just like I thought you would be."

Marlea's eyes shot up to meet the paramedic's. "Pardon me?"

"You're Marlea Kellogg, right? The runner? With Project ABLE?" Her grin went crooked when Marlea nodded. "I thought I recognized you. I'm Tara Morgan. My brother Terrence is a part of your project."

"Terrence Morgan?" Marlea looked down at Rissa and tried to place the name.

Project ABLE had drawn a lot of attention and a real following among athletes since its inception. Born of Marlea and AJ's love of sports, his physical therapy practice, and her competitive nature, Project ABLE had stretched across Atlanta and beyond, helping hundreds of athletes find life after challenge. Being founded and sponsored by an NFL Hall of Famer and a Paralympics' gold medalist had insured Project ABLE's ability to generate press and funding. But it was their success in motivation and support that drew the attention of The President's Council on Fitness, and kept them in touch with athletes like Terrence Morgan.

"Sprinter," Marlea finally remembered, picturing his face. "Diving accident, right?"

"Broke his neck," Tara said. "Came to your program through Piedmont Hospital, and now he's a wheelchair racer." Her crooked grin flashed again. "And he'll graduate from Georgia Tech in the spring. Gonna be an engineer."

"I'm glad." Rissa's moan made Marlea look down. The speeding ambulance took a turn, and she had to plant her feet to keep from rolling off the seat.

Rissa's eyelids were drooping; they'd given her a sedative. "It's over," she mumbled, her fingers tightening on Marlea's. "I messed up. I let him down, Marlea." Shushing her had no effect; she was determined to speak. "He was depending on me . . . All I had to do was . . ."

"She's a little shocky, but stable," Tara explained. Leaning, she looked out the window, then back at Marlea. "We're still about two minutes out."

"Thank you."

Tara's crooked grin flashed again. "Thank *you*, from me and my brother." The ambulance slowed and Tara moved between Marlea and the stretcher. "You're going to have to move now. We're taking her inside."

The ambulance jerked to a stop and the door clanked when the blonde pulled it open. She blinked and stepped back. "What is she doing in there?"

"Relative," Morgan said, sweeping Marlea with her as she pushed past.

A dozen hands moved in to help and Marlea hung close. When they moved, she went with them, feeling a bump in the pocket of her windsuit. Jamming a hand in the pocket, she pulled a cellphone free. For a moment, she wondered where it had come from, when she had gotten it. *Probably Rissa's. Probably grabbed it when I picked up her purse.* The thought of a purse reminded Marlea of her own. *It's at home, with my children.*

The hospital doors were flung open and everything around them seemed to pick up speed. Marlea found herself jogging alongside the stretcher, still holding Rissa's cold fingers. When a woman in plum-colored scrubs and white rubber-soled clogs stopped her outside the ER, she felt breathless and numb.

"I'm Andi Marcus, and I'll be handling intake for Mrs. Traylor." The woman edged a step between Marlea and the double doors, and Marlea was forced to release Rissa's fingers when the gurney slid through the opening. "We're going to need her personal information. Did I hear somebody say you're her sister?"

"Sister-in-law."

"Close enough." Ms. Marcus smiled, apparently satisfied that Marlea wasn't going to keel over in front of her, and indicated a chair in front of the hospital green Formica counter.

Marlea sat. If the woman had given her name, she couldn't remember it, but she tried to answer every question. Opening Rissa's purse, she found medical and social security cards when requested. When the woman paused for breath, Marlea asked, "Can I see her?"

Sympathy crossed the woman's face, and, rising, she nodded. "Let me check."

She walked away and Marlea pulled out the cellphone and scrolled through the phone book. She hesitated, wanting to call AJ first. Determined to do the right thing, she passed his name and found Dench. Glancing at her watch, she tried to screw up her nerve. He would probably be out on the field or something, but he would want to know. He needed to know. Inhaling deeply, she pressed in the number.

"Hey, sweetness."

Marlea's heart broke. "Dench, this is Marlea, and I'm at the hospital . . ."

"What?" Confusion twisted across the line and he was silent for a long second. "Wait a minute, this is Rissa's phone. Why are you on her phone? Did you say at the hospital? Is she okay? Which hospital?"

She heard the hot bright edge of hysteria touch his voice. *I should have called AJ first. He might have taken this better coming from AJ.* "We're at . . ."

"It's the baby, isn't it?"

"I . . . Dench, we just got here and I'm still in Admissions. I don't have any answers for you, but I think you need to be here with her. We're at Southwest Medical Center."

"Yes, of course. I'm at Flowery Branch . . . I'll be there as soon as I can. Southwest—about an hour, okay?"

"Dench, that's fifty miles in traffic . . ."

"About an hour." He was breathless, running, she guessed.

"Of course." She couldn't make herself end the call. "Don't worry, I won't leave her alone. I'll be here when you get here."

"Thanks, Marlea." Fear was pushing hysteria aside. She heard it in his voice.

"Drive carefully." She pressed the button, disconnecting the call.

The politely cleared throat made her turn. The woman in the plum-colored scrubs stood just behind her. "If you need a minute," she indicated the cellphone, "I'll be right back." Marlea nodded and she disappeared around a corner.

Marlea looked at the phone in her hand and pressed the number in.

"Hey, Rissa. What's up?"

His voice was as familiar as her own right hand and comforted her as no other could. "It's me, AJ. I'm just using Rissa's phone." She waited a beat when he covered the phone with his hand and said something to one of the Project ABLE staffers.

"Yeah, Silk, what's up? Everything okay?"

Holding the phone in both hands, she lowered her voice. "AJ, I'm at the hospital with . . ."

Silent alarm raced between them. "Are you all right? The kids?"

"I'm fine, and the kids are with Mrs. Baldwin. They're fine, too." She braced herself. "It's Rissa, she . . . Well, I don't know yet. Can you get here? I'll stay with her, but AJ, please?"

There was silence, and she knew he was nodding. "You already called Dench?"

"He's on the way."

"So am I. Southwest, right?"

Marlea nodded. "Right."

"Hold on, Silk. I'm on the way."

The man was a rock and she was grateful as she closed the phone and dropped it into Rissa's purse. The hand that touched her shoulder made her jump. The woman in the plum-colored scrubs stood beside her and, as hard as she tried, Marlea could read nothing in her expression. "Is she all right?"

"At her doctor's request, we're going to hold her for observation. But in the meantime, she's stable and you can see her now," the woman said and gave her quick directions.

Forcing her feet not to run was a job all on its own as Marlea found herself taking the stairs instead of waiting for the elevator. On the third floor, she stepped out of the stairwell and into the sterile hall. She was nowhere near out of breath, but when a woman pushing a fetal monitor passed her, she felt like she'd been punched. One hand on the wall, Marlea forced herself to stand straight and breathe normally. Putting one foot in front of the other, hand still on the wall, she forced herself to read the room numbers and walk toward Rissa's room.

When she found it, the door was closed. Looking at the door made her stomach hurt and she dreaded opening it, but she knew how much the woman on the other side needed her right then. *Maybe she didn't lose the baby. Maybe it's just a complication. They can fix complications. Maybe . . .* Marlea closed her eyes, wished she could stop shaking, and prayed. *Whatever is on the other side of the door, please help Rissa to bear it. Dench is on the way, Lord. Please let me be enough until he gets here.* Straightening her shoulders, Marlea opened her eyes and pushed the door open.

White, beige, and deep gray shadow dominated the room. Stepping in, Marlea let the door close behind her. Rissa lay on the narrow white-sheeted bed in the middle of the room, silent and unmoving. Plastic tubes at her face and inner arm delivered oxygen and glucose. On the wall behind her, one low-wattage light bar burned and a monitor beeped regularly, verifying her heart rate and breathing. *Whatever else happened, she's alive.* Marlea licked her lips and stepped forward. "Rissa?"

"Here." The single word was filled with bitter defeat.

"I thought you could use some company." Looking around, Marlea found a neutral-colored chair and pulled it from the corner. "I brought your purse, and I called Dench. He's on the way."

The cracked sob and sudden movement on the bed stole the strength from Marlea's legs, dumping her into the chair. "Rissa?"

Rissa pushed the oxygen tube down and pulled the edges of the sheet to her nose. Holding the sheet tightly, she sniffed hard and turned her face to Marlea. "Thank you for getting me here."

"Of course . . ."

"I wish I was dead." The sheet twitched as she pulled it again. Marlea reached for the box of tissues on the bedside table. Rissa pushed them away and twisted the sheet to her face. "I lost the baby."

Though she'd half expected them, the words raked Marlea's soul. "Rissa, I am so sorry."

"All I had to do was hold on." Bitterness slimed her words. "I couldn't do it. I tried and I just couldn't do it."

"Rissa, it's not your fault."

"Who else do you think was carrying the baby?" Rissa snorted and choked. "I should have seen the specialist like they said, but I was so damned tired of doctors and everything was going so well." She turned swollen, red-rimmed eyes to Marlea. "It's my fault, all my fault."

Rissa snatched her hand away when Marlea reached for it. "I wanted this baby so badly. And Dench, he . . ."

Marlea settled for pulling her chair close enough to hold Rissa's gaze with her own. "You already know that man will forgive you anything. He'll never blame you for something that is so clearly not your fault."

Rissa glared, then turned her face away.

"Look, I'm not trying to minimize your pain." Marlea reached out, her fingers touching Rissa's shoulder. "Of all the people you know, I know what it is to wake up in the hospital and have your life irrevocably changed."

A despondent tremor shivered through Rissa's body and she curled in on herself. "Marlea, you got hit by a car and woke up without two toes. You lost a chance to make the Olympic team, but you got a second chance in the

Paralympics. I lost a baby. Now you have a good shoe-maker and I have an empty womb—where's the justice in that?"

Ashamed to say the words, Marlea admitted, "There is none." In her heart, she heard the words she would never say: *This was never about justice, was it? This was about heart's desire and love unfulfilled. This was about investing everything and not having anything but pain and emptiness to show for it. This was about losing faith, and losing yourself in the effort.*

The tremors shaking Rissa's body grew deeper and Marlea hurt for her. At a loss, she pressed both hands to Rissa's back and laid her head against them, wishing she knew how to fix this, how to make it better—but she had nothing. *Please, God,* she prayed, *where is Dench?*

AJ pulled into the parking lot and shoved the gear into park. *If I go into the deck, I'll miss him for sure.* He turned the key and pulled it from the ignition. *He won't get past me here.* The thought had no sooner occurred to him than he saw the truck. Dench made a two-point turn and AJ hit his horn.

Seeing him, Dench angled the truck into a slot and hit the ground running. AJ bailed out of his own truck two steps behind him. The two men ran for the hospital entrance like the wide receiver and running back they had once been. The doors slid open before them, but not fast enough. Dench's shoulder hit one, sending it swinging as he plowed toward Admissions. "Rissa Traylor," he demanded. "Where is she?"

Ike Whitman looked up from his textbook, *The Anatomy Coloring Book,* in time to see Dench take out the door across from the desk. The student's eyes grew wide behind his spectacles and his mouth formed the sibilant word his mother kept telling him not to use. The two big men in front of him were in a hurry and they looked ready to fight. And Ike could tell that the one doing the talking meant every word.

Trying to think fast, to remember everything he'd been told in orientation, Ike heard him make his demand again and didn't have a clue as to how to answer him. The woman he was asking about—what if she was an abuse victim? Lord, what if she had died in an accident or something? *I don't want to be the one to tell him!* Ike looked around and found himself alone. *Now how the hell did that happen?*

Dench's fist landed hard on the counter in front of him. "Where is my wife?"

"Sir, I need to check . . ." Ike stood and looked up at the big man.

Andi Marcus stepped behind the counter and stood next to the student. She gave him a look that made him step back, then turned to Dench. "Did I hear you ask for Mrs. Traylor?" Dench nodded. "I did her intake. Let me get the room number for you."

Grateful, Dench nodded. AJ clapped a hand to his shoulder and he nodded again when Ms. Marcus gave him the number. He turned away, then back again. "Is she all right?"

"She's stable." Andi wiped a suddenly sweaty hand on the hip of her plum-colored scrubs and watched the tall men run down the hall. *The husband has nice eyes*, she thought and a little piece of her heart broke for him, already knowing the news he would get when he reached his wife.

Ike Whitman stood behind her and wondered if it was too late to change his major.

Taking the same path Marlea had chosen, Dench and AJ climbed the stairs to the third floor. Stepping out into the sterile corridor, it took a moment to get their bearings. Dench reached out to the first person passing—a youngish man with an afro in baggy brown corduroy pants, a tired blue shirt and a white lab coat.

Hand on the man's arm, Dench looked into his eyes. "I'm looking for Rissa, Marissa Traylor. I'm her husband, and they brought her here."

"Yeah," the man turned and pointed. "I just saw her. Her room is right down there."

"I still don't know what happened. Is she all right?"

AJ shifted from foot to foot until the doctor pulled them into a small room behind the nurse's station. He propped a hip on the desk and looked down at the clipboard in his hands. He read a page of notes, then looked at the two men. "Okay, here's what I know." The young ER doctor tried to explain, but the medical terms he strung together meant nothing to Dench.

"Look dude, I know football, I don't know medicine. Doctor . . ." Dench peered at the man's nametag. "Griffin. Talk English, Dr. Griffin."

Recognition flashed in the doctor's heavy-lidded eyes. He jabbed a finger in the air and laughed. "That's where I know you from! I should have connected the name—Traylor. You're the coach, right? Defense, yeah."

Dench planted a heavy hand in the center of the man's chest and looked hard. "Tell me about my wife."

"Whoa." The doctor took a step back and glanced at AJ. "Uh, yeah. Your wife is stable, but she lost the baby. Spontaneous abortion."

"Can I see her?"

"She's with her sister-in-law right now." He looked at AJ, recognition ticking behind his eyes. "Your wife?"

"Yeah."

The doctor folded his arms over the clipboard. "Mrs. Traylor was in shock when they brought her in, and she did lose the baby." He sucked at his lower lip. "This happens sometimes, and from all I could tell on examination, there was no specific cause. Depression is setting in right about now . . . She's going to have a lot of guilt, but there is no blame to be placed. She may just want to be alone . . ."

"I'm her husband. She'll see me."

"Let me get the sister out and you can see her, okay?" He looked at his watch, then back at Dench. "Just don't stay too long, okay?"

When he moved along the corridor, AJ and Dench followed. The trio stopped at Rissa's door and the doctor tapped lightly. The door opened and Marlea's face appeared.

"Dench?" She glanced behind her before stepping into the hall to hug him. "I can't tell you how sorry I am."

115

She looked helpless as the doctor left them alone. "She's asleep now. They gave her something and she's asleep. I don't know for how long. Did the doctor tell you anything?"

"He said she lost the baby, that this can just happen sometimes. It's nobody's fault."

"She's afraid it's her fault, you know. She thinks she did something wrong."

"And that I'll blame her."

Marlea passed a hand over her hair and shrugged.

"I don't," Dench said. His big shoulders heaved, moving his heavy jacket, and his hand splayed against the brass doorplate. "I don't blame her for anything and I guess all I can do now is stand by her and keep on loving her." He pushed the door open and slipped into the shadowed room beyond.

AJ and Marlea watched the door swing closed behind him and, needing to do something, drew closer to each other. They stood watching the door while hospital business went on around them.

"Do you want to look in on her?" Marlea finally asked.

"No, I'll wait. Let Dench have this time." His arm went around her shoulders.

"What do you want to do?"

"I want to go home, Silk." His arm tightened around her and his cheek came to rest against her hair. "I want to go home and hug my children and love my wife."

Tipping her head, she caught his mouth with hers and whispered, "You always know the right thing to say."

He nodded and they leaned against each other on the way to the elevator.

Dench stood alone in the shadows and watched Rissa sleep. Her face was tight and her dark lashes moved fitfully along the curve of her cheek. She whimpered and pulled her knees high under the sheet. Then almost like magic, he saw the tear. Silvery in the diffused light, it gathered along the line of her lashes before following the line of her short nose. When it stopped at the corner of her generous mouth, it was joined by another, and as he watched, the flow became steady.

Stepping close to the bed, careful not to disturb her, he pulled tissue from the box and dabbed at the tears. Déjà vu swept him. Was it only last night that he'd watched her sleep and touched her lips? Last night she'd smacked her lips and it had made him laugh. This afternoon, she cried in her sleep and he felt water gather in his own eyes.

Trying to man up, he sniffed and dropped into the chair Marlea had abandoned. Rissa suddenly lifted a hand and cried out. He caught her slender, long-fingered hand in the air and held it. *She's so cold*, he marveled, remembering holding her hand the night she'd told him about the baby. Closing her hand in both of his, he tried to share his warmth with her. Her face twisted and she pulled her hand away, leaving him alone and watching the tears still marking her face.

So much pain. He could see it around her closed eyes and tight mouth. Reaching, he used his thumb to smooth the soft hair framing her face, the tiny bracketed worry lines between her closed eyes, and the tear trickling along her nose. Concentrating, he followed the tear's course to the corner of her mouth. He touched the tear and she sighed.

"I love you, no matter what," he whispered, watching her. "You know I love you like Jesus loved the church."

She sighed again and opened her eyes. Puffy and red-rimmed, her nut brown eyes searched his face before she spoke. His thumb touched the corner of her mouth and she sighed. "We didn't make it. I tried, but . . ." Her voice cracked and more tears fell. "We didn't make it."

He stood enough to slide a hip to her bed. Sitting close, he pulled her into his arms, cradling her like a child. "This time, Rissa."

She hiccupped enough to stop the tears and determination claimed her eyes when she nodded and whispered, "Next time, Dench."

CHAPTER 7

Marlea parked her car and sat thinking for a minute, tempted to turn the key, shift the gears and roll away. What good would it really do to get out and go into a stupid restaurant, anyway? *Go in there and smile and try to choke down a meal with them watching my every move. Especially Libby. That little woman can't figure out whether she's a track and field coach or mother-confessor to the Western world. She's still pissed that we didn't tell her about the baby in the first place. I can still hear her nagging me about keeping secrets, saying I almost kept AJ secret right up until we got to the church.*

Libby Belcher was a great coach and a better friend. She'd been with Marlea since college. As an assistant coach, she'd helped Marlea build a stronger than average college career, then helped her move beyond PAC 10 and onto an international stage. As a friend, she'd been at Marlea's side through both the good and the bad times.

And now this . . .

Grabbing her purse from the passenger's seat, Marlea stalled for time. Pulling tissues, tiny teddy bears, minicars, and the whistle she'd confiscated from Jabari during church last Sunday from deep within her purse, she smiled. They were little things that reminded her of her children.

Damn, she sniffed, suddenly ambushed by small, tender memories that wouldn't matter to anyone else in the world. *Except me. And Rissa would sell her soul for little memories like these.* She swept the toys back into her purse, then dug deep for her lipstick.

She found her lipstick and opened the tube, gliding color over her lips without benefit of a mirror. Touching the corners of her mouth with a finger, she closed the lipstick and wondered what she was going to say. *I walk in there, I have to tell them something. There is no way that Jeannette and Connie are not going to ask for the details that I know Rissa refuses to talk about. And Lord, I know that she's the one with the big mouth, but if she doesn't tell her business, it's not my place to do it for her.*

Across the lot, a square-bodied man in a dark suit and sparkling white shirt escorted a thickly pregnant woman to a small car. Marlea watched him take exaggerated care to install the woman in the car. He even straightened the seatbelt and took the time to make sure that it was fitted to her maternal girth. Smiling, the woman seemed content to let him take care of her. *Kind of how Rissa was with Dench.*

Damn. Marlea's eyelids fluttered, beating back the threat of quick tears. *It's been a month, she's home and even if she's sadder than I could ever imagine, she's with Dench.* Marlea touched the tip of a finger to her eyes to block a tear. *Am I ever going to stop sniveling? It's not like my being weepy is going to fix things for Rissa and Dench. God knows, if I thought it would help, I would carry their baby for them. It's just so sad, and she's still so hurt . . . Guilt is such a heavy load . . .*

The couple in the Nissan were laughing, teasing, his hand rubbing circles on the woman's belly. *That's the way it should be*, Marlea thought, sighing. *That's the way it was with AJ and me. Maybe that's the way it will be for Rissa and Dench . . . someday.*

The sharp rap on the window snatched her from the privacy of her thoughts and made her jump. "Are you going to join us, or what?" Libby's violet eyes and spiky black hair were immediately recognizable.

"A little respect, please. Just give me a minute." Marlea collected her things and stepped from the car.

Libby took a step back and whistled. "You sure do clean up good. Isn't that suit a little fancy for a school teacher?"

"I have a little business to take care of this afternoon, so I'm wearing my official clothes."

Libby cocked her head and grinned. "If I dressed like that for business, my husband would swear that it was monkey business, but you look gorgeous." Her eyes fell to Marlea's feet and she smiled at the simple black pumps, low-heeled, with a tapered toe. She knew they'd been specially made. "How's the running these days?"

"The foot is fine," Marlea grinned, tapping her toe against the asphalt, "and so is the rest of me."

"Smart ass."

"Running is great." Marlea tapped her toe again. "AJ and I are planning a 10K for Project ABLE in a few weeks."

"Good to know." Libby's smile hitched higher. "There was a time, right after your accident, when I wasn't so sure that you were going to continue."

"That makes two of us, but then AJ came into my life." *And he made me two promises—that I would run again, and that I would dance with him. He kept both promises.* "My husband is good at what he does, and therapy worked wonders."

"Something worked wonders." Libby opened her arms and reached for a hug. "And just for the record, I love this suit. You look so smart and sexy—nothing like a runner. You know, you always wear so much blue, it's nice to see you in another color. I love this green on you." She paused and stepped back, then nodded. "AJ bought this one, didn't he? The way it fits and the color, yeah, that's him all over. Girl, you know you hit the jackpot with that man—good looks and good taste. And on top of that he's crazy about you."

"And sometimes, crazy is a good thing," Marlea agreed, looping an arm through Libby's. "Let's walk and talk." Across the parking lot, the square-bodied man finally satisfied himself with his wife's safety and walked around to the driver's side of the car. Marlea kept walking and tried not to think of the couple.

". . . thinking of building a gym so we can stay put," Libby said. "What do you think?" Marlea pulled the door open and they stepped into the City Grille. "Marlea," Libby frowned. "You didn't hear a word I said, did you?"

Starting up the winding marble stairs, her hand on the brass rail, Marlea looked back, knowing that there was no way out. "I'm sorry, Libby, I didn't hear you. What did you say?"

"I *said* that Hal and I are looking at maybe building a training complex, actually a gym with a track, so that I can stay here and we can enjoy being married to each other, instead of our work."

"Works well for AJ and me."

"Yes, but Project ABLE is not the only thing you do. AJ has his physical therapy practice, and you're still teaching. Hal and I would have a 24/7 arrangement—coaching and training all day, but neither one of us would leave at night."

"You wouldn't have it any other way. You know you love him."

"Yeah. For now, but if we were together nonstop, I might become homicidal."

"Please," Marlea laughed. "You two have been married for almost twenty years and you keep finding interesting things to love about the man. You, my friend, will be fine."

"You might be right. That man really is my all day study, and my all night dream," Libby sighed.

"You are so mushy, it's almost embarrassing," Marlea laughed.

"I may be embarrassing, but those two ladies look hungry." Libby walked across the red-carpeted dining room to the table Jeannette and Connie already occupied. Sliding into her chair, she looked around for the hostess and happily accepted the menu she offered.

"Love the suit, girl. Where's Rissa?" Connie's eyes went to the door beyond their blue linen covered table, searching.

"Thanks." Marlea opened her menu. "Don't bother looking, she called to cancel. I got the call while I was on my way. She made a lame excuse about getting herself together to go back to the office—then she hung up before I could say anything. She's been getting ready to go back for the last two weeks."

"So that means she's not coming today, so that she can avoid going back to work tomorrow? We were getting together today to cheer her up. She agreed to come so that she could get out of the house—it's been more than a month since . . ."

"She decided to become agoraphobic," Jeannette muttered behind her menu.

"You don't decide to become agoraphobic."

"She did." Jeannette lowered her menu. "I'm ready to order."

"How is she handling her workload, Marlea?" Libby murmured her drink order to their server and shook her head. "Telecommuting? Working from home?"

"Every day."

"Nice when you can do everything with your computer." Jeannette huffed and planted her elbows on the table. "All we wanted to do was get her out to do something normal, something to get her back to herself."

"Damn." Crushed, all of the women sat silently for a moment.

"You've got to know that losing this baby is killing her," Connie said softly.

"And Dench," Libby said, her voice even softer. "Poor Dench, how is he taking it?"

"He's still not talking about it. I mean, he cares about Rissa, he's taking great care of her, but I don't think he's taking care of himself." When all three women turned to look at her, Marlea pressed her lips together. "AJ's been good about spending time with both of them—for all the good it's done."

"Not easy on you and AJ either, huh?"

"Loss is never easy for anyone, but this is worse than anything I could ever imagine." Marlea let the words die. "And she still wants a baby."

"Bet she can't pull that up on her computer," Jeannette muttered.

Glaring at the computer, Dench double-clicked the mouse and brought up another game of Hearts. It was the twentieth game he'd played over the last two hours. He held his breath as his hand whipped into place, displaying his cards face up. He chose three cards and passed. Still holding his breath, he watched the two and three of diamonds and the queen of spades snap into place. His fist hit the desk, making the laptop bounce. "Sucks."

"Should have listened to Aunt Linda. Never bet on anything you can't guarantee you'll win." He closed the game and was tempted to open another—maybe the next hand would be better. *Don't bet on it. Your track record on bets hasn't been very good lately.*

A week ago, two weeks, hell, a month ago, he would have bet that they would have been past this. A month ago, he would have bet that as much as they both wanted the baby, they would have mourned their loss and found a way to hold onto each other in the process. Instead, she was guilt-bound and locked in depression so deep that he wondered if she would ever find the light again.

And I need for her to find the light. Spending his nights on the cold side of their king-sized bed was torture. Lying there night after night, a hand-span away from the woman who had been more than friend and lover almost from the moment he'd first seen her, was more punishment than any one man deserved. Sharing their bed with the guilt she'd strapped on only made it worse.

And the days were no better. How she managed to actually get work done was beyond him. In the house, she passed him like a ghost, moving from the bedroom to the bathroom, to the kitchen, and into her office with her eyes downcast and her smile missing. She'd pretty much abandoned her stylish wardrobe for his T-shirts and sweats, and when she thought he wasn't looking or listening, she spent hours in the small suite they'd planned as a nursery.

This can't go on any longer. I need her back.

Elbow on the desk, Dench dropped his forehead into his palm and logged off the computer with his other hand. *Stalled as long as I can and I can't keep putting it off; I need to go talk to her now.* He pushed up from the desk, rocking the slate gray leather chair as he stood.

His feet were slow as he walked from the office. Following the low drone of the television, he shoved his hands into the pockets of his jeans and wandered through his house. *Used to feel like a home,* he thought. *Now it's just a house.* He shook off the urge to go back to the computer, back to his game of Hearts, and kept walking.

Any other time, the stark, white-accented chocolates and blues of his home were soothing, but they suddenly reminded him of the muted colors of the hospital. And he'd thought of almost nothing but how she'd looked in the hospital since she'd come home, silent and betrayed.

Turning the corner, he caught her reflection in the dressing room mirror before he entered the bedroom. Rissa sat in the middle of the bed with her legs crossed. His T-shirt tented around her slender form, the short sleeves ending at her elbows, and his gray sweats were rolled up at her ankles, leaving her bare feet exposed. No makeup and her uncombed hair completed the picture and made him sadder. *Should have kept playing cards. At least I would have had a chance.*

"Hey, baby." He walked into the bedroom and she barely turned her head as he sat on the edge of the bed. "What are you watching?"

"Nothing."

"Mind if I watch it with you?" He ran the pad of his thumb along her leg.

"You can if you want to." She moved the leg a millimeter—just enough to lose the contact.

"Rissa . . ."

She kept her eyes on the television.

"I want us to get back to being us."

She dropped her head and inhaled deeply. When she looked up at him, her eyes were brighter. "I want that, too."

127

"You have any idea about how we should go about it?"

"This is hard, Dench." On her knees, she scooted close enough to look into his eyes. "Can we go slow? Real slow?"

"Whatever you want, baby." He opened his arms to her and she came to him. Stiff at first, the closer she came, the more fluid and graceful she became. All warm curves and soft flesh with a scent he knew as her own, she slipped into his lap, fitting like a key to a lock. Her gentle hands were dry and warmer than they'd been in weeks as they lightly framed his face. When he leaned to kiss her, her lids fluttered nervously before her mouth met his.

The kiss began slowly, quiet and sensuous, gifted with patience. His lips were a warm and gentle contact as they felt their way around the kiss, demanding nothing. Nearly a month of sleeping in the same bed and never touching had a cost and a passionate penalty. Without warning, he felt a desperate craving for more of their simple shared human warmth roaring through him. She felt it, too, and her body stiffened in his arms. The pain of threatened rejection was instantaneous, but he'd promised to go slow and, as his hands slipped from her face to her shoulders, he held onto the promise.

"I'm sorry," she said softly.

"Nothing to be sorry about." Dench cursed himself. *She isn't ready for this, and neither am I.*

Her hands covered his and she studied his face. "I should have listened. I should have called the other doctor. I should have been more careful, Dench." Her lips trembled, but no tears fell. "I'm sorry."

Wrapping his arms around her felt like the only right answer, so that's what he did. Then he lost track of how long they sat together, and if she'd asked he would have had to confess that he held her because he was afraid to let her go.

Rissa rested her cheek on his shoulder and sighed. "I've been hiding out in here long enough," she said. "I really am going to go back to work tomorrow. I promised to finalize the BeaconGreen contract for Jimmy and Sierra." She turned her head and pressed her lips to a place beneath his ear, sending a shivering echo of need quivering through him.

Her lips pressed again. "I've missed you so much. I just thought . . . I was afraid that . . ."

'I will bend like a reed in the wind.' The quote caught him off-guard, but it was right. *Now where did that come from?* Then he remembered: *it was from that movie AJ made me sit through the other night*—Dune. But the words were so right. *Whatever it takes.* "It's okay," he soothed. "I'm here and I'm not going anywhere."

"But I . . ."

Dench closed his eyes and moved his cheek against her hair. Inhaling deeply, he caught the scent of jasmine and honey and something else that was uniquely her. He loved her smell and knew that he would willingly sell his soul to hold onto her if he had to. *Whatever it takes.*

Her arms tightened around him. "Dench, I am so ready to get back to us, to what we had."

"That's all I want, Rissa."

Moving enough to watch his eyes, her gaze consumed him. "Can you really love me after this?"

"I always have and I'll never stop. You know I love you like . . ."

"Jesus loves the church," she whispered against his lips.

"It's true," he told her. "Do you have any idea how important you are to me? What I would do to keep things right with us?"

"I do." Her eyes suddenly filled, glittering with unshed tears. She sniffed and her lashes dropped, curtaining her eyes. "See what 'for better or worse' will get you?"

"I could never ask for more."

Scooting deeper into his lap, Rissa curved a long leg around his hips and pressed her hands to his face. Her thumbs traced his lips. Her eyes searched his face and his heart soared when she smiled.

"What?"

I was thinking." She cocked her head and giggled. "Ever thought of shaving your head? How sexy you would look?"

"Shave my head?" He passed a hand over his close-cropped hair and looked at her. "I can honestly say that it's never occurred to me."

"Simply studly."

Her voice poured into his ear so sweetly that he nearly bought it. "Wait a minute. What's in it for me?"

"A new start, for both of us. Shave your head and I'll let my hair grow out." Her fingers flitted over the razor-cut ends of her hair. "I'm overdue for a cut, so I'm a little ahead of you." She arched an eyebrow and his imagination went into overdrive, serving up images of her romping naked with flowing tresses.

Rissa pushed her other leg around him, binding him to her. "How about it?"

We need a new start, he reasoned, and this was as good a way to begin as any other. "Okay," he said, hitching her higher and into his arms, making her scream. "Let's do this."

Rissa clung to him when he stood, laughing all the way to the bathroom. When her feet touched the floor, she was still laughing, the sound soft, intimate, and healing. Dench laughed with her as they collected shaving supplies.

Pulling a small wooden stool from beneath the curving granite vanity, Rissa slapped the seat. "Sit! I want to do this before you change your mind."

With so much at stake? There will be no mind changing up in this camp—not today!

Draping a thick white towel over his shoulders, she flipped a hand towel over her own shoulder and tried to look competent, as if she did this every day. When she stood behind him, appraising the task at hand, Dench felt promise shimmer between them. *This is right.* He knew it as surely as he knew that he loved her.

Her hand brushed his head lightly as she picked up the electric clippers and found his eyes in the vanity mirror. "Are you sure?"

Holding her eyes, he nodded. "Do it."

He sat patiently, accepting her ministrations as she used the clippers to cut his already short hair closer. She hummed softly, absorbed in her task, as she applied hot towels to his scalp to soften his hair. Dench closed his eyes, listening to Rissa whipping creamy soap into rich warm foam. He swallowed hard and vowed not to flinch when her fingers pressed his head forward.

Lord, what the heck am I doing, offering my neck to a depressed woman with a razor in her hand? Have I lost my damned mind? Opening his eyes slightly, he saw her in the mirror and she looked more like herself than she had in over a month. Thinner, maybe, but definitely Rissa and he swallowed panic and decided not to run. *Trust*, he thought. *I'm going to trust us to get through this.*

Taking her time, artfully playful, she lathered his head. Stepping back to admire her beginning, she told him, "You are going to be so beautiful."

He tried not to match the smile he heard in her voice. "I hope so."

He felt her hold her breath when the razor touched his skin. Starting from the rear, she tenderly worked across his scalp. "It is beautiful. Baby, you should see." Head down, Dench reached for a hand mirror. She slapped his hand and giggled. "I said you *should* see, not that you *could* see. No peeking."

"When you do the front, I'll see." He raised the mirror to inspect his head and she caught it in the air.

"No. I have a plan." Rissa stepped from behind him with the razor in her hand. "Watch."

Even with the sagging shirt and baggy sweat pants, he found her compelling as she draped a long leg across him and settled into his lap. Without thinking, he reached for her, one lucky hand sliding beneath the shirt and homing in on the mellow globe of her breast. They both looked down, but Rissa spoke first.

"Guess you're going to try to tell me that's an accident."

"No," Dench looked innocent. "It's just nature taking its course."

She looked down, then back at him. "Then maybe I should get this big shirt out of nature's way, huh?" She laid the razor on the counter and pulled the shirt over her head, letting it drop at Dench's feet. "Think that will satisfy nature?"

"I hope so." *'Cause it's definitely working for me.*

"Fair is fair." Rissa's fingers made quick work of the buttons of the shirt she pushed from his chest and shoulders. Not trusting himself, Dench sat still as she leaned into him, pressing herself close. Her breasts pillowed against his chest as she squeezed him. "I've missed this, my skin touching yours."

Me, too.

"Dench?"

He stirred slightly, not wanting to surrender the moment.

"We need to finish."

"You're right." His hands slipped beneath the band of the sweatpants, cupping her.

She squealed and pulled at his hands. "Don't start something I'll have to finish. I meant your head." Her fingers traced the remains of his hairline, lingering near his ear before she reached back for the razor. "Remember?"

"Right."

He settled for locking his hands behind her bare back as she completed her task. Blotting streaks of soap with her towel, she finished and leaned back to admire her work. Her eyes held him even when she twisted slightly to find the hand mirror. She held her breath when his fingers closed over hers on the mirror's handle.

"It's different." Guiding her hand, he angled the looking glass and moved his head slowly for a full view. "Looks like you got it all."

She nodded and watched him when she released the mirror's handle. His eyes rose to the vanity mirror and he tilted his head. The hand mirror caught the sculptured curve of his head, and subtle light stroked his bare scalp. Satisfied with his inspection, he settled the mirror on the vanity. When his breath rolled smoothly against her cheek, Rissa began to breathe again.

"I like it," he said.

"I'm glad." Trusting him to bear her weight, she relaxed, her eyes finding his and agreeing with everything she saw there. He leaned toward her, his red-touched skin catching the afternoon sun and she met him halfway—giving as much as she took. He covered her neat hand with his own and felt their heat stamp his soul.

"I love you." Her lashes fell against his cheek.

Still holding her hand, he nodded. "I know."

Her hips moved against him and her fingers tightened on his. "I want to love you."

"And I want you happy."

"Then you need to take me to bed."

"I can do that." If he hadn't been sitting, Dench would have fallen to his knees as quickly as the towels fell to the floor. A grateful man, he blessed everything he could think of. Scooping up his wife, he forced himself to walk with her in his arms when what he really wanted to do was whoop with triumph and take her right there on the bathroom floor.

But this was a new start and she'd asked for the bed. He could give her that.

Lowering her to their bed, he slipped her low on her back and found the drawstring holding the sweatpants and the tease of her bikini panties. Loving that her eyes stayed tight on his, he pulled the pants low, revealing the deliciously golden skin he craved. Dench quickly lost his clothes, and heard her moan as he framed her body with his own. Mindful of his promise, hungry and determined to save something for later, he lost focus when she traced the lines of his back, her long fingers memorizing him as much for comfort as seduction.

His mouth against the strong hot pulse of her throat tested restraint, not wanting to take too much too soon. Tasting her, filled with the sweet scent of her, he tangled his flesh with hers and slid deep. Her quick catch of breath answered as her back arched and her hips rose, straining to follow him. Filling her drove thought from him. There was no room for anything more than the heat, the need, and the fulfillment. He plunged deep, accepting all that she was, almost like being swallowed alive, and he heard her cry out as she fell with him.

Cool air on steamy skin led them to drift back, with Dench still buried deep within her. Rissa turned to her side, separating them. The corners of her mouth lifted when her husband's warm arm fell across her. Spooned comfortably in their bed, his cheek pressed hers, Rissa curved her arms over his and enjoyed being satiated.

"It feels good to be us again, doesn't it?" When Dench hummed assent, she smiled. "A new start is good for us. Everything is going to be fine from now on. Everything."

Dench bent his head and kissed her shoulder. Rising on his elbow, he reached for the edge of the comforter and pulled it over them as Rissa's fingers loosened their grip on his arm. Her breathing deepened as she drifted into sleep and rolling onto his back, he pulled her close. One hand went to his newly shaved head.

I hope you're right, Rissa. I hope that this is our new beginning and not some kind of sucker bet, because I don't bet on things I can't win.

CHAPTER 8

Rissa watched the numbers change as the elevator rose. She was grateful to be riding alone and eyed the red emergency button on the panel beside the door. *I could push that button and stop the elevator, get off, and be back in my car before anybody knew the difference. I could be back at home and it would all be okay.* Her fingers itched to touch the button. Then she thought of Dench. *He would know the difference, and I promised . . .*

But damn, when I promised our new beginning, I didn't take all of this into consideration. She raised her eyes to the console above the doors and read the numbers—*my floor is next.* Her stomach turned on itself and she looked longingly at the emergency button again.

The last three days were hard enough. I don't know why I'm going in there to subject myself to this again. A quick flash of frustration threatened to become anger as the elevator slowed. *I walk in there, and I know that it will start all over again.*

Every time I think of how it was when I walked in there on Monday, I could just scream. You would think that since I helped build this agency, I could have a little privacy, but no, there they all were, so solicitous and busy. It's a wonder I got anything done at all. And it was precious little, at that.

And Yvette is the worst. She needs to remember that she's my partner, not my mother. I don't know why she just insists on treating me like an invalid. She shuddered and could almost hear her partner's voice. *'Honey, you look thin . . . Honey, are you all right? Honey, you just take it easy . . .' That crap is going to make me lose my mind!*

The elevator stopped. *Last chance.* Rissa stood there, still wanting to run, as the tall doors opened. Inhaling deeply, she stepped off and faced her office. *I can do this. I promised Dench and myself. I owe it to my clients to be here for them. I can do this, one day at a time.* She lifted her head and stood taller—didn't her mother always say that if you acted like you knew what you were doing, nobody could ever prove different? Gripping her briefcase, she pushed her purse higher on her shoulder and pasted on a smile— they would all feel better if she smiled.

Pushing through the steel and glass doors of her office, she forced gaiety that she didn't feel into her face, eyes and voice. *All I have to do is get past Karee and Yvette, and I'm in my office. Safe.*

"Hey, superstar. You can take off the shades, we all know who you are."

Damn, Yvette! Turning with her smile ready, Rissa waited for her partner to stroll closer. Knowing that she was being inspected, she decided that the best defense really was a strong offense and popped the collar of her rose-colored silk shirt. "Don't hate. You're just wishing you looked as good in them as I do."

"Huh, I wish I looked as good as you do in a lot of things." Yvette scooped up a bundle of mail and waved it

GAIL McFARLAND

in front of her. "Those glasses may look good on you, but I'll bet you can't read all this mail through them." She walked closer, her tapping heels marking her progress. "I know you needed some time, but do you ever plan to get all of this read? Believe me, it didn't multiply like this just because it has a sex life."

Façade dented, Rissa pulled the glasses off and jammed them into the pocket of her jacket. "Satisfied?" Blowing hard, she snatched the rubber-banded bundle, muttering. Flipping through a few of the pieces on top, she dropped random advertisements into Karee's waste-basket and started toward her office with the rest of the mail tucked under her arm.

"Hey!" Yvette watched Rissa's steps slow, and she waited for her to stop and turn. Propping a hand on her hip, Yvette didn't hesitate to radiate attitude—it was expected. "If you've got something to say about me, be adult enough to say it to my face. If you have something to say to me, come to my office. But if you need me to listen, I'm always here—don't forget that."

"Yeah, sure." Lips tight, Rissa turned and stepped into her office. Pushing the door closed, she pressed her back against it and closed her eyes. Her heart was pounding and sweat beaded her forehead and upper lip. *Made it, but I could have gone all year without Yvette throwing a pity party for me. It's not supposed to be this hard,* she told herself again.

Not liking the tremor that shuddered through her body, making her knees weak, Rissa pushed away from the door and headed to her desk. Draping her jacket over the back of her chair she sat with her briefcase and purse at her feet, grateful that she'd had the foresight to check the Weather Channel before returning to work.

Goodness knows how they would have treated me if I'd walked in here with a wool coat and suit on. She edited the thought and turned her chair to look out over the Buckhead skyline. *The weather sure did turn quickly—coats, jackets, and gloves at the end of February, and summer suits in the middle of April. Oh, well, that's life in Atlanta.* She wrapped her arms around herself and leaned back in the chair, denying the cold lump of anguish rolling like an iced marble in her belly.

So much has happened, and in such a short time. I remember Dench asking if I wouldn't rather have a kitten. No, I told him, I want a baby. Wonder if I would still have the kitten. But we're making a new start . . . Let it go, Rissa, let it go. . . .

She had no idea how long she sat like that, thinking and knowing that she had to move at some point. When her line buzzed, her jangled nerves pumped adrenaline through her body, making her jump. Realizing the source of the sound she hit the speaker button on the phone.

"Hey, Rissa. Mr. Clarence is here for his appointment."

James Clarence? His appointment isn't until . . . Rissa's eyes flew to the watch on her wrist. *Eleven-thirty? Where did the time go?* She turned her chair fully toward the desk and tried to sound normal. "Thanks, Karee. I'll be right out."

Haunted by her lost time, Rissa pulled her jacket on and pushed her briefcase and purse under her desk with her foot, and almost laughed at herself. *For a minute, I almost forgot what I was doing. He's here to review the contract for his next fight.* She pulled the paperwork out of her desk and crossed the room to place it on the table between the red chairs. Looking over her shoulder, checking on herself, Rissa left her office and nearly ran over Yvette.

"Now look," the feisty little woman began, "I'm going to need for you to watch where you're going, put on a blinker, sound a horn, or something . . ." Her voice dropped and her eyes evaluated Rissa. "Are you all right? Honey, do you need me to take this for you? If . . ."

The concern in her voice sprinted along Rissa's spine like fast flame on a fuse, setting her temper afire; the words that hissed past her lips when she turned on her partner surprised even her. "Let me tell you what I'm going to need: I'm going to need for you to stop creeping up on me, trying to treat me like an invalid—ever notice the spelling on that word? It's the same as the word that means 'not valid', and there's nothing wrong with me! When I need you to handle anything for me, I'll let you know!"

"Rissa, I didn't think . . ."

"Damned straight, you didn't think. If you had, maybe you'd get out of my face and give me a minute to breathe. I don't want or need your pity, Yvette. That's my client out there, I'll handle him. I don't need you monitoring my mail, my clients, or my productivity. I'm a partner here. I helped build this agency. When I can't hold up my end, you can buy me out. Until then, leave me the hell alone."

Watching Rissa stalk away from her, Yvette finally released the breath she'd held, but her feet wouldn't move—they couldn't. Blinking, feeling almost as if she'd been slapped, she knew something was terribly wrong and she didn't have a clue how to fix it.

At the other end of the corridor, Rissa's fingers went to the wall when she paused for a moment. Feeling Yvette's eyes on her back, she refused to look over her shoulder. Instead, she took a deep breath to calm herself and smoothed a hand over her gray pinstriped skirt and jacket. Satisfied that she at least looked peaceful, she rounded the corner and stepped into the lobby. Jimmy Clarence stood the second he saw her, and she smiled.

"Hey, Rissa, how are you doin'," he drawled.

"How do I look?" She imitated his drawl.

"You look good." He grinned. "Oh, and this is from Mama." He offered a large white bakery box. "She said to tell you that she didn't feel like making chicken soup, but a red velvet cake ought to make you and Dench feel better about everything."

"Thank you." Rissa had to force the weak smile to stay in place as she accepted the box. "I'll have to call your mother to thank her. Come on back to the office."

Leaving the cake on her desk, she sat with Jimmy and struggled to keep her lost child out of the conversation as they reviewed the contracts and the notes she'd gotten from his trainers. Together, they checked all of the caveats and she made the necessary amendments. When he approved the final condition, Rissa gathered all the sheets for reprinting.

GAIL McFARLAND

"While Helen is finishing the contract for signatures, would you like coffee or something else to drink?"

"Nope." The boxer leaned back into the depths of his red chair and grinned. "I don't know if Sierra and I ever said thanks."

"Thanks for what?"

"For setting me straight." Jimmy flashed white teeth. "You and Dench both said that by the time the baby got here, my mother would be all right with my marrying Sierra." His grin went sideways and the boxer looked like a twelve-year-old. "You were right, both of you."

"That's nice."

"Mama's so proud of this baby that she woke us up this morning with breakfast and then she baked that cake for you. She started an endowment for the baby last week, said she wanted the best for her first grandson. Then she said she hoped he was just the first of many."

"Would I be out of line for saying, 'I told you so,' only because I did?" Rissa tried to ignore the boxed cake when she walked to the mini-fridge built into her wall of bookcases. She pulled out a cold bottle of water and twisted off the cap. "Sure you don't want one?"

"No, thanks." He held up a hand and shook his head. "Sierra saw the paperwork on that little policy Mama started, and I thought she was going to go into labor right then. She started crying and making plans . . ." His voice dropped, the words dying on his tongue. "Oh, damn Rissa . . . I'm so sorry." He stood and walked to her, pleading his case. "Look . . . I didn't mean to bring up any . . . uh . . ."

"It's okay." She turned the bottle up and gulped water until he turned away.

Etching the line of his brow with his forefinger, Jimmy looked lost. "Sierra told me that I should wait to see you, and I guess I should have. I mean, this can't be a good time, with you all . . . vulnerable . . . and all."

"I'm fine." *Where does he get off, calling me vulnerable?* "We're here for business, let's just handle this and get it over with." Rissa twisted the cap back on the empty bottle and moved toward her desk. Coding the phone, she hit the speaker and waited. "How much longer, Helen?"

"On the way."

"Uh . . . I wanted to come and see you, but Sierra said we should send flowers and wait." Jimmy blinked when Rissa's chin dropped and she leaned against her desk. "We were both sorry when we heard."

"Thanks, Jimmy."

Helen tapped at the door and pushed it open without waiting for invitation. Rissa knew relief like she'd never experienced before. With whispered thanks, she took the contract copies from Helen and rushed Jimmy through their signing.

On the final page, Jimmy scrawled his name and laid the Mont Blanc pen aside. Standing, he shoved his hands into his pockets and looked lost. "I guess that's it, then. I should be going." He moved toward the door and pulled it open. Halfway through, he turned and looked at Rissa. "I just wanted to say . . . I . . . I'm sorry you lost the baby."

"Me, too, Jimmy."

Water filled her eyes and she never saw the door close as he left the office. The first determined tear broke free, fell and stained her blouse—after that crying became easy. Folding her arms on the desktop, she dropped her head and succumbed to fifteen minutes of heartsickness. She might have indulged in more, but for the buzz of her phone. Swiping at her wet cheeks with the back of her hand, she sniffed before answering.

"Rissa, I have a call holding for you. It's the attorney from BeaconGreen. Shall I put him through?"

Rissa knew her sigh carried over the phone and wished she could take it back. "No, Karee. Please take a number and I'll call him later." She disconnected the call and stared at the phone. Who knew, maybe she really would return the call. Reaching under the desk, she pulled her purse free. Digging for tissue and a mirror, she tried a little positive self talk, and gave up when she felt the tears well up again. She found the mirror and tissue but the phone rang before she could use them.

She saw that it was her personal line—family and friends only—and dropped her purse back under her desk. Not wanting to answer, she let it ring three times before relenting. Clutching the tissue and the shreds of her dignity, she picked up the phone.

"Rissa, hi!" Libby Belcher, Marlea's former coach, was on the line and Rissa could have slapped herself for ever giving her the private number.

The last thing I need right now is overweening good cheer. "Hi, Libby."

"I'm in Phipps Plaza, right down the way from your office, and I thought I could take you to lunch . . . if you haven't already eaten?"

"Oh . . . Libby . . . I . . . can't make it today. You know how it is, just getting back to work and all, maybe another time." Rissa closed her eyes and prayed that the lie would suffice.

"Well," Libby drew the word long. "Maybe another time, then."

"Yes. Another time, but thanks for the offer." Rissa hung up the phone and looked at her watch. It was barely one o'clock on an endless day and all she'd accomplished was the signing of a contract and pissing her partner off.

"But this is a new start, and I can do this." She flipped open the mirror she'd left on the desk and went to work with the wad of tissue, trying to erase the ravages of her tears. She bent and jammed her hand blindly into her purse for lipstick and mascara. She didn't feel much like putting the stuff on, but it was expected.

She looked down at her blouse; the tearstained silk was drying but still obvious. She pulled at her jacket until she was satisfied that the worst of the spotting was covered. Then she brushed her fingers over her hair and pushed away from her desk. Concentrating on her breathing, she picked up Jimmy Clarence's contract and almost called Karee to pick it up, then decided to walk it to the front herself. "I can do this."

At the desk, Karee looked up in time to see Rissa walking toward her. She leapt to her feet and rushed around the desk and accepted the contracts. "Oh, Rissa, I could have come back for that."

"Not a problem." Rissa looked around, surprised at the general quiet around her. "Where is everybody?"

"Yvette wasn't feeling well, so she left for the day. Helen is out, filing some stuff at the courthouse." Karee walked back around the desk and sat. "The interns are at the library, and we still close at three on Fridays." She shrugged. "That's it."

"I guess I'll go back and put my nose to the grindstone, then, do a little catch-up work." Walking back to her office, feeling Karee's eyes, Rissa felt a lick of shame at the things she'd said to Yvette. *I hurt her feelings. She never leaves early, and she left early today because of me.*

Knowing that she would have to apologize, Rissa closed her office door and headed for her desk. The cake James Clarence delivered still sat on the corner of her desk, and she reached for the box. Lifting the lid, she peeked in—the cake was a high, creamy frosted work of art. *I should have given this to Yvette. She likes cake. Maybe she would forget enough of what I said . . . maybe she would forgive me for a cake like this.*

Rissa closed the box and pushed the cake away. *I need to get some work done. That was my reason for coming in today.* She opened a desk drawer and looked at her pending files, then spent the next two hours reviewing contracts for two players who were unhappy with their teams. One of the men was due to become a free agent this year, and all she had to do was keep the other one out of jail—that was enough to keep anyone busy.

Running her fingers through the new, longer hair edging her neck, she read through the files and tried to focus on a game plan. The harder she tried, the foggier her thoughts became. *It's all that time I took off, that and the argument I had with Yvette today.* She turned a page in the file and tried to make notes, but her focus was off. Her stomach rumbled and ached a little. *Maybe if I eat something, I'll feel better. I'll get Karee to pick up a sandwich for me.* She touched the speaker and tapped in Karee's extension. The phone rang six times, and cut off. She tried again, and still no answer.

Going to the door, she was surprised to see the space beyond her office cast in afternoon shadow. "Karee?" No answer made her check her watch—four-fifteen. "And the office closed at three," she remembered, stepping back into her office.

Knowing the sandwich was out of the question, she found yogurt in the mini-fridge and silently blessed Yvette for saving her from starvation. She licked strawberry yogurt from the container lid and tossed it into the trash. Digging into a drawer, she found a plastic spoon. Eating slowly, pacing herself, she tried to think her work through to a logical conclusion—though logic didn't seem to be her strong suit today.

For all the good I've done this week, I could have stayed home. For all the damage I've done today, I should have stayed home. Trying not to think, she spooned more yogurt and almost choked when the phone rang. "Karee must have set them on night mode." She picked up the phone and barely opened her mouth.

"Rissa?" Jimmy Clarence was more than she could take right now and she almost hung up when she heard his voice. "Rissa, please! Are you there?"

"I'm here," she said, against her better judgment.

"I thought it was my phone," he shouted, breathless and nearly incoherent in his excitement. "We just got here! The hospital, we just made it, but we're all here!"

"Jimmy, that's great." Her stomach cramped.

"All of us, Rissa. Sierra, my mother, me, and James Jr."

Thick air clogged her throat and for a second, the room shimmered around her. Swinging an arm behind her, she found her chair, and managed to sit before she fell. "The baby is here?"

"He came at exactly four-fifteen. We almost didn't make it." The boxer laughed. "Everything happened at once: Sierra's water broke, we got in the car, we got here, we got a baby! Sierra, man, she was like a champ—she wasn't in labor ten minutes, and Rissa, you ought to see him. I've never seen anything like him."

The strawberry yogurt soured in her throat and Rissa nearly gagged. Fighting for control, she closed her eyes and held the phone in both hands. "That's wonderful, Jimmy. Congratulations. How is Sierra?"

"She's here. Here, baby."

The phone was passed from hand to hand and Sierra's soft voice came through. "Well, Rissa, we did it. He's here."

"Congratulations, Sierra. I can't wait to see him. What does he weigh? How long is he?"

The new mother's pride was broadcast over the cell-phone. "He's seven pounds, eight ounces, and he's twenty inches long—a lot of baby for me! I'm kind of preju-diced, but I think he's the most beautiful baby ever born, but you'll see him soon. Here's Jimmy . . . oh! You and Dench never gave us an answer, and the baby is here now. . . ." She yawned. "Let us know soon."

"Soon . . ."

The phone passed again and Jimmy was on the line. "They're bringing him in now, Rissa, and I think my mama is gonna pass out from sheer joy. We'll call you later."

Hanging up the phone, Rissa swallowed bitterness and wanted to cry again. Instead she turned to her com-puter and switched it on. When the system booted fully, she did a search for the prewritten press release. The doc-ument came up and she inserted all the details, then saved it to Karee's file. Karee would be in for her half-day tomorrow; she could send it out first thing in the morning.

Tonight though, James and Sierra Clarence would hold their baby in their arms. *And I've got a cake.* Sierra would be able to touch, kiss, and cuddle her child. Elbow propped on the desk, Rissa clamped down on the pain she felt leaking into her soul and refused to think of what Sierra and James Clarence must be feeling right about now—about the feelings she and Dench had been denied.

Intentionally numbing herself and ignoring the white bakery box on the corner of her desk, Rissa reached for her purse and fumbled until she found her wallet. Pulling out a credit card, she turned back to the computer and hit the internet. Clicking on the search box, she searched for flowers. When the sites came up she selected a bouquet and ordered it, then did the same thing for a layette.

Determined to keep moving, to stay busy, she scribbled a note to herself. *Be sure to visit tomorrow.* She almost added a time, then hesitated. Tomorrow was going to be a big day for the new family; maybe a visit should be postponed. Her stomach twisted on a bit of unbidden angst and Rissa suddenly felt empty, a husk of a woman, and she wished again that . . . but it wasn't meant to be. She logged off the computer and swung her chair around to look out the window at the sky darkening over Buckhead.

"Why her? Why not me?" Tears stung her eyes and she felt guilty but justified in asking for an answer. "How did this happen?" She heard the anger in her voice and her soul ached when she questioned everything she'd ever believed in. "I don't smoke, I quit drinking when we started the fertility testing. I've never had an abortion. I guard my health better than the government guards Fort Knox." The threatened tears fell and Rissa heard the hysteria in her voice even as she set it free. "Why? I waited all this time and then I lose what's mine. All this time and all I get is a damned cake."

Her ragged breath tore through her chest when she looked at the cake in its white bakery box, and she hated cake baking Brenda Clarence. Half rising from her chair, Rissa grabbed the box and threw it across the room. The smashed cake, the soiled box, and the smell of chocolate sickened her.

"Why does God hate me so much? Why is He punishing me, denying Dench? Why?"

Folding her arms, she dropped her head to the desktop and gave in to anger and frustration. Silent weeping gave way to sobs and wet, heaving breaths as her passion and pain unraveled. On her desk, her phone rang, and she knew it was her private line but didn't answer—the last thing she needed was an ebullient Jimmy Clarence sharing more good news. Her sad, jealous tears flowed heavier.

The stupid phone rang ten times, stopped, then rang again. When her cellphone rang, Rissa started to reach for her purse, but slipped instead from her chair. Landing on her knees, feeling the pop and run of her hose, she didn't care about the phone. *What the hell can I do about anything?* Her leg shot out, kicking the purse away, silencing the evil phone.

How many unwanted black babies are there in the world? All I wanted was one, only one! Wrapping her arms around herself, rocking, she pressed her back against the desk and wept.

Her cellphone lay amid the debris spilled from her purse, and if her kick had not dislodged the battery, Rissa might have heard her cellphone ring again. As it was, the incessant but now silent phone rang four more times before Dench thumbed the disconnect on his phone when the call went straight to voicemail.

"Where in the world is she?"

"Who?" AJ looked up from his computer, then back down. He might have been an NFL Hall of Famer and an excellent physical therapist, but he still handled the keyboard with a distinctive two-fingered hunt-and-peck style.

"Rissa." Dench ignored the ticking of AJ's typing. "She's not answering her phone. I thought she might have already left the office, so I tried her cell and she's not answering."

"Maybe she's busy."

"Who's busy?" Marlea's windsuit whispered echoes of her energy when she walked into AJ's office and across the room to drop a kiss on his forehead. Waiting for an answer, she parked a hip on AJ's desk and looked at Dench.

"This is not right." Dench sat wide in the chair across from AJ's desk and tried the call again. This time when the call went to voicemail, he cleared his throat and spoke into the phone. "Rissa, baby, this is Dench. I'm with AJ and Marlea and we're waiting for you."

"And you should hurry up," Marlea called across the room.

"Because we're hungry and my kids have to be in bed before nine," AJ added, rising from his desk. Agile and long-limbed, he stretched before collecting the patient file from his desk.

Cupping his hand around the phone, Dench glared at the couple and lowered his voice. "Anyway, sweetie, just call me back—let me know that you're all right."

"You sound worried," AJ said. He jammed the completed file into the cabinet and shoved the drawer closed.

153

"Rissa's a big girl and she's fine, probably just got tied up with something and forgot about the time."

"Yeah, the time." Dench turned the phone between his hands, then flipped it open and called again. He listened and frowned. "Damned voicemail."

Marlea shook a warning finger at him. "Easy on the swearing. You know my children adore you, and they'll repeat almost anything you say."

"Especially Nia. She really likes words and phrases that revolve around the word 'damn.'" AJ grinned.

"I'll keep that in mind." Dench stood, with Rissa clearly on his mind. "Maybe I need to take a ride downtown, just to make sure she's okay."

"It'll probably be a waste of gas. You'll pass her on the way home. You know that my sister not only cannot keep a secret, she's chronically late. That girl has been slow all of her life—all a part of her enduring charm."

"Dude, she may be your sister, but she's my wife. If she calls, tell her that I'm on my way." Heading for his truck, Dench made a quick detour through the kitchen. Mrs. Baldwin worked at the stone sink while Jabari sat on the floor and worked at reading to an attentive and adoring Nia.

Someday . . .

Dench pushed through the side door and climbed into his truck. *Rissa's fine,* he promised himself. *AJ and Marlea are right, she just got all caught up in what she was doing and forgot about the time. That's all.* Turning the key, he set his eyes on the road ahead and stomped on the gas. Following the curves of Cascade and entering highway traffic, Dench held onto the single thought: *She just forgot about the time, that's all. She's fine.*

Working his truck through the evening traffic, maneuvering around a pair of accidents, he tried calling her again—straight to voicemail each time. Pulling into the underground parking lot of the Hanover Building, Dench heard himself muttering under his breath, "She just forgot about the time, she's fine."

Ignoring the RESERVED sign, Dench pulled into the slot next to Rissa's small BMW and climbed out of the truck. The deck was mostly empty. Besides her car, only two others waited on the same deck level and Dench felt his heart bang in his chest. *She just forgot about the time, she's fine.* He refused to consider anything else as he jogged toward the building's lobby. Raising his hand to the security guard Rissa always snagged Falcon tickets for, still muttering, he jogged faster, determined to will her safe and well if he had to.

In the lobby, he jabbed the elevator call button and paced while he waited. Watching the numbers above the elevators descend as the car neared the lobby seemed endless. By the time the car finally reached the lobby, Dench was ready to give in to the urge to run up the stairs, but he stepped on board and pressed the button for her floor instead.

She just forgot about the time, she's fine, he reminded himself again.

He pulled at the neck of his Falcons shirt while the elevator climbed toward the seventeenth floor. Jerry Glanville might have put the Falcons 'back in black' for good luck back in '93, but right now the shirt was the hottest and most uncomfortable piece of clothing Dench had ever worn—and Rissa was responsible for his wearing it. She'd brokered his coaching contract just four months earlier.

A little sick to his stomach, he tried to imagine how he was going to feel when he reached her office. "She's probably sitting there at her desk with a mountain of paper piled up around her," he promised himself. "Got her shoes kicked off and the computer fired up, too." He pulled at his shirt again. "Dude, she's going to be madder than a wet hen when I pull her away from work." The words didn't really make him feel better when the elevator doors opened, but they made sense to his heart.

From where he stood, the offices of MYT, Unlimited looked deserted and his stomach dropped. The office closed at three on Fridays and she was the one who insisted on the monthly dinner date with her brother's family. *She just forgot about the time, she's fine.* Dench held the thought on mental lockdown and pushed at the office door.

Locked, the door didn't budge, and he fought the urge to put his foot through it. Instead, he reached for his keys and sorted through the bunch to find the emergency key Rissa had given him the night he'd asked her to marry him. Turning it between his fingers, he realized how proud he was of the silver key. Somehow, it was one of the ties that bound him to her life. It was proof that she trusted him enough to share everything she cared about with him. And now he was going to use it to search for the woman who represented everything he cared about.

She just forgot about the time, she's fine.

He pushed the key into the lock and turned it.

She just forgot about the time, she's fine. He would have sworn on a stack of Bibles that he believed the words, but as he stepped into the dark and empty office suite, every instinct he could call his own told him that something was wrong. He hit the lights and called her name—no answer. *She's here, and she's fine.*

She was definitely here; he could feel her in the silence. But something was wrong; he could feel that, too. Walking past Karee's deserted desk, he made the turn toward Rissa's office, trying to keep hope alive in his heart—but hope was a lie. He didn't feel any better.

"Rissa?" Feeling every nerve in his body reach for her, he walked carefully through the office. *If she's here, why isn't she answering?* Afraid to wait for an answer, Dench continued through the darkened suite until he came to Rissa's office. Letting himself in, he saw her jacket and briefcase—she would never leave without those.

"Rissa?" he called into the darkened space. "Rissa?" Approaching her desk, noticing the handwritten notes beside her computer, he was tempted to turn on the lights, but it didn't feel right, even as he caught the scent of chocolate on the air.

Chocolate? He blinked against the dusky light coming through the broad windows behind her desk and searched the office until his eyes found the splattered remains of the ruined cake on the floor. *Office food fight?*

It made no sense, especially when he saw her overturned purse. "Rissa?"

This time he heard the small answering moan and his breath stopped. Moving her chair, he looked down to see his wife's long, shapely legs beneath her desk. "Rissa?" Dropping to his knees, he found her crumpled into the knee space like a broken doll. "Rissa? Baby?" Her ravaged face, swollen and streaked with makeup turned to mud, turned to him.

"Dench?" She whispered his name, almost as though she feared being overheard.

"Yes, it's me." He reached for her and was hurt when her arm twitched away from his hand. *Man up*, he scolded himself, *she needs you*. "Come on out, baby." When she looked at him, he opened his arms, inviting her to take refuge in him. She hesitated and he nodded, encouraging her. "I'm here and I'm not going to leave you." She swiped a hand under her runny nose and inched closer to him. "Come on," he urged, waiting.

Her trembling hand reached for him and folded into his when he reached again. Slowly, she inched toward him, bending into his embrace. His hands moved over her body, searching for injury and praying against it. Finding her whole made him weak and Dench found himself sitting on the floor beside her desk. Almost afraid to speak, he wordlessly held her, feeling his shirt grow wet with her grief.

He held her, letting her cry until she ran out of tears. Finally spent, breath hitching through her chest, Rissa sat up in his lap and scrubbed the heels of both hands against her eyes.

"Guess I look bad, huh?"

It would have been funny if he hadn't found her crammed under her desk looking like this. He nodded and rubbed a hand along her arm.

She sniffed twice and rubbed her eyes again. "I kind of made a mess in here, didn't I?" Still rubbing her arm, he nodded again, and she buried her face in her hands. "It's been that kind of a day." His arms collected her and held her close to his heart while she kept her face covered. "Say something, Dench. Please don't just sit here holding me like I'm fragile or valuable or something."

"You are valuable to me," he murmured into the soft, inky darkness of her hair. Still holding her, he began to rock slowly, swaying with her, and the motion calmed them both.

She dropped her hands from her face and used them to hold his. "Ask me what happened today."

"What happened today, Rissa?" He continued to sway.

"I pissed Yvette off—royally."

"Yvette's your partner and a friend. She'll survive."

"Yes, but I owe her an apology."

"You'll apologize and she'll accept. Is that why you threw a cake across the room?"

She drew a sharp breath and stopped rocking for a beat. When she started again, Dench followed her rhythm. "Brenda Clarence baked the cake—red velvet. She didn't feel like making chicken soup."

"Chicken soup?"

"For an invalid. That's why I was so pissy with Yvette. They were all treating me like I'm not able to handle anything since I lost the baby."

Dench half smiled in the dusky office. "So you threw the cake across the room. Guess you showed them."

She sighed, and he thought she smiled a little. "No, I threw the cake later, after I found out that Sierra had her baby." She felt his surprise in the tension that vibrated through his fingers and along her arm. "Today at four-fifteen, the Clarences became the proud parents of a bouncing baby boy, twenty inches long, seven pounds and eight ounces." Turning to face him, she sighed. "We sent flowers and a beautiful hand-sewn layette. Do you think that makes up for the cake?"

Dench kissed her forehead and nodded.

"Am I crazy, Dench? You can tell me. She gets a beautiful, healthy baby, and I get a big-assed cake. How is that right? I'm jealous as hell, but now I'm all cried out and I think I may have damaged our new beginning." Twisting in his arms, she looked into his face. "This would be a good time to tell me if you think I've lost my mind."

"No, baby, I don't think you're crazy, and you killed the big-assed cake."

"And our baby. You can say it. I know what I did."

"Rissa, no."

"I should have listened. I should have . . ."

"Listen to me. The only thing you've done wrong is to keep blaming yourself." His fingers were tender when they stroked her cheek and directed her face to his. His voice when he spoke was balm to her soul. "Baby, I understand that you did everything you knew to do, you did everything you could to be right." Then he sat, simply holding her, breathing with her because there was nothing more for him than her.

When he pulled her desk chair close enough, he leaned on it and stood slowly. Taking her hand, he drew his wife to her feet and stood in the semi-darkness, holding her. Smoothing a hand over her short hair, he smiled. It was longer now, beginning to curl at her ears and over her shirt collar—a symbol of their new beginning.

She rested against him and sighed. "You could run now, and nobody would blame you."

"Yeah, but you would keep the house, and the house has you in it. I could never leave a house with you in it."

"Even if the house has no children in it?"

"Rissa, you're all I need, and I need you like the ocean needs a beach. Without you, there is no definition for me, no place to come back to. You're not crazy, and I'm not leaving you."

She relaxed against him and Dench kissed the top of her head, then looked over her shoulder and out into the blue Buckhead night.

Lord, now what do we do?

CHAPTER 9

AJ cleared his throat and hoped he didn't sound as embarrassed as he felt. It was bad enough to find your best friend on your doorstep first thing in the morning talking to himself and trying to figure out how to work things out with his wife. But when your best friend lived right down the street and was married to your sister . . . well, it was enough to raise more than a little concern. And now he wanted to talk, man-to-man. About Rissa.

"Have you two thought of counseling?"

"Thought? That's been about my only thought since she crawled out from under that desk." Dench blew out hard, the blistering sound rude and loud in AJ's office. He was glad the door was closed. "I sat down last night and told her that I thought it was our only alternative."

"And what did she say to that?"

"Dude, you know her, she's your sister. She told me that she'd lost a baby, not her mind—flat-out dismissed it." Dench turned from the broad window to face his friend. "Dude, I love her more than a fat kid loves cake and damn it, I need her. But I don't know what else to do for her."

"So you took your troubles on the road and walked them down to my house?"

"She's your sister. I figured that you care about her almost as much as I do. I'm looking for a new perspective here." Dench's brow furrowed when he frowned.

"Not trying to make things any worse, but whatever you do, you need to go home and face her. I can't see you fixing this from my house."

"You putting me out?"

"No way, I'm just telling you what I know from experience. You can't fix anything long distance—especially not with a woman." AJ reached across the desk, picked up the gilt picture frame and smiled as he turned it to his friend. "See this? This is Marlea on the day we got married. The pretty white dress, carrying those white peonies she loves so much, and that look on her face. You look at this and all you see is my beautiful, hopeful bride. You don't see her amputated toes, the career she thought she'd lost, Bianca's mess, or any of the other stuff we went through. If I'd run, or let her run and put distance between us, we couldn't have fixed anything—and damned if I would ever want to give up what we have."

Dench swallowed and a half smile sketched across his face. He shoved his hands deep into his pockets and remembered that Marlea Kellogg would forever be the one who almost got away from AJ Yarborough.

Still looking at the photo, AJ sat back in his chair. "A world-class runner, and I went and ran into her at a local 10K."

"Knocked her flat," Dench recalled. "Made her miss her time, knocked her out of the Olympic trials."

"And she tried to hand me my face." AJ grinned, sitting forward, leaning on his desk. "Look, Dench, all I'm saying is that women feel things differently than we do."

"Dude, you think I don't know that? I still remember how hurt Marlea was when you first brought her here—all depressed and betrayed." Dench paused and frowned. "Whatever happened to that doctor, the one who ran into her car and then did the surgery on her?"

"Reynolds?" It was AJ's turn to frown as he ran his fingers over the photo, touching the image of his wife's face. "Not as much as Marlea would have liked, I guess. Parker Reynolds did his time and got married almost the minute he got out of jail."

"Still practicing?"

"Wound up having his license revoked." AJ moved the photo back to its place of honor on his desk. "You know he was in the paper again last week."

Dench snapped his fingers and nodded. "Yeah, I thought that was him. The wife is Desireé, or something like that, right? She's filing for divorce, asking for millions, claiming economic incompatibility. What is that supposed to mean?"

AJ grinned. "Claims he's devoted himself to volunteering and it causes her social duress."

"Yeah, I can see how that would reduce her circumstances." Dench's chuckle rolled into full laughter. "Here she went and married a doctor who refuses to doctor and she's socially embarrassed—what a comedown. And all it will take to make her anguish easier to bear is a few million dollars."

AJ's finger touched Marlea's photo again—for luck.

Warming to the gossip, Dench dropped into the chair across from AJ's desk, one long leg draped over the chair's arm. "What's Bianca up to these days, and are you keeping track of her?"

"Man, I value my life and my wife is fast—you don't play around on a woman who can run like she can." AJ laughed. "Of course, she knows everything I know about Bianca. I learned that lesson the first time around—don't play with Marlea and secrets."

"So what is she up to these days? Still trying to slide into somebody's pocket?"

"You know Bianca." AJ shrugged. "Same old, same old. I don't want to look up and find her finagling her way into my bank account again."

"But where there's a will . . ."

"She'll try to make a way. She's still trying to build a name for herself as a designer, but I hear she's given up on football players. Trying to get with some music folks."

Dench swallowed laughter. "Looking for the next Russell Simmons?"

"Something like that, and as long as she's not looking in Atlanta, and keeps her distance from me and my family, whatever she does is her business."

"I just pity the fool she gets her hooks into, because you know she won't quit."

"No, she won't quit. She wants what she wants and only knows one way to get it. I'm just glad that Marlea came into my life and stayed." AJ watched Dench nod and they settled into companionable silence. Dench's eyes went deep and thoughtful as he turned his face back to the window. They'd been friends long enough for AJ to guess at what was going through the other man's mind.

"So what are you going to do?" he finally asked.

"You mean besides pray?" Dench sighed and shifted his leg from the chair. Standing, he looked like a man wishing he was heading anywhere but where he had to go. "I guess I'm going to head home and check on the roses like I promised Rissa." He shrugged. "Then I'm going to sit down and talk to my wife."

"Ultimatums don't work with her. They never have."

Pushing up from his chair, Dench held AJ's eyes. "I know. That's why I'll be working with a hope and a prayer."

"But you've got no net, so if you fall . . ."

Looking back from the door, Dench grinned. "That's what the prayer is for, dude. Wish me luck."

"You got it." Watching his friend leave, AJ nodded and hoped. Talking helped, but if it was going to work, then Rissa was going to have to listen. Dench was going to need that hope and prayer.

Walking into his home, Dench paused in the kitchen. He could feel Rissa in the house, listening, almost dreading his need to talk to her. In the distance, he could hear the muted sounds of the television, and he wondered if she was really watching it. She said she was going back to work on Monday. *She'll do it to prove her strength*, he guessed. The thought of her returning to a space scented with stale chocolate still made his stomach tighten.

At least that won't happen. The cleaning crew he'd called this morning would see to it. But still, there was the thought of her going back and maybe winding up under the desk again.

Tempted to walk down the hall just to look in on her, Dench stopped when the phone rang. Reaching quickly, he grabbed the handset. "Hello?"

"Hello, Dennis Charles. How are you today?" His mother-in-law's lilting magnolia-drenched voice poured into his ear and Dench pictured Sandra Yarborough sitting in her sunroom enjoying her usual mint-spiked iced tea and a stack of travel brochures.

"I'm fine, how about you?"

"I'm just fine, darlin'. I just wanted to touch base with you all before I leave tonight. I'll miss you all, especially my grands, but I can't wait to get on that plane. This will be my first trip to Kenya." Her soft laughter bubbled over the phone. "I'll be doing a photo safari, so you know I'll be using some of the film you gave me for Christmas."

Dench smiled, recognizing the flirty tone Rissa had inherited. "Are you sure you wouldn't rather take the digital camera?"

"You shouldn't tease your elders, son. Everybody doesn't share my pleasant disposition," Sandra drawled. "I'll take it, though it probably won't see much use. But now the film and flashbulbs, they will come in handy. I'm going to take lots of pictures and bring back lots of souvenirs."

And she will. Like mother, like daughter, Dench thought—Rissa always enjoyed practical gifts, and she enjoyed giving them as much as getting them. Sobering, his eyes went to the hall and he imagined her sitting in the middle of their bed, pretending to watch television. *She lost her chance to give me the gift she thought I would cherish most . . .*

"Dennis Charles Traylor, do you hear me talking to you?"

"Yes, ma'am." His attention snapped back to his mother-in-law and he tried to stay tuned to her words. He'd known the woman for years and had sat at her table for more meals than he cared to count. She was as much mother as mother-in-law, and as mother-in-laws went, Sandra Yarborough was a pretty good one, but she was also intuitive and smart.

"Why are you so distant today, Dennis Charles? You seem to have something on your mind. Is everything all right with the team?"

"Me?" *Her radar's up and on full blast.* "No, I'm not distant. The team is good, especially since we're looking healthy and strong in the off-season. Everything is fine."

"You said that too fast." Weighing his response, her tone changed slightly. "How is Rissa? Is she treating you right? Are you treating her right?"

"Oh, yes, ma'am."

"I see. It's about the baby, then? She hasn't come to terms with the loss yet, has she?" Sandra's sigh was deep and heartfelt. "That's an odd expression isn't it? 'Come to terms.' There are just some situations that have no acceptable terms, and yet, if one is to carry on, there is nothing else to do."

Ain't that the truth? Rissa can't seem to come to terms with the loss of the one thing she wanted most. Sandra's easy philosophy made sense, but left him cold and he said nothing.

"I thought about canceling my trip . . ."

"Please don't." Holding the phone, Dench suddenly realized he was also holding his head and wondered when the headache began. "It's not that we don't love you, but this is something we have to work through on our own." The headache took a turn for the worse.

"She always did take everything personally, even as a child. That was one of the things I worried about when she decided on law school, that she would bring every case home with her. But I can honestly say that I've never once worried about her with you." Sandra was silent for a beat and then she sighed heavily. "Put my baby on the phone, would you, please?"

Dench opened his mouth to speak, then thought better of it. "She's, uh, in the bedroom. I'll get her for you."

He decided against just calling out her name. It would have been too easy for her to pretend not to hear. Putting the phone on hold, he walked carefully into the bedroom where Rissa lay curled on her side vaguely watching the figures moving across the television's flat panel. Trying to keep his voice light, he forced a smile and watched her mirror it. At the bedside, he picked up the phone and pressed the button. "It's your mom. She wants to speak to you."

Rissa's back curved gracefully as she curled more tightly in on herself. Cheek pressed against the pillow she held close to her body, she looked up at Dench and shook her head.

Watching her, he opened his mouth, but on the other end of the line, Sandra beat him to it. "I'm sure she just said that she didn't want to talk, didn't she? You tell that girl I said to get on this phone, and be quick about it."

Caught in the middle, Dench looked at his wife, but before he could repeat the words, Rissa closed her eyes and held her hand out for the phone. *Must be one of those mother/daughter things.* He handed the phone to her and left the room.

Holding the phone, Rissa listened to the pad of her husband's steps retreating across the hardwood floor before opening her eyes. "Hi, Mom." She heard her mother inhale. *Prelude to harangue,* she thought. "Before you start, do I get to at least say that I don't want to talk to you about it?"

Sucking her teeth, Sandra Yarborough counted to ten. "If you don't want to talk, you don't have to, but that means you'll be listening while I talk."

Holding the phone, Rissa mumbled something and pulled her knees up to her chest. Her mother took the ensuing silence as agreement. "I thought you told me that you loved Dench."

Rissa blinked at the phone. "You just called him Dench. You usually call him Dennis Charles. Why the sudden name change?"

"Answer the question, Marissa."

Flinching at the use of her given name, Rissa's eyes went to the door. He was gone, probably back to his office. "I do," she said. "To tell the truth, I always will."

"Then why are you stealing yourself from him?"

"I'm not . . . Things are just hard right now."

"Going to school was hard. Convincing your father that law school was right for you was hard. Managing AJ was hard. Starting the agency was hard. Learning to work with your partner was hard. This is not the first hard thing you've ever done, Marissa."

"Losing a baby is not the easiest thing I've ever done, either."

Both women drew long breaths. "Of all the hard things you've accomplished, you've never done any of them alone. You're not alone now, or at least you wouldn't be if you didn't push him away."

"I never meant to push him away." Furrowing her brow, Rissa was swept with more need than a five-year-old. For a moment, she wished her mother was in the room, that she could climb into her lap, stick her thumb in her mouth and be comforted. "I don't know if we'll ever have our own child, but I do know how much he wants one. He wants a family, Mom, and apparently I can't give that to him."

"Marissa, there are a lot of ways to build a family."

"I know . . ."

"And for heaven's sake, do you realize what a crap shoot pregnancy is? How many billions of chances there are for things to go wrong before just one baby comes into this life?"

"Doesn't seem like it's that hard for the people on Jerry Springer," Rissa grunted.

"Don't be smart with your mother." Brief laughter edged Sandra's voice. "You've been happy with Dench for years without a child of your own. You just told me that you loved him . . ."

Standing, Rissa walked to the window that looked out over her budding rose garden. Bless his heart, Dench had taken to tending the roses when she'd abandoned them. She watched him pull a wagonload of tools into the garden. When he stopped, he looked around, surveying the work to be done. Afraid to be caught watching, she stepped back from the window.

"I do. I love him," she whispered into the phone, "and those three words are my life."

"Then I think it's time you did something to save your life, Marissa. I want you to see someone and work this out."

Rissa sucked her teeth and rolled her eyes. "I'm supposed to go sit in somebody's office and tell them all about what a sucky childhood I had and that will make everything better?" She sucked at her teeth again. "I don't think so—you and Daddy didn't abuse me enough to make that work."

"Keep making jokes, Marissa. Maybe it will, and maybe it won't. But at least you'll have tried and given yourself a chance to get rid of some of the anger and guilt you're carrying."

Rissa's hand slashed at the air before she could stop it and she cursed her mother's intuitive hit. "Who said I felt guilt or anger?"

"I did. I'm your mother and I know you—you can't go on the way you are, not for much longer. Dennis Charles needs for you to see someone, if only to keep you from losing him. You need to find a way to smile again, a way to help him smile again. Whether or not you two ever add to the list of my grandchildren is not what's important now."

So you say . . .

Her mother caught more than a hint of petulance in Rissa's sigh. "Do what you have to do to save your life, Marissa."

Her mother's words felt like prayer in her ear. "I can try."

"Nothing beats a failure but a try."

"I'll try," Rissa promised.

"Then I can travel knowing that I'm leaving you in good hands? That you'll see someone?"

"Yes, Mom. Be safe."

"You, too, sweetheart, and I'll see you when I get back."

"Love you," Rissa whispered, disconnecting the call. Standing back from the window, looking out at Dench as he labored in the garden, she felt her promise take root in her heart. She watched him move the Falcons cap farther back on his bald head and look to the sky, exposing all that he was: just Dench. A man with big hands, big feet, long limbs, sheets of muscle, warm lips, and a heartbeat like music.

Her own heart stumbled when she watched him. Backing up until the backs of her legs bumped the bed, she sat and watched him. On his knees, he tended her rosebushes under the hot Georgia sun. He worked steadily, taking as much care with the plant roots as he did with the tender blushing pink blossoms. She watched him use a small hand rake to fertilize the plant and thought her heart would burst.

He always knows the right thing to do. Pulling her heels to the edge of the bed, Rissa hugged her knees to her chest and rested her cheek against them. From the corner of her eye, she could see their framed wedding photos.

I stood on a cliff in Jamaica and married him, and I felt like a queen. I married him and knew that I'd gotten a gift—a perfect man in paradise.

And it almost didn't happen. Sad as she felt, the memory made her smile. *All we had to do was be at Tensing Penn in Negril in time to get the marriage license, and I missed the plane.* The government required couples to be at the resort at least forty-eight hours in advance. Dench left from Florida, but everyone else left from Atlanta. *And everybody was on the plane except me. I got to the airport in time to see my plane leave without me.*

She smiled when she thought of the people she'd called and the favors she'd called in, determined to get to Dench. *There was no way I was going to settle for not marrying him.* In the garden, she saw him organizing something in the wheelbarrow and her smile broadened. *I would have walked on water all the way to Negril to marry him.*

Thank God I didn't have to. When I'd done everything I could, I called him, frantic and afraid, and all he said was,

'I can fix that.' Then he made a call and I got a private jet. When we landed . . . Her tongue traced her lips. *I can still taste his kiss . . .*

The thought of his kiss brought a sweet surge of memory. *Every time I've ever needed him, ever wanted him, he's been there and his kisses . . .* Unsubtle lust rushed and rambled through her body. *Mom's right. I'm a fool and I've punished him for all the wrong reasons. We both want a baby and if we're ever going to have one, I need to make the next step . . .*

The picture she always referred to as their wedding photo sat in the center of the array on the small table across from where she sat. It was her favorite, one of more than two hundred pictures taken the day they were married, and now it captured her eye and her imagination. In the photo, they stood together at sunset, looking into each other's eyes. Framed by a perfect Caribbean sky, standing on a Jamaican cliff, an ocean breeze flirting with her gown and veil, they appeared to be perched on the edge of eternity and it was the way she wanted to be with him forever.

And if I don't move now, forever could become a lost wish . . .

Her eyes and throat filled with tears and she knew what she had to do. Picking up the phone, she pressed in the numbers and listened to the ring. The second she heard the answering voice, her lips parted.

"Marlea, I need a favor . . ."

"And we both know that I'm pretty much the only one you could ask," Marlea muttered. "Seriously though, I'm glad that you decided to take this step." She turned the business card in her hand and read the therapist's name. "Chris Gordon—is this a woman?"

"Yes." Rissa turned the wheel and steered her car around a truck stalled in the middle of the intersection. "Connie gave me the card a while back and I figured that it couldn't hurt to go in and talk with her." Her eyes moved from traffic to Marlea and back again.

"You know, I would argue with you if this wasn't such a good idea." Marlea flicked the card with her thumbnail as she studied Rissa's intent profile. "But just for the record, I know this wasn't your idea."

"It is my idea, and I know what you think you're doing." Rissa passed Pharr Road and slowed a little, ignoring the shift in the Peachtree Street traffic. Squinting, she read the addresses, then picked up speed. "You're trying to distract me." She slowed and squinted again. Changing lanes, she kept her eyes straight ahead. "Thank you."

Along for the ride, Marlea kept her mouth closed. *If I say one word, it will be one too many, and I don't want to give her any excuses for avoiding this session—she needs it too much, even if only to have the chance to hear herself say things out loud.* Lowering her lashes, Marlea studied her sister-in-law, looking for a clue.

Rissa looked neat and pretty—normal, in fact. Dressed in creamy white slacks and a sleeveless coral sweater, she wore minimal makeup, and her longer hair curling at her cheek made her seem softer. Only her fingers, tight on the steering wheel, gave her nerves away. Marlea didn't blame her for a minute.

When I think of everything she must be holding inside . . . I don't think I could stand it if something had happened while I carried Jabari or Nia. Unconsciously, her hands folded across her stomach and her unseeing gaze veered toward people on the sidewalks. *And AJ would never have blamed me, just like I know that Dench will never blame Rissa. But how do you forgive yourself?* Careful not to let Rissa catch her, Marlea studied her face and saw the tightness around her mouth. *This is hard for her . . . so hard . . .*

"Here's the building." Timing the traffic, Rissa turned and drove through the iron gate fronting what appeared to be an elegant home. Parking in the small lot behind the building, she collected her purse and jacket without so much as glancing at Marlea.

Following, Marlea kept her questions to herself. *I'm just here for moral support,* she told herself. *There will be plenty of time for questions later.* It struck her a bit odd that such a classically built mansion, complete with rolling green lawn and handsome shrubbery, would sit so close to the urgent bustle of Buckhead. *Wonder if this used to be a private home?*

She was still looking around when Rissa marched up the wide, white marble stairs. Keeping pace with her, Marlea stopped at her side when she paused to press an intercom button beside the door. Waiting, trying not to give in to the urge to try to peek through the leaded-glass-paned windows in hopes of seeing beyond the door, Marlea noticed the small brass plaque bearing the engraved names of four women practitioners, including Chris Gordon, PhD.

Hearing the click of the lock when the door opened electronically, she followed Rissa. Impressive antique furniture and what she guessed to be Aubusson carpets filled the lobby. Staged to look like an elegant home, polished wood gleamed, piecrust-edged tables bore what looked like real Tiffany lamps, and etched crystal vases were filled with fragrant flowers. Marlea had the feeling that they had stepped through time.

A lot of money went into this place. Maybe they figure clients will recover better if the surroundings don't look clinical. Marlea felt Rissa's nervous resolve and wondered if the surroundings would work for her.

"Mrs. Traylor?" The voice was gentle and sensitive, and filled with enough authority to make Rissa and Marlea jump. The speaker, with her salt-and-pepper hair, polite smile, and sensible shoes, walked toward them with her hand extended. "I'm Chris Gordon."

Shy for the first time in her life, Rissa took a step back. "I'm Rissa and this is Marlea." She pushed her forward.

Just throw me under the bus! Marlea pasted on a smile and extended her hand. Taking stock of her, Marlea knew instantly that the woman was no athlete, probably never had been. At medium height, she was middle-aged and carrying a few extra comfortable pounds. Though everything about her seemed soft, the therapist's earthy confidence reminded Marlea of singer Nancy Wilson. Her bright eyes were dark enough to be considered black and didn't seem to miss a thing as she looked at the women in front of her.

Chris looked deeply into Marlea's eyes and smiled warmly. She took Marlea's hand and held it in both of hers. The effect was comforting.

"I came along for moral support," Marlea murmured.

"Always a good thing."

"She's the one I told you about, and she's going in with me. With us." Rissa stood ramrod straight and clutched her purse in front of her like a shield.

"Family support is important, and I am very glad that you have such a willing supporter." Chris gave Marlea's hand a pat as she released it. Her eyes watched Rissa. "But this a bit unusual, and I believe that . . ."

"We discussed it when I made this appointment. I told you on the telephone that I was bringing her with me." Rissa's rigid body went even stiffer. "She's with me and I'm with her. I go in there with her, or not at all."

"Rissa, maybe talking about this would be easier if I waited . . ."

Marlea's soft voice seemed to melt the ice in Rissa's spine, but her gaze never left the doctor's. "No. You promised to help me do this, and I'm going to hold you to it. This is hard, really hard, Dr. Gordon. I trust Marlea and I need her with me, if I'm going to do this."

Chris nodded. "Confidentiality is always an issue, but if you're sure?"

Rissa looked at Marlea, and was comforted when she nodded and said, "I'll sign whatever I need to."

"I will, too. I want her with me. Please." Reaching for Marlea's hand, Rissa waited.

"Then I believe we need to get started." Totally at ease with Rissa's new reticence, the caramel-skinned woman gave new meaning to encouragement as she led them to her office, an eye-pleasing space defined by sensitively muted colors, furnishings and artwork.

Chris watched them settle in the pair of thickly upholstered delft blue chairs across from her, and when Rissa sat stiffly silent, she began to speak. "Grief," she said, "is a natural and normal response to loss. It is the internal part of loss, how we feel and thus how we react to loss. All loss is the absence of someone that was loved or something that fulfilled a significant role in one's life."

Rissa pressed her lips together and stole a quick look at Marla. Her head was bowed as she inspected her nails. Rissa cleared her throat and sat straighter in her chair. *I only agreed to do this once, and since I'm paying for it, I might as well try to get something out of it.* "The baby I lost never had a chance to establish a place in my life."

"And yet you grieve for the loss—this is by no means unusual. A grief reaction may be experienced in response to a physical loss, in your case the loss of your child."

Rissa crossed her legs and pulled her purse into her lap. "How do you propose I get over this grief reaction?"

Marlea sighed and never lifted her eyes from her hands. Rissa's leg twitched nervously when she realized that she was the recipient of Chris's gentle smile.

"You'd like the quick fix, wouldn't you? I wish I could offer you one, but grief is best considered a journey or a process. It is not simply a series of events that fit into a structured timeline."

"Then I can tell you that I don't know why I'm here." When Marlea looked up, Rissa was already facing her. "I don't," she said, determination lancing her features. "There is nothing you can do to help me. I want to be pregnant, and that's outside your area of expertise. I want to not have lost my baby, and you can't fix that either."

Relaxed in her chair, Chris looked at the woman sitting across from her. "Then why did you come here, Rissa?"

"Because . . ." *I want to stop hurting Dench.* The story of crawling out from under a desk nearly spilled from her lips, but Rissa folded her hands, squeezing them nearly bloodless as she clamped down on the story. *There is no way I'm going to tell her about Jimmy and Sierra's baby.* "I want to get pregnant again. I want a baby, and I guess I thought that talking to you would help me to go forward."

"The decision to become pregnant again after a pregnancy loss is a difficult one," Chris said.

Rissa slumped in her upholstered seat and glared like a reluctant teen. "Not for me."

Undeterred and apparently optimistic, the therapist plunged on. "Subsequent pregnancies can bring about a whole new set of emotions, and the decision should never be taken lightly. In your case, it's understandable that a pregnancy would be compounded with even more emotions and medical details than normal."

No shit, Sherlock. Rissa pressed her lips into a tight line.

"Let me ask you this: Is it the pregnancy or the child-rearing that's most important to you?"

"It's . . ." *I never thought about that before . . .* Rissa looked at Marlea, remembered her pregnancies, all of those stupid pictures her mother had taken of her belly, AJ's face at the birth of his children. *I want that . . . for me and for Dench.* She thought of Nia's pride in her potty training, of Jabari's face when he took his first steps into Marlea's arms. *I want that . . . Dench wants that . . .* Her mind flashed images of what it would be like to hold her own child.

"It's both," she finally said.

Chris nodded softly. Her voice was understanding and supportive. "What is your husband saying about your decision?"

Dench. "He's supportive."

"Have you asked him what he thinks?"

"I . . . of course I have. Like I just told you, he wants a baby as much as I do." Her quick glance stole Marlea's thoughts and bound her to silence.

"In my experience, some couples choose to try again immediately, while others are left wondering if they ever want to try again. Others will choose adoption because of concerns due to fertility problems or the age of the parents." Chris paused to consult her notes. Looking up, measuring her client, the therapist spent her next words like dollars. "At thirty-two, I can imagine you're eager to try again."

"As soon as possible," Rissa said softly.

"Have you considered taking some time?"

"For what?" Rissa's head jerked up, her eyes dark and sharp. "My eggs are not going to wait forever."

"I'm not suggesting that you cease trying," the therapist said quickly. "Perhaps you might benefit by taking at least a few months to heal a bit emotionally—think about it."

"I have, thank you. At the rate I'm going, my emotions will be healed and my womb will still be empty." Rissa reached for her purse as she stood. "Thank you for your time."

Marlea caught her in the hall.

"Don't say it." Rissa walked faster. "Marlea, if I'm ever going to have a baby, I have to take control over my fertility, and I'm doing that right now."

"Rissa, there are alternatives . . ."

"Sure, there are alternatives, but how many of them are really reasonable for me? Dench and I have already spent years and a truckload of money on fertility treatments that were useless and never guaranteed in the first place."

"Wait, Rissa."

Marlea's fingers closed on her wrist and Rissa stopped to look at her. "You really don't understand that my reality is totally different from yours, do you? You're right, we could adopt, but then it's not like any of the available children would be genetically linked to me or Dench. Foster care? No way can I see bringing a child into our lives, loving it, then giving it back like some kind of rent-a-baby. Don't you think I've done my homework? Checked all this stuff out?"

Pushing through the heavy door, she rushed down the stairs to her car. Jamming her key in the lock, her hand shook, and she hoped Marlea hadn't noticed.

"Have you thought about a surrogate?

"Yeah, right," Rissa snorted, dropping into the driver's seat. "Have you noticed? I'm a black woman living in America at the beginning of the twenty-first century. There is no huge demand for surrogates among African-Americans at this time. African-American women prefer to make their babies the old-fashioned way, Marlea, and you should know that. Even if I wanted one, acceptable surrogates aren't growing on trees."

Marlea crossed her arms and made a face. "AJ is right. You really do have a head like a rock."

"Takes one to know one," Rissa muttered. "What's your point?"

"That was an offer, dummy." On the other side of the car, Marlea dropped her arms open, into full display. "Would I be acceptable? I could be your surrogate." Rissa's mouth dropped and she started to protest, but Marlea cut her off. "We already know that I'm healthy, we share the same blood type—B positive—and I've had two perfectly healthy babies."

"So you think that qualifies you to be a . . . a rest stop for . . . mine?"

"I could be. Rissa, I really could be."

"No. Dench and I are going to try again." Rissa turned the key and the car's engine purred. She pressed her foot to the gas and eased out of the parking slot.

"And if things don't work out? Would you consider adoption?"

"I already told you . . ." Rissa's eyes snapped and her lips tightened.

"Rissa, there are millions of unwanted children of color out there. Children of all ages—I'm sure you and Dench could adopt an infant if you wanted to. You could have all the sleepless nights and diaper changes that would occur if you gave birth to the baby yourself."

"But they wouldn't be blood, Marlea. That whole 'bone of my bone, flesh of my flesh' thing? It's deep, and it's what I want for Dench and me. He doesn't have anyone else, no other blood relatives, and I want to give him that connection."

"You're all the connection that man needs."

"I don't expect you to understand, but I hoped you would. My hardheaded stubbornness cost him everything. When you touch Nia and Jabari, every cell in your body connects to them. When they turn to you or AJ, there is no other human who can and will give them what you do—and that's what I want for us, Marlea. I know that means being blessed with a second chance, but if I had one, there's nothing I wouldn't do to make this real for us."

"Then think about my offer, that's all I'm saying. Flesh of your flesh, bone of your bone. You could have it, Rissa." The hand that Marlea laid on Rissa's arm trembled faintly. "You're the closest thing I've ever had to a sister, and as frustrating as you can be sometimes, AJ and I love you. Dench loves you and we both know that this is hurting him. Give it some thought, Rissa—for you and Dench. Just think about it."

Rissa steered into traffic. "Why does everyone think that I'm so frustrating?"

"Because you are, and personally, I fault AJ. If he'd been a good little boy, he would have been an only child." Marlea laughed when Rissa slapped at her shoulder. "Just promise to think about it."

"Right." Rissa slipped a hand from the steering wheel and crossed her fingers. "I promise."

CHAPTER 10

Rissa was hoping for an early start, normalcy, and a little privacy—even if she was starting her week on Thursday. *But taking the time was the right thing to do, 'cause I was a little stressed. I needed to take a minute,* she told herself when she pushed through the door of MYT, Unlimited, with a full cup from Starbucks in one hand and the Atlanta *Journal-Constitution* under her arm.

But the door was unlocked and the lights were on—proof that fate had conspired against her, and that she was not alone.

Yvette's head lifted and her eyes met Rissa's, almost daring her to speak.

Damn, Rissa realized, *this sister is loaded for bear!* "Good morning."

"Good morning."

That's it? Rissa took a deep breath and walked closer. "How was your weekend?"

"Fine." Yvette's lips thinned when she lifted a stack of folders from Karee's desk and pushed them toward Rissa, but she never mentioned Rissa's extended weekend. "Those are yours. Karee has already finished them." She lifted a second group of folders and held them close to her chest.

Rissa fingered the folder tabs. "Oh, good. She got to the Jimmy Clarence information." She looked up and tried a smile, then nearly shivered from the frost Yvette sent her way. "They, uh, had their baby. It's a boy—James Jr."

"How nice." Yvette opened the file on top of her stack. She found an error and scowled down at it.

Walking closer, Rissa set her purse on the edge of Karee's desk. "Look, Yvette . . ." Her throat closed when Yvette's eyes nailed hers. "Yvette, I'm sorry. There's no good way to say it. I was a bitch the other day and I had no right, absolutely no right, to speak to you the way I did. I don't know how to make it better and I don't even know if I can forgive myself, but I hope you'll accept my apology."

"Yes, you were a bitch." Yvette bit her lip. "Maybe you don't realize it, but everybody in this office knows what you've gone through recently, and, whether you believe it or not, we're all pulling for you."

Humiliated, Rissa's breast rose and fell, but her gaze did not waver.

"I'd be lying if I didn't admit that you were a bitch, with a capital 'B,' and that I was pissed with you." Yvette laid her palms flat against the folders. "Want to tell me what happened with the cake?"

Rissa gasped and shook her head. "No."

The corners of Yvette's mouth turned down, but she nodded. "Okay—for now."

"But can you forgive me for just being nasty?"

"Yeah, I can. I've had a few days to think it over, so I suppose I will." Yvette's hand was warm and comforting on Rissa's arm. "I've never been through the kind of stuff you and Dench are going through, but I meant it when I said that you could talk to me. I'm not just your partner, I'm your friend."

"That's what Dench said you would say."

"Smart man, you should hold onto him." Yvette winked as she picked up her folders and walked to her office.

In her own office, Rissa shuffled through the folders and smiled when she thought of Yvette's words. *I have every intention of holding on to him, and I'm so glad he holds onto me.*

Thinking of him made her look around her office. She looked at the wall and the floor, trying to see evidence of the cake she'd thrown—that nothing was visible was evidence of his hand. She sniffed the air and smelled only the vague clean scent of vanilla instead of chocolate and rancid butter from the red velvet cake. *Dench,* she thought again, knowing that he'd made sure she could work in her office.

I must have scared the bejoogers out of him, and he still found a way to make sure that my office was clean. Pleased and grateful, she was tempted to call him, but he was out on the field today—preseason training, she knew. *But there's no reason I can't text him.*

Her fingers were quick on the keys as she worked to say what she wanted him to know. *I love you like a flower loves the rain,* she began, then spent five minutes revising. Finally satisfied with her message, she sat at her desk and sipped her coffee, wishing she could have said more, somehow reassured him of more.

At least I was able to tell him about my time with Chris Gordon.

It didn't take a lot of imagination to recall the look on his face when she'd walked in from the appointment. Coming in through the kitchen door, she'd caught him standing at the dark granite counter, building a massive and manly structure of turkey, a couple kinds of cheeses, and assorted vegetables. He called it a sandwich. She strolled close enough to stand next to him and steal his potato chips.

Slicing the sandwich, he levered half of it onto a second plate and pushed it toward her. "See, that's proof that I love you," he grinned.

Snagging more chips, she pushed the sandwich back. "No, baby, you eat it. I don't want to take food out of your mouth." No argument from him as he poured two tall glasses of milk. She took one and sipped, before running her tongue over her upper lip. "Can I tell you what I did today?"

"What did you do?" He moved both plates to the other side of the granite counter and she followed him. When he sat on one of the tall stools, Rissa pressed herself between his legs and leaned against him.

"I kind of took your advice. I got Marlea to go with me . . . I . . ." She stuttered when he raised a brow. "I went to see a therapist."

And I don't know what I expected him to do or say, but when he rubbed my arms and held me . . . when he listened . . . promised me that everything was going to be all right . . . She sipped more coffee, looked out over her clean office, and felt cherished. *I told my mother that I loved*

*him, that those three words were my life, and I ain't never
lied about where my feelings are for him. Dench is my life,
whether we ever have a baby or not.*

Lifting the first of the folders she'd brought from the
front, Rissa started to read over the details of a new commercial contract, and was interrupted by the ring of her
phone. She was slightly disappointed that it wasn't her
private line.

Joyce Ashton sounded wide awake. "You've been on
my mind and I thought I would give you a call."

"That's nice, but . . . why?" Anxiety skittered across
her skin, leaving goose bumps in its wake. "Joyce, is
something wrong with me?"

"Calm down, you're fine, as far as I know. I just
wanted to chat a little."

Chat? I've never chatted with Joyce before. "What did
you want to chat about? Is it something legal?"

"No, and it's nothing big." The doctor's smile edged
her voice. "I had a chance to speak with Dench."

Rissa's mouth opened and closed on her shock. "I
can't believe he went behind my back and called you."

"How do you know I didn't call him? Besides Rissa,
he was worried and he wanted to understand what was
going on with you."

"Joyce, you're *my* doctor, not *our* doctor. He should
have at least said something to me first." Rissa turned her
desk chair to look out of her window. In the distance, she
could see the haze of early summer heat rising over the
Buckhead skyline and was thankful for air conditioning.
"Ethically, if I didn't come to you, no one should have."

"You're one of those people who only thinks about ethics when she gets caught in them, aren't you?" Joyce's light chuckle crossed the line between them, smoothing some of Rissa's irritation. "How ethical is it for you to keep details from Dench and then make him an accomplice to a loss he had no control over?"

Rissa groaned and propped her chin in her hand. "It never crossed my mind."

"He told me that you saw a counselor."

"Yes, I did, and I think it helped."

"When are you going back?"

Rissa lifted the lid on her coffee cup and sighed. *Empty. Just my luck.* "What else did he tell you? Or maybe a better question is, what else did you tell him about me?"

"He says you're going to try again."

"We are."

Rissa could almost hear Joyce toying with her glasses, maybe tapping one of the temple pieces against her lips as she framed her words. "I'm sure the sex is enjoyable, but is it fair?"

"Oh, you wait until I talk to Dench . . ."

"And what will you say to him? 'If at first you don't succeed, try, try again?' Rissa, even if you are successful in getting pregnant again, and remember it took four years this time, is it fair to tell him that you'll just keep on trying until you get it right?"

"That's mean."

"No, Rissa, that's real. If you don't find a way to accept and respond to your cervical insufficiency, you will more than likely repeat your loss. Could either of you stand that? Could your marriage survive it?"

Chris Gordon said I was entitled to my grief. She never said it would haunt me like this. "What do you recommend?"

"There are alternatives . . ."

"I know, I know. Anything else?"

"Well," Joyce drawled. "You could call Alexis Stanton, the specialist I told you about. And keep having sex. If you get pregnant, talk to Alexis about cervical cerclage. If you truly want to carry your own child, the procedure might give you a chance. Other than that, just enjoy sex with your husband, stay open to the alternatives, and don't discount the option of a surrogate."

There's that word was again—surrogate. "Have you been talking to Marlea?"

"No, not lately, why?"

"No reason. Maybe I should talk to her."

Ending the call with Joyce, Rissa considered calling Marlea—and it seemed like a good idea until she looked at the time. Not even ten in the morning. She realized that Marlea would be in class at the Runyon School right about now.

And there's no way to call her and work through this. Pacing did next to nothing for her nerves and getting Dench's sexy text message didn't help, either. Rissa looked at the door and debated going to Yvette's office. *She said I could talk to her . . . but this is too much, and way too personal . . . Connie and Jeannette talk too much, and they talk to each other . . .*

Her phone rang and she paced close enough to pick up the receiver.

"Hey, Rissa. I've got pictures."

Oh, goody. Just what I need.

"I emailed them to you this morning. You'll see them as soon as you open your email," Jimmy Clarence enthused. "I sent a set to Dench, too."

"That was really nice, Jimmy. Thanks."

"My mama called this morning, and I thought I'd better give you a heads up—before she tracks you down. She bought a video camera and she's trying to make a film about JJ's first days. That's what she calls him, JJ, for James Junior. He ain't been here but a minute and she's already got a nickname for him." The boxer's voice thickened and slowed. "You know, I owe you a lot. If you and Dench hadn't been there to point me in the right direction . . . man . . . I would be missing out on all of this. So, you know . . . thanks."

"You're welcome, and I'm going to look at those pictures."

Hanging up the phone, she congratulated herself. *I just had a whole five minute conversation about a baby and I didn't have a meltdown. That's progress.*

Determined to make more progress, she opened the files on her desk and tried to prioritize. Marcus Sawyer's file seemed to rise to the top and she flipped through it, shaking her head as she read. Twenty-one years old, fast feet, balance to die for, and the kind of hands that could become NFL legend, the receiver had a drinking problem that could condemn him to a career of regret—*if he doesn't kill himself or someone else in the process.*

Reading deeper into the file, Rissa found herself shaking her head. *I knew from the beginning that this boy had problems.* Her first meeting with him was at a high school football game, at the invitation of his mother. Sawyer's mother was not so different from her own and when Rissa decided to go to the game, she hauled Dench along for backup.

Sawyer was a dream on the field and hell at home. He was a smart, arrogant kid, being raised without a father, and maybe that was part of the problem, because it took the promise of a man with passion for the game they both loved to grab his attention and get him through school. Dench promised him a chance and Rissa used AJ's contacts to get Sawyer into Tech. She'd hoped the rest would be up to him and his talent. Now there was a place on the Falcons for him—if he could ever develop the discipline to hold on to it.

Dropping her head into her palms, Rissa read more. Every problem on Marcus's list seemed based in alcohol. The alcohol issue never showed up in the time he played for Tech. His grades were decent, better than decent, actually. *Addiction,* she thought, *and addiction is not about discipline.* She saw the sticky yellow note Yvette had attached to the file.

José Christopher and Ben Thomas had already called and were waiting to hear something from her. Christopher and Thomas were reporters. Worse, they were damned good reporters and, like sharks, they could already smell blood in the water surrounding Sawyer.

This can't be ignored or left alone in the hope that people will forget about it—memory is just too convenient. Crushing the note into a ball, she turned her computer on and did a search of the Fulton County Jail records. When she found Sawyer's name the first time, a blunt burst of acid shot through Rissa's stomach, and she knew she would have to dig deeper. Her fast fingers moved the mouse and typed in more data, hoping she wouldn't find him. *Hope all you want, there he is.* She tapped the screen with her finger and wished she wasn't seeing what she was seeing.

This was the part of her job that she hated, having to confront a client and issue an ultimatum. Marcus Sawyer was going to have to decide to embrace his life and the career he craved, or take a dive into a bottle and figure out how to live with what he found at the bottom. It wasn't about getting a break. It was about making a choice.

But it's never really that simple, is it? Massaging her temples, Rissa could hear Chris Gordon's voice and knew the truth of her words. It wasn't simple, but Rissa knew that she would connect the player with the therapist, and pray for the best.

It took four calls to track him down and the steel in her backbone to back him down, but Rissa finally got Sawyer to talk to her, and the first thing he did was take the alcoholic's refuge in lies. He lied about the charges, making them all figments of the arresting officer's imagination, reducing them to minor joke status—until she told him that she was looking at them on her computer. He refused to come to the office or to meet her anywhere else. When she threatened to burn his contract, he confessed to being previously arrested under a false name and she was tempted to really burn the contract.

Instead, she stood up from the desk and hardened her voice. Pacing the length of her office, she broke the realities down for him, speaking of rappers in the wrong company caught with guns and drugs in drugstore parking lots, and big-balling football and basketball players dealing with false names and faked realities and learning that they were not above the law. "And you can keep on until it's your turn to be caught, or you can fix this now. Marcus, I promise you that having a former agent and a lost NFL contract won't do you a bit of good while you're sitting in prison braiding somebody's hair."

When he swore, she verbally spanked him and told him what she expected and what he was going to have to do to keep her services and the contract she'd secured for him. He growled at her and she snarled back, reminding him of the morals clause in his contract and what it would cost him to violate it. The Falcons had a one-year exclusive and a first choice option that they were not obligated to pick up. "And if they don't at least make an offer at the end of this year, you're going to be marked for extinction.

"The rest of the world is not as stupid as you want to think they are, and they're not as forgiving as you want to hope they are. Are you willing to blow this shot at a dream for a few drinks, a little crack, and a police record? You get picked up like this again, Marcus, get prosecuted, you'll be looking at federal time and you'll need a better lawyer than me to pull your butt out of the fire." She paused and hoped she had him thinking.

When he finally spoke, his voice was hollow and dull, stirring her suspicions. She closed her eyes and hoped against hope that she was wrong—though she knew in her heart that she wasn't. Walking back to her computer, she listened to his ramblings as she did a more complete search and found what she knew she would: four small alcohol and drug stops—one with a minor female in the vehicle. Two of the stops, including the one with the girl, had resulted in ticketed warnings.

Eyes on the screen, miscreant mumbling in her ear about how the whole world was out to get him, Rissa shook her head and hoped it wasn't too late. He admitted to using the name Marc Sayler, and sticking to the lie even when the arresting officers seemed to recognize him. His celebrity status had kept him safe, so far, but what would happen when he got picked up after a bad game or after he made a bad play? She tapped more keys. The fines had been paid without his having to show up in court. *That's how he'd stayed off the media radar.*

Her next call would be to Dench.

But in the meantime . . . "There's someone I want you to talk to, Marcus. Her name is Chris Gordon. She's a counselor and I think she'll do you some good." She listened to his protests and excuses, and then said, "I'm going to make this simple for both of us, Marcus. See her and I'm still your agent. See her, and I'll tell Dench that you're trying to do the right thing. Don't see her, and I'll shut my mouth tighter than a drum and you're on your own."

She smiled, liking the technique. He called her a "buzz saw in a skirt", but he agreed. She gave him the contact number for Chris, then made him repeat it. Sullen and more than a little shaken, Sawyer promised to make the call.

"You make her your very next call, and have her let me know when your appointment is. Oh, and when you keep it, I want to know that, too."

His brooding, "Yes, ma'am," gave her hope. She made a quick note in the file before she dialed Dench.

"Hey, hot stuff, how's it going?"

"I just love how you always see me for who I really am," she purred into the phone.

"Sexy is as sexy does, I always say."

"Did you wear shorts today? The ones I like?"

"Life is good when dirty girls grow up to be dirty women," Dench said, his voice dropping to pick up the raw edge that always thrilled her.

"I'd better tell you what I called for before I forget." She crossed her legs and cleared her throat as she eased her hips forward on her chair. "One of your new players has got some stuff going on, and without trying to violate his confidence, I can tell you that reporters are sniffing around for information. It won't take them long to ferret it out, either. I found it on the first try, maybe because he's a local boy."

Suddenly serious, Dench moved his hand across the phone, muffling his words. "I'm on it," he said. "Random testing starts in an hour. Just a thought, but maybe I should start with last names beginning with the letter 'S'."

"Good start."

"Oh, and before you go," his voice changed for her, "do you suppose that the dirty girl will be waiting when I get home?"

"Probably not," Rissa's leg pumped a time or two, "but I know a dirty woman who can't wait to see you. I did tell you that the therapist said that I should have lots of sex, didn't I?" She laughed with him.

Hanging up the phone, Rissa liked how she felt— braver and more able somehow. For the first time since losing the baby and returning to work, she felt capable and ready to handle it. *Maybe therapy isn't such a bad idea. I certainly thought enough of my session to recommend it.*

Then she remembered. *I told Dench that the therapist said I should have lots of sex, but it wasn't Chris, it was Joyce who said it. And I forgot to tell him that I talked to her, that I said I would consider the options.* Moving her fingers over the files still remaining on her desk, she debated working, then looked at her watch and figured that now was as good a time as any to try reaching Marlea.

Marlea must have been standing over the phone. She picked up on the first ring and groaned when she heard Rissa's voice. "Where are you going to try to make me go now? Wherever it is, I can't go. I have too much to do at school, the 10K is coming up and I told AJ I would pick up his shoes. Besides that, Nia and Jabari have swimming lessons this afternoon . . . do you have a suit in your gym bag? Maybe you should come."

"Please, with my hair growing out, there's no way I'm climbing in a pool."

"Chicken?"

"Completely. Do you know what my head would look like after playtime in a pool with your two little heathens?"

"Thanks, Rissa," Marlea suddenly pouted. "Are you telling me that I look bad?"

"Girl, no." Rissa sucked at her teeth. "I would never do that."

"Yes, you would."

Gritting her teeth, Rissa managed not to scream. "Actually, I just wanted to talk . . . for a minute."

"I've got about forty minutes." Rissa heard the chair scrape as Marlea pulled it away from her desk. Sitting, her tone relaxed. "What did you want to talk about?"

"I got a call from Joyce Ashton this morning." Rissa ran her fingernail over the edges of the folders on her desk. "Dench called her and she was following up."

"Why did Dench call your doctor? Is something going on with you?"

Rissa ignored the question and her nail traced the edge of the folders again. "She wanted me to consider alternatives. I told her I would and I will, no matter how unnatural or unreasonable they seem." She heard Marlea's breath catch in her throat.

"Are you just using me as a sounding board, or are you serious?"

"I'm serious. Right now, I'm considering everything, even *in vitro* and maybe a surrogate."

"Why do you think it would be unnatural to have an *in vitro* procedure with me as your surrogate?"

"I never mentioned your name." Squeezing her eyes shut, Rissa made a gagging sound, then cleared her throat. "I didn't say that you would be the surrogate, if that was the way to go."

"Whatever. It would be me, and that's that." Marlea suddenly sounded excited. "So you and Dench decided? You're going to do it?"

"No, I'm still a long way from making that kind of a decision. I have no idea what Dench would say."

"Yes, you do. You already know he'll say you can adopt, or you can take me up on my offer."

"I'm still trying to think this through, and I already told you that the old-fashioned method is my preference." Rissa cleared her throat again. "Doesn't the whole thing strike you as trifling with nature? Playing God? Mixing up some kind of Frankenstein baby in a petri dish?"

"Don't be silly, the Frankenstein monster was full grown—made out of man parts. And who would know how your baby was conceived if you didn't tell them? Oh, what was I thinking, you'd probably tell them."

"Have you talked this over with AJ?"

"Not yet, but you can't keep on like this, Rissa."

"That's pretty much what Joyce said. And I said I would think about it, but promise you'll talk to AJ."

"I will, but this is the right thing to do—for you and for Dench."

Rissa's nail rifled the folders again. "You just want to stake a claim on my happily ever after."

"And what's wrong with happily ever after?"

There is absolutely nothing wrong with happily ever after, Marlea thought as she touched the wall panel that bathed her bedroom in soft light. If she had been counting, that would have only made the fiftieth time she'd had the thought since talking with Rissa.

Sometimes happily ever after needs a little help, but all in all, happily ever after is a good thing and I ought to know.

It still made her smile to think of her own fairy tale. Who could have known that a woman who had run all her life would have run into her own handsome Prince Charming in something so ordinary as a 10K footrace? Who could have guessed that, even when the dragon at the door was a doctor who cast a dream-stealing spell over the heroine, she would still find a way to run into the arms of her hero? And that the hero would turn his back on a wicked witch capable of stealing his will with unimaginable skills, to claim happily ever after.

"Hey, Silk." The perfect hero, still wet from the shower, a towel wrapped at his waist, AJ walked into the room and his wife fell in love all over again. She watched as the sweet milk chocolate of his skin flowed complete and beautiful, capturing bronze tones as he passed into the light. Muscle, bold and breathtaking, sculpted by a lifetime of athletics, showed in artistic detail along the eye-pleasing length of his elegantly articulated body, and her knees grew soft. Then he smiled at her.

"Thank you for fairy tales," Marlea murmured, wondering if the time was right.

Her eyes on him made him watch her. Then her tongue traced her lower lip, taunting him. "What are you thinking?"

An easy glance at his towel told her what he hoped she was thinking. "Babies," she said.

"Another baby? Three?" He grinned. "Why not? It's not like we aren't great parents. Another baby might be fun."

"You mean making one might be fun?" He was too close and she couldn't resist, not even if she wanted to— and she didn't want to. Marlea pulled at the towel knotted at his waist and it came away in her hand. Holding the towel aloft, she stepped back. "Oh, my goodness, look what I found." Her lusty interest evident, she danced back a step, but only one when he reached for her. Naked, his palpable and growing need unmistakable, he reached for her again.

"Ooh, I give up." Marlea let the towel drop to their feet, her eyes never leaving his when she stepped into his embrace and feigned innocence. "What are you going to do to me?"

"Give me a minute, I'll think of something."

His mouth found the dusky column of her throat and claimed the sweetness he found there. Fast hands, large enough to snatch a speeding ball from the air, were gentle as he stole the clothes from her body and claimed her. In his arms, kissing and touching, Marlea felt a fleeting whisper of guilt, but the heat of his hands on her skin brushed it away.

Holding her hips, softly kissing her stomach, slowly working his way down to the groove between her thighs, they shared deep and hungry breath. Moving inward, delicately revealing her, accepting her welcome, he felt her quiver. Rocked by the oceans he stirred within her, she called his name and he clung to the silken bands of her flesh.

In AJ's arms, pressed beneath the weight of his body, knowing that he was as necessary and as integral as air, Marlea had one thought as she surrendered to all that they shared: *I'll tell him tomorrow.*

CHAPTER 11

Martha Baldwin was used to the vibe they shared. Goodness knew she'd been around long enough to watch them build their communal bond and to watch them with their children. Not that they were perfect. In fact, some days she wondered why God had trusted them with each other. But other days, it made no sense in the world to wonder if there had ever been anyone else for either of them.

This was one of those days, she noted. Marlea was moving through the kitchen with efficient grace, like a model mommy. But today, Mommy had a bit of an edge. Not one for robes and slippers at breakfast, today was an exception. Her usually sleek hair looked more than a little worse for wear, twisted up from the nape of her neck and clipped high on her head, and every time her eyes touched AJ, the color in her mocha-toned skin went high.

And AJ wasn't much better, though he'd pulled on jeans and a T-shirt. Talking with his son, his voice low and specific, he was a daddy a little boy would always love. He hadn't shaved yet and his eyes were heavy lidded. Daddy definitely looked like he hadn't gotten much sleep last night.

Luring Nia to the table, using her sippy cup as bait, Marlea smiled at AJ and the housekeeper read the subtext. *It must have been a good night, because they both look like they would fall in bed together in a heartbeat.* Martha stirred her eggs and kept her thoughts to herself.

Sliding the eggs onto the warm, waiting plate, she handed them off to Marlea. *So nice to see how far they've come to be together like this. To have and enjoy their children and each other. But it wasn't always like this. No, sir!*

There was a time when it looked like this little domestic scene didn't stand a snowball's chance in Hell. Martha strolled over to the counter and selected a rosy apple from the sterling bowl and found a paring knife in the drawer by her hip. *Yes, child, there was a time . . .* Martha tucked in her plump bottom lip and held it between her teeth.

It was magic for both of them, almost like catching lightning in a jar, the way they found each other. Twisting the knife, Martha scooped out the apple's core, and thought about the man and woman across from her. *She just about ran him off before she understood what he felt for her, but he stuck and stayed, and here they are.* Slicing the apple, Martha slipped a sweet crunchy slice between her lips and considered while she chewed. *Those two were made to be mated, I figure. Rissa and Dench, too, because if the good Lord ever made a woman for any man, then He surely made Rissa for Dench—and vice versa.*

Martha managed to keep her eyes on her apple, but she was fully aware of Marlea and AJ talking, teasing, playing, and engaging their children, even as they connected with each other. Intimate as lover's foreplay, they shared food, newspapers, and coffee and made it look easy and natural in the process.

Feeling every bit the voyeur, Martha Baldwin finished her apple and moved to rinse the plate she'd used. Standing at the granite sink, her back to them, she heard Jabari's quick laughter. "Mommy kissed Daddy!"

"You think that's something? Watch Daddy kiss Mommy."

Nia clapped her hands and laughed, too, imitating her adored brother.

Martha let her eyes drift into the courtyard beyond the kitchen window and smiled. *Sounds like a little privacy might be in order.* Leaving the dishes, Martha moved smoothly to the table and scooped Nia from her booster seat.

Settled on the housekeeper's hip, Nia smiled. "Store?" she wanted to know. When the housekeeper nodded, the little girl's face lit up and she swiped her hands over her face. "Me, too?"

"As soon as I take care of that potty face," Martha teased.

" 'Kay." Any store was Nia's favorite place to be— even if it meant additional face washing. "Come on, 'Bari." She was even willing to share the adventure with her brother.

"Bye, Dad." Jabari climbed down from his chair and grinned up at his mother. When Marlea closed one eye in a slow wink, his grin widened and he slowly squeezed both eyes tight then opened them wide. "I love you, too."

Bending to hug him was easy; standing and releasing him was a good bit more difficult, but Marlea managed and waved when he ran off.

"I wonder if he'll always do that two-eyed wink for you?" AJ opened his arms, then closed them again when Marlea dropped into his lap.

"I hope so," she said.

"You say that now, but when he's thirty-five and his wife is giving you the evil eye . . ."

"I'll still love it." Turning slightly, Marlea linked her fingers with AJ's and they sat together, listening to the sounds of their home.

"Life is more than a little different with kids, huh?"

"But it's a good different, and I wouldn't trade anything for them. I wish . . ."

"What do you wish, Silk?"

"A baby." Leaning forward, she rested her forehead against his and smiled. "For Rissa and Dench." She sighed. "I wouldn't mind being pregnant again."

His fingers, warm and strong, squeezed hers gently. "Another baby is not a bad idea. You look good pregnant."

"Are you sure?" She tilted her head, and he reached out to touch the strands of hair that slipped free to caress her cheek. "You wouldn't mind me carrying another child?"

"I can't think of a single reason to mind."

"I was hoping you'd say that, but . . ." She slipped her slender hand to his cheek and touched him the way he touched her. "AJ, I don't think you understand. I promised Rissa that I would talk to you. If I carried another baby, it would be . . ."

"What has Rissa got to do with us and a baby?"

"A baby?" Before Marlea could answer, Jabari launched himself into the kitchen. "For us?" Climbing onto the chair next to his father, he looked seriously from one parent to the other. "If we have a baby, could it just not be another sister, okay? They're icky, nothing but trouble."

Laughing, AJ locked his arms around Marlea and laid his face against hers. "Well, son, sisters can be fun, after you get used to them."

Jabari made a face. "How long does that take? We've had Nia for a long time and look at her!"

"If you think Nia is bad, you should take a look at your Aunt Rissa, and she's been around a whole lot longer."

"That's mean." Marlea stood, leaning down to kiss both of them. "Sisters are special, and you should both be glad to have them. Daddy loves Aunt Rissa a lot because she's his sister and he will always love her, just like you're going to love Nia for the rest of your life."

"That's a long, long, long time." Jabari frowned and raised his eyebrows. "Nia is a girl. Girls are . . . you know."

Marlea raised her brows and made the face back at her son. "I know, icky."

Nodding, Jabari repeated the word. "Icky."

"Hear that?" AJ laughed. "He learned that in pre-school."

Marlea traced a finger over her son's face, tenderly touching his brow, his nose, and his lips, making him smile. "Yeah, I can't wait to see what he learns in kindergarten."

"Come on, little boy," Mrs. Baldwin called from the door. "If you want to go to the market with me, let's go."

Climbing down, the little boy ran for the door, then remembered his mother and father. Running back, he planted sloppy kisses on both of them and cupped his fingers at his mother's ear. "Becept you, Mommy," he whispered. "You're not icky."

"I know." When she smiled and winked, he squeezed his eyes closed for her. Opening his eyes, he matched his mother's smile, then turned and ran, clattering down the hall behind the housekeeper.

"Doing that two-eyed wink thing," AJ chuckled.

"That's our firstborn, and it's sweet," Marlea sighed, pushing her fingers back into AJ's hand and holding them there. "That's what I want for Rissa and Dench. I want us to help them."

Reaching, AJ pulled her back into his lap and buried his face against her neck, inhaling her scent and absorbing the heat of her.

"I'm serious, AJ. I really want to help."

"Yeah," he murmured against the beat of her pulse. *But how?*

"AJ, I suggested using a surrogate mother to carry a baby for Rissa and Dench."

He felt her draw breath and hold it tight. *Where is this going?*

"You think that's a good idea?"

Still tense, Marlea released the breath and drew another. "For them, yes. Rissa wants a baby. She wants a child that shares her blood and Dench's, and she can't carry it. She needs an alternative, AJ, and she's even trying to work through it in therapy."

AJ felt the quick and dirty thrill of anticipated dread run beneath his skin and tried to dismiss it. He held Marlea tighter. "Still can't believe she went back."

"But she did. She went again yesterday, just like she promised that she would, and over time, the therapy will help. Now, at least, she's thinking about a surrogate, if she and Dench don't . . . can't . . ."

AJ's dread gave up on subtlety and stomped through his soul wearing combat boots. The sudden ache he felt fully qualified as gut wrenching, and only intensified when Marlea stiffened in his arms.

"She wants to try again, but if they can't, then . . . I . . ."

And he understood the words she wasn't able to come right out and say. AJ's hand went to her cheek, cupping, holding, pleading. "No, Silk. I don't even want to hear this."

"Surrogates are not easy to find, and there are so many stories of women doing it for the money and taking families through all kinds of hell. Making it easier for them would be the right thing to do," she said softly. "AJ, honey, it's an offer that has to be made."

That voice, that tone, this depth of her—I wanted this part of her, he thought, hating the idea that she would even consider sharing herself like this. *If she was fooling around with some man, at least I would know what I was up against, I could fight back. But not this . . . not even for Rissa and Dench.*

Marlea pushed her brows high and sighed. "Nothing is certain yet. She hasn't even talked to Dench about it, but if it comes to that . . ." Her trusting brown eyes took a chance and found his. "I promised Rissa I would talk to you. It's just giving them a chance, AJ."

Dread, full-blown, slithered into fear. "Is this what you were leading up to last night? Asking me about another baby? Marlea, this is crazy. We've got two small children to raise. Did you ever stop to think of how this might affect them?"

"No, I . . ."

"Don't you think that maybe you should? How do you expect me to explain something like this?"

"Why do you think you would have to do the explaining?" Confusion followed the sweep of anger in her gaze, but resolution was locked in the set of her mouth. "This is not about you, AJ. And it's bigger than just our little family. We would all be in this together, and the kids would be fine."

"How can you say that?"

"Say what?" Marlea swiped at the drops of perspiration she felt lining her upper lip. "What do you mean?"

"I mean Rissa and Dench live fairly public lives, and so do we. How is it going to sound when the kids hear it? When my mother hears it? Jabari will be going to kindergarten soon—kids talk, they repeat things. How about when some kid walks up and says something like, 'Your mommy is your cousin's mommy, so is their daddy your uncle? Are your cousins your sister and brother?' Our kids deserve better than that kind of confusion. It's wrong."

Deliberately moving his hands, Marlea freed herself from AJ's embrace and stood looking down at him. "I don't know where this is coming from, AJ, but this craziness you're coming up with is wrong and ridiculous. If I did become Rissa's surrogate, would you try to make me wear a scarlet letter, too?"

"Will it still be wrong and ridiculous when our kids are joining my crazy sister for family therapy? Think we'll get a special group rate?" AJ followed her lead, standing to maximize the height difference. He couldn't stop the fear from morphing into anger. "This is none of our damned business."

"Well, I'm making it our business, and don't you call her crazy." Marlea balled her fists and narrowed her eyes at him. How did this man who inspired such love and passion in her manage to be this infuriating? "Don't you dare call Rissa crazy. She's hurt, vulnerable, and scared, but nowhere near crazy, and you know it. Maybe you could dredge up a little empathy if you had been the one carrying the child she lost."

"So now it takes a uterus to have common sense?" AJ threw his hands up and huffed. "Tell you one thing, wife of mine, if I had a uterus, I would keep it to myself. I wouldn't be out there trying to share it."

"Maybe that's why you didn't get one," Marlea muttered. Turning to the table, she refolded the newspaper and began to clear the dishes—anything to end the torture of talking to her husband.

"Look," he said, swallowing his anger. "Look, let's just be reasonable."

"Now you're going to dictate reason?" Marlea's eyes cut him into thin slices. "Whatever."

AJ tried again. "Even if her eggs are viable and could be implanted in you, how could you carry a baby in your body for nine months and then give it away, just set it free, like a puppy or something, even for Rissa and Dench? Marlea, this is not a good idea, and I don't want you to do it."

Her fingers fumbled her daughter's pink sippy cup, splashing juice on the table. "Or what? Are you going to try to forbid me?"

"Do I have to?"

"Selfish," Marlea whispered. "This is not even a real question yet. I only brought it up because I promised I would, and that's the most selfish thing I've ever heard of from you or any other human being."

Turning from her, AJ threw up both hands and started from the room.

"AJ." Her voice was sharp and her head held high when he turned. "You are my husband, and I love you dearly. God knows I love you to a point of utter stupidity and I would probably follow you to the end of the earth for almost anything else, but you are not the boss of me."

Knowing that it was more than his long stride distancing him from her, he almost turned back. Then he heard her say, "When and if the time comes to make a decision, I'm going to be on Rissa's side."

His hand shook when he reached for the door, but he opened it anyway, and managed not to slam it on his way out of the house. He stood on the small stone porch of his home, the home he'd made with her, without an idea in the world of what their next step would be. At a loss, he gazed up at the solid blue wall of cloudless summer sky.

Fourth of July coming up. Peachtree Road Race . . . She didn't accept an apology then, either. Thinking back to his first meeting with Marlea, AJ almost smiled.

She was stubborn then, and she's stubborn now. She has no business getting mixed up in Rissa and Dench's business. If God meant for them to have a baby, well, she'd be pregnant, wouldn't she? He thought of Dench's face the day Rissa lost their baby. *But that's not our business—we've got our own babies, and they're what should matter right now. Besides, Rissa and Dench . . . they could always adopt.*

What kid wouldn't want them for parents?

Stepping down from the porch, AJ bent his long frame to sit on the top step. Reaching out, he plucked at the petals of one of the sunflowers growing nearby and thought of his sister. She'd helped Marlea and the kids plant the flowers.

I don't care. He pushed his sister's face from his thoughts. *I don't want Silk involved. I don't want her hurt.* He fingered the flower petals again. *I don't care what they say about the process, in vitro is supposed to be tricky. It only takes one time for something to go wrong . . . and to spend the rest of her life looking at a child she'd carried but could never claim . . .* His jaw tightened and he felt a small muscle jump from the pressure.

She called me selfish. Silk knows that there's nothing in the world I wouldn't do for her and the kids—how is that selfish? He twisted the petals that came from the sunflower. *It's not that I don't love Rissa, I do. I always have, I always will. And Dench will always be my brother.* For a long minute, he tried to see his wife's point, to try to pinpoint where the fear really lived. *No, it's not worth the chance of anything going wrong, or something happening to Silk. Nothing is worth that.*

Behind him, the door opened, sucking at the air. AJ turned to see Marlea standing framed in the doorway. She'd taken the time to shower and change into running clothes, but he knew her well enough to know that she hadn't changed her mind.

"Hey," she said. She licked her lips and stood with one hand on the door.

"Hey."

"Maybe you should come in, put on some clothes?"

"Or you could come out?" He patted the space on the step beside him.

"And have you do to me what you just did to that sunflower? No, I think I'll keep my distance until you calm down."

She smiled and AJ felt a little better. He moved his bare foot over the broken flower petals and grinned. "I don't know what you're talking about."

"Figures." She crossed her arms and struggled to keep her smile in place. "I don't want to fight anymore, AJ. Can we just set all this aside for a little while?"

"I'm not going to change my mind." He stood and brushed the petals from the step with his foot.

"Neither am I," she said, holding her hand out to him. "But before we fall out over this, can we wait and see if it even matters?"

"I can, if you can." Standing, he took her hand and looked into her eyes. "But I won't change my mind."

"Then I guess it's a darned good thing I love you."

CHAPTER 12

He felt her enter the house, her presence soft on the change of air when she opened the door. The approaching click of her heels on the hardwood floors only added to his anticipation. Holding the razor and his breath, Dench stood before the tempered copper vessel sink in his bathroom and watched the vanity mirror. When she turned the corner, pausing to rest her shoulder on the doorframe, he smiled into the mirror. She was worth the wait.

Standing there in her tailored white shirt and black pencil skirt, matched pearls at her throat and ears, she could have graced the cover of almost any women's magazine—even with that extra button opened. His eyes followed the inviting button and found the shadow of her lacey bra outlining the lush arc of her breasts. Tucked neatly into the skirt's band, the shirt almost dared him to remove it, and he silently promised to take that dare the second he finished shaving.

Eyes still on his in the mirror, Rissa shifted her hips and the magic sent his gaze lower, and his smile widened. The narrow skirt hugged her hips, kissed the sweetly solid mound of her behind before tracing the line of her hips and stopping just above her knees, but it was the stiletto heels that took her outfit to a whole other level for him.

She might not ever work a pole, but if she wanted to . . .
Dench almost had to slap himself to stop the thought.

Still leaning against the door, looking at him with a sassy possession that he had to admit he liked, she moved a hand to her hip and cocked her head, letting her hair fall carelessly over her collar, teasing her cheek.

Damn, Dench thought. *She looks . . . happy.*

The thought surprised him and made him search his memory. Last night, she'd been tired and overworked, a little cranky and not willing to step into the next day. She'd tossed and turned in his arms all night, leaving him sore and his rest broken. Then this morning, she'd run out of the house while he was in the shower, and a trip to the kitchen proved that she'd left without breakfast or a glance at the newspapers. It wasn't like her to schedule anything when she knew that they would be separated for any amount of time, let alone the week he was going to spend up at Flowery Branch with the team.

From her place at the door, Rissa lifted a languid hand to brush back her hair, then let her fingers fall easily against her breast. Dench's hand slowed as he watched her. *Happy looks good on her.* And for the briefest of moments, he couldn't remember why he'd been so very concerned by her unexplained early morning absence.

Wonder what's going on?

Now, seeing her standing here like this, it seemed silly, but that had been his first thought that morning as he stood in the empty kitchen. She hadn't gone off on one those work-obsessed tangents for a while, not since she'd been seeing Chris Gordon. The therapist was good for her and he knew it, even as he made himself calm and reached for trust. Holding onto his faith in Rissa, he'd made coffee and pulled the paper apart. Searching for the sports section, he'd had to shake his head and take a deep breath when he found it.

So that's what's got her so stirred up. And she didn't say a word to me . . .

The photographer had gotten a close-up of Rissa and Marcus Sawyer and the picture really was worth a thousand words. A contrast drawn in steel and clay, she had a fistful of Sawyer's shirt and her face was close to his. Her features were tightly controlled, the lines of her face elegantly etched in light and shadow. In sharp contrast, the young player's face was caught in shades of darkness and remorse, seeming to fold in on itself as he bent closer to hear his agent's words.

Dench eyed the caption above the picture: JUDGED BY THE COMPANY HE KEEPS. Eyes racing across the page, Dench had skimmed the story and found small relief. At least this time the problem wasn't fully caused by Sawyer, but had been aggravated by his poor judgment. It seemed that he'd loaned one of his cars to an old friend for a road trip. Preparing for the trip, the friend had loaded his luggage, and then stocked the vehicle with groceries and a kilo of coke.

Dumb ass.

Wondering why no one had contacted him, Dench read on and understood. Apparently, when the friend was arrested and the vehicle checked, ownership came to light and Sawyer was picked up for questioning. He'd called his agent. *And damn if she didn't go flying in there like Wonder Woman.*

To separate Sawyer from his buddy in his hearing, Rissa had convinced Sawyer to let her introduce his efforts to straighten himself out—that was probably when the intrepid photographer got his shot. She'd dodged a conflict of interest by not telling her husband about the situation and then she'd gone to the player's defense. *But only after she snatched a knot in his ass, as my Aunt Linda used to say.* Dench had to chuckle.

And that's why she flew out of here so early, he'd realized, finishing the article. *She wanted to make sure that knot was tight enough to keep any other mess from getting on Sawyer—or me and the team. Smart.*

"Can I do that for you?" Rissa used her hip to open a space between her husband and the sink, drawing his attention. Slipping close, she blocked the mirror and got shaving cream on her nose when she nuzzled his cheek.

Caught in reverie, Dench had a moment to wonder when she'd moved before he surrendered the razor. "Not too close, okay?"

"Okay." Her intensity was contagious and he dropped to the dark wooden stool in front of the vanity and sat quietly to let her finish working at the back of his head. "Do you know why I enjoy doing this for you?"

"No." He bowed his head to her clever fingers when the razor moved behind his ears.

"Mostly because I never got to touch you like this before we made our agreement, our new start." She paused, her palm warm against his scalp. "I can feel you here," she said. "I can feel you thinking. It's like a pulse, and I never felt that before we did this." She touched her lips to the smooth skin and smiled as she finished. "Are you glad we did it?"

"Decided to get back to being us?" He took the towel from her hands and dabbed at the back of his neck. "Absolutely."

She reached past him to turn the hot water on and his eyes fell on the fullness of her bosom, reminding him of his promise to get rid of the shirt at the earliest opportunity. His finger reached, popping the next two buttons free. When she looked at him, he watched her eyes and flicked open another button.

"I like this shirt," she said.

"I'll buy you another." His fingers closed on the shirt and they both watched the last buttons fly across the bathroom floor when he pulled.

"What the heck." Rissa beat his fingers to the hem of her skirt by less than a second and yanked it high above her hips before she pushed his robe open. Straddling him, she pushed close to find him ready and waiting for her. Anticipating the urge of his hands against the hot skin of her thighs, she caught her breath when his strong fingers traveled higher, breaking the fragile lace that might have kept them from joining.

"I'll buy more," Dench promised against her mouth. Like a woman closed too long from love, she pressed closer, straining to feel him grow, throbbing within her boundaries, and he knew she wasn't listening anymore.

Opening herself to him, Rissa wouldn't have had a clue as to what language she screamed in, if she'd given it any thought. The trails of reddened skin that followed her neat nails across his chest and shoulders would concern her later but for now, for the time that counted, they marked her desperate need to hold him. Clenching tightly, she surrounded him and pulled him deeper, committing him to her heat.

For Dench, the boil began where she sat and would have surged blindly had he not fought for control when she closed around him. Closing his eyes, he took hold of the passion she spilled and gripped her tightly, accepting the wet and the firmly curving reality of her.

Letting her lead, taking the pressure of her body against his, Dench let the world spin as he filled her and pumped heat straight to her brain. Driving deep, the shock of sensation slicing through them, her rhythms paired and danced with his. Quivering, captured by the primal urges of mating, he took her mouth as fully as her body, and still she wanted more as the blood roared through his head, taking him with her.

When the storm that twisted between them smoked to a finish, leaving them sated and panting, Rissa fell against his chest and let her breath come as best it could. Unwilling to break the shared moment, Dench held her, letting her heartbeat slow to find his. Beneath his hands, her cooling skin joined his and he closed his eyes, not wanting to know the difference. Still closed in her intimate embrace, he felt her lashes move against his shoulder. He felt her lips curve and tightened his hands on her when she stirred. Her hands moved higher, skimming his shoulders, locking behind his neck.

When he spoke, his soft voice was husky and warm. "Do you know how much I love you?"

"Tell me."

"I love you more than sand loves the sea."

"Ah, Dench." She let her lips find his. "And I need you more than air."

Contorting slightly, Rissa demonstrated some of the flexibility that Dench admired and pulled her leg across him, leaving her sitting more comfortably in his lap. Leaning against his chest, she toyed with his fingers. "Wouldn't it be nice if we just made a baby . . ." She sighed again and then seemed to realize what she'd said. "I mean . . ."

"It's okay." Dench's thumb traced her shoulder, then toyed with the strap of her lacey bra. "If we can't talk about it, then . . ."

"Then the therapy is useless." She looked at him, then smoothed her hand over his head, her fingers lingering. "Our new beginning would be useless, too."

"Nothing about us is useless, baby. Nothing." Feeling like a man about to push a really big rock out onto precariously thin ice, Dench held her close, resting his cheek against her hair, rubbing a soothing hand along her arm. *I won't let it be.*

"I saw the paper this morning," he finally said.

Rissa nodded. "Another fine mess, but I think it's been contained—for now."

"I'll see him when I get up to Flowery Branch. At least you'll know where he is while he's at camp, and I'll keep his happy ass humping on the field the whole time. He'll be too tired to get into any trouble."

Rissa sighed and nodded. "That'll be good for him. Marcus always seems to find trouble when he has too much free time, but I'm going to miss you. I wish you didn't have to go."

"I'll call you. We'll talk every day."

"Promises, promises. Text messages don't do a lot for a woman left to her own devices."

He frowned and tried to look sad. "You have devices?"

"You know what I mean." She crossed her legs and managed to lean closer, intriguing him. "Can't say I'm looking forward to living on text messages."

"Then I guess I'll just have to work extra hard to keep them interesting, and get back here as soon as I can, won't I?" His fingers turned her wrist enough to see the time on her wristwatch. He didn't need to leave for an hour yet. "Baby, I'll be less than an hour away if you need me, and back next Wednesday."

"Sure." She made a face and stood carefully. "Come on, then. I guess I should at least try to act like a good wife and help you pack." Walking into their bedroom, she held his hand between both of hers.

His traveling bag was open at the foot of their bed and she sat down next to it, watching him. *Damn it,* she thought, smoothing her hands over her ruined skirt. *Sex like we just had ought to produce a whole houseful of babies.*

When I was a kid, I remember my mother warning me that it only took one time to get pregnant. She crossed her arms under her breasts and frowned. *It looks like I only got the one time and blew it.*

"Penny for your thoughts."

"Huh?"

Dench stood in front of her holding his clothes. "I just offered you a penny for your thoughts, but I could pay more if I had to, what with inflation and all."

"You already owe me for a blouse and panties."

"That was money well spent."

She reached out and gave the belt of his robe a tug. "I think you need to go ahead and get in the shower before I find some other clothes for you to destroy."

"I have time—and extra cash."

"Go!" She laughed when he dropped the robe at her feet and strutted into the bathroom. "You think you're funny," she muttered to his naked back, picking up the robe.

The sound of sudden water came from the bathroom when he started the shower and she found herself already missing him. Squeezing his jade green robe in her hands, she brought it to her nose and inhaled. Their combined scent, the musk of passion, touched something in her heart.

Pheromones. They'll do that to you. She inhaled again. *Sex like we just had ought to produce a whole houseful of babies.* The thought caught her off-guard this time and she lowered the robe to her lap.

But when it doesn't . . . Marlea has a point . . . When it doesn't, there are alternatives. Maybe the alternatives aren't that bad . . . eggs, sperm, nine months . . . a perfect baby.

Rising to drop the robe into the laundry basket, Rissa listened to the shower and smiled. He was in there singing an old Stevie Wonder song: "Knocks Me Off My Feet". His voice, a strong and natural tenor, rose above the sound of the water, and he kept repeating the same line, professing love. He sang the song a lot and hummed it even more often, and she never grew tired of hearing it.

As if his love could ever bore me . . .

And suddenly, stubbornly, all of Marlea's arguments all made sense. *With in vitro, the egg would be mine and the sperm would be Dench's, and the baby would be ours. I know I can trust her to carry it for us. Marlea is healthy and has carried two children, and another one for a friend, one for Dench and me to love would be no trial—she said so.*

Stepping from the shower, Dench was still singing the Stevie Wonder song. By the time he wrapped the towel around his waist and walked into the bedroom, he'd toned the song down to a happy hum. He was still humming when he felt Rissa's eyes on him. He stopped and opened his arms to her. "Hoping for an encore? I've got time."

"What you've got is an insatiable libido." She laughed when he frowned. "And I'm not complaining. I'm just sayin' is all."

"As long as that's all." He started to dress.

She watched him pull on jeans and wanted to slow him down.

227

"Something on your mind?"

Her hand flew to her lips. *Did I say something?* She shrugged, started to say no, and changed her mind. "I was just thinking . . . about us." She came back to sit at the foot of their bed. "About how much we really want a baby." He looked up and she hurried on: "People who don't even want children get pregnant at the drop of a hat, but not us. Maybe it really is time to look at alternatives. Maybe we need to think about a surrogate."

She tried to read his face and saw nothing. "With a surrogate, the baby would be ours, truly ours, even if I didn't carry it." Her lashes fluttered and she felt the tears begin to build. "What do you think?"

He pulled the oxford cloth shirt over his long arms and rolled the sleeves. "I don't," he told her. "I don't even see where it's an issue. We've been trying this long, no success, maybe it's just not meant to be."

Not meant to be? Her mouth dropped.

"Maybe we're putting too much pressure on ourselves, making a new start and all. Maybe if we just let things happen in their own time," he shrugged, "it'll just happen like before."

"It took four years for it to 'just happen.' "

His fingers moved over the buttons on his shirt, stopping when her words ended. "Rissa, look, we've been through the testing. We've been through all the pregnancy and loss drama. Hell, I was the one who had to pull you out from under your desk, remember?"

The first tear fell and she hated it for opening the way for all the others that followed.

"Rissa, I'm not trying to talk about your . . . your . . ." Words failed and, reaching out to brush her tears with his fingertips, he floundered.

"Insufficient cervix," she finished for him, brushing his fingers away.

"It's not like anybody is challenging your femininity, is it?" He shrugged and looked at her. "There's so much more to you than having babies. It's not like having a baby has anything to do with keeping us together, right?"

Her chest was too full. The words were squeezed away from her.

"Having a baby doesn't have anything to do with making you who you are, not for me. A baby won't make you a whole woman, right?"

She felt the words wheeze through a crack in her heart. "Would you say the same thing if the doctors determined that the problem was with you and not with me?"

She brushed his fingers away again when he reached for her, and a small muscle jumped when he set his jaw. "Is that what this is about? You're not being perfect? Rissa, I always thought you were perfect for me, and I'm willing to put in the work it takes to keep us together, but I don't want to keep having this same argument about something we can't control."

"Women have babies every day, Dench. Women who aren't me."

"Damn it, I didn't marry you just to have babies. I married you because I love you—you, not your eggs or your cervix. You."

Jamming the last of his clothes into his traveling bag, he zipped it closed. Grabbing it, Dench silently collected his keys and wallet from the dresser and headed for the door. "I'll call," he said, and couldn't even look her in the face when he said the words.

She wasn't sure how long she sat at the foot of their bed, but long afternoon shadows stretched across the room when the telephone rang. In the empty house, the ring was shrill and disturbing when Rissa lunged across the bed to grab it.

"Hello?"

Should have known it wasn't him. I wouldn't call me, either. Closing her eyes, Rissa willed her voice clear and cursed her stupidity for not checking the caller ID first. "Hey, Connie, what's up?"

"Girl, Jeannette found a man! Found him on the internet, but when you're looking, and you've been looking for as long as she has, a man is a man!" Connie cracked herself up and Rissa tried not to scream with frustration. "She's going to meet him tonight and we were thinking that you and Marlea could come along, kind of ride shotgun—you know how we do." She cracked up again. "Okay, so you're in, right? Unless Dench is . . ."

"Away," Rissa said. She dropped the phone to its base, not caring whether Connie heard her or not. "I drove him away. He tried so hard, and I drove him away with my obsession."

The phone rang again and, walking from the room, she ignored it.

The bathroom she shared with her husband looked like a small tornado had passed through it. Collecting damp towels from the vanity, she moved Dench's shaving supplies and ran water in the sink, but her heart wasn't moved by the urge to clean.

Looking up, she caught sight of herself in the mirror. *He's right, you know. Having a baby is not going to make you any more of the woman he keeps telling you that he loves. And you can't very well hate Marlea for offering you what you don't have.* She sighed and almost smiled at her mirror self. *Maybe a shower.* She looked down at her ravaged blouse and wrecked skirt. *Couldn't hurt.*

Sliding the shirt from her shoulder, she let it fall slowly along her arms. *He got out of here before we could finish talking about it.* The shirt joined the towels she'd dropped at her feet. *I can't keep making him crazy like this.* Opening the clasp between her breasts, she released her lacey bra and missed the pressure of his hands.

He doesn't deserve it, and neither do I.

Watching herself, evaluating her image, Rissa unbuttoned her skirt and managed to slide it, with the tattered remains of her panties, down the curving length of her body. Catching her image in the ambient early evening light, she straightened. Letting a hand run across the taut skin of her belly and hip, she sighed.

Marlea said she didn't get any stretch marks with either of her pregnancies, but she did get indigestion. Rissa remembered all those saltine crackers and the gallons of ginger ale Marlea drank during both pregnancies. *Jeannette said she didn't get the stretch marks because she*

*used cocoa butter to keep her skin supple, but she didn't have
a lot to say about the indigestion.*

Twisting, Rissa tried to see behind herself. *I could live
with a few stretch marks and a little gas. If . . .* She closed
her eyes, pushed out her stomach, and imagined.

When she opened her eyes and looked at her mirror
self, she couldn't help the escaping sigh. Her hands
moved over the small mound of smooth skin made lus-
trous in the waning light. Turning, evaluating, she
couldn't temper or control the urge to see and touch her
own potential. *Dench is right, it could happen again.*

*Being pregnant, actually delivering a child, that part
would be my heart's desire.* Relaxing, watching her mirror
self, she let her body flatten. *But if it doesn't happen . . .*
She let her mind flip the thought and found it heavier
than she wanted it to be. *To raise a child with love . . .
that's what I want for us.*

Naked, Rissa moved to the shower and adjusted the
water. *Raising that child with Dench, that's what I really
want. I want toys under the Christmas tree, family vacations
with AJ and Marlea, and a chance to watch Dench teach his
son to throw a football or his daughter to ride a bike,* she
thought. *I want to join the PTA and bake cookies for the
Scouts. Someday, I want to wind up with a cranky, resentful
teenager who can't wait to date and drive.*

How that child gets here is not the issue.

Turning off the water, Rissa grabbed a towel and
walked back to her bedroom, wrapping it around herself.
The phone was exactly where she'd left it and she dialed
quickly.

Coming into his kitchen, AJ heard the phone; he just didn't feel like rushing to answer it. Marlea was out running, or at least that's what her note said. Mrs. Baldwin was in the playroom with the children. He could hear them laughing over the cartoon music. *Probably can't hear the phone over that little video game they like to play.*

Grabbing a handful of grapes from the bowl on the counter, he loosened his tie and tossed his suit jacket over the back of one of the high stools at the granite counter. As good as he looked in the business suit, he was so much more willing to don sweats, and he had every intention of doing so—until he pressed the play button on the answering machine and heard his sister's message.

"Hey, Marlea," Rissa sounded seriously convicted. "I hate to admit that you were right, but I'm swallowing my pride and I guess Dench's, too. Um . . . I want to take you up on your offer. Call me."

What kind of offer? AJ's stomach cramped and he stood staring at the phone. *Aw, my damn. That can't be right.*

"Hey, good lookin'."

Marlea's cool fingertips at the back of his collar made him jump and AJ turned to find her standing close enough to kiss. He jumped again when she popped to her toes and kissed him.

"Hey, Silk."

"Messages?" She leaned to look around him, then hesitated. "Anything special on there?"

"Yeah, the last one, I think." He pressed play, triggering the message and they listened to Rissa's words. AJ

233

looked into his wife's eyes and knew the answer before he asked the question. "Is that what it sounds like?"

She licked her lips and nodded. "I told you that it could come to this."

"But I thought we decided . . ."

She shook her head. "You decided. I chose Rissa's side. I told you I would, AJ, I did."

His head began to throb and he passed a hand over his close-cropped hair. The pain behind his eyes made him step away from her. "Silk, how could you? Why would you?"

"Are you about to yell at me?" She planted a hand on her hip and looked up at him.

"No." Cold-fired anger, wielded like a sword, sliced deep as he turned from her. Long strides carried him down the hall and into their bedroom. Undressing, changing into running clothes, he tried to put her out of his mind and forbid her re-entry. It didn't work, and became impossible when Marlea walked in to stand across from him.

Hair pulled back in her usual sleek ponytail, wearing Adidas shorts and shirt with matching shoes, she jammed her hands against her hips and stood, looking powerful. "Why, AJ? Why are you so determined to be against this?"

"Because it's wrong. Now Rissa's got her hopes up. You had no right to offer to do something this drastic without my agreement."

"What?" Marlea blinked and for a second stood open-mouthed, watching him change clothes.

Recovering, she took a step toward him. "What do you mean, without your agreement? We already had this conversation."

"No, apparently, we had two different conversations." The shoe in his hand flew across the room and bounced off the wall. "Damn it, we're married, and I married all of you—your womb included."

Crossing her arms tightly, Marlea leaned against the wall and refused to flinch. "So now you're the keeper of the family womb?"

"No, that would be you, and you've got jokes." AJ kicked his other shoe under the bed and walked away, leaving her standing with her mouth open again.

CHAPTER 13

Walked away from her and now where the hell are you going? Barefooted, AJ stalked through the house. *Now I look like a fool walking around in shorts and a T-shirt, with no shoes.* Looking down at his hand, he discovered that he was still holding a sock. *One sock?* His wounded pride was still gushing arterial anger when he shoved the sock in his pocket and kept walking. *I'll be damned if I'm going back in there to get the other one.*

Passing through the kitchen, he pulled open a door and headed for the lower level of the house and almost settled in the family room—but that was for families, wasn't it? *And she's damned and determined to change ours forever.*

Why can't she see that we ought to be her priority? Why doesn't she understand that if she's going to go through morning sickness and cravings and labor pains, I'm the one who'll be there with her? Damn it, I'm the one she married, and every time that baby moves, I'll be there. I'm the one who's going to worry about her every time she . . . and if something happens . . . but no, she's already made up her mind.

Fuming, he kept walking until he reached what Marlea liked to call the big kid's playroom. The wide room was actually a game room that AJ had added to the house because it sounded like fun to him. Part of the fun was the pool table, the card tables, and the home theater setup—but that was a lifetime ago. For now, it was a refuge. Crossing the room, he dumped himself into a barrel-backed leather chair at one of the card tables. Throwing one long leg over the arm of the chair, he slouched with an arm draped over his face, determined to breathe and figure out a way around this mess.

Five years it took us to get this far. Five years of trust. I thought she knew that I was with her every step of the way. That ought to be worth something.

With his sister's hopeful message and his stubborn wife's angry eyes echoing in his head, AJ closed his eyes—and got nothing but a headache. Dropping his feet to the floor, he straightened in the chair and debated going for aspirin or ibuprofen.

She keeps it in the bathroom where the kids can't get to it. I go up there, we'll have to talk. I don't want to talk about this anymore. He sighed. *I'll survive, but I can at least rest my eyes for a minute.* Determined, he stood and walked over to the small sofa in front of the windows.

Stretching out, struggling to be comfortable, he twisted and tried to fit his full length onto the cushions of the six-foot sofa. On his back, trying not to hang off the end, he settled for bending his knees and closed his eyes. He felt his breathing deepen just before the sharp tapping sound roused him. Bleary eyed and disoriented, he sat up and looked around the dusky room.

Must have fallen asleep. He yawned and stretched, remembering where he was and how he'd come to be there. *Marlea. Rissa. The phone call.*

The insistent tapping came again. Standing, he walked toward the window and found Dench peering in.

"Why are you out there? Why are you knocking on the window?"

"Dude, how 'bout you let me in and I'll tell you."

"Side door." AJ pointed and Dench nodded. Opening the door, AJ was surprised to find the sun had gone down, leaving the sweet velvet of a steamy July night in its wake. *Must have slept longer than I thought.*

AJ took a good look as Dench passed him. "I thought you were headed up to camp."

"I was, but my heart wasn't in it. I got a few miles down the road and turned around. I was going to try to talk to Rissa again, but I couldn't make myself do it." His shoulders lifted and fell. "I saw a light over here and thought I'd see what you were up to. I parked in the driveway and came around the side—didn't know I'd find you down here in the dark."

"Yeah, guess we could have some light." AJ touched the wall panel, filling the space around them with light. "That better?"

"At least now we can see."

The shirt and jeans Dench wore looked like he'd slept in them, and when AJ looked closer, he saw lines of tension and fatigue wearing into his face. "Well, you look like hell."

"That's a step up from how I feel."

"Must be going around." Leading the way back to the game room, AJ walked over to the small kitchen area. Opening the refrigerator, he pulled out a couple of beers.

"Sit down and talk. How bad can it be—considering that you're talking about my sister, of course." The look on Dench's face made AJ stop and sit. "What is it?"

Dench sat in one of the barrel-backed chairs and twisted the top off his beer. Tilting the bottle, watching the amber liquid move against the cold glass, he had no taste for it and set the full bottle back down on the table between them. "Dude, she's . . . It's the baby stuff, again. She can't let it go, man. And I don't know how to make it any better for her. She's still hurting, dude. She's hurting bad."

"You both are," AJ said. Looking at his friend, he twisted the cap off his beer. Shaking his head, he tapped the beer cap against the table and waited.

"All she wants is a family. Some of that is my fault, I admit that." The rich red tones of his skin seemed to heat and burn brighter as AJ watched. The green and gold flecks of his eyes synched their burn to the intensity buried beneath his words. "You know what 'covet' is, right? Desire, longing, yearning, craving—that's how it was for me growing up and watching you and Rissa with your All American family. I loved my Aunt Linda, but dude, I would have given my right arm to be you."

AJ raised his eyebrows.

"Right," Dench grinned. "I would have given my right arm to be you, right up until I realized how I felt about Rissa, that I loved her, that she was crazy enough to love me back. She's known me long enough to know how much I always wanted what you two grew up taking for granted." The grin died.

"It's what she wanted, too."

"Right. You know, that's why she's still stuck on that 'no more big Christmas trees' pledge of hers. The big trees are for toys, traditions, and family gifts, not for couples on their own. She figures we can come over here and enjoy your tree—and your kids. Unless we have our own—and so far, it ain't happening." Dench lifted his hands, trying to convey more, then dropped them to the tabletop when nothing else came out.

Damn, AJ realized, *my boy is hurtin' big time. Maybe Marlea was on to something.* The headache was back—smaller this time, kind of like a slow-beating snare drum instead of a big bass drum, but definitely back.

Every man who wants a family ought to have one. Raising his eyes to Dench's face, AJ read the loss. *It's not just Rissa that he's missing.* He thought of his own children, bright, healthy, and strong. How they filled his heart, how he almost hurt with love for them, how it felt to hold them, and how much Dench wanted to feel that same boundless, aching love. *He wants this as badly as she does.*

Marlea said I was selfish, and I'm thoroughly pissed with her, but however all this turns out, we'll be okay. I know we will. AJ turned his beer bottle between his fingers when Dench heaved a gigantic sigh and slumped lower in his chair. *I once told Silk that Rissa and Dench didn't have the sense to know that they were in love. He knows now.*

Sitting in silence, each holding his own thoughts, the two men moved the bottles of untouched beer around the table, contemplating the wet rings the bottles left behind.

"So what are you going to do?"

Dench's head came up, the green and gold flecks in his eyes almost lost in the darkness of his troubled gaze. "Guess I'll go home—eventually." He sighed and moved the beer bottle. "Got any suggestions?"

"Yeah." AJ sat up in his chair. "Let's get out of here and go somewhere where a man's thoughts might stand a chance."

"Dude." Dench moved his untasted bottle and almost smiled. "You're in the doghouse with Marlea?"

Half standing, AJ froze. "Why?"

"For one thing, you were hiding out down here in the dark when I showed up. No shoes, shirttail hanging halfway out, and I know you've got food in the house, but you want to go out." Dench snorted, and the smile finally broke through. "It doesn't take a detective to figure it out."

"Whatever."

"That's a girl answer."

"You sound like Jabari. Give me a minute." AJ shook his head as he climbed the stairs, retracing his earlier steps. He was glad not to run into his wife when he walked into the master suite. Changing into jeans, finding shoes and his other sock, he dressed quickly. Collecting his wallet and cellphone, he had a second thought and reached into a drawer for a T-shirt. Dench could use the change.

Walking back into the game room, he tossed the shirt and Dench caught it one-handed. "You trying to tell me something?"

"Yeah." AJ nodded. "You're looking rough, dude. I thought the change might do you good."

Dench looked down at himself, pulled at his shirt to get a better look, and frowned. "Good lookin' out." He pulled his shirt over his head and exchanged it for the fresh one. "Better?"

"Much." AJ patted his pockets. "Keys. I forgot my keys."

"S'okay. My truck's outside. I can drive and drop you off later."

"Good enough." AJ hit the light panel and led the way out of the house.

"You're not going to leave a note?"

"I've got my cell. I'll call if we're out late."

"Yeah." Dench grinned, climbing into the driver's seat. "You're in the doghouse. Don't even want to take the time to leave a note. Dude, you might be *under* the doghouse."

"No, she'll be okay." AJ grinned and clicked the seatbelt into place. "Our last conversation ended with The Loud Sigh."

"You mean The Loud Sigh that means she thinks you're an idiot and she can't remember why she's bothering to argue with you?"

"That's the one."

"You might want to text that message, then." Dench eased the truck down the drive and through the iron gates. "Where are we going?"

"First Down okay with you?"

Dench nodded and turned onto Cascade. Riding in silence, the two men held their own thoughts close, the way only good friends could. Ten minutes later, they walked through the doors of the sports bar.

First Down, sitting directly across from heavily visited Camp Creek Marketplace, was a neighborhood bar with great aspirations. Making the best of its proximity to upscale neighbors, First Down was known for cold beer, thick burgers served with double orders of fries, hot wings, and anything covered in cheese. The walls were covered with sports memorabilia, including autographed photos of AJ in action, a game ball from one of Dench's winning games, and flat-screen high-definition televisions. League and division games were offered nonstop and close-captioned for those needing to watch more than one at a time.

The owners, Jim and Liz Parrish, had laid the Falcons' red and black colors heavily throughout the bar, though a couple of their former investors had insisted on some of the green and gold touches that Liz still lamented. "Makes the place look like Christmas on hard times— damned Packers," she often said.

Tonight, Liz sat at the end of the curving brass-railed bar, surveying her private territory. Her sharp eyes, heavily shielded by the thick fringe of false lashes, were on the trio of long-legged pretty women in short shorts, tight T-shirts, and sandals. Sitting with her tall glass of iced water, the lemon floating on top, her posture was a dare to any of the three. Good-looking, muscular Jim was off limits.

AJ and Dench exchanged quick glances. "Hey, Liz," they said together.

"Hey, boys." She slipped from her chair and offered seductive smiles to both men as she hugged them, pressing her gym-tightened body as close as she could while still pretending innocence.

Maybe Jim was the one who should have been doing guard duty.

"AJ and Dench!" Affable Jim was glad to see all of his customers, but he especially liked this pair. Nice men, all about business, they could talk ball all day—his kind of guys. "So, how's it looking, Coach? Is my money going to be safe with the 'Dirty Birds' this year?"

Shaking hands, Dench grinned. "That would be telling, wouldn't it?"

"I thought we were friends!"

AJ laughed and took the hand Jim offered. "You trying to send your kids to school on Falcon bets?"

Talking from the side of his mouth, Jim looked at his wife as she settled back in her seat. "Can I?"

"You'd better not," Liz called, making them all laugh.

"Let me set you up," Jim offered, reaching for the pair of Coronas Dench and AJ usually ordered. He popped the caps and stabbed lime slices into the bottles. "You want some wings with that?"

"Thanks. Sure," Dench and AJ said, heading for a table.

A tableful of black-and-gold-shirted Alpha Phi Alpha men turned to watch their progress. One thick-bodied brother stood and thumped his chest with a meaty fist. "Yarborough, right? Man, I remember you taking the Heisman, back in the day. We were so proud of you when they inducted you into the Hall of Fame." Moved, he turned to his frat brothers, obviously all over-the-hill former players, and they all lifted their drinks in salute.

A second fortyish man stood, his gold shirt stretched across his abundant belly. Grinning at Dench, he lifted his glass. "And don't forget Traylor. Here's to some big 'D' this year!" He barked loudly and clinked his glass against AJ and Dench's bottles.

"What are you all drinking?"

"We just came to sit a while," AJ said.

"Then your money is no good here," one of the Alphas declared. "Put them on our tab," he shouted to the ever-cooperative Jim.

Thanking the men, they autographed a stack of napkins, laughed when one of the men mentioned 'eBay,' and finally escaped to find a table of their own. Ignoring the pretty women in the short shorts, they sat back and silently watched the end of a televised soccer match.

"Ever wonder if Jabari will want to play pro ball?"

AJ's eyes moved to his friend. "You know I do. Just like I wonder if Nia will run like Silk does." He smiled thoughtfully. "On the other hand, maybe she'll just decide to be a princess and Jabari will be a fireman. You never know."

"You never know," Dench echoed.

Across the bar, determined to garner attention, the three women headed for the pool table and spent a lot of time bent over the table racking up the balls.

"When Rissa came to me with the offer to come to the Atlanta team, I thought it was the perfect thing to support our marriage, but this baby thing seems to be shredding it."

Propping his elbows on the chair, eyes on the television screen, AJ looked focused on the tail end of the soccer match. "She tell you that she talked to Marlea about it?"

Dench toyed with the lime slice. "No, but I figured she did. Probably talked to Jeannette and Connie, and Yvette and Libby, too." He sipped from his bottle. "You know my wife. Her mouth won't hold water."

"But you know Silk is just the opposite. She'll take a secret to her grave."

AJ moved his bottle when the young waitress brought her heavy tray to their table. Smiling, she unloaded wings, fries, and thick sticks of fried mozzarella cheese, along with a bucket of cold Coronas. When she asked if there was anything else needed, both men shook their heads. Dench picked up a celery stick and bit down thoughtfully before he saw the smirk on AJ's face.

"What?"

"Celery sticks?"

Tossing the last bite into his mouth, Dench took a heavily sauced wing and dug deep into the bleu cheese dressing. Tearing into it, he looked at AJ. "Satisfied?"

Taking one of his own, AJ bit into it and savored. "Oh, yeah."

Finishing, AJ set the bones aside and looked hard at Dench. "Did Rissa tell you that she's thinking about using a surrogate?

"Oh, that." Dench licked his fingers and sighed heavily. "We sort of talked about that today."

"That's why you never made it to Flowery Branch."

"Yeah." Dench sucked at his beer. "How did you know? About the surrogate thing, I mean?"

"She wants Silk to be the surrogate."

The double-take would have been funny if the subject had not been so serious. "Where did you get that from?"

"Rissa called today, I guess right after you left. Silk was out and I got the message." AJ watched Dench close his eyes and tighten his lips. "Rissa needs a surrogate mother. She asked, and Silk wants to do it."

Eyes open, Dench looked empty. "And you don't want her to."

"No." AJ said the word like it explained everything. "I don't want her to do it, but she's made up her mind— just completely dropped me out of the equation." AJ's face tightened. "You should have told me, man."

"Told you what? I didn't know she was going to take it there. I didn't know she'd talked to Marlea like that." Dench's hand covered his mouth, the fingers working against the tightly drawn skin of his jaw. "Dude, you know, if you were anyone else, I'd call you a bastard for telling me like this and not backing us up. I don't know if you're a selfish bastard or just a damned lucky one. You have everything I want, everything Rissa and I ever wanted, and you have the nerve to sit here and be mad about it."

"It's not that . . . it's . . ."

"Rissa is your sister, dude."

"Silk is my wife."

"Selfish bastard. If Marlea is willing to try . . ."

". . . and it doesn't work, what next?"

Struggling to breathe, Dench swallowed hard. "I don't know."

"It's not that I don't want this for you . . . for both of you." AJ threw up both hands. "Silk and I have been lucky, blessed, really. I guess I just don't want to press our luck." His hands rose again when words failed. The anger in his friend's face dried up his excuses. "Look, Dench, you're family, you know that. All that's missing between us is blood, and Rissa makes up for that. You know I love you both and that just makes this harder all the way around. I'm way the hell selfish and I know that. I'm as wrong as two left shoes, but . . . damn."

"I didn't put her up to it. You know that, right?"

"I know." AJ dropped his hands and looked hopeless. "I know my sister and my wife."

Across the room, one of the televisions burped static before the Atlanta Braves game flashed across the screen. Dench's fingers worked at his jaw again. "She said she wanted us to try again—insisted on it. She never said . . ."

"Welcome to the Wonderful World of Rissa. Problem is, now she wants my wife to carry your baby. That's the message she left at my house."

"And it left you pissed off."

"Come on, man. Dench, you've got to try to see my side. I marry one woman, make a family with her, and now this. It's not like Rissa asked me for a kidney." Spreading his hands, AJ looked confused. "How does anybody get over wanting something for their whole life, having it within their grasp and then losing it? I can only imagine how you feel and why she did it."

Dench dropped his hand and reached for his beer. He drained the bottle and reached for another. Swallowing fast, he stopped halfway through. "I should have known that there was more to it when she said she wanted to try again. I thought that meant we should . . ."

AJ hunched his shoulders.

"How am I supposed to compete with that?"

"My thought, exactly, but every man has to find his own way."

"That's a nice greeting card sentiment, dude." Finishing the beer, Dench set the empty bottle on the table and pushed it away with two stiff fingers.

"One out of four is not bad. I was wondering if you were ever going to finish a bottle."

"I got thirsty. But that doesn't solve the problem."

AJ winced and sighed. "I thought she was coming around to the idea of adoption."

"For a minute, I thought so, too. Dude, I'm not trying to drag Marlea into anything, but it looks like I thought wrong."

"I know that, besides, you didn't have to drag Silk into anything. She ran into it on her own two feet." AJ's eyes went to the television in front of them and he drew a deep breath. "Look, maybe I shouldn't have . . ."

Dench raised a hand and shook his head heavily from side to side. "No. If the situation was reversed, I would probably feel the same way."

AJ's eyes touched Dench, then bounced back to the game. "Too bad you can't just run off somewhere, get relaxed, and make a baby right quick."

"You know, that could work . . ." Dench looked thoughtful. "Do you think Marlea could kind of slow her roll? Just for a little while?"

"You have an idea?"

"Maybe before all that testing and the implantation process happens, I could sweep Rissa up for a second honeymoon, kind of romantic getaway. Take a chance that we can work this out."

"A second honeymoon is one thing, but a baby-making holiday is something else altogether." AJ snickered.

"Dude, just because you . . ."

"Sorry. I was wrong for that." AJ finished his beer and set the empty bottle next to Dench's. Leaning, he propped his elbows on the table. "Maybe a second honeymoon is not a bad idea—if you can sell her on it."

"Looks like I'm going to have to." Watching AJ open another beer, Dench ran a hand over his bald head. "I'm not trying to shave anything else."

"But what if it doesn't work out? If she doesn't instantly get pregnant, then what?" AJ took a deep swallow from his bottle and shook his head. "Hell of a thing to be sitting here discussing my sister."

"Do it, don't do it. She's your sister, she's my wife . . ." Dench bit into one of the mozzarella sticks. "Careful you don't get chafed trying to straddle that fence, dude. I'm going to take it one step at a time." Thinking, he chewed. "I'll take her back to Negril—back to Tensing

Penn, where we got married. It'll be romantic; she'll eat it up."

"It could work, if a hurricane or something doesn't come along."

"You got anything better?" When AJ shook his head, Dench nodded. "That's what I thought."

AJ broke a chicken wing and pointed a section at Dench. "Man, I've got to give it to you. Rissa always did like heroes."

"Don't cheer yet. I've still got to talk her into it."

"I don't see that as a problem." AJ concentrated on his wing. "I kind of think she likes you."

"Huh. That was before our last conversation. Before I got The Loud Sigh."

"Negril might be your last hope."

"Dude, isn't that what I just said? She loved it at Tensing Penn."

"Except for that night at Rick's." AJ grinned.

"You won't be there this time, we're already married, and I'll promise not to go off the cliff again." Leaning back in his chair, Dench turned to check out the nearest television when the Alphas cheered. The Braves had closed out the final inning of their game with a home run. "Maybe that's a good sign."

"For your sake, I hope so." AJ pushed the wings away and wiped at his fingers with a napkin. "So what's your plan for tonight? Still going up to Flowery Branch, or back home?"

"Flowery Branch, I think." Dench tapped his finger-tips on the tabletop. "Bet I could hit the internet while

I'm up there, make the plans and surprise her with them. She'll like that."

"Then I guess we solved your problem, huh?" AJ checked his watch, then turned to look at the television screen where the Braves' postgame review was showing.

"Guess I'd better get you back home before Marlea starts thinking you've been kidnapped or something."

"Nah, I'll catch a cab. There's usually one in the parking lot." AJ looked at his friend. "You gonna be okay?"

"One way or another." Dench shrugged. "How about you?"

"You know Silk. She's stubborn as they come, but she doesn't hold a grudge."

"Wives. What are we supposed to do with them?"

"Keep on loving them, I guess." Standing, AJ pulled cash from his wallet and waited while Dench did the same. Dropping the bills on the table, he smiled. "With a tip like that, that's going to be a happy little waitress."

"Don't be condescending, dude. You've got a wife and a daughter."

"And a mother, and a sister." He dropped another bill on the table as penance.

The Alphas were still cheering and toasting when AJ and Dench raised their hands for a final farewell. In the parking lot, standing next to Dench's truck, AJ tried to read his friend's face. "You really think she'll go for a second honeymoon?"

"I think I have to at least give it a shot."

"And if she doesn't?"

"Then I'll have to try to convince her that adoption is the way to go, if I'm not enough for her." Dench jiggled his keys and sighed. "Just for the record, I don't think the surrogate thing is right for us, but I'm grateful that Marlea would even consider putting herself through that for Rissa and me."

"Yeah, well, she's special like that." AJ jammed his hands in his pockets and looked up just as a taxi rolled into the parking lot. Raising his arm to hail it, he was surprised to feel the odd warmth in his heart. "She's real special."

He was still thinking about how special his wife was when the cab pulled away from First Down.

AJ stopped the driver at the foot of his driveway. Dench was on his mind when he paid the fare. *Every man has to find his own way,* he thought, adding a tip. *My dad used to say that, and mad as the old man could make me, he was right. Tonight I heard myself say the same thing to Dench. Aww, man . . . please don't let me be turning into my old man.*

He watched the cab turn and drive out of the gated community before turning toward his house. The silence surrounding his home was pleasant and reassuring as he walked the rest of the way to his house.

Letting himself in, he noticed that though the house was quiet, Marlea had not armed the alarm system. She'd also left lights on in several rooms. *She didn't want me to break my neck,* he thought fondly.

Turning the lights out as he walked toward the master suite, he couldn't help hearing Dench's words. *'I don't* know if you're a selfish bastard or just a damned lucky one. You have everything I want, everything Rissa and I ever wanted, and you have the nerve to be mad about it.' For sure, that was the kind of thing that only a friend could get away with saying, and damn it, he was right.

AJ set the alarm system and continued down the hall. Seeing the subtle glow of nightlights coming from his children's rooms, he couldn't resist the urge to look in on them. He used his fingertips to press Jabari's door open and moved silently into the room.

His son, dressed in little blue and white striped pajamas, lay on his back with his arms and legs flung wide. Snoring like a trucker, he had given himself fully over to sleep. Listening to his son's snoring, AJ bent to look into his face and found him smiling. Touching a finger to the child's hand, he smiled when the boy's fingers curled around his. Dropping a light kiss to his son's cheek, he tipped from the room.

Nia's door, directly across the short hallway, was similarly open. Moving like a shadow, AJ entered his daughter's pink and white room. Lying in a swath of moonlight, Nia slept in the exact center of her small bed wearing a tiny white ruffled nightshirt and a glittering tiara.

My baby is a princess, for real.

Reaching, careful not to wake her, AJ lifted the miniature silver crown from her hair. Tenderly, he untangled a few errant stands and smoothed them gently back into place. Her lashes fluttered against her cheek and he froze, not daring to breathe. Suddenly, she sat straight up, looked at him and smiled. Before he could speak, she plopped her head down on her pillow and closed her eyes—sound asleep again. Marveling, he watched her easy breathing and wondered how she did it.

Lucky, he thought. *Next time I see Dench, I'll have to tell him that I am one damned lucky man. This all came so easily that I never fully appreciated it.* Nia sighed and rocked in her sleep. *Dreaming*, AJ guessed.

Charmed by his daughter, AJ was startled to feel Marlea at his side. Looking down at her, he couldn't help being pleased. She wore only the top of his pajamas, with the sleeves rolled to her elbows. *She missed me . . .* When his lips parted, she touched them with a silencing finger.

"I think we'd have to set off a bomb to wake her," he whispered, sliding a long arm around her shoulders. When she leaned against him, he closed the circle of his embrace.

"Did you and Dench have a good time?"

How did she know?

"I saw his truck when you left the house."

Oh. "We watched the Braves and talked." Feeling her warmth, he made himself finish. "Maybe I've taken too much for granted. We have some things to work through, but nothing like Rissa and Dench. You called me selfish, but I was stupid, Silk."

"Promise me that you're not going to make it a habit."

"Promise." Her hair was soft and smelled of something fragrant and clean, distracting him. "If it comes down to Rissa needing your help and you want to do it, I understand and I'll be right there with you."

"And I don't need your permission."

He smiled. She was going to work this for all it was worth—oh, well. "No, you don't."

Her hand flattened against his chest when she lifted her mouth for his kiss, and he let his lips linger. When they parted, she sighed lightly, then smiled when their daughter made the same sound.

Pushing far enough away to look into the face of the man she loved, Marlea's eyes narrowed, appraising him. "It's nice to be loved by someone who's not afraid to be stupid over me. But just don't forget," she rose on her toes to leave a sweet kiss on his lips, "I'm not a democracy, you don't get a vote, and you're not the boss of me."

Convinced she'd made her point, Marlea rested against AJ, taking the comfort he offered.

Nia sighed again and turned in her sleep, looking every bit like her mother, offering a glimpse of the woman she would someday become. Holding the miniature crown and the woman he would love for his lifetime, the little girl's father felt his heart swell with love even as he hoped that just maybe she had not inherited her mother's stubbornness.

CHAPTER 14

Selfish bastard. Love him like a brother, but he's still a selfish son of a bitch . . . and damn it, I wish I could blame him for feeling the way he does, but I can't.

Rolling down the highway, letting I-285 lead him out of Atlanta, Dench eased the windows down in his truck and tried to let the breeze clear out his head, but damn, there was so much in there. *And we both know I didn't lie. He and Marlea have everything Rissa and I want. Everything.*

Truth be told, I never really thought about having kids before I married Rissa. I always liked them, never called them crumb snatchers or rugrats, or anything worse, but I never saw myself as a father—maybe because I didn't have one, didn't quite understand what the father thing was all about. But now, because of her, I want children, at least one. I want the chance to touch eternity in my son or daughter.

He reached, touching the buttons on the in-dash MP3 player and sighed when Nelly's smooth rap, surrounded by Kelly Rowland's sweet voice, filled the cab. He felt his head bob to the rhythm, sucked in a deep drought of the night air and kept his foot pressed down on the gas.

"Dilemma," he remembered, resting his arm on the window frame and starting to relax. That was the name of the song. *It was hot back around the time I was fumbling around trying to make sure that I could really afford to be the right man for Rissa.*

Drifting with the melody, he wondered where the time had gone. "Dilemma" had been playing on just about every radio station in Atlanta when he pulled up in front of Emory University's School of Law that summer day. She was sitting on the white marble steps in front of the main building, with four tall, good-looking guys hanging on her every word—holding court. Wearing a short khaki skirt and sandals, she had her short, wavy hair brushed straight back from her face, and a stack of books rested at her feet. She looked fresh and pretty, and any one of the four men would have picked her up and carried her on his back anywhere she wanted to go.

But she called me. He still felt pride that he was the one she'd turned to when her car was towed. *And that look on her face when I walked up . . . men go to war just to have a woman look at them like that.*

Happily rescued, she'd thrown an arm around his neck and stood on her toes to kiss his cheek. When he'd bent to pick up her books, one of the four men, more aggressive than the others, had the nerve to step into his path.

"Didn't get your name, brother. Are you in school here?"

Stacking the books in one hip-braced arm, Dench had given the man a slow grin. *"Didn't give you my name, brother. And, no, I'm not in school here, but you are right about one thing."*

"What's that?"

"When it comes to her, I'm not your competition. I'm *The One.*"

"The One?"

"For her."

Walking away with his arm draped casually about her shoulders, settling her into the little two-seater he used to drive, he'd been a proud man. She'd toyed with the radio, found "Dilemma" on another station, smiled at him and had sung along as he pulled away from the curb. *Thought law students were supposed to be smart. He should've seen that one coming.* To this very day, he wasn't sure whether Rissa had heard the brief exchange or not, but the song would forever remind him of her.

"Dilemma"—I guess that's a perfect song for us. My baby always brings the drama, whether she means to or not. And AJ is not much better. I still remember when I told him that I was going to marry her . . .

It felt like a lifetime ago, sitting out on the stone terrace that cool November afternoon. Sitting there, kicked back by the firepit, AJ was a man in love and feeling like a million tax-free dollars. *Marrying the right woman and finding out that you're going to be a father will do that to a man.*

Not that I blame him, but how lucky can one man get? Beautiful woman, fantasy wedding, fabulous honeymoon, and he manages to get her pregnant on the honeymoon. I don't think I'll ever forget him sitting there like someone had given him the keys to the kingdom. Dench shook his head and willed the flash of jealousy away.

Deep down, I don't really blame him. If the shoe was on the other foot, I would feel the same way and I would fight to keep what I had, too. He sighed and focused on the road. *Maybe that's what Rissa thought she was doing when she called Marlea.*

And AJ just had to be the one to pick up the message. Dench bit his lip and frowned at the night. *Well, at least now, he knows what Rissa is thinking.*

The song ended and Dench hit replay, humming along with Nelly and Kelly as he slowed to merge onto I-85. Coming out of the turn, he felt a small slow smile cross his lips as he passed a nervous man hunched over the steering wheel of a white Honda.

I can see why he got so worried about Marlea's wanting to do this—AJ's always been so protective of the women in his life. Shoot, I remember that when I told him that I was thinking about marrying Rissa, the first words out of his mouth were, 'Where are you going to live, because man, you are not going to shack up in my guest house with my sister— and my mother will lock her doors on you! Don't play with my sister like that. You love her, you treat her right, and you'd better keep a roof over her head!'

When I told him that I'd already bought the land and was ready to break ground on a new home for her, he was still not satisfied until I showed him the deed to the property and the plans for the house. Then he got mad when I wouldn't tell him how I planned to propose.

Sitting there, trying to look like somebody's daddy . . . 'You know Rissa believes in happily ever after, so you'd better step up the romance.'

And I did, Dench remembered, *that's just what I did.* The light traffic fell easily behind him and Dench's smile broadened. Rissa hadn't been much better than her brother. Romance and fidelity scored big points in her book. *I knew that from the minute I stepped into her lineup. I believe she always knew what I had in mind for us,* he thought, *even though she didn't know the plan exactly.*

I didn't want to do anything like putting the ring in a cupcake, or hiring a singing telegram. So, dinner, I told her, and any other time she would have been wearing one of those slinky dresses, spiked heels, and sexy cologne. But that night, I showed up and she was decked out in T-shirt and jeans—cute, but not what I expected. And there was no way I could say anything about it without giving away the surprise. Never mind that I walked through the door dressed like a lumberjack. I still don't know how I managed to pick the coldest night of the year to propose.

He sighed, remembering how hard he'd worked to come up with the perfect proposal for her. Then there was the setup: *I went all the way to Buckhead to pick up that special meal from Chef Steph at Field Greens Café and then had to hike the food, the flowers, the table, the music, and the lanterns onto the property by coming in the back way . . . It seemed so right though, proposing to her that cold night on the site of our future home. Still seems funny that she trusted me enough to let me blindfold her, drive her around for twenty minutes, and then lead her to that spot, but she did.*

And when he removed the silk scarf he'd used to cover her eyes, she'd gasped and clapped her hands in delight. "We're camping out?"

"Sort of . . ." *Okay, that's not the smartest thing I could have said, but what else was I going to say and still manage not to give away the surprise?*

Turning to him, obviously pleased and laughing, she'd buried her face against his shoulder and held him tightly. *Nice as that hug was, I was determined to say what I planned and all I got to say was her name.*

When Dench held her gloved hands and spoke her name, she'd looked at him with those sparkling nut brown eyes and convinced him that the world was his. Going to one knee, determined to speak the words in his heart, he was stunned to find her kneeling with him.

I must have looked completely crazy, but she said she wanted to be close so that she didn't miss a word. So I just knelt there, holding her hands, looking into those eyes and speaking the words I'd practiced for a year.

And he could still hear her words. *"You don't know what you mean to me. I would cross desert sands for you. I would walk on water for you. I love you more than air, and I will be your wife—forever."*

Dench played Nelly and Kelly again as he steered onto I-985, thinking. He could still see her sitting in the glow of the fire he'd built, staring at the band of diamonds circling her finger. *Even when we walked that property together, stumbling along in the beam of that little flashlight, talking about what rooms would be where, it was the ring that made it all true for her.*

"A perfect circle," she'd said, turning her hand. *"No beginning, no end, just forever."* Firelight had danced in her eyes and gilded her skin. She'd asked for only one other thing. *"Warm."* She'd shivered slightly in his arms. *"Let's get married somewhere warm."* And it had made perfect sense to him. Reliving the moment, Dench felt his heart swell and he drove in silence, enjoying it.

Pulling off I-985, Spout Springs Road came up almost before he realized it. The turns along Thurmon Tanner and Atlanta Highway brought him to the Falcons' complex. Recognizing his truck, Hal Freeman raised a hand and stepped out of the air conditioned cubicle guarding the front gate.

"Hey, Coach, what's up?" Hal tugged the band of his pants over his belly and rocked on his heels. "You're late tonight."

"Yeah." Dench grinned, knowing that the guard would never be NFL prime, but it never hurt to take pride in one's appearance. "Had some business to finish up at home. Everybody else in and accounted for?"

"On board and accounted for, even Sawyer." This coach ran a tight ship and every fan in Flowery Branch appreciated him for it—and Hal was a fan.

"Glad to hear it. Well, I'm going to call it a night."

Hal raised a hand and snapped off a smart salute, grinning when Dench returned it. Stepping back into the air conditioning, Hal closed the door behind him and watched Dench's truck follow the road past the practice fields, heading toward one of the five dormitory-style units that housed the players and coaches. "He's a good guy."

Mike Wilton looked up from his newspaper and nodded. "Coach Traylor? Yeah, he is. He say why he's coming in so late tonight?"

"Guess he wants to get an early start in the morning. Said he had some business to finish up at home." Hal shifted his attention from the window to the refrigerator across the room.

Mike smiled, then laughed.

"What? What's so funny?" Sensitive, Hal straightened from his inspection of the refrigerator's contents. He hitched his pants higher and looked concerned. "What?"

"Ever meet his wife? She's fine, right?" Mike's laughter simmered into appreciation. "Huh, fine as she is, she's the business he had at home."

Hal looked out the window, then back at his coworker. "You think?"

"Yeah, man. A woman looks like that and she's smart, too . . ." Mike licked his lips and smiled wolfishly. "Oh, yeah, she's the business."

Rissa was still on his mind when Dench pulled the MP3 player from the dash—Nelly and Kelly were going inside with him. Shoving the driver's side door open, Dench caught sight of his watch and wondered if Rissa had tried to call him. It was midnight and his cellphone had yet to ring. *I left her just after seven. Maybe she left a message up here.* Stepping out of the truck, he reached back for his cap and traveling bag.

If she didn't . . . I could always call her . . . He hesitated a moment. then slammed the truck door shut and headed into the housing unit. Pushing the lobby door with his foot, he greeted the two linemen who plowed through the opening, nearly running into him. "Hey, dude, save some of that for the field."

Sheepish and definitely caught, the two big men claimed to be observing curfew.

"We're just heading over to the amenities building to break up the pool game," said one.

"Yes, because it's after midnight," the other added piously.

Dench just shook his head and they took it as a reprieve, running out into the night. "Make it quick," Dench yelled after them, shifting the strap of his bag on his shoulder.

"Last thing I need is those dudes hanging out all night watching movies and talkin' smack, and then dragging out on the field in the morning trying to run drills. I need them up and ready to hit that 1-2-1 schedule." He continued to talk to himself as he followed the corridor to his assigned living space.

"Knuckleheads already know that they'll be hitting between ninety minutes and two hours a session, and they're out there running around in the dark talking about playing pool. I'd better not hear any moaning and groaning in the morning."

Sliding the cardkey through the lock on his door, he pushed when he heard the lock click. Inside, his hand brushed the wall switch and the contrast between the relatively Spartan training facility to his home hit him instantly—not that Flowery Branch wasn't a better than average setup. But he missed the tranquil blues and greens, the chocolate browns that colored and filled his home. He missed the sight and sound of Rissa moving through his life.

I've seen worse, he thought, dropping his bag by the desk in the small study. *For that matter, the whole Falcon franchise has seen worse.* He remembered that in the days before Arthur Blank's ownership and the move to Flowery Branch, the Falcons had done their in-season training at Furman University in South Carolina.

Here, he had privacy and it was clean. His bedroom was spacious, the furnishings were good, he had a private bathroom, and the common area was convenient—a far cry from the old college dorms. *Decent*, he thought, kicking off his shoes in the bedroom and sneaking a glance at the bedside phone—no flashing message indicator. Stripping off AJ's shirt, he tossed it across the room and watched it land on a chair. *Couldn't do that at home. Rissa would pitch a royal fit.*

Unbuckling his belt, he had a quick thought. *It'll only take a minute.* The laptop he used for team information was still in the study. *I wonder if I can pull up a website for Tensing Penn?*

It took forty-five minutes to make all the reservations he thought they would need. *Now I just need to make sure about the timing.* It was minutes after one in the morning, too late to make the final calls. *I can check with Yvette and Marlea in the morning—I tell them this is a second honeymoon for Rissa and they'll be on board. If I can get five days with her we can make this work. I know we can.* AJ crossed his mind and Dench trashed the thought. *This time, it's all about Rissa and me.*

Standing, he stretched and tried to think further, but came up dry. *I'm on 'Empty,' time to crash.* In the bedroom, he flipped the spread back across the bed and dumped his body onto the clean white sheets. *These must have a lower . . . what do you call it?* He passed a hand over the sheet and tried to remember what she called it . . . *thread count,* he suddenly remembered, missing the eight-hundred thread count sheets Rissa liked for their bed. *Huh. I like them too. They feel like satin on the skin, so soft, so smooth, and when they touch your bare skin, it's like . . . Damn, I miss her.*

Memories of his wife started to push through, and he let them come. Easy and early thoughts of her would always be cherished, like the first time he'd seen her. She was eleven years old and ridiculously cute in her Girl Scout uniform. *She had those long plaits hanging down her back, and she was as smart as a whip and damned good at selling those cookies.*

Hard not to smile.

Dang, I almost forgot about the time she got me and AJ to jump double-dutch, and I got twisted in the ropes and fell. I broke my wrist and had to sit out most of my freshman year. He smiled. *To make up for it, she baked cookies for me, all by herself.* Five years later, she was a cheerleading hottie and AJ was worried about the string of boys who always seemed more than willing to follow her.

He didn't need to worry, though. She had her share of dates, but never seemed to be interested in much more than fun. It was like Fate or something was always conspiring to keep us together. All that time I spent training, moving up from assistant to full coach. From Cleveland and St. Louis, all the way to Florida, she was always there.

He closed his eyes and tried to remember how long it had been since any other girl or woman had fascinated him the way his wife did—and couldn't. *A billion pretty women on the planet, and not one of them as exciting or interesting as my Rissa.*

Stretched out, his body long and his ankles crossed, Dench laced his fingers behind his head. *She's not the kind of woman any man could ever own, but I'm damned glad she's chosen to make a life with me.* He laughed out loud when he remembered her saying, *"You are the only man in the world that I would willingly cook and clean for. I must really love you."* Those words would always touch him. *And even though she still can't cook worth a tinker's dam, I would kick B. Smith and Patti LaBelle both to the curb for her—any day.*

Staring at the ceiling, he wondered what she was doing, and the words to "Dilemma" ran through his mind again. *There's no point, nothing to gain in my lying here like this, and that damned song is not going to stop running through my head. There's no way I'm going to sleep if I don't at least say something to her. Besides,* he grinned, *I promised AJ that if I married her, I would never leave her hanging.*

Knowing the hour, Dench rolled onto his elbow and reached for his cellphone. His heart lurched when it rang just as his fingers brushed it. Flipping the phone open, the name in the caller ID made him grin.

"Why are you still awake?" Her voice, as sweet and decadently rich as melting Noka chocolate, poured into his ear and scourged his soul.

"I'm horny and I miss my wife. How about you?"

"I don't have a wife, I have no devices, and I'm horny, too. On top of that, the bad news is that my husband walked out on me."

"Foolish man." He heard her breath cross the line and he hardened in response. "I think you should forgive him."

"There's nothing to forgive, because I love him," she said softly. "I only wish he'd kissed me before he left. He didn't, and now I'm left with an old memory on my lips."

"A stale kiss?" Dench couldn't help smiling.

"I didn't tell you which lips," she whispered.

CHAPTER 15

Dench hit the button on the garage door opener and was relieved to see Rissa's car already parked inside. "Good thing traffic was light." Dench checked his watch and climbed out of the truck. He knew they were cutting it close, planning to leave the house by two, but it was the best he could do.

"Got to make that four o'clock flight and my baby is amazing, but being on time is not one of her gifts—I'd better get in there and light a fire under her."

Reaching back, he fumbled for his traveling bag, found the handle and hefted it from the cab of his truck. The shoestrings of his cleats were tied together and he tossed them over his shoulder. He checked his hip pocket and found the computer printouts—itinerary, gate assignments, and reservations. Assured they were in place, he took a deep breath and tried not to do his personal happy dance—pulling this off felt like a major victory, and if he'd been the receiver on the field, he would have done a victory dance and spiked the ball.

"A week alone on a tropical island with the woman I love, and if we're lucky, we'll make a baby." *If we're not . . .* He felt his excitement shiver and refused to let it go. "We're lucky."

And so far, the luck was holding. Last minute reservations for Tensing Penn, the resort setting for their wedding and honeymoon, were secured. And Yvette had come through like a champ. Thrilled to be included in Dench's plans, Yvette made sure that Rissa's calendar was clear and guaranteed her ability to get Rissa out of the office by noon. "And I'll do it, even if I have to set fire to her desk," she'd promised.

Old girl made a pretty good conspirator, he thought, walking past Rissa's BMW. *That's a good thing.*

There would be no missed planes this time around. He grinned, remembering her missed flight and the nearly missed wedding. *But it was my own fault. I knew that running late is more than a character flaw for Rissa. It's a way of life. I should have made her get on the plane with me.*

His grin softened. *She wanted our marriage to be special,* he remembered. *She got all traditional and old-fashioned on me, didn't want me to see her gown, didn't want me to see her until the ceremony. Even made me promise to share one of those thatched huts with AJ the night before, because she wouldn't sleep with me until we exchanged our vows.*

Then she missed the plane and had to call for help. But there's no way we're missing this flight, not today.

Pushing through the kitchen door with cleats over his shoulder and his traveling bag in his hand, Dench wasn't prepared to find her standing in the middle of the kitchen—pretty much naked, unless you counted the silk dress in her hand, the narrow webs of smoky gray lace banding her hips and breasts, and the high-heeled pumps she still wore.

His eyebrows went up and his throat went dry.

"Ink," she said. Holding the turquoise raw silk dress at her breasts, she looked completely amazed to find him standing in the doorway holding cleats and luggage, looking like he was glad to be home. "I got ink on my dress, and they say that milk will remove it."

Walking toward her, he dropped the cleats and his traveling bag. Opening his arms, he looked unsure of where to touch her first. She solved the problem by tossing the dress on the granite counter and stepping into his arms.

The long track of her body seemed to melt, molding her form to his. When she touched him, her fingers were warmer than he'd expected, but her skin was as silky as he needed it to be when she wrapped her arms around him. "I missed you," she whispered.

"If you had promised to dress like this for me, I would have gotten here sooner," he whispered, closing her words with his lips.

Need stirred between them when she tightened her arms around him and allowed her bare leg to insinuate lust. She filled his senses with a smoky sensuality. Edging just beyond surrender, he remembered the tickets and Tensing Penn.

"Baby, we've got a four o'clock flight." *Better not to tell her that the flight was really scheduled for four-forty.* His fingers stroked the curve of her waist. *We'd only figure out a way to use that extra time . . .*

"Everything is already packed," she promised, resting against him.

His fingers found the lace at her hip and he was sorely tempted. Resolving to hold onto strength he wasn't sure he possessed, he moved a step away from her and found the dress she'd tossed to the counter. "Unless you plan on wearing this, you'd better get dressed so that we can make that flight."

She took the dress from his hand and made a face. "Party pooper."

Dench propelled her from the kitchen and into their bedroom. "Are you going to wear that dress or not?"

She faced him with a dare in her eyes, then changed her mind. "Not."

An hour later, Rissa's BMW was parked in Hartsfield-Jackson's long term lot and they were standing at the flight gate. Dench linked his fingers with hers and checked his watch—they were going to make it.

"This is such a perfect thing to do," Rissa whispered, pushing close enough to nudge him with her shoulder as he handed over their boarding passes.

I hope so, Dench thought when she said it again on the plane. Locking his seatbelt in place, he was glad that she liked the idea.

"This is so not the typical 'date with my husband,' " Rissa cooed when the Air Jamaica plane flew low over the northwestern coast of the island, coasting low before bumping the runway at Sangster International airport and cruising to the gate.

"The last time I was here, I was your fiancée. Then I was your new bride," she smiled. Holding his hand, she squeezed Dench's fingers tightly as they deplaned.

"And now you're my wife."

"Lucky me."

"Lucky us."

The handsome sun-bronzed man at the counter in the Immigration Hall passport control station looked up and smiled when the couple reached him. Eyes on Rissa, he considered flirting with the pretty American, even though he saw the rings on her finger. Then he looked at Dench and reconsidered—this one looked like he could read minds. Knowing when to cut his losses, the immigration officer held out his hand for their passports and immigration forms.

"Clearance was quicker than I remember," Rissa whispered, her voice barely loud enough to be heard over the terminal music when she walked away from the counter, hand-in-hand with Dench.

"You came in on a private jet the last time, remember?"

"All too well," she laughed lightly.

Exchanging some of the cash he carried for Jamaican dollars took only a few minutes and Rissa seemed more than content to wait with him. When Dench handed her the wad of bills, she grinned and wiggled her eyebrows at him. "Are you trying to buy my affection? If you are, I'm going to owe you some change, because you could have bought me for a penny."

He jammed a hand into his pocket and pulled out a single penny. Placing it in her palm, he kissed her.

"Sold," she whispered, dropping the money into her tote, "to the man for a penny."

"You honeymoonin'? Of course you are." The easy question and answer came from a full-bodied woman in a floral dress. The island lilt of her voice and bright flash of her white teeth were an invitation to smile, even before she winked at them. "This is a good place for a honeymoon."

Starting from his feet, the woman let her eyes wander, looking hard at Dench. Approval apparent, she held his gaze until he looked away. Still watching, obviously admiring, she pushed a bunch of vividly deep red, yellow, and white hibiscus blooms into Rissa's hands. "For luck," she said. "As if you'll need it with this one." Laughing, their impromptu hostess fluttered her loose flowery skirt and dancing a few steps, bowed. "Enjoy the island and have a lovely honeymoon."

As quickly as she'd appeared, the woman melted into the thick flow of airport traffic. Dench hoped she was a good omen as he and Rissa moved through the Baggage Hall and Customs area.

The car for Tensing Penn waited just outside of the Sangster International Customs Hall and Dench was glad that he and Rissa were the only arrivals for the resort. Closing them into the car's rear seat, their driver made his way around the shining black vehicle. Relaxing, with Rissa's head on his shoulder and her voice in his ear, Dench felt like a rich man living in a world designed only for his pleasure.

Pulling away from the curb, the driver's eyes rose to the rearview mirror and his smile broadened when he saw the kiss Rissa and Dench shared. "I am your driver, Christopher, and we are en route to Tensing Penn Village."

Rolling from the airport and into heavier traffic, Christopher began a practiced and steady monologue, detailing the beauties of the island. "Negril is located across parts of two Jamaican parishes, Westmoreland and Hanover. Westmoreland is the westernmost parish in Jamaica. Located on the south side of the island, you will find downtown Negril and the southern portion of Seven Mile Beach readily accessible. The northernmost resorts on the beach are actually located in Hanover. Both Westmoreland and Hanover are part of the county of Cornwall, and the nearest large town and capital of Westmoreland is Savanna-la-Mar."

Driving easily, Christopher followed a modern and well-maintained road. The car picked up speed and every turn beyond their vehicle provided glimpses of Jamaica's verdant abundance.

"This road we're riding on, it runs all the way across the island between Montego Bay and Negril. While you are here, you must visit our Seven Mile Beach. It has been rated as one of the top ten beaches in the world, so you see, we are justifiably proud of it. This part of Jamaica is called The Cliffs," the driver said, taking a curve and tipping Rissa's shoulder closer to Dench's. "The rock wall here is about twenty feet above sea level and offers a stunning view. There is no pool here," Christopher explained, "but there is access to the water for diving, with ladders to return. It is also excellent for snorkeling here."

Absorbed in each other, the couple in the rear seemed oblivious to the travelogue.

Turning from the main road onto the grounds of Tensing Penn, Christopher seemed proud to offer the arching trellises of bougainvillea, flaming fern-like poinciana, and Jamaican orchids for their welcome. Stepping from the car into the evening's tropical splendor, Rissa exclaimed over the grove of blue mahoe in the distance, and the driver beamed as though he'd planted the trees himself.

"It looks exactly as I remember it. Dench, this is absolute perfection," she breathed. Pulling her sunglasses from her face, she turned in a small circle, taking in her surroundings. Following her from the car, Dench looked from the trees to the sky and made a wish: *Perfection, that's all I want. Perfection.*

Around them, Tensing Penn Village was a unique collection of secluded wood, thatch, and stone cottages, ringing the spacious and private Great House. Surrounded by tropical vegetation as thick and lush as he remembered, he walked with Rissa and the porter through the beautifully manicured grounds.

"Remember when we got married? How beautiful all of this was? Remember when my mother was concerned about the storms? You told her that there wouldn't be any storms."

He couldn't help smiling. "Yeah, and she told me I was a smart-mouthed boy who should be ashamed of himself for daring God just to get what he wanted." Looking at Rissa over the tops of his shades, Dench brought their joined hands to his lips. "I wasn't daring God, I just knew He wouldn't keep me away from the woman He had for me."

"There were no storms." Rissa squeezed his fingers. "And now, you've got me."

"And you know I love you like Jesus loved the church," he whispered.

Walking ahead of them, the porter smiled. Carrying the luggage for this pair was easy work—not too many clothes, he guessed. Tensing Penn saw a lot of lovers, a lot of newlyweds, and even a lot of second and third honeymooners, but these two . . . *Mi ma call dem forever weds*, he thought. These two belonged together and would forever find their way back to each other.

Sitting on a secluded rocky bluff, their thatched hut was a study in elegance, spacious and comfortable as any luxury hotel. When the porter unlocked the door, Rissa took a step forward and stopped. The look of confusion on her face made Dench smile, and he waited for her to either take the clue or move forward for more. Backing up a step, she looked back at the path they'd taken. Finally, still holding Dench's hand, she walked through the door.

Inside their hut, classic Caribbean-style tile floors, stained wooden louvered windows, and cool white plaster walls were accented by tasteful mahogany furnishings, with French doors opening onto a private patio.

"Still beautiful," she sighed. "Still romantic."

Dench smiled as he tipped the porter. The man smiled and winked. Dench handed over another twenty before the porter left, closing the door behind himself.

Touched by nostalgia, Rissa opened closets and doors. When she found the small kitchen, she opened the refrigerator. Fresh fruit and cheese lined a large tray on the center shelf, and several dark bottles of foil-wrapped champagne rested on their sides on the bottom shelf. Opening an inner drawer, she found more tropical fruit, and smiled at the meat and vegetable patties.

"These were a special order, right? I know how much you love those patties." Closing the door, she straightened and looked back at Dench. "You also know that I don't plan to use this little room, don't you? And none of that, 'If you cook, I'll do the dishes stuff,' either. You promised me a romantic getaway and I'm going to hold you to it."

His hands on her shoulders squeezed gently, urging her closer. "There is nothing in there that I want to eat," he said, letting his voice go low and suggestive enough to make her blush. His green and gold-flecked eyes held hers, eroding self control. "Well," his tongue touched her ear and her lashes fluttered low. "Maybe one thing . . ."

"O-kay, that will get you sensuality points." She slipped away from him and moved to the French doors. Opening them, she stepped out onto the stone patio and the view took her breath away. Staring out, she felt herself tremble. "I thought this hut looked familiar. How?" she finally asked. Turning to her husband, her face glowing in the reddened gold and indigo touched light, she asked again: "How did you do it? This is the same one, isn't it?"

When he nodded, she pushed her way off the patio and into the vegetation beyond. Stumbling on the slight loamy rise, she brushed her hands against her jeans and stepped forward. Dench stumbled behind her, but managed to stay on his feet as he followed.

Sliding in her sandals, Rissa counted the dozen steps from the patio and then moved six steps to the left, skirting a large boulder. Counting again, she moved forward and extended her hands. Trying to read with her fingers, she ran her hands over the bark of the first tree she came to. "I found it," she screamed. "I found it!"

Behind her, Dench scooped her into his arms and held her close. "I knew you would."

In the four years they'd been married, the little tree had dug deep roots and weathered raging tropical storms, but right there on the trunk, they could see the heart Dench had carved the morning after they'd exchanged their vows: "R + D = 4 EVR".

"Still here, and so are we." Reaching, she ran her fingers over the rough tree bark. "The tree grew, and so did we."

"So I got it right?"

"Exactly right. Dench, I want forever with you. I always have."

"Me, too." When she folded her hands into his, Dench closed his eyes and wished again: *Perfection, that's all I want. A perfect forever.*

It was fully dark, with the velvety sky painted with stars, when they climbed back onto their patio. Dropping onto a lounging chaise, Dench pulled Rissa with him.

"Wait." She scrambled away from him.

Turning on lights as she went along, Rissa ran into the small kitchen, where she collected the fruit and cheese tray, adding water biscuits and hard dough bread to the wicker basket she found on the counter.

"I think I need help," she called. Rummaging, she found a tin of Jamaican cheese and another of pâté and added them to the basket.

Joining her, Dench found knives, forks, and a large knife for the mammy apple they found resting on the counter. Tucking the large round melon under his arm, he gave the thick light brown skin a solid thump and smiled. "This one is going to be good, sounds heavy and ripe. Too bad we don't get them back in Atlanta—love the taste, that sweet juiciness, like mangoes."

"And speaking of mangoes," she held them up and licked her lips, anticipating their moist, rich taste. Leaning on the refrigerator door, she inclined her head toward the contents. "I see bottles of Red Stripe, Ting, and some ginger beer in here."

"We're celebrating, let's take the champagne." He added the champagne and glasses to the basket.

Back on the patio, she spread the food and handed the bottle of champagne to Dench. He untwisted the wire, aimed the bottle away from them, and popped the cork. Laughing, Rissa held the glasses while he poured.

"Where did the candles come from?"

Taking his glass from her hand, he smiled. "I told you I would always take care of you, and I didn't want you sitting in the dark, so . . ." he swept an encompassing hand in front of her ". . . candlelight for you."

"Did I ever tell you that I love you?"

He leaned close, his fingers stroking the back of her neck. "You might have mentioned it once or twice, but one more time wouldn't hurt."

"I love you."

He kissed her and a tiny shiver rocked the hand holding his champagne when she kissed him back. Scooting closer, Rissa lifted her glass to his lips and took private delight in his mirroring her. Sharing cold champagne on a hot Jamaican night, they sat together and made a picnic, enjoying the food and each other.

"Do you remember that other picnic? When you proposed to me?"

"Never forget." He nodded. "Asking you to marry me was a big deal."

The corners of her lips lifted. "You never had to ask me. You always knew I would. You proposed. You told me what you wanted for us, and I agreed."

"Leave it to a lawyer to break romance down to a contract."

Feeding sliced melon to her husband, Rissa watched him chew. "Did you really think we would make it this far?"

"Always together." He nodded and chewed.

She dabbed a trickle of juice from the corner of his mouth. "Even when you found me under my desk?"

"When you came out, I figured you came out for me." His eyes, darkening with the night, searched hers. "You?"

"I always knew that we deserved to make it." Biting into sweet mango, Rissa sighed. "Delicious." She bit the slice again, then shared it with Dench, laughing when he licked the juice from her fingers.

Suddenly shy, she dropped her eyes. "I've put you through a lot lately, and I know it. I didn't mean to, I just couldn't seem to stop." When she looked up and into his eyes, the green and gold flecks that always charmed her swirled deep and warm. "As much as I love you, I couldn't stop."

"What about now?"

"If we never have children, if we adopt children, I just want us, Dench, perfect and whole forever, because I love you very much."

"I love you, too." He leaned close, brushing his lips across her skin. "That's the nicest apology I've ever heard."

They sat in long silence, sipping champagne. His sudden gasp made her look up to follow his pointing finger. Blue-white flashes of timeless fire, the shooting stars streaked the sky above them. Breathless, Rissa and Dench touched their glasses and closed their eyes. Making wishes, they sat together in hope. Dench recovered first. Opening his eyes, he looked over at her and watched her moving lips.

Baby, Rissa wordlessly entreated the cosmos. Opening her eyes, the word lingered on her lips, so strong that she could almost taste it. She touched her glass to his again and waited for him to sip. "What did you wish for?"

"A winning season." He grinned.

"Really?" Unconvinced, she poked his thigh with her finger. "Thought you said they looked good this year.

Why would you waste a wish on them?" She poked him again.

"Never hurts to have a little heavenly backup." He caught her finger and held it. "I really wished that we would always be as happy as we are right now. You?"

"That we would only get better with time," she said softly. Dropping her eyes, looking at the finger he still held, she lifted her shoulders and let them fall. "I still think that a baby would make us more complete, maybe not better, but would complete our circle."

"We are complete, Rissa—want me to prove it? I could take another knife to that tree."

"The island ecosystem should be scared of you." She giggled and pushed her hand deeper into his. "No, like I said, adoption is fine with me. Besides, I don't want you to get thrown out of paradise for trying to prove your love."

"I would, you know." Dench pulled his hand free to work a damp napkin over their sticky fingers. "In a heartbeat."

"Such a man, and I mean that in a good way." Moving the remains of their meal to the small patio table, Rissa covered them with the cloth napkin they'd used. Climbing into Dench's lap, she pressed her ear to his chest and listened. "I love your heartbeat."

Content, they lay curled together, watching the sky.

Dench felt her fall asleep and let the cadence of her heart lull him. Another star shot across the sky, its freefall touching his imagination as he drifted toward sleep. *Baby.* His hand stroked her arm. *Pregnant*, he wished.

It was the sunrise that woke them. Dench stirred first, smiling when he found Rissa curled against him. He moved his leg and she sighed. Sliding an arm around her, he debated further movement, but hesitated when her lashes fluttered. Her eyes opened to find him and she sighed again.

"Good morning." He kept his voice low and she heard only the tenderness. "Sleep well?"

"I slept with you."

"Out here." He indicated their garden surroundings. "And to think, I promised your mother and your brother that I would keep a roof over your head."

She looked up and smiled. "This little patio has a roof."

Dench looked up. "That it does." He shifted, moving her across his lap, and she giggled. "Anything special you want to do, today?"

"Just be with you. I can do lazy, maybe the beach." She shrugged. "Whatever."

"Dude, the beach sounds good to me."

Rissa slipped from his lap and held out her hand for his. Walking back into the confines of their thatched hut, she squeezed his fingers. "Remember how small the bathroom was?"

He grinned, remembering. "Want to see if we can still fit in the shower together?"

"I'm game." Snatching her shirt over her head, Rissa brushed her hair back from her face and unsnapped her jeans. She waited, looking over her shoulder, for Dench to unhook her bra. Holding her bra in place with both hands, she watched Dench lose his shirt. When he turned toward the bathroom, she cleared her throat and he stopped.

"What?"

"The pants, buddy. Lose the jeans."

"I will, if you will."

"We'll do it together," he said when she walked closer, still holding the bra. "On three . . ."

He counted one and never got to two. She tossed the bra, dragged the pants down his legs and ran for the bathroom. By the time he caught her, Rissa was laughing beneath the massaging spray of water.

"You cheated," he growled near her ear, making her laugh again.

"Aww, don't be a sore loser." Indolent as a cat, she turned her back to him and leaned with her hands against the shower walls. His wet and slippery hands touched her and she gasped. When he braced her, she laughed again. "I thought you wanted the beach."

"We'll be here for a week, and that beach has been there for how many thousands of years?"

"Oh, well, in that case, we have time."

"Lots of time."

The sudden coldness of the water sent them both howling out of the shower. Cold water slapped the heat out of all their intentions and they had no choice but to laugh about it all the way to West End Road and Seven Mile Beach.

West End Road was their destination on most of the days of their retreat. Leading to beach coves, stores, and restaurants, the treasures they found almost made the cold showers bearable.

"Somehow, I forgot about the water doing that, getting cold like that," Rissa said again, "and it's done it every day this week."

"But it's been a good week, right?"

"A really good week. I'm glad we took this time together."

"Me, too. Tell me again why we're walking today?" Dench squinted behind his glasses and pulled his cap lower.

"Because today is our last day here and I just want us to soak up as much of this as we can." Rissa opened her guidebook and traced a line with her finger before stuffing it into her tote bag. "Besides, Rick's Café is close and I want to see what you and AJ thought was so grand."

"You know we only wound up there because he said it was my last night as a bachelor."

"Uh-huh." She pushed her shades firmly over her eyes, gave her short denim skirt a tug and headed down the road. "South is this way."

Mumbling, he followed, making her grin.

"Come on, baby, you said you wanted the fish escovitch, and cold ginger beer sounds good to me. Maybe with rice and peas?"

Dench brightened with the promise of good food and he picked up his pace to walk beside her. "It's been a minute since the last time I saw Rick's."

"Right. I seem to remember standing on top of a cliff hoping you would survive so that I could get married the next day."

"It was AJ's idea," Dench tried.

"Lame."

"Your brother said that it was the last free thing you would ever let me do, if I married you."

"Oh, no, he didn't." Mouth open, Rissa stopped on the side of the road and stared. "Yes, he did. I know my brother. And you believed him?" Dench shrugged and she made a face. "You did."

"Come on, Rissa." He took her hand and waited for her to give in. Walking together, their joined hands swinging between them, he grinned at the memory. "Jumping off that cliff was, like, the freest, coolest thing I've ever done. Hitting that cold water, feeling it move over you after all that air . . . dude, I can't even explain it."

"Really?"

"For sure."

She looked at him, then focused on the road before them. "Would you ever do it again?"

"Definitely."

"With me?" She held her breath when he stopped suddenly and turned to look at her.

"Don't look at me like that. It's not like I haven't been jumping off all kinds of cliffs in the last few months." He pulled off his sunglasses and raised his eyebrows.

"Metaphorically speaking," she amended.

"Forty feet off a cliff, Rissa?"

"With you, Dench." She pulled off her glasses and tried to stare him down. When he dropped his gaze and shook his head, she grinned. "It'll be great," she promised. "You'll see."

"I guess I'll have to, won't I?" He didn't look entirely happy about it.

Crossing the road to Rick's, hearing the music and the crowd, watching people dance their way in and out of the Jamaican landmark, Rissa felt her stomach quiver and decided to keep it to herself. Stepping onto the stone stairs, her first impressions of Rick's Café were of music and endless party. Bright colors, water, wood, stone, and happy people were all around, and their pleasure in the moment was contagious.

An arm draped around her shoulders, Dench guided them through the crowd. Looking around, his smile went a little crooked. "Hard to believe that most of the original place was lost back in the 2003 hurricane season."

"It looks exactly like it did the night you and AJ took your jump." Rissa hoped her voice wasn't shaking because it was taking an act of supreme will to keep her hand steady in Dench's.

Heading for the jump site, checking their bags and stepping out of her skirt, Rissa kept a grin on her face. When she heard a man in the crowd yell, she turned to see him waving and pointing at her. "Do we know him?"

Before Dench could answer, the man jumped to a table top and yelled again. "A girl is taking the jump! The babe in red is going off the cliff!"

"Guess that would be you," Dench grinned, checking out her little red bikini.

"With all the noise he's making, I guess I have to do it now." She plucked at the gold chain circling her waist and made a face. "At least he called me a babe."

Holding her hand, Dench looked down at her. "Rissa, you don't have to do this . . ."

A crowd pushed close, following and urging them toward the jump site, and Rissa heard the questions, the cheers, and the shouts of encouragement. Three men climbed onto a stone wall and hooted their approval, and she tried to ignore them, even as she saw the fear on one woman's face. A stranger's hand touched her bare shoulder and she turned to face envy in the eyes of a deeply tanned blonde who shouted, "You go, girl!"

And at her side, Dench remained solid. "Rissa, you don't have to do this . . ."

"Oh, yes I do. You know good and well that this jump is listed as one of those 'One Thousand Things You Have to Do Before You Die' things, and I'm doing it with you." She stopped walking and looked up at him, determination in her eyes. "I told you, I'm okay about not having a baby now. I can do adoption, but I'm not going to let your memories of the most exciting thing you've ever done not include me."

His hands went to her face and his crooked grin sealed them in a world of their own. "You know I love you like a fat kid loves cake, and there is no eternity for me without you." He kissed her and the crowd behind them roared approval. When she turned and jerked her thumb up, the chanting got louder.

"Let's do this." Climbing to the cliff ledge, Rissa took a deep breath and squeezed Dench's fingers when she looked down at the water. *Oh Lord, that's a long way down . . .* "Together?"

"Together, on . . ." He almost said, 'three,' but shook his head. "Look who I'm about to try to count with. Go!"

Still holding his hand, she went gracefully off the ledge with him. The sound of the crowd was replaced by the hissing rip of unbordered air as they fell. She lost track of her heartbeat and knew only the pledge of his grip on her fingers.

Falling almost forty feet in the sheer whine of air, so far above the ocean, trusting him and their joined hands was everything. Falling into nothing, then timeless thrashing waters, risk was everything. Falling into nothing, with calm sky above and nervous water below with Dench Traylor was the easiest and scariest thing Rissa had ever done.

Hitting the water was like the kiss before heartbreak, hard, shattering, and sudden. Cold moving surf, sudden and incontrovertible, wrenched them apart and stole her breath. The wave that hit her shoved her deep and had her struggling for air. Surfacing, Dench found her easily and pulled her to him, kissing her hungrily. Breathless and gasping, recovering from the jump and his kiss, Rissa pushed hard and slapped water at him.

"You almost killed me!"

"Hey, it was your idea!" Treading against the waves, water glistening in shining beads on his richly sun-darkened shoulders, Dench laughed and Rissa couldn't resist.

"I can't believe we did that!" He looked up, pointing, sighting along the rough climb of sea-carved rock. "Baby, we just jumped off a cliff!"

Leaning, treading, he opened his arms to her and she slapped more water at him, then floated in his embrace. Cool water dripped from her braided hair and she couldn't have cared less as her skin warmed to the water surrounding her. Clinging to him, she ran her tongue across his shoulder, then his neck. In his hands, her swollen breasts were tender, heavy and buoyant in the sea when his fingers moved along her flesh, kneading their lush fullness.

Pressing her lips to his, the sudden urge to mate overwhelmed her and her kiss was desperate for invitation and fulfillment. His lips, soft and hungry as her own, were hers for the taking and she shared his breath as her tongue sought more. Rocked by the ocean, his taste filled her mouth and her mind as she pressed against him with nothing but water between them.

Accepting her closeness, Dench held her, their legs moving against the persistent waves, sweeping the water to keep them afloat. Feeling him growing and lengthening against her, Rissa felt his hands move freely over her skin in the warm water when her hand found the band of his trunks. Breathless, she pushed at the band, freeing him. Desperate for connection, she closed on him with quickening intensity.

Still holding her and trusting the salty ocean not to drown them, Dench's hand slid down, covering her hip, over her thigh and the bottom on her suit. When his fingers dug deep, separating the scant bottom of her bikini from her body and moving it low on her leg. Rissa's legs opened like an automatic gate and she barely registered the quick prayer: *Lord, don't let me lose my bottom.* She felt the bikini hook around her leg and then forgot all about it when Dench's hand moved again. On her own, Rissa led and encouraged him, and he rewarded her efforts fully, finding her, touching her, striking and holding her rhythm.

Somewhere along the shimmering edge of madness and completion, Rissa found enough sanity to grab the tiny red scrap that floated to the water's surface. Mindlessly clutching it, she clung to Dench and took the ride he offered.

Below the ocean's surface, he filled her like liquid light, fast, hard, and blinding. Weightless, no thought touched her as her legs wrapped around his hips, binding them. Eyes locked, bodies pressing together, moving together, lost in each other, aware of nothing but his back, hard and sleek under her hungry fingers, and his skin against hers as he took what was already his, Rissa only knew that she wanted to do this with Dench for a long, long time.

The waves that crashed within and without deafened her and left her weak and clinging. *For always . . .*

"What?" The word was a breathless whisper, so deep in her ear that she wasn't certain it wasn't a thought.

Did I say that out loud? She swallowed hard. "Just promise me that we'll tell our children about this," she whispered, still clinging to him.

Dench's hand slid along her bare hip. "You're going to tell our children?"

"You bet your sweet butt I am." Panting, conscious of the red scrap she still held, Rissa pushed wet hair back from her eyes and began to tread again. "The clean version."

Bobbing closer, Dench straightened his trunks. Always a gentleman, he helped his wife stay afloat as she wrestled with her bikini bottom and pulled the top back in place. "What I want to know is how you're going to make a clean version out of what we just did."

Rissa planted a chaste kiss on his cheek. "I'm going to edit—selectively." Dench's hands went deep, finding her again beneath the water, making her scream. Quick as a fish, Rissa flipped away and began swimming for shore. "You're a bad, bad man."

"But I'm yours," Dench laughed, striking out on his own.

Walking out of the surf together, they climbed the ladder back to Rick's and stood with joined hands raised in triumph at the top. They were greeted by cheers and clapping from people lounging on the deck and a waiter with cold bottles of Red Stripe. Rissa's still cheering admirer tendered an offer for dinner.

"Think they know what we did out there?"

"Shh! What they don't know won't hurt us."

"Well, surely we weren't the first. Or the last."

"But we were the best." Dench's kiss sealed the argument and they accepted the beer but declined the dinner after meeting the cheering man. It was time to get back to real life, and they had a plane to catch.

Leaving Rick's holding hands, Rissa looked up. "I'm glad we did that. It kind of puts things in perspective."

Dench gave their joined hands a little extra swing. "How so?"

"For one thing, I don't care if my hair is all puffy and frizzy, but more than that, whatever happens, it's all good as long as we're together."

"That's what I'm saying."

She stepped in front of him and stopped walking. "Then promise me something, because I don't want to lose what we have and I don't ever want to forget what we did today—not any of it."

He grinned. "I'm not going to forget. I promise you that." She stepped closer to him and he could feel the heat from her skin. "Whatever it is, I promise."

"Let's do it again when we're fifty. Promise."

"You're crazy, you know that, right?"

"But you promise, right?"

"I promise. Whenever you step off a cliff, Rissa, I'll be right there with you."

"You know," her lips pressed his, "I believe you will, and that's good enough for me."

CHAPTER 16

Stepping off the elevator in front of MYT, Unlimited, Marissa Yarborough Traylor took a deep breath and promised herself that she would not skip through the doors and do a happy dance in the lobby of her seventeenth floor offices—that just wouldn't be dignified. Instead, she pushed her shoulders back and lifted her head a little higher.

Her new Ann Klein suit looked good and she was ready to handle business, but she still felt like dancing. Carrying the shopping bag filled with hats, sandals, dolls, T-shirts, a bottle of rum, and bags of Blue Mountain coffee, she struggled to compose herself—there was still just a bit too much island attitude attached to her soul. Knowing that she was headed back to the grind of contract negotiation and high-stakes sports did nothing to dim her outlook.

There is nothing in this world that I can't handle, she promised herself. *After all, I jumped off a cliff in Jamaica.* She had to stop walking and stifle the grin that threatened to consume her when she thought of what that jump had led to in the waters beneath Rick's Café.

We were lucky we didn't drown each other—or get arrested. She had to bite her lips to keep from laughing aloud. *Luck had nothing to do with it—I am just com-*

*pletely, totally, certifiably blessed. How did one man get to
be so romantic? And how did I get lucky enough to find him?*

More than a little giddy, she tried to back some of the
swing out of her step before she pushed through the
doors of MYT, Unlimited.

*Dench told me about Yvette's part in our getaway. No use
in giving her any reason to gloat over her contribution to my
happiness.*

Too late, she spotted Yvette—or more correctly,
Yvette spotted her. Like an information-seeking missile,
Yvette's path changed and she darted across the space
between them, scooping an arm through Rissa's. Pressing
close, she held on, slowing the taller woman's step.

"Second honeymoon." She grinned wickedly. "So?
How was it? Did you have a good time? Did you bring
pictures? You look really tan. Did you hate coming
back?"

Trying to hold onto her purse, briefcase, and the bag
of souvenirs, Rissa stopped walking. "Can I get a minute
to breathe?" She pulled her arm free, pressed a hand to
her breast, and drew an exaggerated breath. "Now, to
answer your questions: fabulous, yes, they're printing,
thank you, and absolutely. Anything else?"

"Did Dench have a good time?" Yvette's slow grin was
sly. "How was he?"

"Romantic, perfect, and better than anything you can
imagine," Rissa said, enjoying the smugness in her own
voice.

"I am so jealous," Yvette sighed, then perked up.
"Can I have him when you get old?"

"No, for two reasons," Rissa snapped. "First of all, I'm not ever going to get old, and second, when I finish with him, he won't be any good for anyone else."

"Well, if you're going to use the man up . . ."

"I'm going to leave a withered husk behind. My plan is to enjoy him while he's young and sexy. That way I won't have to feel deprived later on in life."

"Evil," Yvette muttered, following Rissa back to her office.

"If you only knew . . ." Rissa bit her lip and sighed, earning a curious glance from her partner. "We did do one thing that was completely amazing."

Yvette jammed her hands against the roundness of her hips. "Are you going to tell, or do I have to beg?"

"A little begging might go a long way." Still walking, Rissa handed over gifts and a pound of coffee from her bag.

"Just evil." Yvette smiled at the coffee, shoved the shirt and sandals under her arm and brought her palms together, entreating. "Please tell me what you did."

Rissa grabbed her elbow and pulled her into her office. Closing the door behind them, she pressed her back against it and grinned.

"What?" Yvette's impatience wound through the word.

"We went to Rick's Café. We went off the cliff together."

"Together?" Yvette's mouth dropped and she backed up blinking. "You jumped?" Her breath returned on a small wheeze. "Was it sexy as all get out?"

"Better."

Yvette's mouth dropped again. "And did you . . ."

Rissa nodded.

"In the water . . ."

"Girl, yes!"

"I'm so jealous. I think I hate you." Yvette's hand made little fluttery motions. "And in my next life, I get Dench." She fanned herself and let her imagination go wild.

Satisfied that she didn't have to imagine anything, Rissa carried her bag of gifts to her desk. "Did I miss anything while I was gone?"

"Do you care? I know I wouldn't." Yvette dropped into one of the red chairs in front of Rissa's desk and crossed her legs. "Had a whole week of heaven with a sexy man, lying on the beach and jumping off cliffs, left the rest of us back here laboring like slaves, and now you try to buy me off with some coffee and T-shirts, and want to know if you missed anything. I wouldn't tell you if you had." She drummed her fingers on the chair arm and let her foot pump. "I wouldn't even tell you if one of your clients had a new contract bid . . . with a substantial bonus."

"Yeah, yeah, and his initials are Kadeem Gregg." Rissa simpered when Yvette frowned. "We closed the deal before I left." She stuck out her tongue and made a face.

"No wonder you had such a good time. You could afford it."

"Please. My man has a good job. He didn't need my little commission to make sure that I had a good time."

Unloading her bag, Rissa looked over her shoulder. Her partner really did look like she thought she'd missed out on something good. *But hey, life is hard and we can't all be me.*

"Yeah, that's why you're going to donate your little commission to charity, right?"

Rissa shot her partner a deadly look. "Don't hate."

"It's what I do." Yvette dropped her foot to the floor and sighed. Pulling her skirt lower on her plump thighs, she tried to look disinterested and failed miserably. "So, are you going to tell me more about your trip? You actually look rested and as your partner I feel compelled to ask . . ."

Rissa shook her head. "That's pitiful."

"You know I live vicariously through you." Yvette sighed, blowing through pursed lips. "Off a cliff, huh?"

"You know . . ." The knock at her door stopped her. Pulling the door open, Rissa faced Karee's big smile. "Doesn't the intercom work anymore?"

"Of course it does." Karee smiled brightly.

"So you're at my door because . . ."

"Oh, I just wanted to make sure you were back, and I wondered how your trip was, how you and Dench enjoyed . . .everything."

Yvette feigned innocence when Rissa glared at her. "Why is it so important to everyone to know that my husband is protective, indulgent, and loving? Maybe if you all would get out of my business, I could enjoy him."

"Just so touchy," Yvette muttered, plucking at the T-shirt Rissa had given her.

Taking the reprimand seriously, Karee brushed a hand over her pleated skirt and swayed on her toes. "I just wanted to let you know that Marcus Sawyer is here to see you."

"Thank you, I'll be right there."

Peering at the shopping bag on Rissa's desk, Karee made little effort to conceal her curiosity. "Did you bring back souvenirs?"

"Yes." Rissa grabbed the bag and shoved it into Karee's arms. "There's something in there for everyone. You'll find the stuff for you with your name on it."

Looking like she had something else to say, Karee took the bag and swayed again. Rissa waited. When she said nothing more, Rissa turned to Yvette, who stood and headed for the door with her shirt, sandals, and coffee. Taking Karee's arm, she turned her and stalked majestically down the hall, towing her along.

Best of intentions, Rissa told herself as she walked toward the lobby. *They're nosy because they care.*

Stepping into the lobby, she found Marcus Sawyer sitting in a corner chair. Deep in thought, he sat with his legs wide and his head low, folded hands dropped between his knees. Totally occupied, he didn't see or hear her the first time she called his name.

"Marcus?" She walked closer. "Hi . . ."

"Oh. Rissa." Gripping the arms of the chair, he pushed to his feet and offered his hand. "I know I didn't have an appointment, but if you have a minute?"

There was something about the look in his face that told her that this was a Now Or Never moment for him. "Sure," she said. "Come on back to the office."

He followed her, but looked hesitant when she indicated the red chairs in front of her desk. When she sat, he took a deep breath before following suit. Seated, he immediately dropped his chin to his chest and folded his hands. He tried crossing his legs, then sat with them wide, his feet flat on the floor.

When Rissa parted her lips, he looked up and lifted a hand to stop her. "I came to say I've got to get out. I appreciate everything you've done for me and everything you've tried to do for me, but I can't do this any more."

"Are you asking me to trash your contract?" *Nobody does that!* It was bad enough that he'd spent most of his freshman season dancing on the fine edge of disaster, but who didn't want a second chance? *In his place, I sure as hell would.*

"Rissa, the NFL is a dream, but it's not for everybody." His head swung heavily from side to side. "It's too big, too much for me, and right now I feel like it's swallowing me. You see all the trouble I found just trying to get through the first year? Bad and wild as you used to think I was, I never did any of the stuff I've been into lately.

"I'm not a bad person, really, I'm not." He sniffed hard and shook his head again when she leaned toward him. "Maybe it's a maturity thing. Maybe I'm just not ready." He shrugged. "So I've been thinking about it. I want out—for now. I want to go back to school, maybe finish up a second degree, but I can't survive being pro right now. I mean the money is good, the women are hot, and all the attention is off the chain, but it's all too much. It's too big."

"Have you talked to Dench?"

"Not yet. I wanted to talk to you first." He grinned. "You're tougher."

"I always said you were smart." She grinned back and reached for his hand. "I hate to lose you as a client, Marcus."

He held her hand gently and lifted his shoulders. "Who knows?" He let his shoulders drop as he released her hand. "A year, maybe two years from now, as long as I keep working out, I may come back."

"You know that's rare . . ."

He nodded. "Yeah, but what's for you is for you, and if I do, I'll come back stronger. Oh, and I'm going to keep seeing Chris. Working with her helped me get this far."

Standing, Marcus wiped his hands against his pant legs and smiled. "That's all I came to say, I guess. I'm going to call Coach soon's I leave here."

"He's not going to like it."

Marcus shrugged. "Can't be helped. Like I said, I've got to do what's right for me."

"Okay." Rissa stood and walked him to the door. "I'll draw up the paperwork and we'll finalize everything next week." She shook his hand and opened the door. "Marcus?" When he turned, the quick kiss that brushed his cheek made him suddenly shy. "No matter how all of this turns out, don't be a stranger, okay?"

"Okay." He kissed her cheek and nodded. "It's all good."

And that's the way we want to keep it, Rissa thought.

Turning back to her desk, she had a moment to wonder how things were with James and Sierra Clarence. It had been a while since she'd last spoken with either of them. *The last time we spoke, they asked again about Dench and me standing as the baby's godparents.* The absence of pain surprised her. *I'm getting better at this,* she thought proudly.

Maybe Jamaica really did help . . .

Almost on cue, her phone buzzed. Reaching, touching the button, Rissa heard Karee's voice. "Rissa, the Clarences are in the office to see you, if you can fit them in." Her voice dropped and Rissa could tell that her mouth was close to the speaker. "And thank you, I can't wait to wear it," she whispered. "This bikini is the right size and color and everything, and the little cover-up, omigod, I can't wait to wear it. Thank you!"

The connection broke so quickly that it left Rissa stunned. Oh well, at least she knew that Karee liked her gift. *Now I have to go face Jimmy and Sierra.*

Standing, Rissa was glad that she and Yvette had made personal greetings a part of their corporate policy. Taking her time walking to the lobby gave her a minute to compose herself, but nothing could have prepared her for the sight of James and Sierra Clarence—and the baby carriage.

The Clarences looked every inch like the upwardly mobile little family they were. Sierra and James both wore their tailored True Religion jeans and classic boots with flair. She'd added a flirty little feminine blouse and a blazer to complete her outfit, and Jimmy's trademark flat Ivy cap matched the dark denim of his jacket perfectly. He'd gained a good bit of muscle since the last time she'd seen them, and Rissa had no doubt that if he flexed, she'd be treated to a 'gun show.'

As attractive as they were, the accessory that held Rissa's eye was the stroller between them. Her palms were suddenly sweaty and her mouth strangely dry, and the irony was not lost on her as she crossed the room. "Hey, guys," she said softly, not wanting to frighten the baby— or herself.

The proud young parents stood with their hands on the carriage and smiled. James spoke first. "We thought you might want to meet him in person and since we were out this way, it seemed like a good time for introductions."

Rissa swallowed hard and felt her pulse gallop, but she managed to hold onto her smile. Bending carefully, she lifted the blanket the child's careful mother had placed over the stroller's hood and fell hopelessly in love. Little JJ looked up at her with bright, guileless eyes the color of melting chocolate and sealed himself in her heart when he smiled.

Cherubic, the infant had yet to form the features of his parents, but the healthy beauty of his infantile form was obvious. Touching his hand with her finger, Rissa loved the softness of his skin, and his baby powder scent. Kneeling at his side, she marveled at his flawlessness.

"This is our little JJ," Sierra cooed, kneeling beside Rissa. "Want to hold him?"

Sierra had him out of the carriage before Rissa could speak. Dressed in soft jeans and a cotton sweater that might have been meant for a child's baby doll, JJ's feet did a little stutter kick and he gurgled, the sound calling to Rissa's soul. She opened her arms in self defense and felt love shudder through her when the baby's solid warmth and weight curled close to her breasts. "How is it that he's short and fat, with no hair or teeth, no job and no education, and I'm instantly and totally in love with him?"

"Don't forget, he drools, wets himself, depends on someone else to do everything for him, and he can't talk, either." Sierra laid a hand on Rissa's arm and smiled at her baby. "That's baby power, girl."

"Yes, I guess it is." Rissa touched the tiny hand again and sighed.

"Oh, and look what he can do." Not wanting to be left out, the new father moved the baby's little blue blanket enough to expose a tiny perfectly formed foot. His finger looked large and capable when he stroked the sole of his son's foot. The baby's big toe flexed and the others fanned out while father and son smiled at each other.

"That's called the *Babinski reflex*," Jimmy announced proudly.

Sierra's eyes went to the ceiling and she shook her head. "Every baby does that . . ."

"But they don't all smile like JJ does when they do it." Jimmy was defensive about his young son's physical abilities.

"And he did it very well." Reluctantly handing the baby back to Sierra, Rissa sighed again. "Well, come on back to my office and let's see how can I help you guys today."

Jimmy pushed the carriage as they followed her back to the office asking polite questions about her vacation as they dropped into the red chairs. Neither of them had ever been to Jamaica, and thought maybe it would be a good place to visit after Jimmy's next bout.

"The island is isolated enough that you wouldn't have to worry about reporters, and you have the resort option if you want it, or you could do a small house or a villa near the beach," Rissa explained. "You're not fighting Gervais Tabac until the end of November, so you have some time to plan."

"Maybe your mom might want to come with us." Sierra looked at James.

"Or we could hire somebody to look after the baby while we hang out." He looked at Rissa. "Right?"

She shrugged. "All up to you, but that villa near the beach would be nice, so that you could go back and forth easily with the baby."

"What did you and Dench do?"

"We stayed at a small resort and . . ." Rissa felt her temperature rise when she smiled and had a flashing image of landing in the water beneath Rick's. "We just did the usual tourist stuff."

JJ fussed and the parents sprang into action. Jimmy jiggled the carriage handle while Sierra adjusted the light-weight blanket covering the child. "He's getting sleepy, so we need to get on our way." Sierra turned soft eyes on her husband.

"We just wanted to ask a question," he said. "That was our reason for stopping to see you."

What kind of question couldn't be asked over the phone?

"What can you tell us about adoption?"

She nearly choked. "Adoption?"

"Well, yes, because we figure that JJ needs a play-mate."

"Another little boy," Sierra nodded, encouraging. "We think it would be nice if they were the same age. That way they could grow up together."

The baby fussed again and when Sierra lifted him from the carriage, Rissa felt her arms open of their own accord and was a little surprised when Sierra relinquished him. Settling the child in her lap, loving his dependence and trust, she looked from him to his parents. *What the hell are they thinking?*

"Adoption." Rissa tried to inject finality into her tone and guessed she'd succeeded when Sierra couldn't meet her gaze and looked away. "So far, you're turning out to be pretty good parents, but you've only been at it for a couple of months. You don't know what he needs yet. This little guy is not a puppy or a doll. He's your son, and he needs some one-on-one time with both of you before you go adding another child to the mix."

She looked down and was surprised to find JJ staring up at her, his mouth open and his gaze fixed. Holding him on her lap, loving the warm baby powder and milk smell of him, Rissa smiled at the adorable baby and would have given just about anything to have one just like him. The sudden moist warmth spreading across the lap of her Anne Klein skirt made her lift the baby and look down at the wet spot he left behind.

"Oh, my goodness." Sierra was on her feet and pulling wipes out of her baby bag. Mortified, she grabbed the baby and handed him off to his father, who simply looked confused. "Change him," the mother hissed. "I knew he was fussing an awful lot, and now he's peed in her lap."

"Coulda been worse," James muttered, pulling out a disposable diaper. "You could have spit up, couldn't you, little man?" The baby blinked and obliged his father, to his mother's apologetic chagrin. James tried to smother a grin and went to work on his son's needs.

Rissa took the towel Sierra offered and blotted her skirt. "See? That poor kid is too young to even know how much pressure he's under—adoring parents and grand-mother, being included in the BeaconGreen campaign, and now being potentially elevated to Big Brotherhood by anxious young parents. That's enough to make anyone lose control. I think you need to back off, let time take its own effect, and wait to see if you'll have another baby. Enjoy what you have before you run off looking for more."

And maybe I should take my own wise advice, she thought, feeling the floor slide from beneath her feet. Someone screamed and Rissa would never know who it was—fainting had a way of blurring reality that way.

Lying on the floor, slowly regaining consciousness, Rissa couldn't remember how she got down there, or why all of these people were crowded into her office. Yvette waved something stinky under her nose.

Smelling salts?

"Is she conscious? Breathing?"

Who? Fingers pushed at the base of Rissa's throat. *Not me?*

"Should I call 911 yet?" Karee's face floated in the background.

"Don't move her," Jimmy counseled from his knees.

"Okay, but . . ." Yvette took another swipe with the smelling salts.

Ammonium nitrate. The scientific name for the vile smelling stuff rushed into Rissa's brain. Reaching to brush Yvette away, Rissa blinked and gagged. *Get that stuff away from me!*

"Oh, Lord." Karee sounded like she was begging. "Are we going to have to do CPR on her?"

"She has a pulse. You don't do CPR when people have a pulse," Yvette snapped.

"No, you need to call Dench. Her husband has a right to know if she's conscious or not," Sierra insisted, clutching her son to her breasts.

"Yeah, that sounds good. I would want to know," Jimmy agreed.

Enough is e-damn-nuff, Rissa thought. *And I'm going to swing on Yvette if she sticks that smelly stuff in my face again. They're treating me like I have the vapors or like I'm . . . like . . .* Sitting up, Rissa looked at the faces looming over her. She could smell the baby, noxious vapors from the smelling salts, and the mix of floral and citrusy scents worn by the women in the room. The light coming through her large office window seemed unusually bright.

"Why am I lying in the floor?"

"You fainted." Yvette's hand threatened to swoop in with the horrible smelling salts again. "We think."

Pushing to sit up, Rissa gathered herself. "I don't faint." *Or, at least I don't normally faint. If I was going to faint I would have fainted when we jumped off that cliff. The last time I fainted, I was . . .* Sudden thought snapped her to attention. "I have to go home," she said, ignoring Jimmy's hand and scrambling to her feet.

"Let me get my keys, I'll drive you," Yvette began.

"No, that's okay, thanks, anyway." Rissa brushed off Karee's offered hand and grabbed her purse. Heading for the door, she stopped to trace a single finger along JJ's cheek. When the sweet baby smiled and cooed at her, Rissa took it for an omen—didn't old folks say that babies always knew?

Looking up at Jimmy and Sierra, she shook her head. "You two need to let this little boy be a baby for as long as nature intends. When, if, it's time to have another baby, then there'll be a baby. I've got to go."

Karee watched Rissa and looked worried. "Should she be driving?"

"Probably not." Yvette pushed her lips together and looked at Karee. "Do you want to try to stop her?"

Karee lifted a hand and shook her head. "My mama didn't raise no fool."

"If I'm wrong, I am going to feel like the biggest fool in the Western world." Rissa looked down at her shaking hands as she pulled the BMW into her garage. "But if I'm right . . ." She grabbed her purse and briefcase, carefully ignoring the small white bag sticking from the top of her purse.

Keys in hand, she closed her eyes and started to count, then stopped herself when her stomach fluttered nervously. "Trying to count weeks won't mean anything if I don't know for sure, and if I don't get out of this car, I'll never know." The white bag crinkled when she moved, making her look at it, and she felt a wave of dizziness. "Damn it." She snatched the bag from her purse and looked at it. "I'll never know if I don't check, and for better or worse, the answer is what it is."

Palming her keys, she pushed the car door open and stepped free. Bumping the door closed, she ignored the slight tremor climbing her spine. *I stepped out on thin air and jumped off a cliff in Jamaica. I can do this, too.*

Of course, you didn't jump off that cliff alone . . . She ignored the sweaty slickness of her shaking hand when she turned her key in the kitchen door lock. Stepping into her home, she settled her purse and briefcase on the granite counter and nearly dropped the white bag when she pulled it from her purse. "And I won't be doing this alone, either."

Refusing to be swept away by déjà vu, she grabbed the phone and headed for the small guest bath off her kitchen, punching in the number on the way. Holding the phone between her ear and shoulder, Rissa listened to the rings and opened her bag. *Why is it taking her so long to answer?* "Maybe, just maybe, this time . . ."

"This time, what?"

Rissa's heart jumped at the sudden sound of her sister-in-law's voice. "Marlea, I think I'm late."

"You think? How can you not know? Rissa . . ."

Fumbling with the bag, Rissa dumped six slender boxes into the sink and stared at them. A random thought made her check the expiration dates. *All current—they should work.* "The waistband is tight on everything I own . . ."

"Rissa, you just got back from a vacation, so if that's your only symptom . . ."

"Everything about me feels tender . . ." The sigh carried across the line and Rissa burst into tears. "I just passed out in my office," she sobbed. "That's new."

"Hold on . . ." Marlea was tempted to say more, but dropped the phone and ran instead, grateful again for the love her children shared for Mrs. Baldwin. Running down the street, knowing that she was probably topping her medal-winning 400-meter time, Marlea burst through the Traylors' side door.

"Where are you?"

"In here!"

Following Rissa's voice, Marlea ran to the guest bathroom off the kitchen and snatched the door open to find Rissa sitting on the toilet holding the little plastic wand. Stunned, the two women blinked at each other.

"What are you doing?" they both demanded when they could speak.

"You were crying, I came to see if I could help," Marlea said first. "What are you doing?"

"What does it look like I'm doing?" The corners of Rissa's mouth turned, holding desperation and determination.

"It looks like you're . . . well . . ."

"I'm peeing on a stick, is what I doing." Rissa hitched her skirt a little lower in a futile show of modesty. "And I'm going to sit here and pee 'til I'm pregnant. Get out, give me some privacy!"

"No problem." Marlea stepped back and pushed the door closed. Leaning on the wall at her back, she waited and nearly fell when Rissa flew screaming out of the bathroom. Grabbing Marlea's hands, she danced for joy. "Positive, three times in a row, positive! I'll call Joyce, but this is good enough for me!"

"So maybe you and Dench didn't need Jamaica after all?"

"Hell, no, all I needed was to pee on that stick. Jamaica was a bonus!" Rissa whooped.

Marlea looked down at their joined hands and gasped. "Did you even wash your hands? Ick! What kind of mother are you going to be!"

Dancing back into the bathroom, Rissa turned the water on full blast and laughed. "I'm going to be a fat happy pregnant mother, that's what I'm going to be!"

"When are you going to tell Dench?" Marlea's head came around the corner of the bathroom door. Rissa squirted liquid soap into her palms and looked down at her hands. Suddenly sober, she stood rubbing her hands together beneath the running water.

"You are going to tell him, aren't you?" When Rissa didn't answer, Marlea ran a hand over her sleek hair and nodded. "Look who I'm asking. Of course you're going to tell him. AJ always says that you have a mouth like a sieve, and I know for a fact that you've never kept a secret in your life—especially not from Dench." She crossed her arms and shifted from foot to foot. "When are you going to tell him, Rissa?"

"I guess I'll tell him when he gets in and hope he won't leave me," she finally said.

"Leave you? Girl, don't talk stupid to me." Marlea propped a hand on her hip. "For a smart woman, you sure do get some crazy ideas. What do you mean, leave you?"

Rissa slapped at the wall switch and moved past Marlea, leaving her in darkness. "After all the drama I've put that man through, don't you think he has a right to be tired of me?"

"Humph, maybe in another life. Clearly, you need to make an appointment with Chris Gordon—you have lost your damned mind."

Sliding her hip onto one of the stools at her kitchen counter, Rissa rested her chin on her fist. Marlea stared until she offered her hand. "It's clean."

"You're about as crazy as a . . . a . . . well, I don't know what's as crazy as you are, but Dench is going to be thrilled to know that you're pregnant."

Rissa sniffed and passed a hand across her face. The tears began to roll and Marlea fished tissue from her pocket. Taking the tissue, Rissa twisted it and bawled earnestly into the shreds. "What if I lose this one, too? What if . . ."

"What if what? Why are you crying?" Dench's voice, strong and concerned, made both women turn. Standing with AJ, looking like he would fight dragons for her, Dench closed the door behind them and walked toward his wife. She leaned against him, mopping at her eyes and gulping. He waited. When she calmed, he asked the question again. "What if what?"

Her mouth opened and closed twice before she got the words out. "What if wishing on falling stars worked? What if you really got what you wished for?"

"Then you should be careful what you wish for."

"Remember the falling stars?" Shredded tissue spilled from her palm when Rissa's fingers gripped the cool edge of the counter. "I wished for a baby, Dench. Our baby."

"I thought we agreed on adoption." Confused, he looked into her eyes. "Did you decide on an agency or something?"

Standing behind Marlea, AJ cleared his throat. "Maybe we should go . . ."

"No." Marlea stood firm. "I want to hear this."

"I'm pretty sure that my wish is coming true." Oblivious, locked in a world bordered by his eyes, his smile, and his touch, Rissa couldn't help the grin that spread across her face. "I fainted today," she offered, brightly. "Then I came home and peed on a stick."

"Such a lady," Marlea muttered.

"And that's why she was crying?" AJ's hand went to his ribs when Marlea elbowed him. Then his mouth opened as he realized why.

Dench still didn't get it. "Peed on a stick?"

"The stick was for a pregnancy test. It was positive."

"Well, thank God." Dench collapsed onto the stool next to her. "With you fainting and all, I was thinking . . ." He stopped and looked at her, his next words slow and considered. "Positive? Really? When?"

"The stick said positive, but I don't know." Rissa blinked and shrugged. "Evidently it happened before we went to Jamaica. We'll know more after I see Joyce."

"Jamaica?" Dench's eyes widened and his mouth dropped. "Oh, God, Rissa, are you all right?" His large hand shoved his Falcons cap back, then settled it on his head. Shading his eyes with one hand, he looked at her. "The jump, baby. Are you . . ."

"Fine," she assured him. "I know I said that last time, but really, if anything was going to happen, I think we'd know by now."

"And now you're going to be a daddy." Marlea opened her arms, catching them in her embrace.

"Aw, baby." AJ kissed the top of his sister's head and joined the group hug, wrapping his long arms around them all. "Good luck man, even if you did throw my sister off a cliff."

"Dude, she jumped."

Satisfied to be in the middle of all the love, Rissa's kiss caught the corner of Dench's smile. "Dude, you're going to be a daddy."

CHAPTER 17

It was more than nice to have the morning to herself, and appreciating the sterling silver tea service on her desk, Chris Gordon had every intention of making the most of her leisure. Her tray already held the pot of tea when she added warm cranberry orange muffins on a dainty china plate, and she was still debating the strawberries and crème fraîche when the telephone rang. A little disappointed by the intrusion, she took a deep breath and lifted the receiver.

Her breathless caller barely gave her a chance to speak, so she listened politely. When Rissa Yarborough Traylor paused, the therapist jumped in: "It sounds like you've got quite a lot going on. I have some time this morning. Would you like to come in?"

Rissa was still thanking her for the opportunity when someone knocked on Chris's office door.

Now, who in the world could that be?

"Rissa, could you hold on for just a moment?" Chris set the phone down and crossed the room. Pulling the door open, she blinked and fell back a step. "How did you . . . ?" She looked from Rissa to the phone on her desk and back again. Tilting her head, she blinked. "Why did you . . . ?"

"I was in the parking lot when I called. I thought I should take a chance that you were free." Sheepish, Rissa displayed her cellphone, then folded it into her palm. "May I come in? Please?"

She's wearing that suit like armor, Chris noted, stepping back from the door. The mandarin collar of Rissa's long-sleeved olive green suit was buttoned all the way to the base of her throat, and the sleek pencil skirt grazed her knees, just inches above the highly polished shafts of her tall black boots. *Whatever is going on with her, she doesn't intend to let it do her any damage.*

Rissa took her usual chair, perching on the edge of the seat. She crossed her legs and folded her hands into her lap. *She's ready to run or fight, and she doesn't care which one she has to do to protect herself.*

"Have you eaten?" Chris smiled and tried not to jump ahead as she approached her desk. "How about some tea? I have several herbals, including chamomile, my personal favorite."

"Chamomile is fine."

"And a muffin? They're cranberry orange, and I was just about to indulge myself when you called."

"Yeah, a muffin is fine, but about that call . . ." Rissa worked her phone from hand to hand and looked uncomfortable. "I didn't mean to just . . ."

"Nonsense." Chris flipped a hand and set another cup on her tray. "I'm glad to have the company." Watching as she poured, Chris noticed Rissa's teeth closing on her lip and the nervous pump of her booted foot. Her keen eyes saw the trembling hand that accepted the china cup.

The silvery tinkle of Rissa's spoon moving against the fine china followed Chris across the room to the small refrigerator secreted in what had once been a closet. "Could I tempt you with strawberries from the Farmer's Market? They're beautiful and I have crème fraîche to go with them . . ."

Rissa's head came up. "Crème fraiche? I love crème fraîche."

"So do I." Chris brought the small bowls back to her desk and sat patiently while Rissa served herself. Breaking her muffin, sipping her tea, she waited.

When Rissa finally reached the bottom of her bowl, she licked the back of her spoon and sighed. "That was delicious. Thank you." She set the bowl and spoon on the silver tray, and suddenly remembered her now cool tea. She took the cup and saucer in hand and sat looking at them.

"You don't have to drink that, you know." Chris took another cup and lifted the silver teapot. "I can pour you another . . ."

"No, that's okay, I'm fine." Rissa drank quickly, then set the cup and saucer aside. Looking at Chris, she twisted her lips and sighed, then crossed and recrossed her legs when the odd little tremor in her belly coursed along her inner thighs. "I'm not fine," she finally said. "I'm not bad, but I'm not fine."

Chris raised her eyebrows and folded her hands on the desktop.

"I'm pregnant, and that's good."

"I thought your figure looked fuller." Chris nodded and smiled. "I guessed as much."

Biting her lips, Rissa tucked her shoulder-length hair behind her ears and stared at the floor. "I took a home test a few weeks ago and it was positive. I went in to see my doctor . . ."

"Joyce Ashton."

"Yeah, her. She confirmed the test, did some others and she figures that I am right at sixteen weeks." Rissa's eyes came up for a second and dropped again. "You know Dench and I went to Jamaica in August and now this. I guess more than the weather changed in September, huh?"

"So you were pregnant when you went to Jamaica. What a lovely surprise."

"Surprise. Yeah, you could call it that." Rissa laughed softly and she sat back in her chair, pressing her knees close. "I mean, I've always had irregular periods. That's just normal for me, but I've been totally healthy so I didn't really pay any attention. Then, I'm suddenly fainting and pregnant." Her eyes wandered and Chris sensed the tears that Rissa refused to shed.

"So you turned up here."

"I did." Rissa used the back of her hand to whisk away quick tears. "I came here because I couldn't think of a better place to go. I needed to hear myself say some things out loud and I couldn't let myself put Dench through it." Her eyes flashed upward, gathering and holding Chris in her gaze. "He hasn't called you, has he?"

"No, he hasn't. And this is not something I would ever discuss with him, not without your permission."

"Good," Rissa sighed. "Well, Joyce said that I have an insufficient cervix. Do you know what that is?"

Caught off-guard, Chris plucked at the collar of her pink shirt and looked thoughtful. "Isn't this the condition that caused the loss of your . . ."

"Yeah. Anyway, that's what I have." Rissa sighed again. "She recommended that I see a colleague of hers, and I'm going to do it—this time. I even went back to my office and spent an hour looking her up on the internet. Her name is Alexis Stanton, and she's supposed to be tops in her field."

"This makes you feel not even the least bit better." Chris nodded when Rissa shrugged, then twisted her hips in her chair. "Do you want to tell me why?"

"No." Rissa took a deep breath and shifted again. "No, I don't really want to tell anyone, but it's one of the reasons I came here today. This is the doctor I was referred to . . . the first time. If I had done what I was supposed to, when I was told to . . ."

"There is an old saying that applies perfectly here. 'If IF was a fifth, we would all be drunk.' " Chris pushed her lips together and frowned. "Rissa, that was then, and this is now—a completely different set of circumstances. You've been referred to someone who will help you to give your unborn child a fighting chance and you're acting on that referral. Beyond that, has it occurred to you that this entire process is out of your hands? That as much as you wanted a child, you couldn't will one into existence, and now that you are expecting, you will need to turn yourself and this baby over to the care of another person?"

"And it's not Dench."

"No, it's not Dench, but that doesn't mean that he'll stop loving you or that you two won't have a wonderful life."

"I know that."

"I know you do, it's just that sometimes we all need a little bit of a reminder, just to stay on track."

"Is it reasonable for me to say that I'm scared? I mean, I'm thrilled, but in the back of my mind I just can't help remembering . . ." She uncrossed her legs and sat with her feet flat on the floor. "I can't help it."

"You're entitled to be unsettled by this new development. You don't have to be in charge of everything."

Rissa made a face and sat forward in her chair. "Apparently I am in charge of nothing. Did I tell you all this happened after I made a wish on a falling star in Jamaica?"

"No," Chris laughed. "No, you didn't, but I've heard that mysterious and magical things can happen on the island."

"Oh, for real? Did I tell you that Dench and I jumped off the cliff at Rick's Café?"

Chris's eyes widened and her mouth fell open. "No, you never wrote that on the postcard you sent. What was it like?"

"Life affirming," Rissa grinned, standing.

"That's a very good term, and I think you should remember it the next time you feel afraid." Chris stood and gave her arm a squeeze.

"You're right, I just want to check one more source before I make a real commitment."

"You're pregnant. That's pretty committed, if you ask me."

"You have a point, but just for peace of mind . . ."

"Whatever it takes," Chris agreed.

The words sank into her heart and Rissa could still hear them an hour later as she pulled her BMW into the lot at The City Grille. When she handed her keys to the uniformed parking attendant and stepped from the car, the little quiver that raced through her belly teased her thoughts. *Wonder if I should start telling people that my unborn baby has been trying to communicate with me.* The little rush tapped her adrenaline again. *Guess that's a no.*

Sidestepping single-minded Georgia State University students, she made her way across the street to the City Grille's glass-enclosed brass- and marble-accented foyer. As much as she'd hated plowing through city traffic to get back downtown, it was worth it to have lunch in such elegant surroundings, even though the two Grady Memorial Hospital nurses were on duty and could only get away for an hour.

"At least here the food is worth the trip." Connie flipped her napkin open and dropped it into the lap of her green scrub suit.

Feeling obviously out of place in her scrubs, Jeannette pulled her sweater closer and hid behind the menu. "Everything looks good—especially when you're dieting."

"It's that new man." Connie lifted her eyebrows wickedly and whispered, "Whatever it takes."

"He's not that new."

"He's new enough that you're still trying to find ways to keep his eyes on you."

"Can you make her stop," Jeannette begged, blushing. "She's always teasing me like this, and it's getting old."

"Stop fighting, children." Rissa dropped her elbow to the table and cocked her head. "Let's use our indoor voices and act like adults because it seems to me that since I'm the one paying for this lunch, I should be able to get a word in edgewise."

The nurses pressed their lips together and looked at her. Blinking, Connie raised her eyebrows and waited. Jeannette was not as patient. "What did you want to say?"

"Before I say anything, I want you to promise that what we say here stays here, that you won't say anything to Marlea or AJ, and you cannot tell Dench. Whatever you do, you can't tell Dench."

"Are you running around on Dench?" Jeannette hissed. "After that second honeymoon? How could you?"

"Don't be silly, she's not running around on him." Connie crossed her arms and flopped back in her chair. "It's a baby's mama, isn't it? Who would have thought that Dench would have a baby's mama lurking in the shadows?"

"I'm serious." Rissa's hand slapped the table and made both nurses jump. "Fools, nobody is running around on anybody, and the only baby's mama Dench has is me. Now, just promise me you won't tell."

"Oh." The nurses sat back, appraising. Connie narrowed her eyes and took a deep breath. "You're pregnant again?"

Rissa nodded. "Four months."

"Are you going to ask about the baby's sex?" When Rissa shook her head negatively, Connie huffed. "What about the baby's heart rate? You know if you look at the fetal heart rate, you can predict the gender of your baby. The old saying is that if it's above one hundred forty beats per minute, it's a girl, and below that, it's a boy."

"Don't push. If they don't want to know, that's their business. I'm betting Dench was thrilled." Jeannette handed her menu to the young woman who materialized at their table side. "Seems to me that all the hard work has been done. What's the big secret you want us to keep?"

Rissa focused on her meal order. When the waitress left, she glared at the two nurses. "I thought you were my friends." The tremor was tiny but definite, *and sympathetic?* "What I need from you now is advice, not abuse."

"Aw, honey. Come on, we were just teasing. We're sorry."

"What do you need?" Jeannette pulled her chair closer.

Cautious, Rissa shook her head. "Not until you promise that you won't say anything."

Connie looked at Jeannette, then Rissa. "Us, not say anything? How about you not say anything?"

One look at Rissa's face nearly silenced Jeannette. "Not a word," she promised, and Connie nodded.

"I need to know about a doctor. Her name is Alexis Stanton."

Food arrived, and they waited for service to be completed before Connie spoke. "Isn't she the fertility specialist?"

Rissa nodded, and both women turned when Jeannette cleared her throat. "Don't you remember when Mavis Lawson had all those problems? She went to Dr. Stanton, and now she has two totally rotten spoiled kids. Oh, and didn't Elizabeth Winder see her, too?"

Connie's fork stopped in the air and recognition painted her face. "She did. I remember Alexis Stanton now. She spoke at the National Black Nurses Association conference last year—pretty impressive, too."

"Her articles have appeared in the *American Journal of Obstetrics and Gynecology,* and her practice is devoted to women's general health, pregnancy, labor and childbirth, prenatal testing, and genetics. The procedure she's best known for is cervical cerclage." Jeannette squinted, trying to think. "That's what Elizabeth Winder went to her for."

Rissa held her breath when both nurses looked at her. "Why are you asking us? Didn't your doctor make a recommendation?"

"She did." Rissa pushed her fork through her food and suddenly the orange sauerkraut, gruyère cheese, and roast duck topped with orange ginger dressing that she usually lusted for lost its appeal. She settled for picking at the accompanying rye bread.

"Well, good luck getting an appointment, because she's tops in the field." Jeannette lost interest in her food and poked her fork into Rissa's. One taste of duck, and she switched their plates, abandoning her scallop-topped watercress salad, with its chanterelle mushrooms and creamy Dijon sauce.

"There goes the diet," Connie grinned, turning her attention back to Rissa. Digging into her purse, she produced her cellphone and punched in a number. Eyes on Rissa, giving her best impersonation of discretion, she murmured into the phone, copied a number, and punched it into the phone. She murmured again, nodding all the while, then passed the phone to Rissa. "Talk to her."

Almost afraid to refuse, when the mild tremor rose from her stomach to her breasts, Rissa took the phone. "Hello?"

"Yes, Dr. Stanton here. Are you Mrs. Traylor?"

"Yes. Yes, I am." Rissa's wide eyes locked on Connie. *How did you do this?* she mouthed. Connie blew on her nails and proudly polished them against her scrub blouse.

"Congratulations on your pregnancy. I understand that you have a referral and that you'd like an appointment."

"Yes. Yes, I would." Rissa clutched the phone in both hands and willed herself to something other than the word 'yes.' "I'm wondering what your earliest availability would be."

"It happens that I have a cancellation at four. Will that work for you?"

"Four? Today?"

"Yes, today." The doctor's laugh was musical. "I know they say that you have to wait months for an appointment with me, but little accidents do happen. My four o'clock is still fogged in at Kennedy, leaving the slot available for you—if you want it."

"I do. I'll be there. The Prado, right?" Rissa gripped the phone harder. "If you . . . can you add me to your patient load?"

The bell-like laughter chimed again. "Consider yourself in. I'll see you at four."

"At four," Rissa echoed, folding the phone closed. Connie was diligently studying the dessert menu, but paused long enough to blithely take the phone from Rissa's hand. When the nurses looked at her, Rissa brought her palms together in brief silent prayer. "I have an appointment. How did you do that?"

"It's not always what you know, it's who you know." Connie turned her attention back to the waitress and returned the menu. "I'll have the chocolate lava cake," she breathed reverently.

"And I'll share it with her," Jeannette grinned, wiggling her fork.

"The hell you will—she'll have her own." The waitress smiled and Connie frowned. "I mean it."

Rissa grabbed her bag and stood. "Thanks guys. It's almost three now and I'll have to make it around the perimeter to be there on time. Connie, I can't thank you enough. Thank you from me and Dench—and the baby."

Both nurses looked up.

"No worries," Rissa grinned, pulling out her credit card. "I've got you. I'll run the card on the way out. Enjoy."

Time seemed to blur as she raced through the restaurant, but she took her time descending the marble stairs, and she gripped the polished brass rail every step of the way to street level.

Less than a twenty-minute ride and, this time of day, it can take an hour or more, if traffic is bad. Belting herself into the driver's seat, she tried to think of the fastest route to the doctor's office. *The shortest distance between two points is a straight line. Dang, I could never remember that in high school . . . maybe this baby will be better at math and science than I was.* The random thought pleased her as she backed out of the parking slot. *Don't worry, baby, you will be.*

Aiming the little black and silver BMW north on I-85, Rissa was surprised and pleased to find cooperation on the part of Atlanta's naturally cantankerous drivers. Not a single accident, crime, or "sunshine slowdown" impeded her progress. "I'm going to make it on time," she congratulated herself, ignoring the nervous quiver in her belly. Pulling out her sunglasses, she shook her hair back and covered her eyes. The distracting little quiver touched her again. "Hey, stop that." She kept driving.

Merging onto GA-400, she flipped coins into the toll basket and immediately began to watch the traffic signs. Her belly quivered with a quick wave of warmth. "I told you not to do that. I'm the mother and the driver. I'm also very responsible. I'll get us there in plenty of time—trust me."

Rissa managed the turns onto I-285 and Ashford-Dunwoody without further input from her baby and was relieved to find Dr. Stanton's office. "See, I told you we would make it." She pulled into the parking space and glanced at the time. "And with fifteen minutes to spare." Suddenly, the quiver was back, much lower and deeper this time. Probing and sizzling with the intensity of a low-density pulsar, it left her breathless and sinking into her leather seat.

"Whoa! When did you learn to do that?" Eyes wide behind her shades, Rissa blew out hard and pressed her hand to her instantly sweaty brow. "I thought only your daddy could do that trick."

Recovering, still trying to breathe and regulate her heartbeat, she peered out of her windows, hoping nobody had seen her ride the hormonal whip the baby generated. Satisfied that she was alone, Rissa made fast repair to her makeup in her rearview mirror, and tried to compose herself.

"Now, you're going to have to stop that. We're going in here to see the doctor, and I want you on your best behavior, okay?" Smoothing lipstick across the fullness of her lower lip, Rissa had another thought. "You know what, on second thought, we are going to see a doctor, a really good one. If you have any other new tricks, this would be a good time to trot them out, okay?"

Nothing. "Now you want to be contrary?" When she felt no response, Rissa decided that it was a sign of cooperation. "Better that than an outright rebellion in utero. Let's go."

Slate, chrome, and glass defined the lobby of Dr. Stanton's building, but entering her office transported Rissa to an entirely different place. Subtly relaxing shades of mauve, crème, and sage, augmented by beautiful furnishings and healthy plants, greeted her eye. Soft edged window treatments and curving furniture as well crafted and carefully chosen as that in her own home quieted her nerves.

Simple but eye-catching paintings of women on what looked like the Georgia coast worked to make Rissa smile. Woven baskets and a wall of collectibles gathered her attention, and she longed to touch them. *But my mama raised me better than that.* She kept her hands at her sides and crossed the elegant room-sized carpet to speak to the charming receptionist.

Round-faced with beautifully locked blonde hair twisted high, she looked completely understanding and welcoming. Giving the woman her name was easy, and she waited for the baby to send a signal, but none came. *Trying to make Mommy look crazy?* The receptionist, Lydia, spoke with a sweet island clip as she pointed out the information needed on the medical forms she handed across her desk.

Good thing we're early. Rissa took the forms and found a chair. Sitting, she found the chair every bit as comfortable as it looked. She pulled reading glasses and a pen from her purse and went to work on the pages, finishing as a tall, athletically built woman materialized in front of her. *Big girl is fast. Wonder where she played ball?*

The tall woman smiled, a hint of recognition in her eyes. "I'm Paula Griffin, Dr. Stanton's nurse. If you're ready, I'll show you to the examination room." Her eyes tried to place Rissa's face as she turned away.

Leaving her paperwork with Lydia, Rissa followed Paula. *She's over six feet,* Rissa guessed, walking with the nurse. *We're about the same age, I wonder . . . Paula Griffin . . .*

"I know." Paula stopped suddenly, her voice soft and amused. "You went to Clark College, right?"

"Yes." Feeling disadvantaged, Rissa studied the taller woman's face and sucked at her teeth when the memory clicked into place. One hand on her hip, she pointed, and shook her finger accusingly. "You were Paula Charles, and you were playing for USC when you hip-checked me into the bleachers that time."

"And you were Marissa Yarborough, a known ball thief. It was my job."

"I was bruised for a month."

"And my team took a loss because of you."

They glared at each other for a long second, then burst into a flurry of girlish giggles.

"Hard as you hit me, I'm not surprised that you're a nurse. Somebody has to be able to take care of your victims."

"Fast little thief. Did I see that you're a lawyer now? That is what was on your paperwork, right? Huh, probably because you finally figured out that what you were doing on the court was a crime." Paula laughed, offering her hand.

Rissa accepted the hand and smiled when she shook it. "It's good to see you."

"Yes, you, too." Paula's smile was sweet to the point of tenderness. "I'm an MSRN and you're about to be a mother. Small world."

"You're not kidding." Rissa wrapped her arms around herself. "I figured you for the WNBA."

"I thought the same about you. What happened?"

Rissa shrugged. "I wasn't tall enough, or good enough. Then I fell in love."

"Makes perfect sense to me. I'm still waiting for Mr. Right and refusing to settle for Mr. Right Now, especially after a divorce. Come on, let me get you settled."

When she pushed open the door to the exam room, Rissa was a little disappointed that, while the colors were soothing and the temperature was comfortable, it was set up for a gynecological examination—stirrups and all.

"Here's your gown, and the doctor will be right with you." Stopping at the door's edge, Paula looked back. "I am really glad that I got to see you again. Congratulations on your pregnancy."

"Thank you." Rissa would have said more, but the smooth-voiced woman had already disappeared as the door whispered shut behind her. The room seemed empty in Paula's absence and Rissa stood alone, holding the soft lavender gown she'd been given. *It's a doctor's office,* she reminded herself, unbuttoning her jacket and sliding it off her shoulders. *This is not some medieval torture chamber.*

I'm here for a routine visit—if you could call trying to find a way to hang onto your baby routine. She hooked the hangar holding her suit and shirt on the hook behind the door and slipped out of her tall boots. Feeling vulnerable and debating whether or not she should make a quick call to Dench, she slid her arms into the gown and sat on the edge of the exam table with a hand resting on her stomach. When she felt no tremors, she looked down and waited—nothing.

A little jealous of the baby's apparent ability to sleep through the tense situation, she let her feet swing off the end of the table and tried to think of good questions for the doctor. Her mind went completely blank when she heard the light knock at the door.

"Yes?"

"Are you ready for me, Mrs. Traylor?"

Hardly. "Come in," Rissa called with more poise than she felt.

Dr. Alexis Stanton was a sturdy, square-built woman in her mid-forties, and she wore her wire-framed glasses with the same authority that she accorded her stethoscope. Soft, dark hair, fluffy and natural, curled around her strong, copper-colored face. Carrying enough pounds to pad her medium frame comfortably, the doctor pulled at the lapels of her lab coat and closed the door behind herself. When she moved closer and tapped the corner of Rissa's file against her palm, Rissa noticed that, though she had square, capable hands, her fingers were long and agile.

Surgeon, she recalled. The doctor tipped her head, looked up at her and smiled. Rissa smiled back, liking the bright twinkle of the doctor's eyes behind the glasses. *Maple syrup. Her eyes are the same color as maple syrup.*

"You look a little nervous, but don't worry. About the worst thing we have here would be a speculum," the doctor laughed. "Most of my work involves consultation and support. In your case, I'll be working closely with Joyce Ashton."

"And we have to do this? Even though I just saw Joyce?"

"That's a joke, right?" Washing her hands at the corner sink, the doctor looked over her shoulder. "Mrs. Traylor, if you took your car in for repair, would you want to rely on someone else's description of the work to be done? Or would you expect the mechanic who was actually going to do the work to do an inspection?"

"Good point." She slid down on the table and held her breath, waiting for the baby to protest—again, nothing. The exam was brief and specific and over almost before Rissa realized it. Closing her eyes, she waited for the baby to do something when the doctor spread cool gel on her skin as she prepared for the ultrasound scan, but nothing happened.

I'm keeping my mouth shut, Rissa decided. *You're not even here yet, and you're already confusing me.*

"That will do it." The doctor smiled, retracting her equipment. Happy to dress, Rissa climbed down from the table and met the doctor in her office for further consultation.

This office looks like my sitting room, she thought, easing into a pale blue velvet wing chair. When the doctor poured herbal tea and offered a savory cup, Rissa took it and endured a humbling wash of déjà vu. *Was it only this morning that I was sitting in Chris Gordon's office with a cup of chamomile tea?* "Is this when I get to ask what your verdict is? Or do I have to wait for tests to come back?"

"No, there's no need to wait. I've made measurements and observations, and we can talk right now. In fact, I think we should."

Rissa's stomach lurched, and it had nothing to do with the fetal-generated tremors. *That one was all me—all nerves.*

Stanton took the matching wing chair and angled her body to face Rissa as she sat. She took an easy sip of her tea and paused to appreciate the brew. "You already know that you're facing a diagnosis of an insufficient cervix. In your case, it means that you have approximately a quarter of the space needed to successfully carry your baby to term."

The cup and saucer clattered in Rissa's shaking hand, until the doctor reached to take them from her.

"That's the bad news." The doctor returned to her seat. "The good news is that you're healthy, the fetus is healthy, and there are some options."

"Options?" She hated herself for hoping, but that was why she was here, wasn't it?

"Bed rest, cervical cerclage, or tocolytics."

"Drugs?"

"To prevent premature labor, but in your case," Stanton shook her head, "I believe that would be con-traindicated."

"So I have to stay in bed for five months? How?"

"Don't look so scared. That would not be the full therapy for you. In your case, I believe that cervical cerclage is an appropriate treatment. You're an active woman, with a thriving business." She smiled when Rissa looked surprised. "Joyce told me about your agency, and my husband and I are Falcon season ticket holders—big fans."

"Guess it's a good thing I married well," Rissa joked, not quite managing to laugh. "Seriously, what is cerclage? Who does it? Where do you, I mean, would I have to be hospitalized? And . . ."

Stanton chuckled and set her tea aside. "A cervical cerclage is a minor surgical procedure in which the opening to the uterus, the cervix, is stitched closed in order to prevent miscarriage or premature birth."

"To keep the baby from falling out." Rissa fought to shut down the gag reflex and felt no relief when she won. "So it's real surgery, and it takes place in a hospital? Under anesthesia? Will Joyce do it or would you?"

Stanton looked amused. "I can tell you were a good student. The procedure would be performed in a hospital, and you would be placed under general anesthesia. Unless you'd prefer another practitioner, I would perform the procedure."

"You're good at this, right?"

"At the risk of sounding vain," Stanton smiled, "I'm the best. Look, Rissa—may I call you Rissa?" When Rissa nodded, the doctor stood and faced her. With her hands on her full hips, she looked fearless. "Rissa, I do three to six of these procedures weekly, more than a hundred a year. I promise you, every one of them is different because every woman approaches her pregnancy differently. I know that you wouldn't be here if you didn't believe that I can help you."

"Complications?" The word came out on a whisper.

"Yes, there are risks associated with the procedure, and they can include things like bleeding, premature rupture of the membranes, premature labor, and the general risks associated with local or general anesthesia."

Rissa looked like she was ready to curl up in the chair and cry. Watching the emotions crossing her patient's face, the doctor paused.

Tight-lipped, Rissa straightened in her chair and inhaled deeply. "After the cerclage is in place, how does that alter my day-to-day routine? And what about . . . you know . . ."

"Honey, please," the doctor laughed. "Your husband is going to hate it, and if you're as active as that question leads me to believe you are, it won't be a great treat for you, either." She laughed again when Rissa looked sad. "You'll be able to handle the day-to-day aspects of your business for the most part, but I'm afraid that you'll be storing up a lot of sexual energy over the next four or five months."

"No sex?" Rissa looked bereft.

"Not until the cerclage is removed, and that would be done at thirty-seven and a half weeks."

"I'm only sixteen weeks now." Rissa's eyes moved as she did quick calculations. Her heavy sigh made the doctor smile. "That's an awfully long time."

"Think of how interesting week thirty-eight will be."

"Right." Rissa offered a small smile. "So when do we do this?"

"I have two openings for next week."

"You don't need to check your appointment book or anything?" Rissa looked impressed.

"I have specific hospital time at Crawford Long and Northside, so that makes it easier to keep things on track. As it stands, I have eight o'clock openings on Monday and Tuesday at both hospitals."

Rissa thought of her baby and waited for an answering tremor—nothing came and she guessed the baby was depending on her. *So is Dench.* She swallowed hard and forced a determined smile. "The sooner the better. Monday at Crawford Long."

Sitting in her car, Rissa debated running back across the parking lot and into Alexis Stanton's office. *But my baby's life depends on this.* Looking down, reading the sheet of instructions, she read: *No food or drink after midnight before the surgery, avoid tampons, avoid sexual intercourse . . . Avoid?* She smoothed a hand over the page as Dench crossed her mind.

He's home tonight, so that only gives us three days to . . . A little moan escaped her throat when she pictured him: Big hands, big feet, long limbs, sheets of muscle, warm lips, and a heartbeat like music. *I miss him already.*

And he'll come to the hospital with me on Monday. I'll tell him that he doesn't have to, that he doesn't have to stay, but he'll be there when I open my eyes. I know he will because he's Dench, and because he loves me. The sudden warm rush that filled her body was soft but emphatic enough for her to bring her hands to her heart in response.

"You're right. He'll be there because he loves us both."

CHAPTER 18

This baby is a girl. Rissa was almost surprised when the clear and easy thought finally occurred to her. *But it makes perfect sense.* She pulled her car door open and carefully inserted herself into the driver's seat. *I just don't know why it took me so long to figure it out, although with the surgery and all, I have had a few other things going on . . .*

Moving gingerly, testing herself, Rissa reached for the button at the side of her seat. Pressing, she waited for the BMW to obey and slide her a few inches closer to the steering wheel. *No point in rushing. I promised Dench that I would take it easy and I did, all the way to Chicago and back. Chicago, whew! This was the little trip that almost didn't happen. Your daddy pitched a fit when I told him that I still intended to go. It's a good thing Alexis convinced him that it would be all right, and that we could safely travel.* Satisfied that she had enough room to comfortably maneuver, she tossed her coat and messenger bag into the passenger seat. She felt the tiny tremor, almost too small to be anything more than imagination. *Don't start. Mommy's had a busy day.* She adjusted her sunglasses and ran her fingers through her hair. *Dench likes the hair,* she thought, tossing her head, *so maybe it's here to stay.*

When she pulled the car door closed, her nerves fluttered and generated second thoughts. She reached across to pull the messenger bag into her lap and snapped it open to finger through the enclosed documents. *You're right, it wouldn't do for me to get all the way home only to discover I'd left something undone in Chicago.* Satisfied that everything was in order, she snapped the seatbelt into place.

Nothing to say about that, huh? Satisfied that she and the baby were in accord, Rissa turned the key and powered the BMW out of the lot and onto the highway. *Funny how easily I've slipped into these conversations with you, little girl. I even expect you to answer me—and you do.* She sighed and eased the car over into the next lane.

I have to admit that I'm kind of surprised at how easy you are to talk to—kind of like your daddy. She smiled. *That's a good thing, because your daddy is a special kind of man. I can't think of a lot of men that I would have trusted to be as understanding and supportive as he has been.*

Everything must be happening so fast for him, and he must feel so out of control. Less than a week ago, he walked in the door from his away game, and I hit him with all of the news about the surgery and what it meant for you, our baby, and he took it all in stride—most of it anyway. He had to take a seat when I told him about the no sex prohibition. Rissa laughed and tapped her brakes as a car cut in front of her. The baby sent a querulous flutter across her lap and Rissa laughed again. *No, sweetie. We will not indulge in road rage—Daddy wouldn't like it.*

And we want to keep Daddy happy. Laughter simmered into a contented smile. *Daddy sure worked overtime to keep Mommy happy.*

Telling him about the surgery had not been the easiest thing she'd ever done, and yet he'd taken one look at her face and found the strength to sit and listen. Knowing instinctively that she needed him to hear and understand every word the first time around, he'd listened, generous, patient, and kind.

Kind. Is that even a word that a woman expects to use when it comes to her husband?

But it was the right word to use for Dench when he sat there looking at her with those deep and accepting green and gold flecked eyes. When she moved close, he opened his arms, letting her melt into his warmly secure embrace, and she felt anchored. When his voice stroked her ear, reminding her of who he was, she was ready to defy the world for him.

"I love you, Rissa. We've come this far together and we'll see this through, all the way through, together." The words were exactly right, echoing the promise she saw in his eyes, and she loved him even more for having the faith to say them out loud.

Faith. That's what we're about. Rissa couldn't stop the smile when the baby sent a tiny ripple through her. *That's what you're going to be born into.* She drove the last mile to her home in silence.

Faith. Watching her garage door rise, the word skimmed her consciousness again. *Faith. Is that your name or your mantra?* The baby sent no signal, leaving Rissa wondering as she made her way from the garage.

Jamming her key into the door left her with an anxious shudder that had nothing to do with the baby and everything to do with the housekeeper Dench had insisted on hiring. *Like I couldn't keep my own house clean. The last thing I need is some other woman fanning around my home, rearranging things, and trying to fix things that aren't broken.* But it was his house, too.

She pushed the door open and smelled lemon polish. Stepping in, she pushed the door closed behind herself and locked it. *Bet she forgot to turn the alarm back on.* Moving to the wall panel, Rissa's fingers had to move quickly to disarm the system before the alarm triggered.

Okay, so she followed instructions. Looking down at the gleaming hardwood floor, she moved her foot. *Not slippery, and they look good.* She was going to have to work harder to find a reason to hate this housekeeper. Never one to give up easily, Rissa took a quick tour of her home and wound up wondering how a single woman had accomplished so much in six hours. Mirrors were clean, laundry was done, and there wasn't a dirty dish in the house. Whoever this wonder woman was, she'd even gone to the grocery store and stocked the refrigerator as fully and neatly as Rissa would have herself, if she'd had the time and energy.

Score one for Dench.

And I get to come home to a clean house. She looked around, appreciating. *I'll have to be around to meet this paragon of domestic virtue the next time Dench schedules her.* The baby telegraphed a funny thought her way. *Right. She'd better be a little old lady.*

As much as she would have liked a glass of wine, Rissa settled for a tall glass of cold grape juice. Dropping her coat and the messenger bag on the floor beside her chair, she sat and suddenly realized how tired she was. Looking down at her belly, she smiled. *But I'm not complaining. You are so very worth it.*

Sipping slowly, she lifted her feet to the chair across from her. Kicking off her shoes, she thought about the woman on the plane. Her hand wandered to her stomach and circled. The baby shifted beneath her palm and her smile broadened. "Mommy is not blaming you for anything, little one. Taking off for Chicago this morning was my silly idea, but I'm glad you went along for the ride." When the baby shifted again, Rissa felt her body clench around the movement and felt a thrill that bordered on sensual.

"Second time you've done that to me today," she sighed. The first time was on the plane as it circled Chicago before landing at O'Hare, and the little thrill had come so quickly that she hadn't controlled the escaping moan. Clapping a hand over her mouth, hoping no one had heard, she scrunched low in her business class seat—*I'm going home first class*, she promised herself, hoping no one had heard her.

No such luck. The woman next to her had looked at her belly and her embarrassed eyes and laughed out loud. Tall and long-limbed, with knees that pushed into the seat in front of her, the coffee-colored woman displayed her beautiful and oddly haunting thick-lipped smile. "I know you don't think that's unusual? Honey, before it's all over, that baby is going to have you making all kinds of sounds." She laughed again. "How are your feet and hands?"

345

Rissa blinked when the woman twisted in her seat and frowned down at her low-heeled pumps.

"Swollen? Huh, that's normal—especially in shoes like those. You need to put those in your purse and travel in something more sensible. Next time you fly, sit on the aisle and make sure you get up about every twenty minutes or so. Sit with your feet up every time you get a chance." Reaching, she gripped Rissa's hand in her strong fingers and looked at it. Her forefinger touched Rissa's wedding band and she smiled. "Pretty rings, but tight. You need to move your hands around more."

Is she calling me lazy? Rissa bristled, pulling her hand back. *My own mother doesn't call me lazy, and having a housekeeper was never my idea . . .*

"And you need to drink lots of water, even though that means more bathroom time—keeps you from bloating."

Rissa wondered if she looked stupid, because her seatmate just kept on talking.

"I went through this seven times. I have six children, so I'm kind of an authority on being pregnant." The woman laughed. "What are you, anyway? Six months or thereabouts?" She nodded, accepting her own judgment. "Yes, about six months."

"Almost seven." Rissa found enough nerve to sit up in her seat.

"Your first?"

Your business? "Yes."

"We lost our first one." The woman pulled at the breast of her sweater and her gaze wavered for the first time as she looked at Rissa. Heartbreak hid in the shadows of her dark eyes. Rissa's heart and brain nearly burst with the gravity and the depth of the questions that nearly spilled from her lips when she looked into her seatmate's face. *Did he blame you? How did you learn not to blame yourself? How did you hold out until the next time?*

The woman looked as if she'd heard every question and her face creased. "I like to have never gotten over it— thought it would kill me."

"I know." Rissa bit her lip and touched the woman's hand. "I know."

The woman smiled bitterly as her eyes touched Rissa's. She looked at her for a long moment, but then the smile changed. "I believe you do." She closed Rissa's hand between both of hers and sat straighter. "I did tell you that I have six now, didn't I?"

"I'll be happy with this one."

"I believe that, too." The plane bumped as it touched down and Rissa gasped again when the baby reacted. "Might be a little uncomfortable, but you should enjoy it while you can. It won't last forever. Nothing ever does."

Rissa was still thinking about her seatmate as she hailed a cab and headed to Shula's Steakhouse on East North Water Street. The drive was longer than she'd anticipated, but definitely shorter than it would have been in Atlanta. The fact that DeJuan Fisher was waiting in front of the restaurant made the trip better.

"You made it." He smiled, helping her from the cab. He tossed a handful of bills to the driver and ushered her inside. "I thought that you would get a kick out of this place, especially since AJ Yarborough is your brother and your husband coaches Atlanta."

"Yes, but that's not why I'm here."

"I know." Fisher grinned. "But can I just show off for a minute?"

Rissa raised a finger and looked stern. "One minute."

"Dang, you're tough. Now I have even more respect for Coach Traylor." Taking her elbow, DeJuan led her through the restaurant, talking every step of the way. "I know you probably don't remember the Dolphins in '72, but that was the year they went seventeen and 0, a perfect season—the only team in NFL history to finish with a perfect season. So, to honor that, it's the theme of every Shula Steak House restaurant. The menus here are hand painted on official NFL game balls and signed by Coach himself."

The big man sounded like a fan, but he looked as proud as a little boy. "It's like one of the top five steak house restaurants in the country, and there's one in just about every NFL city—except Atlanta." He stopped at their table and pulled out her chair.

This boy's mama raised him right. She smiled gracefully and sat. "In Atlanta, we have Bones and Chops, both outstanding restaurants in their own right, but I've heard that the Shula franchise is shopping space with the Ritz-Carlton in Atlanta," she smiled, flirting just a little, "if you're interested."

"I am interested." Fisher rubbed his big hands together and leaned forward. "So I guess that brings us to business."

Rissa looked at her watch. "It does if we can do it before my five o'clock flight leaves."

"I'm not trying to move to Atlanta."

"Nobody is asking you to. You told me that you needed commercial representation, someone to vet and field offers, make your name bankable, and help you ensure a life after the NFL."

"Word is, you did well for AJ and you've hooked Traylor up, but you have a vested interest there. What about Kadeem Gregg?"

Rissa looked at him over the rim of her water glass. "What about him? He's got a guaranteed second and a third year option, and eight million in endorsements. If he stays with me, I believe we'll more than double that over the course of a year. Of course, if the Super Bowl becomes a factor . . ." She set the glass aside and let her face go blank. "Is that what you meant by bankable?"

His toothy grin went wide and Rissa's briefcase held the sheaf of signed documents when DeJuan Fisher helped her into the cab for her ride back to O'Hare.

Knowing that she was about to knock Yvette's socks off and pump up their corporate bottom line at the same time, Rissa was happily congratulating herself when she felt the tiny stab low in her body. Much like a menstrual cramp, it was enough to make her gasp and close her eyes in shock as she headed toward the train that would deposit her on Concourse C.

Her feet stopped directly in the path of two rushing men at the same time that her hand moved to identify the pain. The shorter of the two men looked as if he had a hair-trigger temper and opened his mouth to harangue her, until he noticed her belly. Taking full advantage of the moment, Rissa turned big eyes and a radiantly helpless smile into the face of his frustration.

"Oh, my dear, are you all right?" Gray haired and paunchy, he looked as if he were more used to giving orders and having them obeyed than taking care of pregnant ladies, but he did his best. "I am so sorry, I should have been more careful." When he reached to solicitously pat her arm, his taller blue-eyed companion ran his fingers through the remnants of his blond comb-over and gawked.

Assuring the man that she was fine took a minute and she did have to swallow her pride when he asked her due date and the baby's sex, but she decided it was worth it as he left her with a smile and a wave. Sierra Clarence called it Baby Power.

And I do feel fine, she assured herself. The odd little cramps were rare and would only last another day or so, according to Alexis Stanton. They were a byproduct of the cerclage. But the doctor had already instructed her to limit her time on her feet in order to minimize pressure. *If that's what it takes to get the baby here healthy, I'll do what I have to. At least she didn't order me into a wheelchair.*

The sound of Dench's key in the door should have roused her, but Rissa was too tired to even realize that she'd dozed off.

"Hey, Sleeping Beauty." His voice was soft and liquid to her ear.

"Welcome home, Prince Charming." Her lips curved into a welcoming smile even before her eyes opened with her sigh. "The castle looks good—I already inspected it. You were right and I was wrong." She opened her eyes and stretched, liking the sight of him. "A lot got done today. What was she? Some kind of gymnast?"

"Is that jealousy?" Dench grinned as he squatted beside her chair. "Here I go and find you a household ninja, and you get jealous?"

"How did you find her?"

"Ouch, I'm hurt." Dench placed a hand on his chest and grimaced. "Do you really have that little faith in me? You don't think that I could have found the right person to help us out all on my own? Dude, I'm crushed." He dropped his eyes and shook his head sadly. Rissa waited until he finally raised his eyes to hers. "Mrs. Baldwin found her."

"A-ha, dude, the truth comes out."

"Well . . ." His lips brushed her forehead as he stood. "Her name is Rose Kirkwood, she's over fifty, and I only know that because she told me. She's been handling households for more than thirty years. She looked around and said that she could already tell that we would be easy." Rissa raised her eyebrows, and Dench raised his right hand. "Honest. Her words."

"Well, everything looks good . . ."

"And since she did the cleaning, dinner is on me tonight."

"You're going to cook?" Rissa sat straighter in her chair. "You know I love it when you cook. It's one of the sexiest things you do."

"Sexy?" Chagrin crossed his face.

She grinned and winked. "I said *one* of."

"Then I guess I'm going to have to do what I can to amp up sexy." He crossed the room to open the panel secreting the stereo system wired throughout the house. Dialing quickly, he listened when the sound came up and "Dilemma" filled the room. Turning back to his wife, he opened his arms. "Let's dance."

"Dance? You must be kidding. I'm tired. I lugged myself and a baby all the way to Chicago and back today. This chair is it for me."

"Come dance with me. If sex is out for the next four, almost five months, then we have to do something, and you are the one who brought up sexy." He moved his hips, danced a step or two closer, and then stood with his arms stretched in invitation. "I'm just saying."

Feeling almost sorry she'd introduced the topic, Rissa decided to be intrigued by the man she'd married. "Why dancing?"

"Because it's a 'vertical expression of horizontal desire legalized by music.'" He grinned. "George Bernard Shaw."

"Smart man."

Reaching for her hand, Dench drew her from her chair and smiled when she moved into his arms, matching his sway. Meeting his hands, she folded her fingers into his. Between them, the hard mound of their child pressed and joined them when she let her head fall to his shoulder. Her voice was low and persuasive. "I think I like this. Can we do it more often?"

"I don't know." He pressed his cheek against her hair and smiled. "You were so hard to convince."

She could feel his heat as her hips met his. "Promise me and I'll be your friend."

"I've already got a lock on your friendship. You're going to have to come better than that."

"If that's what it takes." Dench grinned as she moved their joined hands low and between their bodies. Bodies close, moving in tandem, they danced. Her cheek touching his, his lips touching hers, they danced and Rissa wished the song would never end. Nelly and Kelly gave way to Alicia Keys and Rissa sighed against the open front of Dench's shirt. Standing together, lost along the proximity of potential, Rissa and Dench stood breathing against each other.

"You know, this is kind of working for me."

"Me, too." His grin went sloppy. "Maybe we'd better think of something else."

"You were going to cook," Rissa reminded him.

"In a minute. I'm not ready to let you go." His arms pressed her tighter. "If that's all right with you?"

"Depends. What were you going to cook? Sorry, that's not romantic, is it?" She fluttered her lashes at him and laughed when he fluttered his in response. "No complaints from me." Swept by a wave of well-being, Rissa trusted his strength and leaned against the length of Dench and let the music lull her.

"I talked to Marlea the other day, about what it's like—giving birth, I mean."

"What did she have to say?" Holding her hand, he turned her gently, then let her relax into his renewed embrace as Alicia Keys promised that no one in the world could fill that special place in her heart.

"It was nice, just having the chance to ask the questions and hear the answers to things I wouldn't dare ask my mother. She told me about having AJ in the room as a coach. She said that he cried every time she did."

"That's AJ for you." He smiled into the softness of her hair when she slapped lightly at his shoulder.

"Dench?" She waited and he felt her body tighten in his arms. "Why haven't we ever talked about . . . the other baby?"

The deep breath rushed from his body and his hand moved from her back to her hair. "I wondered when this would come up."

Rissa stopped moving and simply rested against him. "Then why didn't you say something?"

"I figured that you were carrying enough guilt and hurt for the two of us, and that when you were ready to lay the burden down, I would be there to take it for you."

"I guess I should have known that, shouldn't I?" When his hips shifted and his feet moved, she stirred with him, her head lifting just enough to look into his eyes. "Maybe I missed the boat on the big one, but I figured out something else today."

"That you love me?" He turned her again, then settled her against the broadness of his chest.

"I've always known that, and I thought you did, too."

"I just like hearing you say it. Tell me what you figured out."

"We're having a girl." He was silent, smiling when she looked up at him. "You're not surprised?"

"I already knew."

"How?"

"I just know, and I have faith that I'm right."

"Funny you would say that," Rissa sighed. "Faith."

He nodded. "I think it's pretty, too. Are you thinking Faith or Imani?"

"Maybe both." She blinked and looked up at him. "I don't know."

"Well, she's told us everything else. Let's wait and let her decide." Dench's hand moved on her back and as he watched, Rissa's face flushed and her eyes brightened. Her lips parted and she panted slightly.

"She's decided?"

"I think Faith Imani works for her," Rissa whispered, her hand circling the baby's curve.

When she lifted her other hand, her fingers beckoning, Dench offered his hand and held his breath. When she pressed his palm to the firm mound, he smiled when the baby moved. Kneeling, he framed the rounded shape of his child between his large hands, his fingers curving to trace her. Needing to be close to them both, he brought his mouth close to Rissa's belly and whispered, "Hello, Faith Imani Traylor. I'm your daddy."

CHAPTER 19

Wandering through her home again, Rissa found herself fluffing pillows, straightening pictures on the walls, and missing Dench, even as she tiptoed past the spot where he'd decided their Christmas tree would go.

"I've got to get used to this," she told herself when she pulled open the hall closet door. "The season's going well, the players are healthy, and if they make it to the playoffs, he'll be gone that much longer." She looked at the spot near the fireplace and tried not to think about last year and the promise she'd made.

Last year, though, it seemed like the promise was on the verge of fulfillment. Last year, there had been a huge tree with family and friends decking the halls. There had been the promise of a baby and a hell of a lot of hope. *And then there was none.*

She turned away and jerked open the door of the hall closet, refusing to give the pain any energy. Determined, she spent the next ten minutes shoving things around, rehanging jackets and sweaters, turning all of the hangers in the same direction. "Okay, baby, this is what not to do with your law degree," she muttered. Closing the closet, she went in search of her next make-work project.

The tiny thought ambushed her, worming its way into her consciousness. *We didn't make it this far before, did we?*

The simple answer wasn't easy and almost dropped her prayerfully to her knees. *No, we didn't. But this time is different. Seven months we've made it, and every day that you stay put is one more day to our advantage. One more day to the good.* The baby moved, and Rissa's path changed. Anything to avoid that damned space and the thought of another Christmas tree.

Because this time . . . She squelched the thought.

On the way to the kitchen, she found a stack of magazines and catalogues. "Wonder how the household ninja missed these?" Collecting them, she took them to the kitchen and flopped them on the high granite countertop. Touching the wall panel bathed the room in more light than she wanted, so she turned it down so that she could read at the counter.

Pulling one of the high stools close, she pushed her hip onto the stool and heard herself puff when she settled her bulk into it. That was something new, the thickness of her body and the effort it took to move it, but to tell the truth, when nobody was looking, she liked it.

When nobody was looking, Rissa loved everything about being pregnant. She'd taken to keeping a private journal where she logged daily weight changes and listed weekly waistline and hip changes. She kept shorthand notes of every doctor's visit and had a special place tabbed in the book where she noted every move the baby made. And she guarded her little book jealously, not even sharing it with Dench. *Let him get his own book. This one is mine.*

She was still smarting from the day Nia had pulled it from her purse and sat in the middle of Marlea and AJ's kitchen turning the pages. When Marlea took the little pink and blue book from the little girl, she'd flipped through it, finding Rissa's notes.

"So what is this?"

She'd held the book, teasing, just out of reach. When Rissa reached for it, Marlea had lightly tossed the book to AJ. Sensing a game of Keep Away in the making, AJ caught the book and held it just out of reach, leaving Rissa stomping and screaming.

Thank goodness Dench came along when he did. Using his height and a little stealth to good advantage, he'd come up behind AJ and snagged her book, which she'd promptly hugged to her breast and hustled out of their house.

Thank goodness for Dench. Looking down at the heavy swell of her breasts gave her a little thrill. Letting her hand fall just a little lower to find and comfort the bulge of her baby drove the thrill deeper, touching her at her very core, and she couldn't stop herself from curving her hands around the tight ball of her baby.

Warmth, a wave of sudden undeniable love, swept over her, leaving a comfortable smile in its wake. *I'm glad we did the ultrasound before he left.* It was funny, Dench had been the one to ask for the pictures, to insist on having one at each visit with Alexis Stanton, and to keep the scrapbook. *Who would have thought that this little girl would have captured her father's heart so quickly?*

Still smiling, Rissa reached for the television remote and pressed the buttons. She kept the sound low and watched the images move until she grew bored. Ignoring the television, she reached for the stack of magazines and catalogues. Flipping the top one open, she saw Dench's notes scribbled across the corner of the pages and shook her head. "How is it that the man who is responsible for erecting a moving wall of men can take the time to make sure that we choose the precise shade of delicate pink for your nursery?"

She felt the little bubble of happiness and smiled. "Yeah, I like him, too."

Trading one magazine for another, she yawned and turned pages. Bored, she closed the book and pushed it away. "Well, Faith, here we are on a Saturday night and it looks like everyone in the world has something to do except the two of us. And if I hadn't been told to take it easy, I would find something for us to do. But I won't, I'll sit here just like I promised Dench—and you."

Though the baby sent no psychic message, she did send a bright flash of pleasure straight to Rissa's heart, making her smile and sigh aloud. Faith Imani Traylor was an emotional little girl, even though she wasn't here yet. "But soon, sweet girl, soon." Both hands went to her stomach and she felt the quickness of the baby's movement and the flush of pleasure renewed itself.

"You know your name," Rissa whispered, comforted and amused by the thought. "It was kind of funny that Dench and I came up with similar names. Faith seemed so right because I believe in you, little girl. I believe that you are ours and that Dench and I are destined to love you for our whole lives. And he loves the name Imani because he's as confident that you belong with us as I am.

And your grandmother wanted me to be sure that you know that 'faith is the substance of things not seen.'"

Rissa didn't mention the look her mother gave her when she tried to explain the baby's communications. As a matter of fact, every time she mentioned it, people seemed to give her an odd look, and it was getting old—she'd written that in her little journal, too. "Maybe I should just keep you to myself."

Leaning against the high kitchen counter, she reached across and flipped through another set of catalogues. It seemed that the more they bought, the more catalogues and magazines showed up at the door. Even Rose Kirkwood, the household ninja, had begun to complain about their sheer volume and overwhelming frequency. "And on top of that, I am just getting flat-out sick of looking at baby furniture and amenities." She looked down at her belly and gave it a pat. "No offense."

Apparently none was taken as the baby was still when Rissa walked across the tile floor and shoved the catalogues into the recycling bin. "So now what do we do? The only person I know who would be hanging around is Yvette, and I am so not about to call her and play Twenty Questions all night."

And that's exactly what a phone call to her partner would become. Yvette still couldn't get over Rissa and Dench first refusing to ask about the baby's sex, and then deciding that the munchkin was a girl. When it turned out that they were right, the woman went into curiosity overdrive. 'How did you know? When did you know?

What was the first clue?' *I swear, I ran out of answers for her after the first hundred times she asked. And then when she started to tiptoe around my feelings, I thought I was going to have to choke her!*

Rissa grabbed the remote and went to stand in front of the television. Thumbing the buttons, she started to flick through the channels. *Eight hundred channels of programming, and I can't find a single show to watch.* She stopped on a channel featuring a doctor talking about childbirth. When the program didn't seem to offer any new or relevant information, she started to press buttons again.

Going to the premium channels that Dench swore were work related, she flicked through football, wrestling, and some kind of extreme cage fighting— nothing she wanted to see. She waited long enough to watch a preview of Jimmy's fight, and approved when the full shot of him zoomed onto the screen. He looked good, rather like a hero compared to his older opponent, and the announcer made "The Showdown in the South" sound exciting.

But I have to wait an hour for the excitement.

It was nearly ten, and she'd already talked to Dench. He wouldn't care if she called again, but he might worry if she did, and he had a game tomorrow. Rissa looked from the clock to the phone, and decided against the call. Marlea and AJ were speaking at a Presidential Fitness Council event in Washington. Connie and Jeannette had taken Libby up on a visit to her timeshare in the mountains. Sierra Clarence was probably already at Phillips

Arena. "And my mother is on a date. Everybody has a life but me," she sulked, folding her arms over the baby bump.

Unwilling to be forgotten or overlooked, the baby telegraphed a quick reminder of her presence, making her mother burp and slap her chest in response. Then the baby moved, a silky little stroke. "Okay," Rissa amended, taking the hint. "Everybody has a life, except us."

Her eyes went back to the clock. Almost ten. "If we can stay awake another hour, we can watch Jimmy's fight." The idea filled her with a quick sense of purpose and she left the remote on the counter and turned her attention to assembling snacks and building a tray for her viewing pleasure.

Waiting for corn to pop, she scoured the kitchen cabinets until she found the hoped-for ingredients, and she silently blessed the household ninja. For a few guilty seconds, she was glad that Dench was out of the house as she poured a box of Milk Duds into hot popcorn. He hated the combination, and since her pregnancy, she couldn't get enough of it. She and the baby were almost giddy with anticipation when she dipped her hand into the bowl and shoveled the chocolate and caramel-coated popcorn into her mouth.

Letting the salt, sweet, and crunch tease her tongue and fill her mouth was an almost sensual treat and she stood chewing, savoring it. "Some things are not meant to be shared, even when you love a man," she said aloud. She scooped another handful and stood with her eyes closed, chewing. A few more kernels left her licking her fingers and giggling. "I know that this is not what Alexis Stanton had in mind when she told me that I would have to find a sexual alternative."

And goodness knows *that* hadn't been easy on either of them.

The whole idea of not being able to completely share themselves was frustrating, to say the least. The dancing had worked at first, and it was still nice, but . . . Now Dench, who hated running, was running with AJ and Marlea every time he got the chance. *And I'm stuffing myself with popcorn and Milk Duds.*

It was growing more and more frustrating to be so intensely close, to touch so profoundly, to move so intimately, and to have the freedom to do everything *except* to cross the lines of physical intercourse. "Thank God I love the man for so much more than his body. And that he loves me for more than just my physical charms. Who knew that sexual congress was really *that* big a deal?" Then she thought about it and giggled again. "It got Adam and Eve in a boatload of trouble, though.

"Better stick to popcorn. Oh, and maybe a hotdog." The thought turned her to the refrigerator and she again blessed the household ninja for stocking up on hotdogs, chili, and coleslaw. Quick and greedy, Rissa nuked the hotdog and chili while she toasted the bun. Even the smell made her lick her lips as she assembled her sandwich.

She added the bowl to her tray and took her time maneuvering it and herself to the table in front of the television. Setting the tray in easy reach, she grabbed the remote and levered herself down onto the sofa. The championship bout was in Atlanta, and Phillips Arena was going to be filled to capacity—one reason she was staying home and watching it on HBO. "All I need is to get down there, pushing and shoving through a crowd like that."

Stimulation, of all sorts, was on the prohibited list, too. *The last thing I want or need to do is break the stitches of the cerclage,* she thought. *Especially since we've come this far. Only five more weeks, and we're into the 'safe' zone. Six weeks and we'll be right at Christmas and close to the start of a new year. I can do five weeks easy.*

Five weeks sounded like an eternity.

Pulling a nest of cushions around her body, Rissa punched a fist into the pillow at her hip and pulled at it. When that didn't help, she moved and shoved it into the curve of her back—better. A second pillow went under her knees as she curled into her corner of the sofa. Remote in hand, cellphone, popcorn, hotdog, and ginger ale in easy reach, she settled in to watch.

Billed as "The Showdown in the South", this was Jimmy's first serious fight as a heavyweight and Gervais Tabac, the current champion, had done his best to dominate and intimidate him in all of the prefight interviews. To his credit, Jimmy stood his ground with grace, dignity, and a quiet smile.

Watching shots of him preparing for his fight, Rissa couldn't help feeling a little rip of pride. Reporters spoke well of his record, liking his stats. Contrasting his time in the ring with the current champion, they lauded him as a 'clean' and skilled young fighter, and were charmed by his modesty. Regular comparisons to Thomas "Hitman" Hearns kept cropping up, and he was humble enough to reply that while he was flattered, Hearns had established himself as a legend and the kind of fighter that he hoped to become.

Enjoying her hotdog, Rissa half-listened to what the announcer had to say. A lot of it was canned, a script that she'd reviewed endlessly, but some of it was genuinely interesting and featured shots of Jimmy running and sparring. There were other shots, taken earlier in his career, that chronicled his growth as a fighter. Some of them were really cute, like the one from his days as a welterweight, and the one with him holding his tiny son in the palm of his boxing gloves.

"And tonight, this young man is ready . . ."

"More than you know," Rissa told the announcer.

Over the months leading up to the fight, Jimmy had bulked up, adding more than thirty pounds to his lean frame. *And he wears it well.* Rissa smiled, finishing the hotdog. *No wonder Sierra is so proud of him.* He'd trained intensely, learning to alter his fighting stance and speed to accommodate his increased size, and Rissa watched with interest as he entered the ring.

Tabac, in black shorts, was long-limbed and thick, square and menacing as he prowled the ring. Jimmy, in white shorts with a bright red side stripe, was calm and attentive as he stood in the center of the ring waiting to do the job he'd come for. On the referee's command, the fighters touched gloves and moved toward each other.

Rissa pulled her knees close and clutched a pillow.

Commanding the ring, Jimmy was fast and as graceful as ever, firing shots from both the left and the right hand with deadly accuracy. He moved in with telling blows and scored easily, but it was evident that he'd learned something that she'd heard Dench tell his defensive linemen—*the best way to avoid a hit is to get out of the way.* And Jimmy had it down to a science.

By the start of the third round, Tabac was sweaty and showing the wear of his effort. Jimmy was points ahead, and his style showed in the refinement of every finished move. Rissa reached for her popcorn, munched and smiled. *Dench was right. My boy is a gentleman boxer.* Moving with a breezy, almost choreographed energy, Jimmy drove strong punches into the body of his bigger opponent. Desperate, Gervais Tabac swatted at his challenger who kept stepping out of range.

"Uh-huh. Can't lay a glove on him, can you?" Rissa taunted the screen. There had been a lot of ugly talk from Tabac before the match, but watching the fourth round, it was easy to see that the talk had been just that as he swung and failed to connect. "Hey batta, batta, batta, swing!" Rissa crowed.

Jimmy danced close and delivered a series of flawless jabs and a hook to Tabac's chin as the bell signaled the end of the round. Rissa applauded loudly. "Ha! Training will tell," she shouted when the instant replay tried to track the speed of Jimmy's punches. Even slowed down, they were a blur. Tempted to call Sierra, she grabbed her bowl of popcorn and settled in for the remainder of the match.

She didn't have to watch long. Tabac went down in the seventh round. *Nice of Jimmy not to have embarrassed him*, Rissa thought, spilling popcorn as she clapped and cheered. *He could have finished him in the sixth—the man was definitely outclassed.*

Calling the match, the referee moved toward the center of the ring, and all hell suddenly broke loose in the ring. The still-stunned now former champ climbed to his feet, shook his head like an angry bull and lurched toward Jimmy. With his back to Tabac, Jimmy seemed oblivious. Men from both corners seemed to panic and scrambled urgently over each other. As Rissa, twenty-one thousand ticket holders, and millions of viewers watched, the champ lunged forward and slammed a massive fist into the back of Jimmy's head.

Rissa watched in horror as Jimmy's eyes rolled back, showing only slits of white, and his knees buckled. The commentator's voice was lost in the roaring and screaming of the crowd. People were moving, the crowd surging toward the ring, while in the ring, the final swing seemed to have cost the champ everything as he fell forward, his face hitting the canvas.

The moment seemed to replay endlessly as the reality dropped thickly between Rissa and the television screen. The popcorn bowl spilled from her lap and landed on the floor when she started up from her place on the sofa. Greasy nausea slid through her stomach and made her grab for the sofa's arm. "I know," she muttered. "And I will take it easy. I promise, but I have to go."

The thick shove of too much popcorn in her stomach almost forced her to sit. Grabbing her cellphone, she pushed away from the sofa and went to the closet for her coat. "Look, baby, this is not just my job. This is about our friend, and I'm going."

The unexpected wave of guilt made her stop. "I would never hurt you, Faith. Please trust Mommy. Please." Catching her breath, she pulled the coat over her arms. Car keys and her purse were on the granite counter in the kitchen and she snatched them like a relay runner taking the baton as she headed for her car. The cellphone rang in her hand as she turned the key in her door. She didn't bother to look at the caller ID. She already knew who the caller was. "Hey, Sierra, I'm on my way. Which hospital?"

"Thank you. Grady, they're taking him to the trauma center at Grady Memorial. Oh, God . . ." Her voice cracked and a ragged sob escaped. "I . . . thank you, Rissa . . . I'll see you at the hospital."

She's so scared, so very scared. I would feel the same way if it was Dench. Worse, Rissa admitted, realizing that Sierra's fears were not for herself but for her husband and her son. Biting her lip, Rissa stood where she was, waiting for something from her own baby. When nothing came, she moved her bulky figure down the three stairs to the garage floor.

In her car, she couldn't stop herself from wondering. *What if it was Dench?*

But it's not. She wasn't sure whether she was promising herself or Faith. *It's not.* Staking a claim on calm and purpose, she reached for the car radio and pushed buttons until cool jazz filled the car. She touched the button raising the garage door and backed into the night.

She kept her mind intentionally blank and focused on the road in front of her all the way to Grady Memorial. Turning into the hospital parking deck, Rissa kept her stranglehold on calm as she rolled past the vans of two national news affiliates.

Determined to have nothing to say and refusing to be confronted, she turned the collar up on her jacket. Looping a long scarf over her hair, she took the long way around the building to find the Emergency entrance.

And almost made it.

"Rissa?" José Christopher stepped from the shadows and touched her arm. She jumped and glared. Christopher grinned. "I knew you'd show up. Had a bet on it." Ben Thomas stepped up beside him and offered a single bill, which Christopher quickly pocketed. "So what's the word? What can you tell us?"

Fixing his swarthy features, he looked concerned and downright solicitous, but Rissa would have bet Faith's college fund that he had a recorder in his pocket—so she didn't call him what she wanted to. Choosing her words carefully, she let the scarf slip from her hair, drawing the attention of two other reporters. "Gentlemen, as you know, the recent turn of events in Mr. Clarence's life are exactly that—recent. I have no further details. When we know more, I assure you, the information will be released."

"Aw, come on, Rissa! How are you going to try to play us like that?" José twisted his lips. When Rissa pivoted toward the admissions desk, he moved with her. "You're here and not at home with your feet up. What's going on?"

"Neither one of us will ever know anything if you don't get out of my way, José." Her eyes narrowed and she might have said more if the tall young man in the security uniform had not cleared her path and ushered her onto the elevator.

Christopher watched her back—and the icy little smile that played across her lips as the elevator doors closed. "Mercenary little . . ."

"I wouldn't call her that, if I were you," Ben Thomas whispered. "Pregnant or not, I think she can take you."

"Whatever." Christopher slunk to the bank of gray plastic chairs along the wall and sat down to wait. "Sooner or later, there'll be some news."

"Have you heard any news?" Rissa folded Sierra into a hug and held on.

"Nothing," Sierra sniffed.

Rissa released her and stepped back, feeling useless in the middle of the hospital corridor. "Where's the baby? Where's Mrs. Clarence?"

Sierra wrung her hands and looked up. Her eyes were red and her face was swollen when she licked her lips. "JJ is with his Granny Brenda." Sierra's lips trembled, and, for a second, Rissa wondered if she would get the words out. "I called her and she told me that her family is strong, that Jimmy has a hard head—she said he inherited it from her father. She promised me he would be fine. But how can she know? How can anybody know?" Sierra's composure broke and her face crumpled. "What if he's not . . . Rissa, I can't lose him. JJ needs him too much . . ."

"And JJ is going to have him." Rissa felt her baby stir and her hand moved to her stomach, circling without hesitation. "You'll see. Jimmy fought brilliantly tonight, he's young and strong, and he's going to be fine."

"You have to say that because you care about us." Sierra's head dropped to Rissa's shoulder and she sniffed. Her hand moved to cover Rissa's and she smiled when the baby moved between them. "They say babies always know . . ."

"Then I am going to take this as a definite confirmation and you should, too. I am not going to raise my child to tell lies." The baby moved again. "See? He'll be fine."

She was spared from making more conversation when a lovely, fine-boned woman wearing an open white lab coat stepped close. "He's awake," she said softly. "Would you like to see him?"

Rissa was left to chase the women down the green-walled corridor as Sierra went to her husband. Standing beside the door, the dusky young woman looked at Rissa and smiled again. "I'm sorry." She offered her hand and deftly shook Rissa's. "I should have introduced myself. I am Dr. Jemma Kasmaridan, the neurosurgeon on his case. I was called in when he arrived." Before Rissa could introduce herself, Kasmaridan continued, "You are the agent, the law lady, and the friend. Mrs. Clarence described you," her eyes went to Rissa's belly, "perfectly."

Across the room, James was propped in bed with an iced pillow. Speaking to his wife, he kept his voice low and looked embarrassed. Rissa knew before she asked that her question was a cliché, but she asked anyway. "How is he?"

Kasmaridan shoved her hands into her pockets and looked thoughtful. "We have diagnosed Mr. Clarence with a mild concussion and plan to hold him overnight for observation."

"That's it? I was watching, I saw him go down. He was hit hard."

"What can I say? He has a hard head." Kasmaridan smiled and gave Rissa's arm a pat.

Well, thank goodness for that. Rissa moved closer to the bed and took a good look for herself. Jimmy's eyes were red and the right side of his face was puffy from the fall he'd taken. Other than that, he looked fine, though sorely embarrassed.

"Here I whip that dude in front of how many million people, then I go and turn my back on him and get slammed in the head. What was I thinking?"

"Baby . . ." Sierra's fingers were tentative when she touched the bandage at the back of his head.

"Every school kid in the world knows better than to turn his back. Any drunken fool in a barroom knows better." He threw up his hands and frowned when they fell back in his lap.

"On the positive side, you beat him like he stole something. You won." Rissa rubbed her fingers and thumb together. "That's bank, brother."

James looked confused. "For real? I lost consciousness so fast, I don't remember what happened between the last punch I threw and waking up here."

"It was a very fine contest," the petite doctor said. "You fought well, but you should know that it is not uncommon to lose time when you sustain even a mild head injury."

Soothing, Sierra passed a hand along his cheek. "I'll show you the DVR, baby. I recorded it."

Jimmy's intimate gaze was so grateful when he looked at his wife that both Rissa and the doctor took steps toward the door. When Sierra said she would stay with him, Rissa felt like an intruder. She made an excuse and eased from the room, doubting that they would even notice her absence. Dr. Kasmaridan directed her to a soft drink machine, and Rissa followed the instructions, promising herself that she would leave in an hour and write a press release the second she got home.

When I write the release, I'll need to say something about Tabac. Wonder if they brought him here, too? It would make sense, since this is the closest medical facility and he looked kind of goofy before and after he hit Jimmy . . . Wonder if he was on anything? Wonder if I could find out before José does?

Ignoring her nervous stomach, Rissa looked up and down the corridor and found no sign of ambushing reporters. *Good. At least this will give Jimmy and Sierra a little time to calm down and organize their thoughts before they have to make any kind of public statements.*

Jamming a hand in her pocket, she felt for coins and sorted them with her fingers as she approached the drink machine. Deciding on juice and drawing quarters from her pocket, she felt startling heat arc through her chest. She heard the coins hit the floor at the same time she heard the cry escape her lips. The little pain that knifed through her side traveled raggedly upward to settle between her breasts, bringing tears to her eyes. It was sharp enough to make her suck air through her open mouth and lean against the wall.

Hot salty water flooded her mouth and she wanted to howl in protest. *Not again!* Scared to do anything else, Rissa stayed where she was. *I'm in a hospital, Faith. We're safe.* Waiting, praying that the pain wouldn't come again, Rissa was afraid to move even her head when she heard her name.

"Is that you, Rissa?" Brenda Clarence came close enough to put an arm around Rissa and push her face close. "Lord, child, you don't look so good."

Like a portly angel decked out in a floral sweater and brown corduroy jeans, and smelling like fresh baked cookies, Brenda was determined to stand by Rissa's side. Looking around, seeing no one, she pushed her shoulder under the taller woman's arm and invited her to lean. "You look sick, and you need some help. Right now."

Ever efficient, Brenda managed to move both of them away from the wall, and hooked a foot around a wheel-chair waiting beside the door where Rissa had stopped.

Pulling the chair close, she helped the younger woman to sit. With her heavy brown jacket draped over the handle of the wheelchair, she hooked her purse over the other handle and began to push.

When Rissa moaned and slumped to one side, Brenda brusquely righted her and kept pushing. "Did you see Jimmy? I haven't seen him yet. They say his condition is good, but you know hospitals. If you can breathe on your own, they'll say that you're in good condition."

Steadily talking, Brenda Clarence pushed the wheelchair up to the nurses' station and looking into the faces of two nurses, slapped a hand on the counter. "We need some help over here." She looked down at Rissa. Judging the molten gold of her skin to be pale, Brenda frowned and slapped the counter again. "Did you hear me? I *said* we need some help."

"What seems to be the problem?"

"The problem *seems* to be on this side of the counter," Brenda insisted.

One of the nurses walked around the desk and looked down at Rissa, who now understood how Jimmy must have felt around his mother. If she hadn't been so scared, she might have said so.

"Does she look pregnant to *you*? She looks *very* pregnant to me, and I didn't go to medical school." Brenda's face tightened. "This woman is pregnant and when I found her, she was in pain. That sounds like a problem to me. Help her!"

Rissa ran a hand over her sweaty face and looked at the nurse when the pain surged and climbed through her chest. "Is there someone? I had a cerclage . . . but my chest . . ."

The nurse's green eyes went wide and her dark head bobbed with sudden understanding. Ten minutes later, Rissa found herself on an exam table in the Emergency Room, facing a female doctor she'd never seen before. From where she'd been deposited, she could see Brenda Clarence, armed with her big purse and heavy brown jacket, waiting beyond the door. Pacing, peeking, and keeping watch, Brenda had no intention of abandoning her. Hoping that her self-appointed guard had not called Dench, Rissa submitted to examination.

When the doctor finally snapped off her nitrile gloves, Rissa found herself able to breathe normally. "Everything is normal, there's no spotting, and the cerclage is still firmly in place," the doctor said. Stopping, she turned back to Rissa with a half-smile. "We see a lot of pregnant women in here for a lot of reasons, but the one question that gives us a lot of answers is, what have you eaten in the last four to six hours?"

"Eaten?" *Oh.* Rissa explained her penchant for Milk Dud infused popcorn, and hotdogs layered with chili and coleslaw.

"Really?" The doctor appeared nonplussed. "Together?" Rissa nodded.

"Well, no wonder you have gas."

"Gas? Are you kidding? That's a joke, right?"

"You're sitting in the Emergency Room at Grady Memorial Hospital. Did that pain feel like a joke to you?"

Stunned, Rissa tried to explain, but wound up with a warning: Lay off the Milk Duds and popcorn, and leave the hotdogs, chili, and coleslaw alone.

"First no sex, and now this? I just don't get to have any fun."

"Live with it." The doctor laughed and left.

The second the doctor emerged, Brenda Clarence burst into the exam room and eyed Rissa. Satisfied that the doctor's diagnosis had been reasonable, she handed Rissa her clothes and helped her to put on her shoes. Eager to check on her son, she kissed Rissa's cheek, demanded that she go straight home, and elicited a promise of an early morning call.

Still buttoning her jacket, Rissa remembered José Christopher and Ben Thomas. *The way my luck is running tonight, they're still waiting.* She caught her breath and imagined them lurking in the waiting room. *Or worse, they've heard about my little episode and their reports will claim that Jimmy was so horrifically injured that I went into premature labor.*

No way am I putting us through that. She turned and made her way back to the nursing station. "Excuse me, there was a guard in Emergency when I came in . . . tall, young . . ."

"And pretty as the day is long?" sighed a small brown-skinned woman, fluttering her false lashes and fingering her pixie cut hair.

"Yes, you could say that." *But I wouldn't.* "He was really nice. Do you think I could see him?"

"Marlon is nice," the woman said, running her fingers through her hair. "Let me get him for you."

She made a call and Marlon Givens came around the corner minutes later. "How can I help?"

"I need a favor." When he agreed, Rissa promised him Falcon season tickets and exchanged car keys with him. He drove her BMW from the Grady parking deck to the parking lot for Underground Atlanta. She pulled up in his Explorer five minutes later and handed him a business card with a reminder to call her when he was ready for his tickets.

"Think I might be able to get some for the playoffs?"

"Just tell us where to send them," she promised.

Grateful for the help and missing Dench, she climbed into her BMW. Driving slowly through the streets of downtown Atlanta, she carefully made her way west. *What would I do if someone called to tell me that something had happened to Dench? What would I do if I was watching a game and saw him injured?*

What would I have done tonight without Brenda Clarence?

I don't ever want to know, she decided. Pulling off Cascade, driving through the iron gates, passing her brother's home, she was tempted to stop. But Marlea and AJ were out of town. Even Mrs. Baldwin's apartment was dark.

"That just leaves you and me," she told her baby. Pulling into her own driveway, she pressed the button and watched the garage door rise. Inside, she closed the door. Removing her seatbelt, she sat looking down at her rounded stomach, home of the child she craved. "You should know that this kind of thing doesn't happen all of the time," she whispered. "This was a crisis for Jimmy and Sierra, but everything worked out okay. They still love each other and JJ will have them for a very long time, just like you'll have me and your daddy for a very long time." She sighed and wondered if she was trying to convince her unborn child or herself.

She jammed a hand into the pocket of her jacket and pulled out her cellphone. Maybe it was too late. She tried to figure out the time difference and couldn't remember if it was a central, mountain, or western time zone. And he had to be up early in the morning . . . And she didn't want to scare him . . . The phone rang in her hand. She flipped it open and smiled when his voice touched her heart.

"Hi, Dench. I was just thinking about you . . ."

CHAPTER 20

Rubbing her soapy hands together under the hot water, Rissa wondered how many miles she'd covered in these bathroom runs. It seemed that she was headed to the bathroom, on average, every five minutes. She wondered whether Dr. Stanton ever considered these little side trips when she sentenced her patients to bed rest. *Probably not. If she actually wanted pregnant women to get any real rest, she'd have to insert catheters.* Rissa shuddered at the thought as she opened the door. *I've been in bed with my feet up for more days than I care to count, and yet they're swollen.* "Week thirty-seven is starting to sound really good to me," Rissa puffed, trying to settle into a comfortable position on the king-sized bed. "She said that we needed to get to week thirty-seven to be safe, and I can't get there soon enough."

"And that's why Dr. Stanton confined your active ass to bed. All because you couldn't sit still on your own," Yvette muttered, shuffling through the files on Rissa's table. "Out there running around in the middle of the night, trying to take care of a boxer. I don't know who you think you are—oh, yes, I do. Wonder Woman Black."

"Look, I'm his agent, and you know how that is."

"Right, and you should remember that you are his agent, not his mother."

"I think everybody should calm down and remember that it was gas and nothing else."

"This time," Yvette warned, looking up to shake a finger at her partner.

"Well, you didn't have to shuffle your merry self all the way out here . . ."

"Yes, I did. I am not about to have our agency go down in flames because you can't get into the office for more than one day a week for the next two weeks, and the stuff on your desk was leaking into my stuff, making us both look bad." Yvette clicked a series of commands into her laptop, then leaned to look at Rissa's. "Here's the change," she pointed.

"I see it." Rissa highlighted a section of DeJuan Fisher's proposed shoe contract and smiled. "He said that he was interested in working with us for more than our 'boutique' clientele services. He said that he thought we could help him realize his true value, and looking at the numbers, I have to say that we have done our job."

"And we have done it well." Yvette grinned and high-fived her partner. "Tell me the truth, did you just happen to have that sponsor list in your pocket all along, or did you make it up on the fly?"

"You know how I do." Rissa grinned back. The baby added a swirl of delight and her grin broadened. "I'm just glad he had all of those Florida tie-ins. That made things a lot easier all around."

"Easy is a good thing, sister-girl. I still can't believe that you managed to link him with the Citrus Council." Yvette reread the highlighted clause and nodded. "Have you heard any more about Jimmy Clarence? How is he doing?"

"I guess his head really is as hard as they kept saying it is. He's home, doing fine and apparently no worse for the wear. He's not scheduled to fight again for the next six months, so training and playing with his wife and baby are the next big things."

Yvette giggled. "Playing with his wife? Was that a Freudian slip?"

"Whatever. I'm so horny, it might have just been wishful thinking."

"That's a hormonal byproduct of your pregnancy. Anyway," Yvette cleared her throat and typed quickly before looking up. "So, what's up with the other one, the guy who hit him?"

"Tabac?" Rissa read the changes quickly and approved them with the click of a computer key. "Would you believe he got off with a warning from the commission? The thought is that he was dazed and not thinking clearly when he attacked Jimmy from the rear. The sanction he got was pretty much a slap on the wrist. I guess his penalty would have been stiffer if Jimmy hadn't been blessed with that hard head."

"So he lives to fight another day," Yvette said softly. "God is good."

"And now that Jimmy has taken a title bout and recovered from his attack in the ring, he's even more popular than I ever imagined. A couple of magazines have contacted him for interviews, and BeaconGreen wants to add a new series of commercials since JJ is crawling and

Jimmy is the new champ. Two soft drink companies are bidding for his time and the contracts need to be reviewed." Rissa picked up the folder she'd laid beside her on the bed and flipped through it, then passed it to Yvette. "All in all, it was a night to remember."

"And you wound up on bed rest."

"Give me a minute to get back to you on that." Rissa slid to the side of the bed and made her way to the bathroom, frustrated by the trip and the thought of the return. "I swear, my bladder must have shrunk to the size of a thimble."

"That's because you're such a dainty lady," Yvette teased.

"I've got your dainty lady, right here." Rissa closed the bathroom door on her partner's laughter.

"Excuse, please." Rose Kirkland appeared in the doorway, pushing a heavily laden rosewood teacart, complete with a china teapot, linen napery, and covered dishes. She stepped to the side and waited for Rissa to make her way back to the bed. When Rissa sat and pulled her legs up on the bed, Rose reached behind her to fluff and place pillows. Rissa eased back onto the pillows with a grateful sigh and Rose smiled as she stepped back.

"I thought lunch might be in order, so I took the liberty . . ." Rose let the words drift as she brought the tray closer.

"Oh, how lovely." Yvette cast hungry eyes on the tray as she rose to wash her hands.

"Thanks." Rissa smiled thinly, knowing that there would be no hotdogs or Milk Duds and popcorn on that tray for her.

"Girl, I am going to have to get me one of those household ninjas," Yvette said, slipping back into her chair and lifting the cover from one of the plates. Thinly sliced beef, homemade mashed potatoes with just the right amount of gravy, green beans, and baby carrots waited fragrantly, and she inhaled deeply. "It's like she just slips through the air anticipating your needs. Yes, honey, I am definitely going to get myself a household ninja."

"Household Nazi is more like it." Rissa frowned at her plate. Instead of beef, she had some kind of baked fish that she already figured would taste like cardboard. Not that the ninja wasn't a good cook, she was a really good cook, but she was also following Dr. Stanton's orders and doing everything she could to support Rissa's newly prescribed bland diet.

She watched Yvette uncover her dessert—Key lime pie. *Mine will be fruit—probably applesauce.*

"Don't be mean." Yvette's eyes rolled heavenward as she savored her mashed potatoes. "These potatoes are glorious, and you didn't even have to ask for them." Yvette's fork was busy as she sampled everything on her plate, then went back for more.

When she finally looked up from her plate, Rissa's eyes were fixed on her. "If you're going to stare at me, you could at least smile." When she didn't, Yvette laid her fork to the side and sat straighter. "Look, you're getting the best of all possible worlds, and all you have to do is sit here and wait for it to happen. Instead, you're glaring at me like I'm the villain in this piece, and I'm not, you know. What's wrong?"

"That I've been exiled to this crappy bedroom is a big part of what's wrong."

Yvette's eyes were quick to flit around the room. A pretty part of a small suite featuring garden-facing windows along two walls, the 'crappy bedroom' was bright and sunny, and the small bathroom, positioned only a few steps from the bed, was a bonus. Filled with classic Broyhill cherry wood furnishings and colorful bedding and cushions, it was easily the kind of space she would have begged to be exiled to.

"Okay, now I really don't get it. What's wrong with this 'crappy bedroom'?"

Rissa sighed. "It was the household ninja's idea. She heard Dench and me talking about my being confined to bed and thought that this room might make a nice change of scenery."

"Oh, that evil, evil witch. Let's send her to the dungeon and have her boiled in oil."

"You're an evil, evil witch." Rissa sulked. "And this room might as well be a dungeon. My daily commute is from the bed I share with Dench to this room and back again."

"Your house has how many bedrooms? Five, six? You're only on bed rest for a few more days, right? Choose another bedroom if you hate this one so much."

"I can live with this one until I see the doctor." Rissa shrugged.

""My Lord, you're just bound and determined to be contrary, aren't you?"

"No, I'm just tired of being stuck at home. It's fine when you're here and I can focus on work. It's okay, I guess, when Marlea or Libby are here, or even when Jeannette and Connie drop by. But when it's just Dench and me . . ." Her lips twisted and she looked down at her plate. "When it's just Dench and me, I want us like we were, but that can't be."

"For now." Yvette sipped her tea, then set the cup aside.

"When I'm here alone, just sitting in bed and not working, then I get scared for what might have happened that night. What if it hadn't been gas? What if Brenda Clarence hadn't come along when she did?" Rissa sighed and fanned a hand at her partner. "I know, it's silly, but I can't help wondering."

When Rissa continued to push food around her plate without eating, Yvette pushed the tall glass of milk closer to her and watched her drink until the glass was nearly empty. "After the baby comes, things will settle. You'll see."

"I know. We're in a good place. In the meantime, I feel like I'm never going to have sex again. It's been so long. What if I forget how to do it? Have you taken a good look at Dench lately? Oh, God," she moaned, covering her face with her hands. "He looks so good that I could just scream."

"He's always been a good-looking man—I know, because I've been watching."

"Good looking? That's an understatement." Rissa moaned again. "Most men are struggling to get a six-pack, but after all the running and working out Dench has done lately, he's got an eight-pack. Every time he steps out of the shower or I walk in on him dressing, I almost want to slap myself just to keep from jumping on him. Then, on top of that, there are all those other little sweet things that I love about him."

"Sucks to be you."

"You think? I remember Marlea talking about something that used to happen between her and AJ. How every time he touched her, she would . . . I mean her whole body would . . . Well, I promised I wouldn't tell, but you get the idea. And now it's happening to me. He looks at me and I'm so hungry for the man, I just want to rip his clothes off."

Across from her, the slice of pie was rapidly dwindling, thanks to Yvette's judicious use of her fork, but she stopped eating long enough to appreciate her partner's words. "I can't imagine why he would mind that."

"He probably wouldn't, except that the doctor says that I can't do that. Sex is out for now—I told you that. We can't even make out like a pair of teenagers—I might get too excited. She says that intercourse or even masturbation could cause my uterus to contract, especially in orgasm."

"And that would be bad, because?"

Rissa's shoulders sagged. "The contractions could pose a serious threat to the stitches of the cerclage, and I can't put Faith at risk like that, Yvette. No matter what I want and how badly I want it, and I want it badly, I can't do that to her."

"And daddy-to-be is walking around looking fine as all get-out, just tempting you." Yvette shook her head in sympathy as her fork pressed against her clean dessert dish, collecting tender crumbs.

"Fine as hell and humming Christmas carols. Did you notice that my whole house smells like a pine forest? Did you see the big tree next to my fireplace? Did he just forget about last Christmas?"

"Last Christmas was a year ago, a whole lifetime ago. Besides, you were the one who made the vow about the trees, not him." Lifting the cover from Rissa's dessert, Yvette found applesauce and pulled a spoon from her place setting.

"I knew it would be applesauce—I'm really starting to hate applesauce. Would you rather have more pie? I'm sure there's more."

"Nope. I'm good, and the tree is beautiful. I saw it when I came in." Yvette went to work with the spoon. "Go ahead and let him decorate it if that's what he wants to do. It's not like you don't have something to celebrate this year."

"You're right." Rissa pushed her food away and picked up one of the folders she'd pushed to the side.

"Aren't you excited?" Yvette licked the spoon and set the empty dish aside. "Isn't Faith Imani excited?"

"Don't start with me," Rissa grumbled. "Faith has suddenly developed a preference for her daddy."

"You're kidding. How can you tell?" Yvette's raised eyebrows said most of what she would not allow to pass her lips. There was nothing wrong with a mother thinking that her child was exceptional, but most mothers at least waited for the children to be born.

"I think she recognizes his voice. The second he gets anywhere near me, she starts her show, and she especially likes to perform at night—all night." Rissa gave her belly a poke and frowned. "Mean little thing, she can apparently tell the difference between day and night and seems to prefer staying awake all night." Rissa poked the mound resting in her lap again. "Don't you know that I'm the one carrying you, and if I don't get to sleep, things are not going to be good?"

Watching, Yvette crossed her arms and legs. "What did she say?"

Rissa stared down at her belly. "Nothing. She doesn't seem to care about anything I do, unless I decide to go to the office. Then she spends her time generating untimely bouts of gas for me."

"Everybody has gas sometime or another. You're in your eighth month. That's when pregnancy is supposed to get easier."

Rissa's shirt twitched and she looked down at it as the baby stretched and turned. "Faith Imani Traylor couldn't care less."

"So cute when they do that," Yvette laughed, reaching to touch the active baby. True to her mother's words, the baby flipped and kicked, moving beneath Yvette's hand. She cooed and clucked softly, and when her fingers tapped lightly, the baby kicked back, making her smile as she eased from her chair to sit on the side of the bed.

"Is she dancing for you? We thought about getting lessons, but her talent seems to be natural," Dench laughed from the doorway.

Turning her face to him, Yvette hoped she wasn't staring, especially when she felt the sloppy grin spread across her lips. Rissa was right, the man had definitely been working out, and it had definitely done his body good. Dressed casually, he wore his jeans and boots the way some men wore Armani. Framed in a shaft of golden afternoon light, he stood with one arm braced against the door, draped in careless confidence. Her grandmother would have said that he looked like "two drops of Lord Have Mercy," and Yvette would not have disagreed.

Shooting a quick glance to the side, she caught a flash of her partner's face, and damned if Rissa didn't look like a woman in love. Her nut brown eyes, already bright from the heat of her pregnancy, had gone soft at the sound of his voice. When Rissa lifted a hand to brush back the fall of her hair, Yvette caught sight of the throbbing pulse at the base of her throat and almost smiled. *Yes, a man like Dench Traylor could make a woman's heart beat faster.*

When he entered the room, Yvette felt her own heartbeat pick up, skip a beat. Bending to kiss Rissa's cheek and to touch her stomach, he was so tender that Yvette heard herself sigh and tried to cover it by flipping through one of the files she and Rissa had already reviewed. When his forehead touched Rissa's, and his hand stroked a long line down her arm, lingering at her fingertips, Yvette told herself that she could live a lifetime without that kind of connection.

And I'd be lying like a rug. She watched him leave, waving her fingers in farewell. He'd barely cleared the door when she turned back to her partner.

"Girl, that man is so close to perfect that I can't stand it. If I thought I stood a chance with him, I would hate you." She rested one hand on her breasts and sighed. "That bald head? So sexy."

"I know. Didn't I tell you?" Crossing her arms, Rissa rested her cheek in her hand. "Can you believe that I picked a fight with him?" When Yvette shook her head, Rissa nodded. "Over the tree. When he insisted on dragging it in the house, I pitched a fit." She could still hear his words.

"Just stop, Rissa. I thought we worked through this, and I've had enough. We haven't celebrated much of anything between last Valentine's Day and now. We missed your birthday and mine. We missed Nia and Jabari's birthdays, and I swear, if we hadn't gone to Jamaica, I would have forgotten our anniversary. And now you're determined to kick Christmas to the curb. Rissa, you're humping your frustrations around and pushing all the joy out of our lives like you couldn't care less.

"You know that I love you like Jesus loved the church, but damn, baby. Enough is enough, and I'll be damned if I'm giving up Christmas—even for you. Now, if you'll excuse me, I'm going Christmas shopping. I'm going to spend too much money, watch kids sit on Santa's knee, and bring back a bunch of stuff in pretty boxes to put up under that tree. You can open yours if you want to, and I don't care if you need it or want it. Christmas is coming to this house with you or without you."

"And when he left, he slammed the door. I swear, the door shook in its frame when he slammed it behind him.

I couldn't believe it. He said all that and never even raised his voice."

"Did he really go shopping?"

"Yes. I never got a look at what he bought, I just saw him dragging bags and boxes from his truck."

"I don't believe it." Yvette shook her head. "You didn't creep out there and sneak a peek?"

"I told you I didn't. Besides, the household ninja helped him hide them. He's determined to have his Christmas."

Yvette shook her head again. Bending, she began to collect the files she'd brought with her. Rissa handed her the ones stacked at her side on the bed and watched her fit them into her briefcase. When she finished, she marched to the closet and pulled her coat out. She pulled it on and began silently buttoning it.

"What?" Rissa finally asked.

"You've got a lot of nerve, you know that?" Yvette's fingers stopped moving and her eyes held Rissa's. "Talking about, 'He's determined to have his Christmas.' That man is determined to have *your* Christmas, fool. He's determined to make a memory with you, show you some promise for that little girl you're carrying—and he's going to do it if he has to carry you through the holidays, kicking and screaming every step of the way."

"Maybe I have a reason for feeling the way I do."

Rissa's voice sounded so suddenly and completely haunted that it caught Yvette by surprise. "Reason? Like what?"

"Like maybe . . . you know, we never really talked about the baby I lost. It wasn't like with Faith. She's real, she has a name, and whether you believe me or not, she has a presence. She's already a part of our family. That didn't happen before and . . . and I don't know how he feels about it."

"It sounds like he's put his faith in you and God." Yvette sucked her teeth and planted a hand on her ample hip. "It sounds like he's happy with your foolish behind and like he understands that he can't remake the past. It sounds like he's ready to throw your old 'jinx' theory out and get on with making the future as good as it can be for his family—and that includes you."

"So I'm the Grinch, huh?" Rissa tugged a pair of pillows behind her and flopped back on them.

"Call yourself whatever you want. Just stop trying to steal that man's joy." Yvette tossed her scarf over her shoulder. "And how about you find a little private joy and quit moaning about what you don't have and what might have been? Be grateful for what you do have with Dench. Share that with him."

"What do you propose that I share with him?" Pushing her bottom lip out, Rissa was the picture of petulance. "Maybe I should start with this lap full of baby, or my perpetually overfull bladder. Or do you think he'd prefer to share my swollen hands and feet? And don't forget, I have itchy stretching skin, and stitches where the sun don't shine."

"You're pitiful. A few months ago, you would have given this house and every dime you'll ever earn to be right where you are, right now. But instead of being thankful and helping your man to enjoy his little tree, you're in here sulking like some kind of spoiled brat. I said it before, and I'll say it again. It sucks to be you!"

"It does suck to be me." Rissa ran a hand through the hair she'd twisted high on her head. "Aren't pregnant women supposed to be beautiful? Aren't they supposed to glow? When is it going to be my turn? And why can't he wait until next year to have his tree?"

"Just determined to whine, aren't you? Well, remember this: Nothing is promised, not even tomorrow. That tree is a little thing, and it's for right now. That man and your baby, those are big things, and they're yours right now."

"You're trying to make sense out of my pettiness."

Yvette sucked her teeth and shook her head. "Girl, please, you'll have to have your pity party without me. Don't those stitches come out in a couple of weeks?" Rissa nodded. "Honey, if it was me, the second they let me out of that bed, I would dust off my credit card, get my hair done, buy some lingerie, and seduce my husband. You said it was safe after the stitches came out." Yvette tossed her head and picked up her briefcase. "I would make a date with that man, and remind him of who I was—the hell with a tree."

"You've got a point," Rissa said slowly. "And the tree isn't all that bad."

"Hell with the tree," Yvette repeated. "What about the man? Did you hear what I said to you?"

"I heard you. I'm thinking about it."

Rissa was still thinking about it an hour later as she returned from yet another bathroom break. Rose Kirkland slipped into the room and silently collected the remains of lunch. She lifted Rissa's glass and mutely disapproved of the remaining milk with a sidelong glance. When Rissa refused to meet her eyes, she pointedly set the glass on the bedside table and rolled the tray from the room.

Listening to the sound of the retreating cart's wooden wheels against the flooring, Yvette's words sank deep and Rissa had to admit that the longer she thought about them, the more sense they made.

He loves me and he's been right here beside me through it all. He's never once blamed me or even had an ugly word to say to me, and God knows I haven't been easy to live with. He had to have been scared when he heard about Jimmy, and he knew that I would go to see about him, and he has yet to get mad at me about it.

And I got pissy about a tree. She sniffed lightly and let the thoughts continue to flow. *I can smell the tree from here, and I have to admit that it smells fresh and brings good memories—even if the toys under it are not for our child.*

But they will be soon. She sat a little higher in the bed and her face brightened. *Dench deserves a break and a hell of a lot of consideration.* Picking up the bedside phone, she dialed the number for Alexis Stanton's office from memory.

"This is embarrassing," she said when the doctor answered, "but I need an answer, and I want to do the right thing."

"Certainly. What's your concern, Rissa?"

"I want to . . . make a date with my husband. I . . . miss him, and I would like for us to . . . reacquaint ourselves."

"Nice euphemisms, but I hear that one a lot." Rissa could hear the doctor's smile threaded through her words. "As long as the cerclage is in place, I'm afraid you're going to be limited. But we're due to remove yours soon."

"And when they're out?" The words were drenched with hope.

"When the stitches are removed, you may have some light bleeding, but that's normal and won't last long. At this stage of pregnancy, your baby should be fully developed and ready enough to be born. Sex may induce contractions, which could lead to active labor, but if you're ready to have this baby now, and it sounds like you are, I'd say go ahead and make that date with your husband."

Rissa smiled and leaned back on her pillows. "Thank you, Doctor. That's exactly what I'm going to do."

CHAPTER 21

"All you have to do is read the instructions," Marlea insisted when she stood over the men and their manly display of tools.

"Yeah," Rissa said, picking up the instruction sheet. Skimming the page, she looked at the heap of parts dumped in the middle of her living room. "It says here that all you need is a screwdriver."

"A Phillips head screwdriver," Marlea read over her shoulder.

"I may only be a pregnant woman, but isn't that a hammer?"

"And those are pliers," Marlea pointed. "Needle nosed pliers, if I'm not mistaken."

Irritated, AJ rolled his shirtsleeves higher, then leaned back to look at the picture on the box of the little pink stroller he was responsible for. "You act like this is the first thing I've ever built," he grumbled, sitting down on the floor.

"Maybe not built, but how about finished?" Marlea high-fived Rissa.

"Your wife, dude." Dench sat next to him and turned the box for a better look. "Sounds like a challenge to me."

"Yeah, AJ. It sounds like a challenge to me, too. Why don't you put your money where your mouth is?" Rissa was ready for the dare. When Marlea nodded, she looked straight at Dench and charged ahead. "And dude, your wife will bet you fifty bucks that we can build Barbie's Dream House before you finish putting that stroller together."

AJ looked up from the stack of toy parts in front of him. "Be wary, man. There's a catch. There's always a catch."

Marlea hummed agreement as she snapped the instruction page at her husband. "The catch is that we'll read the instructions."

"Everybody knows that the instructions are a trick."

"Scared, AJ?" Marlea stepped close and bent to let her fingers caress her husband's cheek. "Don't be scared, baby. We know that you guys have been shopping, so we're going to make it easy on you, only fifty dollars—each."

"You can afford that, can't you?"

Reaching, AJ was quick to capture Marlea's fingers. "Wait a minute, Silk. Cash might be okay for you two, but what if Dench and I win?"

"Like that might happen."

"There's always the teensiest chance." Rissa brought her thumb and index finger close together. "You know what they say about getting a roomful of monkeys together and having them come up with the complete works of Shakespeare."

Twisting her fingers lightly in AJ's grasp, Marlea smiled. "Okay, then, if you should just happen to win, what do you want?"

"I'm thinking a date, something nice and private, for New Year's Eve." AJ raised his brows and lowered his voice, "And you have to wear the stilettos and the corset."

Dench turned to look at Rissa and grinned. "I'll take the date, with a rain check on the stilettos and corset."

She kissed the top of his head. "You have to win the bet first, sport."

"Promise me the date and the bet is as good as won."

"Give us a minute to get over there to that table, and we'll start." Rissa walked toward the table and settled into a chair. "On your mark, get set, go!"

"Silk cheats," AJ warned.

"I do not," Marlea called back, sorting through the pile of screws, nuts, and bolts.

Across the room, Dench held a small wheel in both hands and didn't appear to have any idea what to do with it. AJ looked ready to use his hammer on anything close enough to hit. Rissa turned precut pieces on the tabletop and smiled. "What if they win?"

"Are you kidding? Look at AJ over there. He's trying to build that toy the same way he played football—hit it until it does what you want it to do."

"Then let's let them win," Rissa whispered.

"What?" Marlea's head snapped up and her eyes sparked. "First of all, they'll never let us live it down. Secondly, you know we'll have to go over there and help them." She glued a wall in place, and then referred to the instruction sheet.

"Well then, how do we make it a tie, at least?"

Marlea looked at her sister-in-law. "Does it really mean that much to you?" Rissa nodded and Marlea sighed.

"You know you want to wear that corset and those stilettos."

"He likes them." Marlea fused another Dream House wall and looked at Rissa again. "Why is this 'date' such a big deal to you? You see the man almost every day."

"You know about the cerclage, right? Well, the stitches came out a week ago and things are fine, but the doctor told me to be careful for another week. That brings me right up to New Year's Eve, and I can't wait to date my husband." Leaning close, Rissa's voice was low and expressive. "Do you know how long it's been since we've had sex? Do this for me, Marlea, and I'll pay off the bet. Girl, I'll give you the fifty dollars."

"Shame on you, trying to get me to pimp Dench out."

"I'm not doing any such thing." Rissa sent a sour look across the table, then turned her attention to painting tiny shutters. "I remember a time when you needed some help, and Dench and I were right there for you. I remember when a certain hateful wench was trying to play games with your head, and I was right there for you. I remember when . . ."

"You've made your point," Marlea replied. "Here's what we'll do: You paint all of those little pieces while I finish with the walls and the roof. We'll tell them that we can't do anything else until this dries, and then we'll talk them through the stroller and the bikes. By then, everything will be dry and they can 'help' us finish. That way . . ."

"We win!"

"It won't be as much fun if they know we helped them out." Marlea drew a finger over her lips when the men turned to look at them.

And a win is a win, Rissa thought.

Rissa still didn't know how Dench and AJ built that stroller in reverse. As she showered she reviewed the events. Initially unwilling to believe that they weren't being sabotaged, the men had insisted that the women keep their distance. They had struggled valiantly in their effort to deal with pieces meant to fit a small girl's hands, and AJ had reminded Dench that someday, they would do this again for his daughter.

"No way, dude. I'm going to buy my baby's stuff pre-assembled."

When the wheels fell off for the third time, Dench and AJ had looked at each other and thrown their hands up in surrender. The women had flattened out the crumpled instructions and sorted through the pieces. Marlea had unscrewed several pieces while Rissa made sure they were still usable. Together, they had talked the men through the instructions and had the stroller, complete with a baby doll passenger, under the tree in fifteen minutes.

Rissa turned the water off and stepped free of the shower. Pushing the door closed behind her, she took the soft blue bath sheet from the bathroom vanity and wrapped it around the fullness of her body. Everything about this holiday was good—better than she ever expected it to be. A tiny sliver of regret shivered beneath her skin when she thought of her first reactions to Dench's determination to have a Christmas tree. *But I gave in.* And now she was glad she had. Yvette was right, she thought, giving her baby an inclusive pat. *The tree will only be up for a few more hours, and if that's all it takes to make him happy, he deserves it.*

When she'd gone in for her shower, he was removing the last of the lights. He'd packed all of the ornaments away, all except for one. It was a delicate crystal cherub she'd found in a shop at Lenox Mall. From the second she'd seen it, she'd known that it was the perfect peace offering, the perfect beginning to her apology.

Opening the small gift box on Christmas Eve after Marlea and AJ had gone, he'd said nothing, but she saw the happiness in his eyes. He simply lifted it by its golden cord and silently admired its delicately precise rendering. When he surveyed the tree, taking time to find the right spot for it, Rissa promised herself that there would be another ornament to mark each year. *No, better make that two ornaments,* she amended, looking at herself in the vanity mirror, *one from me and one from Faith.*

Beneath the bath sheet, the baby moved, flushing Rissa with a sense of well being. *And you,* she gave the baby another little pat, then let her fingers linger. *Nice to have you back on my team.* It seemed that the baby had forgiven Rissa's rash of tree angst. No more gas attacks and no problems since the removal of the cerclage. *And trust me, Mommy is grateful.*

Removing the oversized towel, dropping it into the bathroom hamper, Rissa took her time, luxuriating in the fullness of her body. Turning, she admired the curve and tilt of her heavy breasts with their dark aureole, and the weighty swell of her stomach. Her fingers surrounded the baby and she proudly watched the response she drew.

When her eyes returned to the mirror, the flash at her throat made her smile. The open platinum and pavé diamond heart pendant was a gift from Dench, and her fingers traced it now. *"Just so that you don't forget that you hold my heart,"* he'd said.

And I hope he knows that he'll have to bury me wearing this. I'm never taking it off.

Filling her palm with scented lotion, anticipating the touch of Dench's hands, her own fingers trailed pleasure along her skin. Warm to her touch, her body tensed and flowed with the movement of her hand and she heard her doctor's voice again.

Filled with amusement, Alexis Stanton had said everything except 'Go get him!' *That's not exactly true,* Rissa reminded herself. *What she actually said was that Faith is fully developed and ready to be born. She said that the strong contractions of sex could trigger full labor. She said that Dench and I could be together. Finally.*

And Yvette said that I should seduce my husband. The lightly scented body spray chilled her skin and filled the air around her. *Never let it be said that I can't follow directions.*

Finding her makeup, watching her face in the mirror, Rissa was careful. *Not too much.* She moved mascara across her lashes and debated more. *How long has it been since I did this just for him?*

Jamaica? Has it really been that long?

She tried to count and days moved into weeks, which became months. *Never again,* she vowed, touching her lips with lipstick. *I dress for everything else that's important to me, and that's everything from work, to church, to hanging out with Connie and Jeannette. The least I can do is dress for Dench.*

The baby sent a wave of approval surging through her breasts. Slipping into her panties, Rissa decided that it was a good omen. Moving with lazy grace, Rissa pulled the red and gold velvet dressing gown from its hanger. Gathering it in her hands, she lifted it high and let it fall over her body, covering herself from shoulders to her bare toes. Watching her image, she buttoned the long row of gold buttons fronting the gown and tried not to wonder how long it would take Dench to undo them.

I don't think I've ever been this nervous about being with Dench. Not even our first date. She pulled the silk scarf from her hair and let it fall into a dark, shoulder-sweeping drift. *That date was just a quick dinner and a movie. Nothing big, and the only thing that made it special was Dench. He took me to see* Spiderman, *and I don't recall a single thing about the movie, except that he held my hand.*

Her toes went quickly into golden slippers and she pressed her hands together, trying to quiet her nerves when she faced herself in the mirror again. *One day, Faith is going to ask me how to know if she's in love, and I'm going to tell her that she'll know when a man makes her feel like this.*

Rissa's fingers touched the wall panel and the bathroom darkened around her. Opening the door, she stepped into the hall and heard music. *I'm going to tell Faith that love is based on caring, friendship, commitment and trust. I'm going to tell her that love is shared between two people who have a vested interest in one another's happiness.*

And I'm going to tell her that I know all of that is true because I love her father.

Kneeling, laying the wood for the fire she wanted, Dench smiled and watched Rissa move carefully around the room lighting candles and rearranging the red and white roses set among the pine boughs. She wore the red and gold velvet dressing gown he'd taken so much care in selecting, and though she said nothing, he knew that she was pleased with his notice. The gown flowed softly from her shoulders, drawing his eyes to the delicious study in contrast—the high richness of her breasts, the lowering fullness of their child—and he felt the pleasure rise.

"Dench?"

Music played around them, softly mellow jazz, and when he looked up into eyes the shade of ripe pecans, he smiled. *Maybe the baby will have her eyes.*

"Did I tell you that I liked the Christmas tree?"

Better late than never. "I'm glad." His lips quirked when the thought crossed his mind. "Did you like the tree, or what was under it?"

"That's not fair. You know that I loved having all the toys under the tree. Santa dropped off nearly as much stuff here for Nia and Jabari as he did at their own home."

"AJ and I were up all night putting those bikes and wagons together."

"You had help, and Marlea will never forgive you for spoiling her kids." Rissa came closer and smiled down at him when his arm slipped around her legs, holding her close.

"If she can forgive your mother, she can forgive me."

"Well, I forgive you."

He looked up quickly. "For what?"

Rissa fingered the open heart-shaped diamond pendant resting against her skin. "For giving me another reason to love you and the tree that inspired you. Thank you."

"You're welcome." He released her long enough to stand and collect her hands in his. When she fumbled with the matches, he took them from her and left the box on the mantle. Leaning close enough for a chaste kiss, he drew back as her eyelids dropped sleepily. Softly feminine and vulnerable, she stood with her eyes closed, holding his hands and waited.

When he kissed her again, taking his time, tasting her mouth, enjoying the softness of her lips, and feeling the tremor of her hands in his, he watched her. Her golden skin took on the blush of a ripe peach and her breathing quickened when she stepped closer, settling their joined hands atop the swell of their baby. Feeling like a man on the rare side of drunk, Dench brushed her lips with his.

Opening her eyes, she smiled. "I hope that's not all you've got, because I'm expecting a really great kiss to welcome in the New Year."

"Got one in my pocket," he told her. "But I have something else. Come here, I want to show you."

"We're not going to dance? Because dancing with you is really nice, and I really love this music, but I have to tell you that it makes really nice foreplay but it doesn't really replace . . . you know . . . and since the doctor has cleared me for . . . you know . . . for everything we might want to do, maybe we should . . ."

"Rissa?"

She looked up at him, question in her eyes.

"Shut up and let me lead. We're not dancing, and I've got this."

"Okay." Pressing her lips together, Rissa let him lead her to the sofa in front of the fire he'd laid, and watched as the flames sparked color and heat. Pulling his knee onto the cushions, Dench produced a small blue Tiffany & Company box. Offered from the palm of his hand, the box was identical to the one he'd given her on Christmas morning.

"I don't understand," she said, "what is this?"

He opened the box and she blinked in surprise. Unable to stop herself, caught in the magic of the moment and the charm of her husband, she put forth a single finger and touched the pavé diamonds of the open heart, a smaller version of the one she wore.

"You already gave me one. What is this one for?"

"For Faith," he told her. "If diamonds are forever, then it only seems right that you should both have one, and that they should match."

"She's a baby, Dench."

"Our baby." He looked at her as though those two words were the answer to everything. "Our baby," he said again when he folded the box into her hand. "I figure she'll love this when we give it to her for her sixteenth birthday. In the meantime, hold it as a part of our promise to her."

"You are so corny, you and your dumb promises," Rissa said against his lips. "Could you do anything to make me love you more?"

"I'll work on it." His hands squeezed her shoulder and he felt her tremble. Around them, the music changed. "Stand By Me" vibrated through the air and Dench pulled her closer, thanking the nameless angel who delivered the little musical miracle. Taking the Tiffany & Company box from her hand, he closed it and set it on the table beside the sofa.

Curling close, her belly snug between them, Rissa laid a hand on his chest and marveled in his strong heartbeat. His pulse traveled through her fingers and the connection called to her very essence. But there was one more thing to say before the elemental lines of basic lust were crossed. Rissa twisted herself to look into his face and her tongue darted across her lips.

"Before the New Year comes, I have . . . a question, and I need an honest answer." He frowned, and she saw the green and gold flecks swirl in the depth of his eyes.

"What's the question?"

"This has been a long year, a hard year, and I want to know how much of it . . ." Her voice failed and her eyes fell.

"Rissa, we lost one and gained another. We're stronger, together. We're better, together. I can't think of anybody I'd rather have faith in." He smiled suddenly, the flash of teeth and the touch of his hand making her blink. "There's not a soul in the world that I would rather have faith in. Only you."

"And there's not a soul in the world that I would rather have Faith for, Dench." When he stretched his long legs toward the fire, she sighed and listened to the music that still spun through the air around them—"Mr. Magic."

"You know, earlier, I was thinking of some things that I want to be able to say to Faith when she's older, but I just thought of something I want to say to you. Dench, I want to tell you that you are my rock, now and forever. When we lost the baby, you held me and refused to let me lose myself. When we jumped off that cliff in Jamaica, you held me and didn't let go. Whether your team wins, or loses, I still get the best of you." Her hands were warm when they closed on his cheeks. "Dench, I'm not ever going to forget that again."

Between them, the baby flipped and bumped. The touch of his hand seemed to calm the baby, but his wife wanted more. "You know, you'll have to take a rain check on that corset and the stilettos, but I can think of other things that we can do."

His breath was hot and moist against the column of her throat and his voice, striped with low growling hunger, scraped at her core. "Girl, you don't know how much I missed you, 'cause you know I love you like . . ."

"Jesus loved the church," she whispered, crushing her mouth to his. The taste and feel of him was everything she remembered, wanted, and craved. "Dench," she whispered, needing to say his name.

"Tell me you missed me."

"I did, I do. Always and endlessly."

Her teeth closed lightly on his lower lip and he saw the hunger surge through her gaze when her hand found skin beneath his shirt. Desire fanned intent and heat licked at his soul. She felt it steam between them, from his hands as they touched her, from his skin against hers. His fingers were quick and nimble, easing the buttons of her red velvet gown open, freeing her when it slipped from her shoulders.

Suddenly modest, his fingers paused to gather the cloth at her breasts. "I want to do this right," he said. When she offered her hand, he took it and drew her to her feet. "When it comes to you, I want to do everything right."

Rissa bit back her usual quick retort and settled for leaving her fingers in his care as he led her back down the long hallway. In their bedroom, cast in ambient light, she was warm and yielding, letting him lead her. For the briefest of seconds, their eyes met and they were caught in the wash of déjà vu. The first time together, it had felt exactly like this . . .

She felt the ache burn and their appetite grew and strained when he kissed her, and her urgency aroused him, made him more than he'd ever meant to be for anyone. Wanting more, fearing for her and the baby, Dench pulled back, would have released her if she had not moaned and clung to him.

Rissa's fingers pressed his flesh, found ridges of muscle, and pulled him to her. Her fingers gliding along the planes of his back branded him. Her eyes were soft, her smile languid, as her fingers committed his face to memory. Tracing his eyes, the bridge of his nose, his lips, she sighed softly, feeling the rise and fall of his chest against her breast.

Shedding the red and gold gown, letting him take the panties he might once have simply ripped away, she looked too fragile for touching. Her belly, heavy with life waiting for expression, seemed too vulnerable for the passion he held so close to his surface. With heavy breasts that still lifted their nipples to his lips and the supple skin his greedy hands could not resist, Rissa was a wanton goddess of fertility and yearning, and he didn't know what to do with his hands.

"I'm not sure of how to do this."

"Let me help."

Taking his hands, she drew him with her onto a bed of silky sheets and smooth rhythm. He moved with her and even from the beginning, she was hot, wet and trembling. She moved into his arms, as close as a dream, and his muscles tensed under her impatient hands, fueling them both, making them greedy for each other. With the lift of her hips, his body quivered against her, fighting for control, until it shattered under need and pleasure.

Flesh pressed and she took him inside her, holding tight as the thrill rushed after him. Blood pounded in his ears as he gathered for her, again and again, and like a legendary Valkyrie, she rode the storm he powered. Between them, the flume of color and scent, thrown hard against desire once denied, now spilled wet and wild until the storm inside them was spent.

On his side, feeling his body cool, his desperate heartbeat slow, he smiled and watched the curve of his wife's cheek as her smile echoed his. Somewhere beyond their home, celebrants chanted, fired guns, and popped champagne. But in their bed, safe in their home, even their child found peace in the womb and rested.

Dench curled himself around his wife, spooning her perfectly and pulled the sheet higher over their bodies. The molten gold of her skin still warm and flushed from their love, the soft waves of her dark hair falling over her shoulder, and the closing of her fingers over his imprinted themselves on his heart.

"Happy New Year, Rissa."

"Happy New Year, Dench."

If this moment was his destiny, Dennis Charles Traylor knew that he would never regret an instant of the time that had brought him here. Not even when his beautiful wife closed her eyes and snored.

CHAPTER 22

"She calls you a *what?*"

"Household ninja." Rose Kirkland smiled and flipped hot muffins into the basket on the counter. "I rather like it. It sounds very modern. I think it sounds like I'm a highly efficient household operative."

Martha Baldwin's hands froze. "I think it sounds like you ought to be working for Jackie Chan. She couldn't call me that—no, sir."

"I'm sure that Mr. Chan is a perfectly fine gentleman, but Dench and Rissa are quite an interesting pair, and I'm enjoying them."

Shaking her head, Martha couldn't help clucking as she made coffee. "Interesting is one way of describing those two. Personally, I have a few other terms. You've only known them for a few months, I've put in a lot more time with them."

"Where do you keep the cups?" Rose turned from side to side, opening cabinets along the way. She finally found the cups on a shelf in a corner cupboard and held one up for approval. "How many do you think we need?"

Martha's eyes rose with her thoughts. "Let me see . . . there's you, me, Marlea oh, and Libby, Jeannette and Connie . . . and I think that Sierra Clarence will be here, and Sandra, too. Eight should do it."

"But not her partner? I would have thought that Ms. Trask would have been here with bells on."

"I think they want to plan something to surprise her, and Yvette is going to try to keep her occupied for a while." Martha said softly. Sandra offered to run interference, but since this is her daughter, and this pregnancy has been special, Marlea wanted her here this morning."

"Oh, I absolutely agree, and I think that if Rissa had any input, she would want her mother here, too." Rose set the cups on the counter and lowered her voice. "You know she says that the baby communicates with her?"

"Shut up!" Martha's mouth dropped open and she forgot all about the coffee.

"Yes, she told me that the baby lets her know things, and that she's very opinionated."

"Things? Opinionated? What kind of things, and Lord help me, opinions about what?" Martha lifted her hands, then gave up and settled for crossing her arms again. "Look, I told you when you took the job, that girl is . . . different."

Rose leaned thoughtfully against the counter. "But they're so sweet together. Especially now, him flying back and forth, making every one of those childbirth classes with her, determined to be her coach. But now that you mention it, whoever saw a woman married for almost five years and still trying to cook?"

"This one." Martha blew hard air and rolled her eyes when Rose took one of the hot muffins and broke off a piece to munch. "Got the nerve to plan a brunch this morning and I don't know what we're going to eat, beyond coffee and muffins. Married all this time and left to her own devices, Marlea is still burning up the pots."

"It's either the style or it's contagious, but it's a darned good thing for Rissa that Dench's aunt taught him to cook. He does pretty well, too."

"Maybe he should give AJ a few lessons."

Rose popped the last of her muffin into her mouth. "It's okay, we'll never let them starve, will we?"

Martha rolled her eyes again. "I would starve Rissa if she called me the—what does she call you?"

"The household ninja."

Martha shook a pointed finger at her friend. "I'm telling you now, I would let that little minx starve."

A quick blast of wintry air crossed the warm kitchen and both housekeepers turned to see Marlea and AJ pushing into the house. "Which little minx? We took Nia with us. She and Jabari are at Tiny Gym this morning."

AJ moved to the high granite counter and dumped his load of bags, then reached for Marlea's. "It's not Nia. It's Rissa, right? I know my sister. Whatever she did, could you just forgive her?" Marlea dropped her heavy jacket into AJ's arms and headed for the sink.

"We know how she is." Martha strolled over to the counter to watch Marlea strip Field Greens Café bags from the boxes and plastic containers. She cast a knowing glance over her shoulder, then looked back at Marlea. "What's that?"

"Brunch."

"With all that restaurant cooking, you'll need serving dishes." Martha smirked, turning to Rose, who was already searching the cabinets. Finding pretty bowls and matching platters, she rinsed and dried them, then passed them over to Marlea. Martha smirked again. "Lots of serving dishes."

"I am so not supposed to be here." AJ eased from the room.

"You made coffee?" Marlea noticed. "I brought coffee."

"Bought coffee is more like it." Martha sniffed and smiled, suddenly forgiving. "Would that be French vanilla?"

"And would there be more of it?" Cool air swirled through the kitchen again as Connie stepped across the threshold.

"AJ let us in," Jeannette added. Libby and Sierra pushed into the door behind her and began pulling off layers.

"Warmth," Sierra sighed, stepping more fully into the kitchen and heading straight across the pine flooring for the fireplace. "Can you believe how cold it is outside?"

"It's January, Sierra."

"Like I don't know that." She walked to the source of the warmth and held her hands out to the fire. "It's going on three weeks after Christmas and the tree is down, but I'm still pulling tinsel and pine needles out of the carpet. I sure do love this fireplace." Rubbing her hands together, she smiled at the flames and sniffed the fragrant burning wood.

Martha and Rose shared a glance and a private laugh when Marlea waited for her to turn her back, then swept bags and carryout containers from the counter and into the trash compactor. She might not be a great cook, but she wasn't trying to advertise it. Knowing the woman she'd coached for so many years, Libby simply collected her coffee and went to stand next to Sierra. Being helpful, Connie and Jeannette quickly washed hands and moved dishes to the counter for serving.

"Pretty much everybody is here, right?" Libby made a quick swing by the counter and picked up orange juice. Seating herself at the table, she crossed her legs and looked comfortable.

"Except me, and since I'm going to be the grandmother, you wouldn't want to start without me." Sandra Yarborough swept into the room, dropping cool kisses and warm hugs along the way. Shrugging out of her long red coat, she left it on a chair and gratefully accepted the coffee Martha offered. She took a sip and accepted a still warm muffin with a wink. "Chef Stephanie and Field Greens Café, right?"

"She knows what's up," Martha whispered to a nodding Rose.

"Before we do anything else, I brought my camera." Sandra struggled to pull her ancient Hawkeye and flashbulbs from a brown leather case. Screwing the bulb in, she dug in the camera case again and pulled out a small telescoping tripod. Snapping the tripod together with a practiced hand, she mounted the camera and organized the women for a group photo. She set the timer and hurried to take her place in the center of the group—she barely made it as the flashbulb popped, temporarily blinding them all.

"Why did we just do that?" Sierra squeezed her eyes together, then stretched them wide.

"For the Dream Keeper." Sandra blinked rapidly and waited for her vision to adjust.

Sierra put her hand out in front of her and felt her way across the room to sit next to Sandra. "What's a Dream Keeper?"

"A photo album, right?" Marlea grinned when her mother-in-law nodded. "Rissa and AJ both have them, and AJ's is going into volume six. Does this one have the little silk bag with it?" Sandra nodded again and Marlea's grin widened. "We keep adding to the little bags with AJ's Dream Keeper. It's where he keeps his high school and college class rings. We added mine when we got married. He even added a shoelace from the first race I ran after my accident. And then Mom made one for Jabari and another one when Nia was born. Rissa is going to love having this."

"I'm going to add this picture and all of the ones we took over Christmas. This is what I have, so far." Sandra pulled the book from an oversized leather tote. Covered in pale pink silk, the book was already several inches thick. Opening the cover, Sandra smoothed her fingers over the first page and looked up with a gentle smile. Seeing the look on her face drew the other women close enough to look at the page. A small card, embossed with a tiny garland of roses framed the announcement of a baby girl's birth.

"This is for Rissa's birth." Jeannette laughed when Sandra smiled. "Hard to believe she was ever anybody's 'little bundle of joy.' "

Connie nudged her hard. "Girl, you don't tease a mother about her child like that. Any pictures to go with the announcement?"

Happy to oblige, Sandra turned the page.

"Oh, my goodness, look at her!" Chubby, toothless baby Rissa sat happily in the middle of the page wearing a frilly dress, lacy socks, and white high-topped shoes. "She hasn't got five hairs on her head. How did you get that big bow to stay on?"

"Scotch tape," Sandra replied proudly. "What did you think? That I was going to staple it on?"

"Girl," Connie whispered, "I told you about teasing mothers."

"All I'm saying is that she has all that hair now. Who would have thought she would have been a bald-headed baby?"

Sandra glared and Connie hid her mouth behind her hand. "Jeannette, you'd better hide your eyes before she blinds you with her heat vision." She giggled when Jeannette looked away quickly.

"Anyway," Sandra finally huffed, "this book is actually for the baby, so that she'll always know that she was special and the dreams that keep her special." She turned a page and displayed an eight-year-old Rissa in pink tutu and ballet slippers. Next to her, resplendent in his full Pop Warner football gear, was a photo of ten-year old Dench. "She'll know that they always had dreams and hopes."

Sandra turned another page: Rissa in a red and white jersey and shorts, with tube socks pulled to her knees, holding a basketball. Dench, sitting formally in full uniform, with a hand resting on his helmet. The next page held several pretty photos of Rissa dressed for formal dances and parties. Dench and AJ were shown together, standing stiff and reserved in suits, holding corsages— proms and homecoming dances. "She'll know that they had to learn what she had to learn."

Other pages showed Rissa and Dench dressed for summer jobs, and with friends. There were shots of Rissa on her high school debate team and a few of her law school mock trials. More photos of Dench chronicled his rise from player to coach. "She'll know what her parents have learned to value."

When she opened the recently developed holiday photos and began to slip them into place, all of the women, even Martha Baldwin, cooed softly. The pictures of Dench and Rissa standing in the glow of the huge Christmas tree made them sigh, but the shot of him fastening the pavé diamond heart at the back of her neck brought tears to their eyes.

In the picture, fast-talking, quick-thinking Rissa had bowed her head and lifted her hair, her eyes nearly closed, leaving her vulnerable to the man who stood behind her, and Dench stood frozen in time, focused and protective. Sandra had captured the moment, but good fortune had captured the couple in a golden haze of reflected candlelight, softening the moment even more. "She'll see this one and know that her parents dared to dream, that she has always been loved, and that love is worth having."

It was a good shot, but Sandra knew that she had an even better one. She turned the page and lifted the next picture, turning it to expose what had been a simple photo—maybe the best one she'd ever taken. She'd had the snapshot enlarged, and loved it even more. At her side, Marlea gasped as she dropped her hand to her mother-in-law's shoulder. Sandra had managed to find Rissa and Dench in a private moment.

In a small chair, with the emerald dressing gown she'd worn on Christmas draped around her, Rissa sat with Dench kneeling before her. With their joined hands cradling the rounded firmness of their creation, she looked into his eyes with the passion and expectancy of a madonna, and gazing up at her, his face was framed in fierce devotion. Humor and something undeniably beautiful passed between them at the exact second her mother pressed the button on her camera. Every one of the women looking at this one perfect moment knew that there would be other photos for this little family, but nothing so telling and exceptional as this one.

"She'll see this one and know why they chose her name and the hope that they will always have for her."

"And we'll be in the book, too," Sierra breathed. "She'll know that friends are worth having." A tear fell and she sniffed loudly. Dropping her head to Libby's shoulder, she sniffed again when Libby hugged her. "I want a Dream Keeper for JJ, too. I'm going to start as soon as I get home."

The other women made soothing sounds as Sandra put the book away, and they settled around the table.

Marlea moved to the head of the table and cleared her throat. "I'm glad we'll all be a part of Faith's book and her life, but I wanted you all here this morning for another reason, and we have to finish before Rissa gets back."

"I told you I didn't see her car when we drove up." Jeannette's elbow hunched Connie sharply. "Where is she?"

"Rissa is at the office—she's only going in twice a week for a half day right now. In fact, I watched her car roll down the street when AJ and I were coming in. She won't be gone long, so this little meeting has to be quick."

"What about Dench?"

"He's up at Flowery Branch. They didn't get to the Super Bowl, but two of his players will be in the Pro Bowl and Rissa is pushing him to take the nod for coach."

"This has been a big year for them." Libby's eyes glowed when she folded her hands together. "Any coach would love to get that kind of nod from his peers. Coaching for the Pro Bowl is a big deal."

"But Dench doesn't want to miss the birth of this baby."

Connie sucked her teeth. "Do you blame him? After all it took to get to this point? I know that I don't blame him even a little bit."

"So, this is about a shower, right? What are we going to do for a shower?" Libby demanded. "She needs one, and he deserves the celebration."

Connie frowned. "I'm a little scared."

"It's not your baby."

"Doesn't matter, Jeannette, this is not easy."

"Which is why we're not going to call it a shower." Marlea raised both hands for attention when the curious women muttered and shifted in their seats. "We're going to call it a good night with people who love her and Dench, and want to see them through to the end. That will work, so I came up with this." She pushed a stack of shiny brochures across the table toward the other women. Together, they flipped the thick papers open and smiled.

"This is so exotic, I don't know why none of us thought of it." Sandra's forefinger tapped the corner of her eye as she gave the menu another check.

"It says here that they will provide the décor and staff for an authentic experience. If we can get her down there, she'll never get up off those cushions," Connie giggled.

"They'll wait on her, hand and foot. She won't have to."

Libby cocked an eyebrow at Marlea. "Did you forget how often you went to the bathroom when you were pregnant?"

"Oh, and there's a belly dancer, too." Martha looked interested. "You all know Rissa, she'll have to try dancing."

"And probably send herself into active labor," Rose Kirkland decided. "It's a good thing you two are nurses."

"I've never done this outside of a restaurant. How does it work?"

"Oh, I love Ethiopian dining." Sandra turned to Sierra and took her hand. "The guests are seated on a low comfortable divan or on cushions and a mesab, an elaborate handmade wicker hourglass-shaped table with a designed domed cover, is set before them. Then someone, usually a tall, stunning woman dressed in a shama, brings a long-spouted copper pitcher in her right hand, a copper basin in her left hand, and a towel over her left arm. She pours warm water over the fingers of your right hand, holding the basin to catch the excess, and you wipe your hands on the towel that hangs over her arm. When she finishes, the mesab is taken out of the room and returned shortly, with a second domed cover. She removes the dome and this time, the table is covered with what looks like a gray cloth overlapping the edge of a huge tray. The tablecloth-like thing is the *injera*."

"It's the what?" Libby looked completely lost.

"*Injera* is the sourdough pancake-like bread of Ethiopia," Sandra explained. "Food is brought to the table in enamel bowls and portioned out. When the entire *injera* is covered with an assortment of stews and other dishes, you tear off a piece of the *injera*, and roll the food into it like a huge cigarette. Then just swoop it up and pop it into your mouth."

"Maybe a couple inches wide, like a little square mini-fajita?" Libby took little comfort from Sandra's wise nod.

"I've got the staff of the Blue Nile on hold." Marlea fanned one hand at Libby and covered the phone with the other. "Pick a menu. I know that AJ and I love the *doro wat* and the *sega wat* and . . ." The other line beeped in her ear. "I'm sorry," she said to the Blue Nile's event planner. "Another call is coming through." She tapped the button and the line changed.

"Marlea? This Yvette Trask, and I'm pretty sure you can cancel that shower-thing."

Marlea's stomach clenched and she turned to see her mother-in-law watching her. "What's going on, Yvette?"

"I would have called sooner, but she just told me. Her water broke. Rissa's having contractions and they are about three minutes apart, lasting about thirty seconds or more, and she's been having them for the last thirty or forty minutes. We're headed to the hospital—I'm driving."

Marlea's eyes went wide. "On the way."

Sandra stood and took steps toward Marlea, but was still too slow to catch the phone when Marlea tossed it and ran for her coat purse and keys. Libby caught the phone in midair.

"Call Dench and AJ," Marlea called over her shoulder. Sierra and Rose Kirkland pulled cellphones from their pockets and Martha Baldwin began reciting phone numbers from memory. Anticipating, Connie and Jeannette jumped down from their chairs and grabbed their purses and coats. They had the side door open when Marlea ran past them.

"So what's going on? Why are we in such a hurry?"

"Rissa's in labor, dummy." Jeannette swung into the front seat of Marlea's car as she gunned the engine. Connie fell into the back seat with Sandra Yarborough and managed to get her legs in and the door slammed shut as the car roared down the driveway.

Dench scrubbed his hands over his face and took a deep breath. AJ's voice startled him.

"Nervous?"

"Dude, there is no way that word can tell you how I feel right now." Dench sucked in a big breath and released it in a huge, almost solid rush. "I go in there and come out with a baby."

"She'll be little, man. You'll have years to get nervous. I'm still gearing up for the first time my son plays ball or takes a hit on a football field."

The corner of Dench's mouth ticked. "But Faith is a girl."

AJ clapped a hand on his friend's shoulder and smiled. "Then you get to be her hero for a while before some hardheaded boy comes along to break her heart. You're going to be a hell of a dad, dude. Go on in there and do right by your ladies. I know Rissa is waiting."

"Dude." Dench brought the knuckles of his right hand up to meet AJ's, and somehow the gesture wasn't enough. Leaning in, not caring if anyone saw him, Dench opened his arms to hug the man who had been his friend and his brother for so long.

"Go on in there and take care of my sister and my niece," AJ whispered, releasing his brother-in-law.

Turning away and making the brief walk down the hall gave him little time to think. Dench gave thanks for all that he had. This time, his wife was conscious. This time, he would be with her. This time, their baby would . . . He refused to think farther as he pushed the door open.

The birthing suite was large. Brightly painted walls, healthy green leafy plants, and cozy oak furniture made it homey and not at all antiseptic. Complete with television, DVD player and a state-of-the-art birthing bed and monitoring equipment, the ambiance was wasted on Rissa. Her lap covered by a pale pink blanket, she sat up with her hands propped against her knees, biting her lips.

"Praise Jesus," Yvette all but screamed, jumping up from her bedside chair and freeing her hand from Rissa's grip. "She's waiting for you, Dr. Stanton is on the way, and I swear this woman has been holding this baby hostage waiting for you." Catching her purse and coat on the fly, she headed for the door and took only a moment to glance back. "Good luck," she whispered and eased from the room.

"Well, I'm here now." Dench stepped close and pressed his hand against Rissa's. She looked into his eyes and smiled, just before she levered his fingers into a death grip. Surprised by her strenghth, he bit back the gasp as pain surged through his hand. *No wonder AJ cried every time Marlea did.*

"Where's the doctor?" Rissa's eyes were suddenly wide and panicky.

"On the way, but I'm here." Shifting slightly, he moved behind her and began to massage her back, feeling tension run through his hands when she sighed and began to breathe deeply. *Like they said in that class . . .*

Mouth wide, Rissa moaned deeply, making Dench work faster. *Where the hell is that doctor?*

"It's time, Dench. I'm ready to push."

Does it really happen this fast? "Rissa . . ."

"Hey all." Alexis Stanton breezed in fully dressed for the occasion, all smiles. Dench wished the nurses with her would disappear so that he might strangle her in private. The nurses didn't disappear, and the doctor gave him no chance to act on the intention as she rushed him off for preparation. Making quick measurements from the foot of the bed, she smiled over her shoulder at him. "You'd better hurry, though, this little girl can't wait to meet you."

She shows up late and now she's rushing me? I might strangle her AND the nurses!

Forty minutes later, Dench changed his mind. Faith Imani Traylor rested in his hands, warm and perfect. Dr. Alexis Stanton would live to deliver other babies.

"You did it, baby. You really did it." Wonder filled his face and voice when Dench looked up at his wife. Standing, he held the quivering, squalling mass of his infant daughter and looked into the eyes of the woman he'd always loved.

"We did it, Dench." Rissa yawned, smiled and closed her eyes.

"Rissa?"

Her name was a whisper, but her eyes popped open and her arms reached. "Can I hold her now?"

"In a minute . . ." one of the nurses began. She stopped and took a step back when Dench glared at her.

"I'll be quick." Rissa proudly counted fingers, toes, eyes, and ears, then nodded, letting Dench pass the baby to the nurse. Rissa and Dench watched their baby cleaned and warmed, while magic hands helped Rissa into a fresh gown and changed her bedding.

Across the room, the baby was weighed and measured. Dench wanted to know if Faith's seven pounds was correct. The two women exchanged amused glances when he grinned at her twenty-inch length. When they offered to let him hold her again, he promptly drew the room's rocking chair close enough to the bed for Rissa to watch and opened his arms.

"Are you okay?" he finally remembered to ask doting Rissa.

"Sleepy and hungry," she replied softly.

"We brought food." Marlea's face in the doorway made them smile. She held a wicker hamper in front of her like a peace offering. "We left Connie and Jeannette parking my car, but since we brought food, can we see the baby?"

AJ pushed in behind her. "My niece."

"My new granddaughter." His mother's hands at his back nearly made AJ run over Marlea. Paying them no attention, Sandra left her son and daughter-in-law to sort themselves out. *They like falling over each other,* she thought as she threw her red coat over the back of a convenient chair. *First things first.*

Managing to get through the door, Marlea and AJ rushed to Rissa's bedside. When the nurse placed the baby in Rissa's arms, they stared breathlessly until Sandra pushed between them. She held out her arms and Rissa carefully passed the infant to her. Cradling the baby, Sandra wordlessly flipped back the little pink blanket and inspected the tiny fingers and toes. She peeked under the little pink cap and nodded. *Bald, just like her mama.*

"She's perfect." Holding the child toward her daughter, Sandra was surprised by how reluctant she was to release her. *Because she's a miracle,* Sandra decided. *Because she's proof that dreams come true.* Swallowing tears, she kissed Rissa, then Dench, and touched the baby's pink cap. "She's just perfect."

Suddenly all business, Sandra pulled at her sweater to straighten it and stood. Crossing back to her bag, she pulled the ancient Kodak Hawkeye free and screwed in a flashbulb. Checking the exposure, she smiled when she set it, then passed the camera to the waiting nurse. "Press here when I tell you."

She crossed the room and gave her children, all of her children, a critical glance. "We have one more thing to do. Stand here, AJ. Marlea, you're here. Dench, sit here with Rissa and the baby, and I'm here." Satisfied, she turned three-quarters front, her best position. "This is for Faith's Dream Keeper. Okay," she nodded to the nurse. "Everybody say, 'dream.' "

The flash caught them smiling, sharing a dream for posterity.

EPILOGUE

One year later . . .

"This is so not the typical 'date with my husband,' but I have to tell you that I like it," Rissa murmured when the Air Jamaica plane flew low over the northwestern coast of the island. "Isn't it funny how quickly life changes? The first time I was here with you, I became a wife. The next time, I became Faith's mother. What do you think will happen this time?" She smiled.

"You mean besides needing to find a place to change a stinky little girl?" Dench held the baby away from his body and wrinkled his nose when Faith cackled merrily.

"Watch a pro at work." Rissa shifted her tote to the other side of her seat and took the baby. "What do you want to bet that I can finish before we land?"

"Can't be done."

"Bet me, or I'll give her back to you." Rissa touched her nose to the baby's and they laughed together. "Watch Mommy take Daddy's money," she whispered, and the baby cackled again.

"Whew, I'll take that bet!" Dench dug into his shirt pocket and found a twenty. He held it out and Rissa's fingers snapped it from his hand. Working one-handed, she flipped the baby in her lap, unsnapped the romper, and managed to simultaneously wrangle the diaper, wipes, and powder. The baby gurgled and Rissa convinced the flight attendant that the plastic wrapped bundle was not toxic.

"See? We're still in the air." She handed the baby back to her father and rested her head on his shoulder when the plane dipped on the air current as it circled Sangster International airport.

"Guess you win." He looked down as Faith curled against his chest and closed her eyes. Warm, soft and trusting, she smelled like baby powder and he was grateful. "Lucky me."

Rissa pushed her hand into his and smiled as the plane landed. "Lucky us."

Walking into the Immigration Hall, Dench couldn't help feeling pride in his wife: tall, slender, strong, and beautiful. "You're making life look easy these days, buying Yvette out, handling the larger caseload, and finding time for this little getaway."

"And don't forget Faith."

"I wouldn't dream of it." He was thoughtful as they approached the passport control station, then looked at her again. "Are you sure you want to do this?"

"Dench?" Rissa raised an eyebrow and looked at him. "You picked a fine time to ask me that. I'm pregnant now. There will be no turning back. And I expect a Super Bowl win this year—it'll help me secure that raise for you because we'll be putting two children through college when the time comes."

"Dude, I'll do my best. Doing that Fox pregame show is going to take up a lot of time . . ."

"And don't forget the fundraising work you promised AJ and Marlea that you and the team will be doing for Project ABLE." She bumped him with her hip. "So we'll commute, because I'm not going for that 'absence makes the heart grow fonder' stuff."

"It'll have to work, dude, because I need you like the ocean needs the shore, and I'm not going far without you."

"Sweet talker." She bumped him again and laughed when he bumped her back.

The handsome bronze-skinned man at the counter smiled when the couple reached him. Eyes on Rissa, he considered flirting with the pretty woman, even though he saw the rings on her finger. Then he looked at Dench and reconsidered. Even with the sleeping baby in his arms, this one looked like he could read minds—and wouldn't hesitate to act on what he found. The immigration officer made his face blank and held out his hand for their passports and immigration forms.

"Clearance was quick," Rissa whispered, her voice barely loud enough to be heard over the noise in the terminal, when she and Dench walked hand-in-hand away from the counter.

"Maybe he didn't want to hold us too long, what with the baby and all."

"Sierra Clarence calls that Baby Power." She laughed lightly.

Exchanging some of the cash he carried for Jamaican dollars took only a few minutes. Dench handed her the wad of bills. She grinned and wiggled her eyebrows at him. "Still trying to buy my affection?"

"Can I still get it for a penny?" He jammed a hand into his pocket and pulled out a single penny. Placing it in her palm, he kissed her.

"Sold," she whispered, dropping the money into her tote.

"You not honeymoonin' this time, are you?" The voice, strong in its island lilt, happy in its certainty, made them turn. "You have the little one with you, I see." The easy question and answer came from a full-bodied woman in a floral dress. The island lilt of her voice and bright flash of her white teeth were an invitation to smile, even before she winked at them.

"The same woman?"

"Looks like, but . . ."

" 'Course I'm the same and I remember you, but I see some things have changed with you," the woman laughed, looking around Dench's shoulder to see the baby's face. "She's pretty like her mother and her daddy."

Starting from his feet, the woman let her eyes wander, looking hard at Dench. "Looks like the honeymoon worked." Approval apparent, her eyes lingered on his, and she held his gaze until he looked away. Still watching, obviously admiring, she pushed a bunch of vividly deep red and yellow hibiscus blooms into Rissa's hands. "For luck," she said. "Though I already told you, you'll never need it with this one."

Laughing, their impromptu hostess fluttered her loose flowery skirt and danced a few steps. She bowed as Rissa took her picture. When Rissa showed her the digital frame, the woman's laughter simmered lower. "You let me take one of you now."

Handing over her camera, Rissa moved close to Dench and the baby. The woman nodded and looked into the viewfinder. Satisfied, she clicked the shot. "You put my picture away with vacation souvenirs. But this one is for you, Dream Keeper. This man, this baby, this is the dream you keep forever."

"I will," Rissa promised when the woman smiled directly into her eyes.

The woman melted into the crowd and Rissa looked into the green and gold flecked eyes she loved. Her hand smoothed the baby's hat and then her husband's shaved head.

"She called you the Dream Keeper."

"She did, didn't she?" Rissa's hand slipped to Dench's cheek and she loved the firm feel of his skin against her fingers. "I mean that, you know. You are my dream, and I'm keeping you forever because I love you like Jesus . . ."

". . . loved the church," he finished with his lips on hers.

"And that's good enough for me."

Dear Readers,

At the end of *Dream Runner*, I got lots of questions about Rissa and Dench, most of them wanting to know more about their relationship, their marriage, and their future. Hopefully, in *Dream Keeper*, you've enjoyed learning more about them and sharing their growth.

Thank you for sharing the continuing lives of the Traylors and the Yarboroughs as they find and realize their dreams. While they don't always have an easy time of it, they are always interesting. I am hoping that you enjoy them as much as I do, as I look forward to their individual and combined futures.

And I love hearing your thoughts and look forward to hearing from you. Please feel free to contact me via email (the_fitwryter@yahoo.com) or via US mail at: P.O. Box 56782 / Atlanta, GA 30343.

Thank you, again.

Gail McFarland

ABOUT THE AUTHOR

Born with a passion for reading, Gail McFarland is
the published author of more than 100 short romantic
confessions and short stories and several novels including
Dream Runner (Genesis Press 2008). A dedicated well-
ness-fitness advocate, Ms. McFarland is currently an
active fitness instructor and consultant. She happily
admits that while *Dream Runner* was the first of her
novels to combine her love of sports and fitness with the
passion of romance, *Dream Keeper* is her first sequel.
Dream Keeper reintroduces the readers to Rissa and
Dench Traylor, and updates the lives of AJ and Marlea
Yarborough.

A native of Cleveland, Ohio, Ms. McFarland
attended Glenville High School and Cleveland State
University. She now makes her home in Atlanta, Georgia.

2009 Reprint Mass Market Titles

January

I'm Gonna Make You Love Me
Gwyneth Bolton
ISBN-13: 978-1-58571-294-6
$6.99

Shades of Desire
Monica White
ISBN-13: 978-1-58571-292-2
$6.99

February

A Love of Her Own
Cheris Hodges
ISBN-13: 978-1-58571-293-9
$6.99

Color of Trouble
Dyanne Davis
ISBN-13: 978-1-58571-294-6
$6.99

March

Twist of Fate
Beverly Clark
ISBN-13: 978-1-58571-295-3
$6.99

Chances
Pamela Leigh Starr
ISBN-13: 978-1-58571-296-0
$6.99

April

Sinful Intentions
Crystal Rhodes
ISBN-13: 978-1-585712-297-7
$6.99

Rock Star
Roslyn Hardy Holcomb
ISBN-13: 978-1-58571-298-4
$6.99

May

Paths of Fire
T.T. Henderson
ISBN-13: 978-1-58571-343-1
$6.99

Caught Up in the Rapture
Lisa Riley
ISBN-13: 978-1-58571-344-8
$6.99

June

Reckless Surrender
Rochelle Alers
ISBN-13: 978-1-58571-345-5
$6.99

No Ordinary Love
Angela Weaver
ISBN-13: 978-1-58571-346-2
$6.99

2009 Reprint Mass Market Titles (continued)

July

Intentional Mistakes
Michele Sudler
ISBN-13: 978-1-58571-347-9
$6.99

It's In His Kiss
Reon Carter
ISBN-13: 978-1-58571-348-6
$6.99

August

Unfinished Love Affair
Barbara Keaton
ISBN-13: 978-1-58571-349-3
$6.99

A Perfect Place to Pray
I.L Goodwin
ISBN-13: 978-1-58571-299-1
$6.99

September

Love in High Gear
Charlotte Roy
ISBN-13: 978-1-58571-355-4
$6.99

Ebony Eyes
Kei Swanson
ISBN-13: 978-1-58571-356-1
$6.99

October

Midnight Clear, Part I
Leslie Esdale/Carmen Green
ISBN-13: 978-1-58571-357-8
$6.99

Midnight Clear, Part II
Gwynne Forster/Monica
Jackson
ISBN-13: 978-1-58571-358-5
$6.99

November

Midnight Peril
Vicki Andrews
ISBN-13: 978-1-58571-359-2
$6.99

One Day At A Time
Bella McFarland
ISBN-13: 978-1-58571-360-8
$6.99

December

Just An Affair
Eugenia O'Neal
ISBN-13: 978-1-58571-361-5
$6.99

Shades of Brown
Denise Becker
ISBN-13: 978-1-58571-362-2
$6.99

2010 Mass Market Titles

January

Show Me The Sun
Miriam Shumba
ISBN: 978-158571-405-6
$6.99

Promises of Forever
Celya Bowers
ISBN: 978-1-58571-380-6
$6.99

February

Love Out Of Order
Nicole Green
ISBN: 978-1-58571-381-3
$6.99

Unclear and Present Danger
Michele Cameron
ISBN: 978-158571-408-7
$6.99

March

Stolen Jewels
Michele Sudler
ISBN: 978-158571-409-4
$6.99

Not Quite Right
Tammy Williams
ISBN: 978-158571-410-0
$6.99

April

Oak Bluffs
Joan Early
ISBN: 978-1-58571-379-0
$6.99

Crossing The Line
Bernice Layton
ISBN: 978-158571-412-4
$6.99

How To Kill Your Husband
Keith Walker
ISBN: 978-158571-421-6
$6.99

May

The Business of Love
Cheris F. Hodges
ISBN: 978-158571-373-8
$6.99

Wayward Dreams
Gail McFarland
ISBN: 978-158571-422-3
$6.99

June

The Doctor's Wife
Mildred Riley
ISBN: 978-158571-424-7
$6.99

Mixed Reality
Chamein Canton
ISBN: 978-158571-423-0
$6.99

2010 Mass Market Titles (continued)
July

Blue Interlude
Keisha Mennefee
ISBN: 978-158571-378-3
$6.99

Always You
Crystal Hubbard
ISBN: 978-158571-371-4
$6.99

Unbeweavable
Katrina Spencer
ISBN: 978-158571-426-1
$6.99

August

Small Sensations
Crystal V. Rhodes
ISBN: 978-158571-376-9
$6.99

Let's Get It On
Dyanne Davis
ISBN: 978-158571-416-2
$6.99

September

Unconditional
A.C. Arthur
ISBN: 978-158571-413-1
$6.99

Swan
Africa Fine
ISBN: 978-158571-377-6
$6.99$6.99

October

Friends in Need
Joan Early
ISBN:978-1-58571-428-5
$6.99

Against the Wind
Gwynne Forster
ISBN:978-158571-429-2
$6.99

That Which Has Horns
Miriam Shumba
ISBN:978-1-58571-430-8
$6.99

November

A Good Dude
Keith Walker
ISBN:978-1-58571-431-5
$6.99

Reye's Gold
Ruthie Robinson
ISBN:978-1-58571-432-2
$6.99

December

Still Waters...
Crystal V. Rhodes
ISBN:978-1-58571-433-9
$6.99

Burn
Crystal Hubbard
ISBN: 978-1-58571-406-3
$6.99

Other Genesis Press, Inc. Titles

Other Genesis Press, Inc. Titles (continued)

Other Genesis Press, Inc. Titles (continued)

Eve's Prescription	Edwina Martin Arnold	$8.95
Everlastin' Love	Gay G. Gunn	$8.95
Everlasting Moments	Dorothy Elizabeth Love	$8.95
Everything and More	Sinclair Lebeau	$8.95
Everything But Love	Natalie Dunbar	$8.95
Falling	Natalie Dunbar	$9.95
Fate	Pamela Leigh Starr	$8.95
Finding Isabella	A.J. Garrotto	$8.95
Fireflies	Joan Early	$6.99
Fixin' Tyrone	Keith Walker	$6.99
Forbidden Quest	Dar Tomlinson	$10.95
Forever Love	Wanda Y. Thomas	$8.95
From the Ashes	Kathleen Suzanne Jeanne Sumerix	$8.95
Frost On My Window	Angela Weaver	$6.99
Gentle Yearning	Rochelle Alers	$10.95
Glory of Love	Sinclair LeBeau	$10.95
Go Gentle Into That Good Night	Malcom Boyd	$12.95
Goldengroove	Mary Beth Craft	$16.95
Groove, Bang, and Jive	Steve Cannon	$8.99
Hand in Glove	Andrea Jackson	$9.95
Hard to Love	Kimberley White	$9.95
Hart & Soul	Angie Daniels	$8.95
Heart of the Phoenix	A.C. Arthur	$9.95
Heartbeat	Stephanie Bedwell-Grime	$8.95
Hearts Remember	M. Loui Quezada	$8.95
Hidden Memories	Robin Allen	$10.95
Higher Ground	Leah Latimer	$19.95
Hitler, the War, and the Pope	Ronald Rychiak	$26.95
How to Write a Romance	Kathryn Falk	$18.95
I Married a Reclining Chair	Lisa M. Fuhs	$8.95
I'll Be Your Shelter	Giselle Carmichael	$8.95
I'll Paint a Sun	A.J. Garrotto	$9.95
Icie	Pamela Leigh Starr	$8.95
If I Were Your Woman	LaConnie Taylor-Jones	$6.99
Illusions	Pamela Leigh Starr	$8.95
Indigo After Dark Vol. I	Nia Dixon/Angelique	$10.95
Indigo After Dark Vol. II	Dolores Bundy/ Cole Riley	$10.95
Indigo After Dark Vol. III	Montana Blue/ Coco Morena	$10.95

Other Genesis Press, Inc. Titles (continued)

Other Genesis Press, Inc. Titles (continued)

Naked Soul	Gwynne Forster	$8.95
Never Say Never	Michele Cameron	$6.99
Next to Last Chance	Louisa Dixon	$24.95
No Apologies	Seressia Glass	$8.95
No Commitment Required	Seressia Glass	$8.95
No Regrets	Mildred E. Riley	$8.95
Not His Type	Chamein Canton	$6.99
Nowhere to Run	Gay G. Gunn	$10.95
O Bed! O Breakfast!	Rob Kuehnle	$14.95
Object of His Desire	A.C. Arthur	$8.95
Office Policy	A.C. Arthur	$9.95
Once in a Blue Moon	Dorianne Cole	$9.95
One Day at a Time	Bella McFarland	$8.95
One of These Days	Michele Sudler	$9.95
Outside Chance	Louisa Dixon	$24.95
Passion	T.T. Henderson	$10.95
Passion's Blood	Cherif Fortin	$22.95
Passion's Furies	AlTonya Washington	$6.99
Passion's Journey	Wanda Y. Thomas	$8.95
Past Promises	Jahmel West	$8.95
Path of Fire	T.T. Henderson	$8.95
Path of Thorns	Annetta P. Lee	$9.95
Peace Be Still	Colette Haywood	$12.95
Picture Perfect	Reon Carter	$8.95
Playing for Keeps	Stephanie Salinas	$8.95
Pride & Joi	Gay G. Gunn	$8.95
Promises Made	Bernice Layton	$6.99
Promises to Keep	Alicia Wiggins	$8.95
Quiet Storm	Donna Hill	$10.95
Reckless Surrender	Rochelle Alers	$6.95
Red Polka Dot in a World Full of Plaid	Varian Johnson	$12.95
Red Sky	Renee Alexis	$6.99
Reluctant Captive	Joyce Jackson	$8.95
Rendezvous With Fate	Jeanne Sumerix	$8.95
Revelations	Cheris F. Hodges	$8.95
Rivers of the Soul	Leslie Esdaile	$8.95
Rocky Mountain Romance	Kathleen Suzanne	$8.95
Rooms of the Heart	Donna Hill	$8.95
Rough on Rats and Tough on Cats	Chris Parker	$12.95
Save Me	Africa Fine	$6.99

Other Genesis Press, Inc. Titles (continued)

Secret Library Vol. 1	Nina Sheridan	$18.95
Secret Library Vol. 2	Cassandra Colt	$8.95
Secret Thunder	Annetta P. Lee	$9.95
Shades of Brown	Denise Becker	$8.95
Shades of Desire	Monica White	$8.95
Shadows in the Moonlight	Jeanne Sumerix	$8.95
Sin	Crystal Rhodes	$8.95
Singing A Song…	Crystal Rhodes	$6.99
Six O'Clock	Katrina Spencer	$6.99
Small Whispers	Annetta P. Lee	$6.99
So Amazing	Sinclair LeBeau	$8.95
Somebody's Someone	Sinclair LeBeau	$8.95
Someone to Love	Alicia Wiggins	$8.95
Song in the Park	Martin Brant	$15.95
Soul Eyes	Wayne L. Wilson	$12.95
Soul to Soul	Donna Hill	$8.95
Southern Comfort	J.M. Jeffries	$8.95
Southern Fried Standards	S.R. Maddox	$6.99
Still the Storm	Sharon Robinson	$8.95
Still Waters Run Deep	Leslie Esdaile	$8.95
Stolen Memories	Michele Sudler	$6.99
Stories to Excite You	Anna Forrest/Divine	$14.95
Storm	Pamela Leigh Starr	$6.99
Subtle Secrets	Wanda Y. Thomas	$8.95
Suddenly You	Crystal Hubbard	$9.95
Sweet Repercussions	Kimberley White	$9.95
Sweet Sensations	Gwyneth Bolton	$9.95
Sweet Tomorrows	Kimberly White	$8.95
Taken by You	Dorothy Elizabeth Love	$9.95
Tattooed Tears	T. T. Henderson	$8.95
Tempting Faith	Crystal Hubbard	$6.99
The Color Line	Lizzette Grayson Carter	$9.95
The Color of Trouble	Dyanne Davis	$8.95
The Disappearance of Allison Jones	Kayla Perrin	$5.95
The Fires Within	Beverly Clark	$9.95
The Foursome	Celya Bowers	$6.99
The Honey Dipper's Legacy	Myra Pannell-Allen	$14.95
The Joker's Love Tune	Sidney Rickman	$15.95
The Little Pretender	Barbara Cartland	$10.95
The Love We Had	Natalie Dunbar	$8.95
The Man Who Could Fly	Bob & Milana Beamon	$18.95

Other Genesis Press, Inc. Titles (continued)

Order Form

Mail to: Genesis Press, Inc.
P.O. Box 101
Columbus, MS 39703

Name _____
Address _____
City/State _____ Zip _____
Telephone _____

Ship to (if different from above)
Name _____
Address _____
City/State _____ Zip _____
Telephone _____

Credit Card Information
Credit Card # _____ ☐ Visa   ☐ Mastercard
Expiration Date (mm/yy) _____ ☐ AmEx   ☐ Discover

Qty.	Author	Title	Price	Total

Use this order form, or call

1-888-INDIGO-1

Total for books _____
Shipping and handling:
  $5 first two books,
  $1 each additional book
Total S & H _____
Total amount enclosed _____
Mississippi residents add 7% sales tax

Visit www.genesis-press.com for latest releases and excerpts.

WIN A
FREE
GENESIS PRESS BOOK
Please fill out this form with your email address and send it to us at:
Genesis Press,
Post Office Box 101,
Columbus, MS 39703
or email it to
customerservice@genesis-press.com
and we will put your name into a drawing for a free Genesis Press Book.
WRITE EMAIL ADDRESS HERE
Winners will be chosen on the first of each month. ONE ENTRY PER CUSTOMER